GOD SWORD AWAKENING

To my first
signature and
~~the~~ best fan

A. A. Mullane

ISBN 978-1-64300-198-2 (Paperback)
ISBN 978-1-64300-199-9 (Digital)

Covenant Books, Inc.
11661 Hwy 707
Murrells Inlet, SC 29576
www.covenantbooks.com

Acknowledgments

This goes out to my mom and dad, for reading every step of the way. Your input and encouragement got me here.

To my brother and sister, for supporting me in their own ways.

To the friends who took time to read my rough drafts. Your perspectives helped shape my story.

Chapter 1

ANTHONY

*B*lack. Everything around him was black.

Anthony stood in the center of the void, sword drawn against an unknown enemy. He had no idea whom he was facing, or if he was facing anyone at all, but the fear he felt was all too real.

A cackle erupted from the depths of the darkness, a cackle that would make children cry and grown men cower in fear. Strength left Anthony's body as he used all the willpower he had left to not drop his katana. He had never felt fear like this before, not since he became a Divine Blade.

"Who are you?" Anthony shouted, his voice filled with fear and apprehension. "Show yourself."

A silence followed, which hurt even more than the laugh. He could feel the tension building, like his assailant was simply watching him suffer; enjoying the fear and cowardice that Anthony was failing to contain. This only scared Anthony more as the thought of some dark psycho toying with him to get his kicks was both humiliating and terrifying.

"Who am I?" a sinister voice purred out to him.

The voice was deep and commanding and would have soothed him in any other situation. But here, each word stabbed into him like an icy dagger.

"I am the one that will end this world as you know it."

The outline of a man formed in the nothingness, his presence being blacker than the void they stood in. But this was no ordinary man. A pair of ghastly wings sprouted from behind him, spreading like a canopy over the two of them. Anthony froze in absolute terror. He had never seen one, but he knew exactly what it was.

A Zankrex.

Anthony fell to the ground, dropping his katana in mortal fear. The shadow seemed to get a kick out of this as he tilted his head back and released a laugh that almost stopped Anthony's heart. The apparition knelt toward Anthony as two bloodred eyes stared into his soul.

"Yes, soon I will make my move. And when that time comes …"

The shadow smiled and glided up close. Anthony couldn't move. His whole body had seized up. All he could do was watch in horror as the black presence came within inches of his face. The bloodred eyes stared deep into Anthony's soul like he was trying to see Anthony's very center.

"I'll very much enjoy seeing that fear in real life … Anthony."

The shadow began to cackle again as the floor gave out from under them. The shadow hovered and laughed as Anthony plummeted into the black abyss. He tried to scream, but no noise came out. He reached for his katana, but it tumbled out of sight. All he could do was fall as the shadow's last words echoed all around him.

"Anthony … Anthony … Anthony …"

"Anthony … *Anthony!*"

Anthony shot up from his desk, sending his chair clattering to the ground as he came to from his dream.

Now standing, he surveyed the room as he gathered his thoughts.

"Having a nightmare, were we, Mr. Multan?"

Anthony stood drenched in sweat as he realized where he was. He breathed a sigh of relief, thankful that it was just a dream.

"Sorry, Mr. Hazblazen," Anthony said, more relieved than apologetic.

The rest of the class began to laugh, which put Anthony back at ease.

That's right, he thought. *It was only just a dream.*

Even still, his heart refused to calm, and his palms remained sweaty.

Mr. Hazblazen sighed as he walked back to the front of the class. "It can't be helped, I suppose. Returning from our summer hiatus is always the hardest part of the new semester. But let's try and keep this from forming into a habit, shall we?"

Anthony nodded as he picked his chair up. Hazblazen continued on as Anthony scooted back up to his desk.

So much for staying out of the spotlight this semester, he thought to himself.

All he wanted was to blend into the faces and not stand out, but his time in college had been anything but. It had all started about a year ago when Anthony was chosen to be a Divine Blade. His potential for a quiet life was blown out the window on that day. His destiny had been written for him at that moment. He would become a Divine Blade and protect the people from the dark energy and the demon beasts it created.

Thinking of the dark energy caused flashbacks of his nightmares. He started sweating again as the images played through his mind. He knew he couldn't be sure of it, but he was almost positive he knew what that horrible apparition was. Even thinking the name caused shivers to run down his spine.

I've never seen one. No one has. Why do I feel so confident I know that my nightmare was about one?

Anthony was deep in thought when Mr. Hazblazen's wooden pointer slammed down on his desk. Anthony jerked back, toppled over his chair, and came crashing to the ground. The roar of his classmates' laughter brought him back to reality. He stood, his face burning with embarrassment, and brushed himself off.

"Well, Anthony, I'm going to assume that since your head is still in the clouds, you're feeling confident about the material," Mr. Hazblazen said with a mocking tone as he walked back to the front of the class. "So, I would like you to recite everything you know about divine blades. If it is insufficient, then I may just have to punish you."

The class snickered as Anthony stood at his desk, gathering his thoughts.

When the class got quiet, he took a breath and started. "Divine blades are swords that were sent down from the Divine Paradise for us humans here on Tertalla. These swords contain the very power of the Creator in them and give the wielder great physical strength, along with certain skills that are specific to each sword. No two sword skills are alike, and each sword skill can be improved depending on the aptitude of the wielder. These swords can only be wielded by one person at a time. If someone tries to use a divine blade that has already picked a wielder, it will feel like an anvil in their hands."

Anthony paused to take a breath and look at the class. He enjoyed this part of school since he was quite knowledgeable on the history of the divine blades.

"If a divine-blade wielder dies, then the blade will find another to replace its late wielder. Blades can also be used by someone other than their wielder if the wielder gives that person permission to use their blade."

Mr. Hazblazen nodded, seemingly impressed by Anthony's knowledge. "That's a good synopsis, but what about the divine blade's purpose?"

Anthony half-smiled as he realized that Mr. Hazblazen was attempting to push some of his teaching duties off on him.

"The Divine Blade's main purpose is to rid the world of the dark energy that inhabits the land. The dark energy takes over animals and form what we call demon beasts. Divine Blades are supposed to dispatch these demon beasts and protect the people who can't protect themselves."

Hazblazen looked up. "And?"

Anthony knew where he wanted him to go with the explanation next, but hesitated. On any normal day, he would have had no problem explaining the topic as he considered it a fairy tale at best. But now it felt as real as his class.

Anthony swallowed hard and continued, "And the Divine Blades were thought to have a more important purpose. That they were supposed to combat a greater evil that the dark energy created: Zankrex."

The class chuckled at the mention of the name. In any other situation, Anthony would have been the first to join in, but right now he felt annoyed. He wanted to yell at them, but he held his sudden anger in check.

He shook his head. *That nightmare got to me.*

Hazblazen's wooden pointer brought the class back to silence. He looked them over once. "Regardless of how you feel about the Zankrex, it would behoove you to study up on them. We will have a portion of class dedicated to them, and it will be on the final exam."

A collective groan escaped the class. The amount of material on Zankrex was surprising considering how the whole of the Divine Blade community considered them myth.

Once the class got quiet, Mr. Hazblazen focused back on Anthony. "Delightful. That will do for divine blades. If you can explain the God Swords to everyone, then I shall consider your punishment levied."

It got real quiet when he said that. The God Swords were the most powerful beings in the entire world and the object of every Divine Blade's admiration.

Anthony didn't miss a beat as this was his favorite topic. "The God Swords are the most powerful of all the Divine Blades. They fall into their own category because of the massive power difference. They were said to be the leaders of the Divine Blades back when the Zankrex were a problem on Tertalla. There are five in total, each one having a certain element connected to his or her sword. Right now, there are four God Swords: the water cutlass, the wind rapier, the fire broadsword, and the lightning gladius. The missing God Sword is the earth katana, and it's said to be the most powerful of the God Swords. While all the divine blades came from the Divine Paradise, some say that the Creator himself forged the God swords."

The silence was palpable for the next couple of seconds. To everyone there, the God Swords were the greatest of heroes, capable of doing anything they wanted. Everyone in that room respected them in one way or another, which is why no one felt right saying anything after the explanation.

Hazblazen walked closer to the class. "The strength of the God Swords is no joking matter, as I'm sure all of you know. Clancy is our academy's finest Divine Blade. No one in this room can even compare. He sparred the water cutlass Vanessa and lost in four seconds."

This shocked the class. Clancy was the strongest Divine Blade any of them had ever seen, but to hear that he lost in such a short amount of time brought the God Sword power into a new perspective.

One student raised his hand. Hazblazen looked surprised to see a question but pointed at him nonetheless.

The student stood up. "I've been curious about this for a while now, but do the God Swords just have that much more divine energy in their swords, or do they also have another power?"

Hazblazen nodded at the kid. "An excellent question. Unfortunately, we do not possess an excellent answer. There was a fairly valid rumor floating around at one point in time that the God Swords also possessed a second power that they fused with their divine energy, and that was why they were so much stronger. That was only a rumor, but it does make one wonder."

Anthony sat in silence as the teacher nodded. "Well, I see no holes in your explanation. You're off the hook for today, Anthony, but I don't want to see you slacking off anymore, okay?"

Anthony sighed. "Yes, sir."

Mr. Hazblazen stared at the class for a couple of uneasy seconds and then clapped. "Well, we still have an hour left in class, so I suppose I can begin the lesson."

Everyone groaned as he turned and started to write away on the chalkboard. Anthony smiled, thinking about how the semester may not be as bad as he thought it would be.

"All right, class," Mr. Hazblazen said, erasing all the notes off the chalkboard, "that will end today's lecture. Be sure to get here on time tomorrow as we won't be starting off each day in the same manner as we did today."

He stared at Anthony to drive the point home, but the day-dreamer was oblivious. The class chuckled as the teacher just sighed.

"In any case, don't forget that your swordplay class starts tomorrow. I would urge all of you to clock some time in the practice arena, so you don't feel too rusty. Also, tomorrow will begin with your start-of-the-semester physical exam. Be sure to arrive with plenty of time to warm up."

With that, everyone got up and began to talk among themselves while the more antisocial ones packed up and left as soon as they could.

Anthony was still lost in thought, reminiscing on his dream. No matter how hard he tried, the imagery wouldn't leave his head.

It was just a dream, he tried to reassure himself, but his unease only grew.

The tip of a sword tore him from his thoughts.

Anthony froze and followed the blade to see his attacker.

It was Hannah.

"Hey there, loser," she said in the harshest tone she could muster. "I don't like the way you space out like you already know everything. You keep that up, and I'll have to bring you down like I always do."

The room got very quiet. Even the teacher was a tad uneasy, but no one dared step in to help. That could be attributed to two things: the first being that Anthony was just not popular or liked enough to be saved, but the main reason was that Hannah was by far the strongest student Divine Blade on campus, even stronger than some of the teachers. She passed the physical entrance exams with flying colors and would be much further along in school if she wasn't so horrible with the written parts.

Ever since last semester, she had hated Anthony. He wished he knew why. The only reason she ever gave him was that she hated weak people. At first, he figured it was because he was far more book smart than she was, but later he heard a rumor that it was due to his base physical skill.

Each physical exam contains a portion that uses the Divine Blade powers and a portion that assesses the wielder's physical abilities without the use of their divine blade powers. Hannah had always been a bit of a prodigy when it came to Divine Blade powers, but her base physical ability was about average. Anthony, on the other hand, had always excelled at the base physical-strength portion while doing less than decent on the Divine Blade–skills portion. He had never understood why she hated him for that, but that was what he had heard from someone who was very close to Hannah.

Anthony sighed. "You know, if you would just study instead of training your powers all day, you would know as much as I do."

Everyone gasped, and for good reason. Hannah was the daughter of the noble family Lillitania, and as such, she was used to everyone she encountered just rolling over for her and not standing up to her. Anthony didn't know that when he met her and said she was childish the first time she made fun of him for being weak. That was where his bad luck started. After that day, he became her favorite punching bag for the spars the teachers made them do. It was annoying at first, but Anthony learned that if he just lost without reacting, it would annoy the heck out of her.

He knew what was coming next after making that comment. Hannah's face was contorted in anger as she pushed her blade closer until it was a hair's breadth from his face.

"I won't tolerate a comment like that from a loser like you," she said, seething more and more with every passing second. "The next time you step into that gym, you better be prepared. I'm going to beat you so bad your mother won't even recognize you!"

With that, she whipped her blade back into its sheath and stormed out of the room.

Anthony sighed again. "Yeah, yeah, I know."

The class remained silent for the next few seconds, until one of the boys there said, "Well, it was nice knowing you, Anthony."

That brought a good laugh to everyone there, and even Anthony managed to crack a smile.

Well, he thought, *time to go die.*

The workout complex drew the most attention out of all the buildings on the campus. The building was a giant rectangle, which was a stark contrast to the domes that sprinkled the campus and contained a massive gymnasium on the first and second floors.

The first-floor gym was lined with special materials that could handle the holy power that was used in the Divine Blade spars. The second-floor gym was used only for basic physical training. There were wings off the main building that contained meeting rooms and other various workout rooms, but the main part was the giant gyms.

Anthony snuck into the boys' locker room and made his way to the second floor. Hannah was always on the first floor practicing her sword powers, so the second floor had become his safe space from her.

Might as well get some reps in with wooden swords before I take her on again, Anthony decided. *Though I kinda wish I had brought my workout clothes. Oh well, looks like I'm fighting in street clothes today.*

He resigned himself to the fact that they would be ruined after his fight with Hannah.

He shook his head and retrieved his wooden katana out of his special locker. The katana was a prize he had won for a high school sword-fighting tournament. The sword was supposed to be made out of a special wood that made it unbreakable, and as far as he could tell, there wasn't a dent or scratch on it even after all the spars he had been through.

At a young age, Anthony had taken a liking to sword fighting. The popularity of the Divine Blades had made sword fighting a big sport in Amaraitia. He had always enjoyed practicing, but he didn't get good at it until his sophomore year of high school. He hit his growth spurt, and his ability skyrocketed. That was when people started talking about how he should be a Divine Blade. The only problem was, Divine Blades were passed down through families. Even though the blade picked its master, it still kept its choice inside that family. There had never been a Divine Blade in any of Anthony's family, extended or otherwise. He was the first in his bloodline to become a Divine Blade. The only reason he got a chance to hold the sword was due to a recent archeological find. They had uncovered the tomb of a wealthy man from ancient times, and in that tomb was the lost divine blade. They couldn't track it back to any family that was living today, so they took the blade around to various children who showed promise as future wielders. When the blade made its way to Anthony's city, the committee was hesitant to allow him to try. They wanted the new wielder to be younger so as to be able to properly train them. But the head of the archeological find pulled some strings to get Anthony an audience, and sure enough, it chose him to be its wielder. He was a week away from graduating when that happened.

Anthony couldn't help but chuckle at the absurdity of it all as he remembered the past. His plans for the future were dashed in a moment. He had no say in his life anymore. He had to become a Divine Blade, and being a Divine Blade meant that the only thing he could be was a protector of the people. He got a full ride scholarship to one of the only two Divine Blade academies in the world. And his life had been a mess ever since.

Anthony strode out of the locker room and observed all the activity that was taking place around him. Many people were running laps, some were practicing their hand-to-hand combat skills, and others were whacking away at each other with their wooden swords. Anthony let a smile out; he could never stay mad here. This gym was his haven, and he always came here when he had to get some things off his mind.

From across the room, he spotted Clancy. Clancy was the sparring judge for the upstairs gym and was also an incredible sword fighter. As a Divine Blade, he was ranked in the top 100 strongest last year. When it came to pure swordsmanship, Clancy was the only one at Anthony's level. An interesting rivalry had developed as a result of this.

Anthony walked up behind Clancy and waited for a bit. Clancy was focused in on a spar between two trainees. Their moves were clunky and rough, but they hacked at each other nonetheless. It didn't take long for one to get the upper hand, and he jumped in for the "kill" blow. The disarmed fighter stumbled and fell down as Clancy blew his whistle.

"All right, fellas, that's enough for today. You're both are at a high-enough level to pass the exams tomorrow, so don't sweat it."

The two fighters smiled in relief and left for the showers.

"Pass or not, that fight was pathetic," Anthony stated.

Clancy chuckled. "They swing swords like they're wet noodles, but not everyone has the grace and finesse that we have."

He turned around and faced Anthony; both of them were on the mat.

Anthony smiled. "No, I suppose they can't."

A drawn-out pause floated between them as the gym got semi-quiet. Most of the people there had been to the gym enough times to know what would happen next, and a small crowd began to gather around the mat.

"But I didn't come here to chat. I'd like to knock some of the rust off before the exams tomorrow, and I was wondering if you could help me out with it?"

Clancy raised an eyebrow and hefted his wooden sword up. "I don't know if we'll have enough time to get that much rust off."

Anthony cracked a wry smile. "Keep thinking like that. It will make beating you easier."

The gym became silent. The fighters took their stances and readied themselves. Anthony took the first move by charging in and slashing at Clancy's left side. Clancy blocked the slash and countered with a thrust that Anthony knocked away. From there, a flurry of blows rained down on both sides, with neither fighter seeming to get the upper hand. Anthony spun, hacked, and stabbed in all the moves and combos that he knew but never once managed to hit his target, much the same for Clancy as he pulled out all the stops to touch Anthony but never succeeded. The onlookers watched in total awe as these two titans matched each other blow for blow.

Anthony was in heaven. His mind saw and reacted to every move that Clancy's body made. He loved the simplicity of the fight; that no matter how hard he tried, he could never land a single blow on him. It had always been like that. Clancy had trained Anthony since high school. At first, Anthony could never get close, but it all changed his sophomore year. In the blink of an eye, he caught up to Clancy's level. Now their spars always looked like this. Two cyclones of blades hacking away at each other.

Anthony pivoted hard and feinted low, but spun off it for a high arching strike. As always Clancy's blade was there to stop it. Anthony pushed as hard as he could to get the sword to go down, but he would have had better luck moving a brick wall. He refocused his energy and pushed off the guard, flying a few feet away from Clancy. His breathing wasn't too labored, but he could feel the strain of the battle on his body. Any more, and he would start to get seriously exhausted. He checked the clock and saw that thirty minutes had passed by. He laughed and lowered his guard.

"Well, I'd say that all my rust is gone."

Clancy smiled and said, "The first layer, at the very least."

They met in the middle and exchanged a handshake, but before either could say anything, the gym door slammed open. Hannah stood in the entrance looking furious as she stormed over to the mat. Anthony rolled his eyes as he knew what was coming.

"You know what happens next, Anthony. Now get down to the first floor so I can put you in your place."

Anthony shook his head. "Yeah, yeah, I know. Would you mind refing this match for me?" he asked Clancy.

"Of course," he said, trying to act nonchalant about it, but the worry was written all over his face.

Anthony turned to a livid Hannah and said, "All right, Ms. Lillitania, let's get this thing over with."

The first-floor gym was packed with people, but you wouldn't know it by the silence that filled the room. A large caged arena stood in the center of the gym, fenced off by special materials that repelled most of the blade powers. The stands on all sides were full of students waiting on the edge of their seats to watch Hannah in action. She was a celebrity on the campus ever since a prestigious magazine ranked her in the top five of rising Divine Blades.

Anthony couldn't help but shake his head. Word of their impending spar had spread like wildfire through the classes. If the stands were full, it meant a complete turnout from the students. Even for a spar like this, the turnout was always huge. That was the problem that Anthony had. Divine Blade skills were considered the thing. No one cared about physical prowess here. Anthony could never dream of a turnout like this for a simple spar upstairs. That was also part of the reason he was so unpopular. No one cared about his physical skill here. The only thing that mattered was divine skill, and his was the bottom of the barrel.

Anthony sighed as he tried to let it go and looked over at Hannah. She stood opposite of him, her sword already out of its sheath. The sword was brilliant to look at. It shined like the moon, and its shape was elegant, to say the least. The handle guard looked like angel wings, and the pommel was a beautiful crystal that shone with all the colors of the rainbow. It was a hand-and-a-half sword, but she always fought with both hands on the handle.

Anthony unsheathed his sword and took his stance. His sword was ugly by comparison. His katana was a simple sword, but the blade itself was a dull metallic-gray color. The guard was an off-color bronze, and the handle was straight up wood. Everything about it screamed pathetic. Regardless of all this, he still liked his sword, but even he felt jealous when it was out next to Hannah's.

Clancy stepped out in the center of the ring and addressed both of the fighters. His usual joking demeanor was gone. He focused on the two combatants with an odd intensity.

"You both know the rules, but I'll cover them again, just so we are clear. This fight allows all Divine Blade powers and abilities. Minor cuts and bruises are excusable, but serious wounds will lead to the attacker receiving punishment from the school council. The match will end when one fighter either gives up or is unable to fight. Fighting will also cease if I step in. Do you understand?"

"Yes, sir," both fighters shouted, causing the tension in the room to skyrocket.

"Prepare," Clancy announced.

Both fighters drew their energy out of their swords. The air got heavy as the sheer weight of Hannah's power filled the room. Anthony's energy was a soft breeze to Hannah's hurricane.

Clancy looked at them both one more time then shouted, "BEGIN!"

Hannah bolted straight at Anthony and slashed at incredible speeds right for his throat. The physical boost that Hannah's sword gave her was far better than the boost that Anthony received. If Hannah had been even half as good as Anthony at sword fighting, the battle would have been over in an instant, but Anthony was far superior to Hannah in swordplay. He managed to see her movements and, in the nick of time, block each of her strikes. Hannah continued the flurry of uncoordinated blows, and Anthony managed to block each one of them. He could see the frustration growing on her face until he found the opening he was waiting for.

Hannah struck the right then left side, but Anthony predicted the move and ducked under the swing. He thrust his sword with all the power and speed that he could muster, but he already knew it was no use. As his blade got an inch away from her stomach, a light barrier appeared in between the point and her flesh. This light shield was the ability that made her such a strong opponent. No student on the campus had been able to penetrate the light shield ever. All he managed to do was push her back a couple of feet, but not a scratch lay on her.

Still, the fact that she had to use her light shield seemed to piss her off even more as she jumped back a couple more feet. Anthony flexed and bent his knees in anticipation of her next move as he already knew what came next. When Hannah got upset, she resorted to her signature move. Her blade glowed as she brought her sword back. She swung it forward, as if slashing an invisible opponent, and sent her light wave flying straight at Anthony. Like a flying curved blade of concentrated light energy, this attack was easily the strongest ranged attack on the campus. Anthony had seen it a thousand times before and had already planned this step.

People flinched as the blade seemed to crash right into him, but were confused when nothing happened. The light wave crashed into the fence and exploded on impact, covering the stands in a thick layer of smoke. When the smoke cleared, everyone gasped as they saw that Anthony was on the complete opposite side of the arena.

Anthony's only special ability was the speed step. This allowed him to move from one point to the next in the twinkling of an eye. Of course, the range was limited, but he had practiced it enough to where the span of the arena was nothing for him.

Hannah spun in a disjointed motion and loosed another light wave. This time, Anthony didn't wait for the wave, but used his speed step the instant the wave was loosed to get to the side that Clancy was on. There he stood straight up and faced Hannah.

Her face was crimson with rage by the time she turned around. She screamed a death cry as she loosed a third wave at Anthony. This time, he didn't speed step; he stood there with his sword ready like he was going to block it. The wave crashed into Anthony and held against his sword for a second before it exploded, sending him flying into the fence. Anthony landed hard and gritted his teeth as he reached for his leg. Streaks of pain came from his calf, but before he could look at it, a scream drew his attention to the sky. Hannah was flying straight at him with murder in her eyes as she swung her sword for his head. Anthony closed his eyes and heard the clang he was hoping to hear. When he opened his eyes, he saw the back of Clancy. He had blocked Hannah's killing swing with one hand on his broadsword.

The crowd gasped as the murder in Hannah's eyes turned into fear. Power began to radiate from Clancy as he stared into Hannah's eyes. Everyone felt suffocated as Clancy's energy blanketed the arena. Even Hannah's energy was blotted out.

"Ms. Lillitania, I know you weren't trying to kill Anthony just now, right?"

Clancy's tone was calm, but it couldn't cover up a rage that seemed to drown out any anger that Hannah previously had.

Hannah attempted to regain her composure, but still stumbled over her words as she tried to speak. "O-of course, I wasn't going to kill him. I planned on pulling up at the last second to give him as big a scare as I could before I won."

She leapt back and sheathed her sword. She took one last look at Anthony then turned around and hurried out of the arena.

Clancy's power subsided as she walked out the doors. Gasps could be heard around the arena as the onlookers were relieved from Clancy's pressure and allowed to breathe again. Anthony let his own pent-up breath out and looked down at his leg. He sighed in relief as he saw it was only a mild cut from the light wave on his calf.

Clancy tuned and took a knee to wrap up his leg. "That's a nice cut you got there, buddy. All you need now is a matching one on the other leg."

Anthony smiled through the pain and chuckled. "Yeah, well, I suppose it's not the worst thing that could have happened just then."

Clancy's face got very serious as he finished the wrapping. "You know, if you could use your speed step more than twice, you might have stood a chance in that fight. Or in any fight for that matter."

Anthony stared at the ceiling as Clancy stood back up. "I know, but this is the lot I've been stuck with. It's not going to change if I complain about it, so I might as well continue on and perfect what little I have."

Clancy looked at Anthony with admiration in his eyes. He shook it out before Anthony could notice it and helped him up. "Well, hurry up and get strong. It's embarrassing having my trainee get his butt kicked in every spar."

Anthony rolled his eyes as he tested his weight on his injured left leg, but found that he could walk just fine. His pants were ruined, though, as the wave had torn off anything below the cut on his leg.

Anthony sighed and stared at the door. "Yeah, I'm not looking forward to my parents seeing this."

Chapter 2

CONFLICT

*A*nthony pulled into his driveway and shut off his vehicle. He sat in silence and stared out the window at the now-browning trees.

Fall's here, he thought, looking forward to the cooler weather. The sweltering summer heat had grown old long before season was supposed to end.

He looked down at his leg again to inspect the damage. He had visited the nurse's office to get his wound all cleaned out and wrapped with proper bandages, but his pants were useless now. The left leg was torn off from midway calf down, and there were burn marks all over. He was thankful that they were a throwaway pair. If his favorite pair had been ruined, he would have been depressed beyond reason.

Anthony stepped out of his trito and stood for a while in his driveway. He gazed at his house with a fondness that he didn't have for most things. This was the house that he had grown up in. Every good memory he had could be traced back here in one way or another. The dome was whiter than his neighbors', and its unique half-circle shape was more pleasing to him than the other shapes his friends' houses took.

He looked in the garage to see his parents' tritos, and his heart sank a little. He was hoping they wouldn't be home, so he could change and clean up without them seeing the damage that he had sustained.

Guess it can't be helped. Though it's not like they're going to be mad at me.

But that wasn't what he was worried about in the first place. It was true, his parents never got on to him for being weak. In fact, the topic of his Divine Blade status never came up in the house unless he was the one to start the conversation. He just didn't want his parents to worry about him. They had enough to worry about with their own jobs and getting his brother through high school; he didn't want to give them anything else to fret over. They weren't poor by any means, but that didn't mean that life wasn't still tough for them.

Anthony walked up the driveway and in through the garage. He kicked off his shoes and walked into the kitchen where his mother and father appeared to be having a conversation. His mother paused to smile at him, but her smile faded into a look of panic and concern.

"Oh my goodness, sweetheart, what happened?"

Anthony looked at his father, who was also wearing a very serious face. Anthony sighed and recounted his battle with Hannah.

His father shook his head. "Hannah again, huh? That girl is nothing but trouble."

"I absolutely agree. In fact, I'm going to call the school about her and have the—"

"Mom!"

She got quiet and looked at her son with confusion.

"It's all right, Mom, you don't have to call the school. These matches are never mandatory, and I can decline her challenges any time I want to. And whenever I do fight her, I always make sure Clancy is the one to ref them."

His mother relaxed a little bit as his parents both knew Clancy.

"But what if one day Clancy isn't around?" his mom questioned.

"Then I won't fight. Like I said, I'm never forced into these battles. I just accept them because I know that at the end of the day, it will help me get stronger."

His parents got quiet as they thought about what he said.

His dad smiled and put his hand on Anthony's shoulder. "All right, we'll trust you with this. Just promise that you won't accept a challenge if you don't feel like fighting, okay?"

Anthony smiled back and nodded.

Anthony jogged upstairs and headed to his room. He found his brother James in the family room sprawled out on the couch watching TV.

"Hey, James," Anthony said as he passed by the couch.

His brother nodded his head without looking away from the TV. "What was all that commotion downstairs?"

Anthony stepped in front of the TV as he showed off his wound to his little brother. James's attention snapped away from the screen and down to Anthony's leg.

"Whoa! What happened to you?"

"Hannah," Anthony stated, and James just laughed.

When his laughing subsided, he turned back to the screen and just said, "Women."

Anthony laughed as he turned to his room.

"Oh," he said, turning back toward James. "Could you tell Mom and Dad that I'm going to bed now? They don't have to worry about me for dinner. I already had it."

"Okay, I'll let them know," James said without looking away from the TV.

"Thanks," Anthony said and closed the door to his room.

Anthony couldn't help but shake his head. *Of course, James wouldn't get riled up about that incident.*

His brother was one of those "gifted yet lazy" students. That had sort of bled over into his personal life. If it wasn't about something he cared about, it was tough to get him excited. But both brothers enjoyed many of the same things, so conversation would always flow. Anthony could recall many nights where they would stay up late playing video games or talking about said video games.

I'm just blessed with a great family, Anthony thought as he changed out of his ruined pants.

He put on his pajama pants and flopped onto his bed, passing out from the exhaustion of the day.

Anthony's eyes shot open as he found himself standing outside a building. His mind tried to process what was going on. The last thing he remembered was falling on his bed. Now he was standing in the courtyard outside the main lecture hall on his campus.

Is this one of those lucid dreams I've heard about? he wondered.

A friend had told him about lucid dreams, saying they were dreams that you were aware of and could control.

Well, pondered Anthony, *if this is a lucid dream, I should be able to fly or do whatever I want.*

Anthony jumped several times, flexing every muscle he had in his body in an attempt to fly, but only succeeded in wearing himself out.

A student trudged along in Anthony's direction, so he decided to interact with the people in his dream to see if maybe they could help him out.

"Excuse me," he said, running up toward the unknown student.

The student never looked up or acknowledged him. Anthony stood in his way, thinking that he would have to talk to him whether he wanted to or not, but the student kept coming. Anthony braced for an impact, but none came. The student walked straight through Anthony like he was a ghost.

Anthony froze in absolute shock. He couldn't do anything in this dream. Once he had accepted this fact, he began to walk off toward the main lecture hall.

A large explosion shook the entire campus. Anthony spun around to see students fleeing in all directions in complete terror. Even as the explosion died down, commotion could be heard in the distance. Anthony ran toward the smoke cloud to see what was happening. His progress was halted by a shadowy figure rising above the buildings. One turned into two, then two into twenty, and before Anthony knew it, the sky was filled with hundreds of black figures flying through the sky on their sickly black wings. Their eyes were bloodred, and their fangs were long and snow white. Anthony stood in horror as he realized what was happening.

The Zankrex were attacking.

Anthony stood frozen as the grim scene unfolded before him. The Zankrex swooped down on the students, killing any who were unfortunate enough to be standing outside. Many Divine Blades fell before they could even pull out their swords. Even when the rest unsheathed their blades, the battle was still one-sided. Most of the Divine Blades were surrounded and murdered before they could find allies, and those who managed to group up could only sit and defend. Very few found shelter, and those who were left outside were dispatched after some resistance.

Anthony tried to process what this meant. Was this a premonition? Was this just a nightmare? He grabbed his head in utter confusion of what this all meant.

"Are you enjoying the show, Anthony?" asked a painfully familiar voice.

Anthony turned in dread as he knew whom that voice belonged to. His eyes were met by the bright-red gaze of the shadow from his first dream. It stood there staring into Anthony's soul with a grin on his face, like he was enjoying every second of this massacre.

Anthony stumbled and fell in complete terror. He didn't know why this thing scared him so much. He knew it wasn't real, but that thought offered little comfort.

The shadow cackled at Anthony's display. He advanced on him as the scene around them faded to black.

"So do you like it?" asked the shadow. "It won't happen as you see it now, but this massacre is going to be the start of my grand takeover. It all starts with your little university. I hope you survive it because it would be an immense pleasure if I got to kill you personally."

With that, the figure disappeared, and Anthony once again felt himself falling straight into an unknown abyss. As he fell, the shadow's voice whispered down one last taunt, "I hope you're ready Anthony." It cackled again. As the voice faded out, Anthony plunged screaming down the abyss.

Anthony shot straight up from his bed, flailing as he woke. He calmed down and inspected his dark room. The clock's dim light shone in the far corner, letting him know that it was midnight. His breathing was heavy, and he was drenched in sweat. He sat there for a couple of minutes, trying to gather his thoughts.

That was no dream. It was more like a premonition. Or perhaps a warning? But why would the bad guy warn me of his plan?

Anthony grabbed his head in confusion as too many questions bounced around for him to think straight. Soon his breathing slowed, and his sweat dried off. He allowed himself to lie back down.

Should I tell anyone about this? he pondered. *Even if I did, no one would believe me, and how could I blame them? I have no proof and no reasonable idea of when this will take place.*

He replayed the scene in his head. It was during the day, and the students were still wearing light clothing. If he were to take that information, he could assume it would happen soon.

But the shadow said that wasn't how it would happen. So that scene was more of a warning than the actual event itself?

Anthony continued to think about it until his brain hurt. In time, the adrenaline worked its way out of his system, and he fell back to sleep.

The next morning, Anthony woke up not feeling much better. His muscles were still stiff from all the commotion that happened yesterday, and his experience last night had kept him from getting the deep sleep he needed.

Anthony dragged his feet down the stairs and got his breakfast. After eating, he grabbed the newspaper to read up on the latest from the Divine Blade world. It was a slow day in the way of demon-beast attacks, which didn't make Anthony feel any better. But that wasn't the part he wanted to read about.

There was a whole page dedicated to the God Swords that Anthony had to read every single day. First up was the Fire Broadsword Brandon from Eufrin: he was in the news because he was constructing a city that would be used to train Divine Blades. It had neared completion, and the ribbon-cutting ceremony would be tomorrow. Quotes about Brandon's amazing leadership were littered across the article.

The next write-up was on the Water Cutlass Vanessa. She was in the news because she had once again skipped out on an important meeting with political figureheads. The meeting itself was pointless, but the politicians wanted photo ops with a God Sword for their campaigns. Vanessa was the most free-spirited of the bunch. She lived life on her own schedule and never stayed in one place for long. This brought the ire of the figureheads, but also brought the admiration of the general public. Anthony always loved reading up on her. He wouldn't admit it to anyone, but he had a giant crush on her. He had participated in a sword-fighting tournament, and she was a guest of honor there. After his final match, he looked up at her, and she nodded at him with an impressed look on her face. He had been smitten ever since.

The next article was on the Wind Rapier Hizaki. Her write-up was small as it was about her taking control of the Hinoromi house. Hizaki was probably the weakest of the God Swords in terms of raw strength or energy, though that still put her leagues ahead of all the Divine Blades and was the one who stuck hard to tradition. She and Brandon had some beef because she refused to see him as the leader and had openly opposed him becoming anything in the form of a leader because the leader of the God Swords was the Earth Katana.

The last little bit was on the Lightning Gladius Robert. The article was about a party that he was seen attending and nothing else. Robert was the most laid-back of all the God Swords. Every day, he was in the papers for some party or just being spotted lying around all day. No one had ever seen Robert fighting all out, but those who knew him were always saying he was a force to be reckoned with.

Anthony folded the newspaper back up and set it on the table. He sat back in his chair and imagined meeting any of the God Swords. He knew it would never happen because you had to be somebody in this world to get an audience with them.

Still, thought Anthony, *it's always fun to imagine.*

He stood and went back up to his room to get dressed and ready for the day. He had already prepped a bag for the physical exam that morning. Street clothes were okay for a duel, but not for what he was about to go through that morning. The physical exam was by no means easy and would leave even the most in-shape participant out of breath.

The running and sword-skill parts would be no problem, thought Anthony. *But I've never done well on the push-ups, sit-ups, and hand-to-hand combat skills.*

Anthony had also heard that more swimming exercises would be on the test as more fish and aquatic animals were becoming possessed by the dark energy.

Well, at least Hannah won't be bugging me today, Anthony realized.

Hannah hated the base physical exam, and by the time she got done with it, she was far too tired to even think about challenging Anthony.

He smiled as he walked outside. *Maybe today won't be too bad after all.*

Anthony parked his trito closer to the gym than he was used to being. He couldn't help but chuckle. On any other day, he would have had to park out in the boondocks, but today was different. Everyone hated the base physical exam. On test day, everyone slept as long as they could before heading off to the gym.

Anthony walked with pep in his step as he strode into the gym. He put his stuff up in a locker and changed into his workout clothes. Today both floors would be used for the physical exam. Anthony walked out on the first floor and took a look around. The arena that he had fought in yesterday was gone, and several pads had been laid out with spaces in between them. Each pad would be used for a different exercise for the different groups. The layout was the exact same upstairs. Anthony scanned the room for a face he recognized. It didn't take him long to find his one friend.

Christian spotted him from across the gym and trotted over. He smiled with his goofy grin and tilted his head back.

"Aye, yo, waz up?" he joked. "I was wondering if you planned on coming or not."

Anthony gave him a quizzical look and asked why.

"Why? I thought you would be recuperating from your battle with Hannah."

Anthony laughed. "No, no, that battle didn't get too serious. Besides, I had Clancy there to make sure that everything would stay clean."

Christian nodded. "A smart move. From what I heard, you would have been in slices if he hadn't been there."

Anthony tried to laugh over the fear, remembering the murderous intent in Hannah's eyes as she flew in for the attack.

"Yeah, I'd like to think she would have pulled up at the last second, but ..." He trailed off, not wanting to finish his thought.

Christian looked at his friend in concern. "You know she may not be joking around with that. Have you ever thought about filing a complaint to the board?"

Anthony laughed hard at that one. "Yeah right, like the board would take up a complaint from a low-level Divine Blade plus a commoner about their star student and the daughter of an influential aristocrat."

Christian couldn't argue with that one. "Well, when you put it like that ..."

They both sat in silence for a while, stretching before getting up and jogging laps around the perimeter. The longer they went, the more people started to show up, and soon the gym was packed with people warming up.

Once they finished, Anthony sat against a wall while Christian went to the top floor to take the exam with his class. Anthony pondered about how he was going to finish that sentence.

Do I really think she would have killed me? No ... there's no way she would have killed me. Even for someone of her status, she would have gotten in a whole mess of trouble. But why do I still feel like she would have.

Anthony struggled to understand but was interrupted by the whistle of the examiner. Whatever thoughts he had were pushed aside for the start of the exam.

Anthony sat at his desk, exhausted in his class. It had been about forty-five minutes since the physical exam had ended, and he was still out of breath. He had believed himself to be more in shape, but the exam proved otherwise. He didn't want to admit it, but the two battles from yesterday really had worn him out. The shower he took after the exam felt like heaven.

The downside of the long shower was that he had only left himself ten minutes for lunch. He managed to scarf something down, but it wasn't enough to fill the void in his stomach. Now he sat in class exhausted and hungry. The only positive thing was that he was getting off his feet for the first time of the day.

His eyes kept closing as he tried to stay awake. His poor night's sleep was coming back to haunt him. His whole body was mad at him, and all he wanted was to close his eyes and nod off. He knew better than to fall asleep in class again. If he did, Mr. Hazblazen would call him out for it, and Hannah would confront him again.

Then Anthony realized something. He hadn't seen Hannah all day. Even in the physical exams, which she hated, she always made sure to stand out. But he hadn't heard anything from her all morning.

They must have put her on the second floor, Anthony decided, but that still didn't make any sense. All those in the same class would participate in the physical exam together on the same floor.

Oh well, Anthony thought, *no point in looking a gift horse in the mouth. If I can go one morning without Hannah, then it's a good morning in my book.*

His train of thought was derailed as Hazblazen walked in the room. Everyone returned to their seats and got quiet.

Hazblazen looked around the class and smiled. "Well, look at all these cheerful students I have in class this fine morning."

A collective groan filled the room as all the students remembered the exam they had just gone through. Hazblazen laughed and waited for the groans to stop.

He scanned the class but frowned as he looked. "Does anyone know where Ms. Lillitania is today? I received a report from the exam instructor that she was not in attendance for the physical this morning."

Murmurs floated through the class as everyone shared in the same shock that she hadn't shown up.

Then, as if on cue, the class door flew open, and Hannah strode into the room. She looked pristine, as if she had just woken up from a long night's sleep. Mr. Hazblazen looked at her with understandable confusion.

"Good morning, Hannah. What brings you tardy to class?"

Hannah smiled with her stuck-up I'm-more-important-than-you smile and said "Oh, I'm sorry, Mr. Hazblazen, but my father needed me at the house this morning so that's why I'm a tad late for class."

The class sat in disbelief as they all knew that was a lie but in no way felt bold enough to call her out on it.

Hazblazen sighed. "I suppose that is also the reason why you couldn't be at the physical this morning?"

"Yep," she stated, puffing her chest out even further. "And since it's my dad's business that kept me, I won't have to make it up."

That sealed the deal. The class knew that her father's business was not something she could help out with. The only reason she skipped was because she begged her father to get her out of it. And everyone knew that her father spoiled her rotten, so that request would have been granted in a heartbeat. Even Mr. Hazblazen seemed to understand what was going on, but knew there was nothing to be done but accept it.

"Well then, my confusion is cleared," he stated and gestured to her seat. "Now, if you would please take your seat, we can begin class."

She walked up to her seat in the middle of the class and noticed Anthony in the very back with his head down. She paused for a second and then walked up the back row with an evil smile on her lips.

"Hey, Anthony," she said, condescension dripping off her words.

He looked up at her without sitting all the way up and sighed. "Hello, Hannah."

Yesterday, that sentence alone would have been enough for her to declare war; but this time, she brushed it off and continued the conversation.

"I'm surprised you showed up today, considering how badly I beat you up yesterday."

The room got silent as students and teacher alike held their breath in anticipation.

Anthony chuckled and turned his head back into his arms. "Yeah, yesterday was rough. I dueled Clancy and fought you. But I still made it in for the exam and passed with flying colors. What was your excuse again?"

No one dared move at that point for fear of drawing attention to themselves. Hannah had the look that she always did the moment before she went off. Even Hazblazen looked hesitant to say anything.

Hannah clenched her fist in an attempt to hold back. "I told you, didn't I? My father needed my help with his business."

Anthony laughed and turned his head to look her in the eye. "You? Help your father? Oh yeah, that's a good one. Your father imports advanced hardware to the far corners of Tertalla. What did you help him with? Refilling his drink when it was empty?"

Everyone stared at Anthony with mouths agape, in complete and total shock. Even Hannah took a step back as she tried to process what he had just said. Anthony had never told her off straight up like that before. His comments were always underhanded and had double meaning to them. But this time, he wasted no words in dissing her.

Hannah shuddered in rage as she gripped her sword. "Looks like I didn't beat you hard enough yesterday. Well, no matter, come to the gym after class, and I'll make sure to put you in your place this time."

"No," Anthony stated. The bluntness of his reply had tangible weight to it.

Everyone gasped at his comment. No one had turned down Hannah's challenge before. Hannah was considered a noble. No one was supposed to ever deny a noble's request. There was no inherent law about it, but it was considered social taboo for anyone to deny a noble's challenge. The class stared on in disbelief as Anthony was now sitting straight up and staring Hannah straight in the eyes.

Hannah's face contorted in furry "*You* decline *my* challenge? A lowlife like yourself declines *my* challenge?" She whipped her sword out and charged at Anthony, the same murderous intent filling her eyes. "I'll kill you right now, you scum!"

Just then, a sword came out of nowhere and blocked the swing. Anthony looked over and saw an arm sticking out of a small wormhole, then looked down at the chalkboard. Mr. Hazblazen stood there with most of his arm in the other end of the wormhole. Even in the heat of the moment, Anthony couldn't help but enjoy the opportunity to see Hazblazen's Divine Skill in action.

Hazblazen's gaze was stern as he met Hannah's eyes. "Ms. Lillitania, unless you desire an audience with the president on this matter, you will march back to your seat and not talk again for the duration of the class."

They stared at each other as all the students held their breath, hoping for a peaceful ending to the tense situation.

Hannah turned her head and sheathed her blade. She stomped back to her seat and sat down without a word. Everyone released their pent-up breath and relaxed. Mr. Hazblazen pulled his arm out of the wormhole and sheathed his own sword. He took a breath, regaining his composure, and smiled at the class. "Well, shall we continue where we left off from yesterday?"

Mr. Hazblazen finished writing his last point on the chalkboard and turned to the class. "All right, students, that concludes for today. Tomorrow we will not be having lecture due to the Divine Blade skills test and the address by the president afterward. Next session will occur after tomorrow."

The sound of screeching seats and mumbles prevailed over the room as everyone got up and headed back home. Anthony kept his head down and waited for Hannah to leave. He didn't have to wait long as she got up and left without even a look back toward him.

She must still be worried about Hazblazen if she didn't even look at me, Anthony realized. He was relieved that nothing happened. He still couldn't believe he had said those things to her. *I wasn't thinking at all. I know she's been extra mad at me, so why did I provoke her extra hard?* He shook his head, attributing it to his extreme exhaustion, and began to pack up.

"Anthony," Mr. Hazblazen said, getting Anthony's attention, "would you come to my office?"

Anthony nodded and followed Hazblazen to his office on the second floor. Anthony was too tired to worry about what this was about—that and he kind of knew what the topic of their discussion was going to be. They walked into Hazblazen's office, and he shut the door.

"Please have a seat, Anthony."

Anthony gratefully accepted his offer and flopped into the nice, comfy chair.

Hazblazen smiled at Anthony's exhaustion. "I see the reports on the exam's difficulty were not fabricated."

Anthony groaned. "It was crazy tough. Last year's exam couldn't hold a candle to this year's."

Hazblazen laughed. "Yes, the president noticed that last year's exam was a tad on the easy side. But I think we may have overcompensated this year." Then his face got serious. "But that is not what I called you in here for. And I'll get right to the point: What is the trouble between you and Hannah?"

Anthony sighed as he sat up in his seat. "Well, last year was my first year, and no one knew who I was, which was okay for me as I was very new to this whole Divine Blade thing. But one day Hannah came up to me and said I wasn't a true Divine Blade. She challenged me to a duel, and I lost. After that, I didn't hear from her again until after the base physical exam last year. Word got out of my exceptional score on the test, and on the sword skills in particular. The day after that, she started to make fun of me again and would always challenge me to fights. After a while, I got used to it because the fights never got real serious. But after I aced the finals, she cranked that hate up to ten. I didn't notice it right away since it was the end of the school year, but over break, I would receive e-mails berating me and reminding me of the beating I was going to get when I got back. Then this year, she changed. She becomes livid the moment I say anything, and our last duel was much more intense than our normal ones. In fact, Clancy had to step in and stop her at the end of it. And then you saw what happened this morning."

Anthony got quiet as he remembered the look in her eyes as she charged at him in the classroom. It was like he was reliving the same moment from yesterday.

Hazblazen sighed. "I suppose I wasn't helping anything by putting you on display like that yesterday."

Anthony laughed. "Oh no, she would have called me out on it either way. She always watches me during class to see if I do anything wrong, so she has a reason to get on to me. It wouldn't surprise me if I'm the reason why she does so poorly in lecture."

Hazblazen chuckled. "Oh, I doubt that very much. She was doing lackluster in lecture the year before you even became a Divine Blade. And she never picked on anyone either. This is weird because there are other students here that are in the same boat as you. They became Divine Blades even though their families never passed one down. I'm just trying to figure out why you're so special."

Anthony could only shrug. He wasn't the weakest of the weak, and even among the weak, there were those who did far better than him on test scores. There just wasn't a logical explanation. Then he remembered the dreams he'd been having. He hesitated telling Hazblazen about them, but decided that it couldn't hurt if he did.

"Uh, Mr. Hazblazen? There's something that I want to tell you."

He then recounted the two dreams he had in the past two days. When he finished, Hazblazen could only sit there with a blank look on his face as he tried to process what Anthony just told him.

He blinked out of his thoughts and looked at Anthony. "And Hannah's violence has followed each dream?"

Anthony nodded. "Yeah, the first dream happened in your class yesterday. Right after that, Hannah and I had our little death match. The second one came last night, and today Hannah almost kills me right in front of the entire class." Anthony realized what he was saying. "Ah, but I'm in no way saying that Hannah is connected with the Zankrex."

Hazblazen continued to stare at his desk. "I wonder though if that isn't too far off," he mumbled to himself.

Anthony raised his eyebrows as he didn't hear what it was that he just said.

Hazblazen shook his head and looked at Anthony. "In any case, I don't believe that your dreams and Hannah's odd behavior is evidence enough to bring action—since the board is a bunch of stubborn old fools that wouldn't believe a Zankrex existed even if one were to smack them with fishes."

The room got quiet as they both tried to think of what to do from here.

Hazblazen stood. "Well, there's nothing to gain from sitting here fretting over it. For now, I'll be sure that you take your Divine Blade skills test on a separate floor than Hannah."

Anthony could only nod. He felt unfulfilled with the outcome of the conversation. Hazblazen let a tired half smile cross his lips before walking over to Anthony. Anthony was lost in thought and didn't see his teacher looming over him. A solid thump to his chest tore him from his trance. He looked down to see Hazblazen's finger laid square on his chest.

"This isn't the Anthony I've come to know. Cheer up. We'll sort this mess out. You have my word on that, but until then, you must buck up."

Anthony couldn't help but smile. The gesture was small, but it held a lot of meaning. Every time Anthony had begun to doubt himself, Hazblazen would thump him on the chest and offer words of encouragement. That was the reason Anthony looked up to Hazblazen like he did. No matter how low he got, his teacher always believed in him.

Anthony stood up and shouldered his backpack. "Thanks, Mr. Hazblazen. I'll keep my head up, promise."

Hazblazen smiled and waved as Anthony left the room. Anthony walked out of the office and continued down the hall.

Hazblazen's right, thought Anthony. *At this point, there's nothing I can do about Hannah. Thinking about it will only drive me nuts. For now, I'll concentrate on the exam. The rest can come later.*

He stepped outside and headed to his vehicle, looking forward to the comfort of home.

Chapter 3

Overrun

*A*nthony went about the rest of his day pondering his conversation with Hazblazen. It wasn't abnormal for him to be coming out of Hazblazen's office with a lot on his mind. Because of his status as weakest Divine Blade but strongest student, he had talked with Hazblazen more than a few times throughout his university tenure. Due to this, a relationship had formed beyond that of just a simple teacher and student. Hazblazen respected Anthony as a hardworking student the same way Anthony respected Hazblazen as a teacher and a mentor. That was why Hazblazen picked on Anthony the way he did. Anthony knew that Hazblazen had no idea about Hannah at the time, so he didn't blame him for anything. But it had appeared that Hazblazen had come to the same conclusion as Anthony: something wasn't right with Hannah.

Anthony sighed as he lay back on his bed. *Oh well, worrying about it isn't going to solve anything. Hazblazen was right when he said that we couldn't do anything right now. I guess we just sit tight and wait for this thing to solve itself.*

Anthony closed his eyes and fell into a deep sleep.

Morning brought along with it a thin fog. The grass had a light coating of frost: the first sign that fall was in full swing. Anthony awoke feeling far more energized than he was used to feeling. He had slept well that night, and for the first time in what seemed like forever, he didn't have a strange nightmare.

Though I suppose I've only had two of those dreams, so I can't say it feels like it's been forever.

Anthony decided not to think about it too much and just enjoy his peace of mind.

He had awoken three hours before the exam was supposed to take place. His family wouldn't even be awake for another hour, but Anthony wanted to get to the gym early to stretch and prepare. He was feeling closer to full strength than he was yesterday, but he was still sore enough to need an ample amount of time to get ready.

He took his time eating breakfast and preparing his gym bag with his workout clothes. Soon he was off, leaving his house with around two hours until the exam.

With it being as early as it was, the parking around campus was wide open, and it took Anthony all of ten minutes from his house to park.

He stepped out into the brisk morning air and took a deep breath in. He always enjoyed this season. It was just cold enough to make you shiver, but still warm enough that you didn't need to bundle up real thick.

He walked over to the gym and checked the test list. The list would tell everyone which floor they would be on to take their test. On a normal day, it would be divided up by classes; but when Anthony found his class, his name wasn't with them. They were on the first floor, but Anthony was listed to take the test on the second floor. He pondered this development as he walked up to the second-floor changing area.

Why would they separate me from my class? wondered Anthony as he changed into his workout clothes.

His conversation with Hazblazen flashed through his mind. *He was serious about switching what floor I would be on. Well, all the better, I guess. If I can avoid even one confrontation with Hannah, it would be a blessing.*

Anthony finished changing and stuffed his street clothes into his locker. This time around, he buckled his sword around his waist since the whole test was about Divine Blade power. He stepped out onto the gym floor and looked at the few students who had shown up. They all seemed ready to fall asleep but trudged along regardless.

Anthony started his warm-up jog alone as Christian wasn't at the gym yet, and even when he did get there, he would be assigned a different testing group.

Alone to his thoughts, Anthony couldn't help but wonder about Hannah. When they first started school, she was always picking on him, but it never seemed to be evil. Even when she got pissed off, she never had murder in her eyes.

Why is she so hell-bent on killing me now? I've never done anything to her. And I know I haven't annoyed her that much. If anything, I should be the one that wants to kill her.

Nothing made sense to Anthony at the moment. He couldn't find one legitimate reason as to why Hannah would hate him so much.

Anthony continued to ponder this topic throughout his warm-ups. As test time drew closer, the gym began to fill up with tired and sluggish students. Anthony finished his routine and waited for the exams to start.

Regardless, thought Anthony, *I'm very glad I won't have to spar Hannah again.*

The eight-o'clock bell rang out, and the exam began. They split the students up into groups according to the results of the test last year.

The test itself was comprised of two separate parts: the physical upgrades of the sword and the divine skills of the sword. The physical-upgrade part of the exam wasn't a big problem. All you had to do to pass was show that your reflexes and strike speed had raised at least one level. Anthony's strike speed and reflex speed level were both at three, and he knew for a fact that he could block and give a four-level strike.

The problem for Anthony came with the divine skills. To receive a passing grade, you needed to show that you had made some progress with enhancing your divine skill. Anthony's divine skill was the speed step, and he could only use it twice. No matter how hard he trained, he could never get it to go any higher. The only way he could get a passing grade would be to show that he could effectively use this skill in combat. The last test, he wasn't able to land a strike on the dummy, but he was able to use one more speed step than last time, so he snuck by with a passing grade. But even after a year, he could still only use his skill twice, so he had to rely on his ability to use this skill for actual combat. The only problem with that was, he was still unable to use his speed step to deliver a legitimate blow to his opponent.

Anthony was still trying to convince himself he could do it when his name was called. With a reluctant sigh, he stepped into the testing ring. Before him was the dueling dummy. It had several arms that were programmed to deliver blows from a multitude of different angles. These blows could be programed to strike at several different speeds. The strike couldn't be blocked by those without divine energy. Divine Blades were tested on their reaction times using this dummy. The computer would choose a random arm to attack with and would even wait a random amount of time in between each strike. The dummy would pull the attacking arm back one inch and then strike from that side. The pullback was what they were supposed to see, and that was how to block the attack. The strikes themselves were at the same speed and power for all levels. What it tests is how a Divine Blade reacts. Only a Divine Blade could see the quick pullback and react to it in time.

Anthony requested that the dummy be put to level four as he took his stance. He needed to block three consecutive strikes to pass that level. He stood poised and stared at the center of the dummy so as to get a full view of all the arms. A twitch from one arm alerted Anthony of the incoming strike, and he blocked the first blow. The second strike came from up top, and Anthony managed to stop that attack as well. The third strike came right after the second and was a sweep to the left leg. Anthony brought his sword down and blocked the strike an inch away from his leg.

The whistle blew, and the judges gave him the thumbs-up sign.

"All right," a voice from the intercom said, "you passed the level-four reflex test. Now, if you would please strike that same dummy with a side slash. You must strike it with a level-four strike to pass. Good luck."

The intercom went silent, and Anthony took a stance against the dummy. He concentrated his divine power and drew back his sword. He slashed with all his strength and struck the dummy on the side. The blow caused the dummy to wobble a bit, but it was made out of very sturdy materials so as to deflect sharp divine blades.

Anthony exhaled and sheathed his sword. He turned toward the judges and awaited the results. A few tense seconds passed as the judges kept their eyes glued to the results screen. They looked up and gave the thumbs up sign. Anthony breathed a sigh of relief as he had passed the physical part of the exam.

The voice crackled from the intercom again. "All right, you passed the physical portion. Now please show us the progress you've made with your divine skill."

The judges sat and stared at Anthony as they watched him walk to the other side of the ring. The distance he would traverse would be much greater than last time, but he knew that if he wanted to pass for real, he needed to land a blow on the dummy.

He steadied his breathing and dipped back into his divine power. He concentrated on the dummy as he strained his energy. He unsheathed his sword and crouched. Anthony speed-stepped from his spot, appearing in front of the dummy in an instant. His slash had happened right after his speed step, but it had caught nothing but air. Anthony was still three feet away from the dummy. His walk back to the starting spot felt like a marathon. The judges' stares bored into him the whole way back. Once he had returned to his starting spot, he crouched and prepared for his last try.

A bead of sweat rolled down his cheek. He couldn't mess this up. Failing the divine-power portion of the test brought far worse than just a failing grade. This time, he used just a tad more power to propel him, and he shot forward for his last attempt. Once again, he appeared in front of the dummy, and silence overtook the ring as he waited in the finishing stance of his strike. Just when he thought he

41

hadn't touched his target, a thin scratch appeared on the dummy's chest. He had managed to lightly slash the dummy. Anthony's heart sank. He assumed that the scratch wouldn't be enough.

A pathetic cut like that wouldn't kill anything. There's no way I'm passing this.

Anthony turned around with dejection in his heart and awaited the overwhelming rejection. To his surprise, they seemed to be arguing among themselves.

Anthony stood in the ring for what felt like an eternity, watching the group almost come to blows over whatever it was that they were arguing about. Soon one of the judges stood up. His face seemed uncertain and rather upset, but he gave Anthony a thumbs-up nonetheless. Anthony, too shocked to do any real celebrating, forced a smile and walked off the floor.

Anthony was sulking in the corner when Clancy saw him. He strode over to the agitated Anthony and plopped down next to him. They sat there, not looking at each other or saying anything as other students showed off their divine skills to the judges.

Clancy broke the silence. "By the skin of your teeth, huh?"

Anthony sighed and put his head into his arms. "That's a nice way to put it. I failed that test, but a technicality pulled me through. You should have seen the judges. You would have thought that they were debating politics with how heated it got in there."

Clancy continued to stare straight ahead. "Well, hey, that means some of the judges didn't think you sucked right?"

"Oh yeah, right," Anthony said as he looked at Clancy. "The only reason they argued for me is because their devotion to the letter of the law is greater than their disdain for me. Since technically I hit the dummy, that technically counts as progress from the time I never hit it. But that scratch I made wouldn't have killed a cat, much less a demon beast. Why? Why is it so tough for me to use my divine skills? No one else in the history of ever has had as much trouble as I have getting their divine skill down. Why does it have to be me that can't make any progress?"

Clancy looked worried as he studied his flustered student. "What's wrong with you?"

Anthony didn't understand. "What do you mean?"

Clancy stood up and brushed himself off. "Well, last year, you never came close to hitting that dummy, but you were ecstatic about passing the exam. Every single time you've sparred Hannah, you've lost, yet every time, you walk off with a smile on your face. But this year, when you hit the dummy you've been whiffing at for over a year, you're off sulking in a corner. So, I'll ask it again, what's wrong with you?"

Anthony put his head back in his arms. He knew exactly why he was mad, but how could he tell Clancy. *He's my friend and all, but even he would think I'm crazy if I told him about my dreams.*

"Is it about Hannah?" Clancy asked.

Anthony's head shot back up, and he looked at Clancy. "Did you …"

"Yeah, I talked to Hazblazen."

Anthony sighed and pushed himself up. "You know all about my dreams and the way Hannah's been treating me then?"

Clancy nodded. "I'm sorry I kind of made Hazblazen tell me. He kept making the sourpuss face he makes when he's thinking about something serious."

Anthony brushed the gym-floor dust off his shorts. "What do you think? Pretty crazy, right? The fact that I think Hannah and a Zankrex invasion are connected."

Clancy sighed as he crossed his arms. "I don't think your dreams are insignificant, and I'm sure if I was in your place, I would think the same thing. But you have to look at it from my perspective. It's not that I think you're a liar, but Hannah is a Divine Blade. No matter how angry she gets, it's impossible for her to ally herself with the Zankrex, and that's *if* the Zankrex even exist. In fact, there aren't even myths of Divine Blades becoming Zankrex. I want to believe you, but right now I would need something more substantial than your dreams. You understand, don't you?"

Anthony stared at the gym floor, not wanting to look at Clancy. He knew that what Clancy said was true. If he was the one listening to Clancy tell tales of a Zankrex invasion, he would doubt it to. But that didn't make him feel any better.

Anthony never looked Clancy in the eye and just nodded. Clancy half-smiled and patted Anthony on the back before he walked off. Anthony continued to stand there, staring at the floor. The feeling of loneliness was nothing new to him, but this time was different. The feeling of dread was overwhelming, but no one would believe him. He stewed in his loneliness and helplessness for a while longer before trudging off the locker room to take a shower.

Anthony leaned against the wall outside the gym. He was waiting for Christian to get out as he promised to have lunch with him after the exam.

The shower had made him feel better, and the bright sunshine washed away his despair. *I need to get this matter out of my mind. I didn't have any dreams last night, so maybe this whole thing was just a random nightmare.*

He tried to convince himself, but no matter how hard he tried to push it aside, he couldn't get it out of his mind. The doors swung open, and Christian walked out. He walked toward his friend, but his mind was elsewhere.

"Anthony? Anthony!"

Anthony came to from his daydream and stared across the table. Christian sat on the other side with a half-worried, half-amused look on his face.

"Dude, are you okay? You haven't said anything since we sat down. What's on your mind, bro?"

Anthony sighed as he looked at his plate. His burger had one bite taken out of it, and he hadn't even touched his fries. He was hungry, but his thoughts had him far too occupied.

"I'm sorry. It's just that a lot has happened in the past two days, and I just can't seem to get my mind off it."

Christian shrugged as he bit into his pizza. "Well, I'm all ears if you want to talk about it. In fact, I would like to hear about it because whatever it is has you and Hazblazen in a funk."

Anthony half-smiled. "Even Hazblazen can't get it off his mind, huh?" he said to himself.

Christian raised his eyebrows at his mumbling friend.

Anthony shook his head. "Okay, I'll tell you, but please just promise you'll keep an open mind through all of this."

"All right," agreed Christian as he set his pizza down and folded his hands under his chin in preparation for the story.

Anthony took a deep breath and started his story. He was hesitant at first but gained confidence as he described his fight with Hannah and the intense dreams that he had been having. Christian listened and never broke his silence even when Anthony stopped to take a drink. By the end of it, Anthony felt a lot better having explained everything to someone. Even though he had told Hazblazen, he still felt bottled up about it. This time, he was talking to a true friend, not a teacher, and it felt a lot better to let his friend know. Once Anthony finished, there was an awkward silence at the table for quite a few seconds. Anthony waited in suspense for his friend to tell him what he thought of the whole situation.

Christian stirred, moving his hand to grab a drink. After two long gulps, he set the drink down and exhaled in satisfaction. He stared at Anthony, almost like he was analyzing him just to be sure that he wasn't pulling some joke on him. Anthony remained stoic, confirming that he was indeed telling the truth.

"All right, I believe you," Christian said.

Anthony sat for a moment in disbelief. "Really? You believe me? Just like that?"

Christian raised his hand. "Well, wait just a second. I believe that you had those dreams and that Hannah has been acting far stranger than normal, but I'm not sure I believe this theory you have on the Zankrex invasion. And I have a harder time believing that Hannah could be part of it. I mean, you know as well as I do that even if Zankrex were real, their power could never inhabit a Divine Blade because we wield the very power of the Creator. The dark energy and the divine energy can never inhabit the same vessel."

"I know, I know. I have no real evidence to support any of my theories, but that doesn't mean I can just ignore them. I can't explain to you why, but my gut is screaming at me that Hannah is somehow connected to the Zankrex invasion."

The two friends stared at each other for a while, Christian trying to comprehend the information that he had just learned and Anthony trying to figure how he could explain himself any better.

Christian broke the silence. "All right, I'm not going to not believe your theory, but that's the best I can do right now. Give me a chance to think about it and see what my gut tells me, and then I can give you a clearer answer."

Anthony nodded, but he didn't feel like he had won anything. "I just hope you figure it out before anything happens."

The two finished their meal in silence as those final words left a dreary cloud around the table.

The two walked out of the dining area. The sun was high in the sky, and the wind carried a cool wave of refreshment. Fall had just begun, and the weather was amazing. Both guys wore shorts but had long-sleeve pullovers to protect them from the cool breeze. They remained silent for a while as both of them had no idea how to follow up on the conversation they had during lunch.

Anthony stretched out in the sunlight, letting its light bathe him in reassuring warmth. As he walked, his mood improved, and Christian began to look visibly better as well. The silence was still there, but it no longer felt awkward.

As they rounded the cafeteria building to head toward their vehicles, a group of girls walked past. They all got quiet and whispered things to one another as they passed, giggling once the two boys were behind them. Christian looked back then elbowed Anthony in the side.

"Duuude!" he said in a shrill tone. "Those girls were totally checking us out, man!"

Christian grabbed the sword on his side and pointed at Anthony's katana. "We should carry these around with us more often. Come on, let's turn around and talk to them."

Anthony winced and rubbed his side. "Yeah right, man. You can go ahead and do that. I don't have the confidence to go talking to random women."

Christian groaned as he had heard that excuse far too often. "Come on, dude, you could totally score those chicks. Everyone on campus knows who you are thanks to Hannah, and most of the women feel bad for you due to the way she treats you. You could use that to get a pity date."

Anthony let out a sarcastic laugh and shoved his friend off the sidewalk. "Ha-ha, very funny. Because that's just what I want: to get a date out of pity. No, if I get a date, I want it to be legitimate. And I want to do it off my own power, not with you breathing down my neck."

Christian rolled his eyes. "Whatever, you won't talk to women because you still have that weird obsession with Vanessa. If you think you could date a God Sword, then you're far more delusional than I thought you were."

Anthony rolled his eyes. Ever since Christian had found out about his little crush, he had never let Anthony live it down.

Anthony shrugged his shoulders. "Well then, it seems you have underestimated my delusionality."

There was a pause; then both friends started laughing.

This is how it's supposed to be, thought Anthony.

Ever since he had his first Zankrex dream, happy moments didn't seem to come, and the Hannah incidents hadn't helped his mood either. Before all of this, it was considered weird if he ever had moments where he wasn't smiling, joking to a point where everyone around them would get annoyed. It was a product of being around each other for far too long, and Anthony enjoyed every second of it. He had let the current situation control his mind and had missed out on these interactions.

I should have done this sooner.

He felt ten times better than he had all week. *Who knew acting like an idiot would be the best thing for me.*

The two would have walked off campus like that, but a sudden scream tore them away from their happy moment.

Anthony and Christian sprinted around the corner. The screams got louder as they got to the clearing between the two buildings.

What stood before them was something that Anthony had never seen on campus before.

Three large cats stood before the women whom they had just passed. The cats were far larger than they should have been. They came up to Anthony's thigh. But it wasn't the size that caught Anthony's eye. Black markings ran up and down the cats' bodies. Their eyes were bright red and were full of hate. These were demon beasts.

"Demon beasts?" Christian said in confusion. "What are they doing on campus?"

Anthony had no answers. All he knew was the women were in trouble. Killing humans was all a demon beast ever thought about. It was the only thought driving them. The beasts could kill the women with a flick of their claws, and if they hesitated any longer, they were going to. Anthony whipped out his blade, and Christian followed suit.

"We don't have any time to think about it. How many light spikes can you fire?"

Christian bit his lip in apprehension. "I can still only do it twice in a row. I need some cooldown time after that."

Anthony gritted his teeth. *That won't do. Even if he kills two of them, the one left over could kill all three girls. I'll need to help.*

This made him feel extra nervous. He hadn't rested long enough to be able to pull of his move twice yet. He had only rested long enough to have regained enough energy for one speed step.

Anthony's mind cleared as he realized the situation. *I can't be doubting myself. I have people who are counting on me right now. I have to throw away my doubts and act.*

Anthony looked over at Christian with newfound determination. "We can do this. The divine energy in our swords should be enough to kill them. They look big, but I'm sure the amount of dark energy in them isn't much."

Anthony remembered reading that small animals can grow to be very large even with just the smallest amount of dark energy in them. The beasts in front of them now were normal house cats. The amount of growth they had gone through by no means indicated that they had a massive amount of energy in them. This gave Anthony confidence.

I can do this. I just have to slice the beast a little bit. The divine energy in my sword should do the rest.

Anthony looked over at Christian. His sword was drawn as well. It was a one-handed double-sided sword with a thin blade. It was perfect for his thrusting attacks.

Anthony half-smiled at Christian. "You take the two closest to the girls, and I'll take the furthest one away."

Christian nodded and looked back to the fight. The beasts had long since noticed their presence and had turned around to face them. The women were far too afraid to run away and just stood there and watched. Anthony took a deep breath in and let it out. Christian's divine ability was called light spike. It worked like Hannah's in that he could send spikes of divine energy flying from his blade by thrusting it forward. Of course, it was less powerful than Hannah's, and he couldn't do it as often as she could; but in this situation, it would do just as well.

Christian closed his eyes and slowed his breathing. The beasts stood there staring at them for a few seconds; then Christian's eyes flew open. He let out a small roar and thrust his blade forward twice as quick as he could. The two light spikes shot forward and struck the two targets dead in the center. The beasts let out a cry and crumpled to the ground. Anthony took that moment and released his energy. He shot forward and slashed. This time was different. His concentration was higher. His confidence was higher. His strike was better. The blade cut an inch deep into the cat's side. Anthony felt triumphant. The divine energy should eat the dark energy from the inside and kill the beast.

They stayed there in that position for a time. Then Anthony realized something was wrong. The cat landed on the ground and cried out in pain but wasn't dying. Anthony didn't understand it. He didn't know why the beast was still alive.

The cat turned back at Anthony with murder in its eyes. Anthony was struck with fear and confusion at that point. He couldn't move.

He could only watch as the cat pounced forward, claws glistening in the light. He was certain it would end there.

A sword flying out of nowhere stopped it from happening. The cat cried out even louder in agony as the sword held it in the air. The blade then began to work on the dark energy. A black dust began to rise out of the beast, almost like it was disintegrating. The black marks faded, and the life drained from the animal until it was dead on the sword.

Anthony looked down the blade to see a wormhole floating in the air. The sword tilted, and the cat slid off it and hit the ground. Anthony looked off in the distance to see Hazblazen standing there. His breathing was labored, as if he had been sprinting for a while. Clancy was in front of him, running toward the scene with sword in hand. Anthony realized the fight was over and fell to his knees, baffled by the events that took place.

Clancy went about making sure the girls were fine. They had no scratches or marks of any kind, but were still shaken up. A few nurses helped them along to a bench to let them recover.

Anthony sat on the curb, still staring off into space with a confused look on his face. Christian stood next to him, but had no words to offer him. He had watched it happen as well. He saw a good bit of blood leave the cat. Some of it was still on Anthony's sword as it lay next to him.

Christian shook his head. "Any idea what that was back there?"

Anthony knew he was talking about his fight. There were no doubts that the sword went into the cat. The divine energy in his sword should have ended it right then and there. Christian's light spike had been more than enough to finish one off.

All he could do was shake his head. "I have no idea."

Hazblazen and Clancy walked over at that moment.

"Good job there, guys," Clancy said with a large smile. "I'm impressed you're both not dead right now."

Christian sighed, unamused by the joke, but Anthony still wasn't paying attention. Clancy looked down at Anthony and smiled in sympathy. He couldn't help but feel sorry for him. "Did you miss again?"

All Anthony could do was motion toward his sword. The two teachers looked at his blade. Realization dawned on them.

"Wait, you mean you didn't miss?"

Anthony nodded.

Hazblazen had a very serious look on his face. "Anthony, may I inspect your sword?"

Anthony nodded.

Hazblazen reached down and picked up the katana. He inspected it with a trained eye. "This was by no means a shallow cut, was it, Anthony?" It wasn't a question; it was a statement.

Anthony still shook his head. "I thought I got a good inch into the cat."

Clancy was almost beside himself. "That makes no sense. Sure, Anthony has a puny amount of divine energy, and he was drained from the exam, but even then, these beasts should have been eaten alive by just a drop of divine energy."

Hazblazen nodded. "I have to agree with you. And if what you say is indeed true, then there is no reason why the animal shouldn't have died by your hand."

Anthony looked up at the two teachers. "Do either of you know what could've happened there?"

Hazblazen and Clancy looked at each other like they both had the same thoughts.

"Eh … no," said Clancy, avoiding eye contact.

Hazblazen cut in, "We will look into it and have something for you tomorrow. For now, try not to let it trouble you."

Hazblazen put the sword back next to Anthony, and the two teachers walked off, whispering to each other along the way.

The walk to the tritos was quiet after the incident with the girls. The Zankrex topic was far behind them now with the new question now taking center stage in their minds.

They parted ways with a wave, and both got into their own vehicles. Anthony had nothing else planned for the rest of the day, and he was thankful for that. The past exam and demon-beast interaction had drained him of all his strength. Even small tasks proved to be exhausting.

He drove straight home and went to his room. His father was back at the university teaching, and his mother and brother were still in school. He sat down on his computer and went about scrolling through various sites. He wasn't paying any attention, though. His mind was a veritable hornet's nest of thoughts and questions. Zankrex, Hannah, and his sucky power were the topics that floated around. He started to think so hard that soon he developed a headache.

He groaned and rubbed his temples. He realized that this was doing him no good.

I'm getting no answers just sitting here stressing about it. I need to do what Hazblazen said and try not to think about it till tomorrow.

The task was easier said than done. On a normal day, he would go and do some reps with his sword on the striking post out back, but he had no energy for that. All he had was his thoughts.

Even if it kills me, I need to do something. I'm going to have an aneurism if I think about these things any more.

He decided to do something that needed little energy to do and went to polish and clean his sword collection.

He had always been fascinated by swords and used every cent of his spending money to buy every sword that caught his fancy. Thanks to that, he had amassed a sizable collection. Including his own divine blade, he had replicas of all the current God Swords and then a few extras from different movies. Polishing these swords always made him feel better, and soon his mind was focused on other things.

The sound of the garage door opening signaled the return of his father. That meant that his brother and mother wouldn't be too far behind either. The night passed for Anthony as he ate dinner with his family, listened to his mother argue with his brother about homework, talked sports with his father, and ultimately stayed up a little late talking video games with his brother. The night was perfect and had succeeded in taking the topic of Zankrex off Anthony's mind. His family was his safe haven. He could always recharge here, no matter what happened that day. He went to bed feeling better than he had ever felt before.

Anthony's eyes opened to a pure-white room. The wall and floor blended together, and it seemed like he stood in the center of an ever-expanding space.

Confused, he looked around for anything that he could recognize. This wasn't like his normal dreams; there was no overwhelming fear or sense of foreboding. He simply stood in this room, feeling relaxed.

A soft, deep voice broke the silence and washed over Anthony like a cool wave.

"Anthony, you stand on the precipice of a great calamity. Only you will have the strength to overcome it and save humanity. But you will not be alone. You will have allies, but in the end, only you can decide the future of Tertalla. Believe in yourself, and you can accomplish great things."

Anthony was at a loss for words. This voice had just informed him of the apocalypse, and he felt calmer than he had ever felt in his entire life. He couldn't form any questions for the mysterious voice, but he wouldn't have had time for them anyway. He began to sink down as if falling back down to the ground. All the while, the voice's message echoed in his head.

Anthony awoke and shot straight up. The vision was still clear in his mind, but that's not what he was worried about. His skin crawled, and fear bubbled up inside of him. Something was wrong that night.

In the distance, what sounded like screaming and sounds of battle could be heard.

Before Anthony could check the window, a noise emanated from the other side of his door. Anthony got out of his bed and tiptoed to the front of his room. He cracked the door open and looked across the hall.

Anthony's eyes widened, and his breath escaped him as he saw the horrible scene unfold before him. His brother, beaten and bruised, was being bitten by a shadowy figure. The creature unlocked its fangs from his brother's neck and let him fall to the ground. The body hit the floor and lay there unmoving. Anthony let out an involuntary whimper at the sight of his brother's limp body being discarded like trash.

The creature looked straight at Anthony. Anthony sucked in his breath and slammed the door shut and jumped to the back of his room. A split second later, the door exploded into shards as the creature walked into the room. Anthony scrambled for his sword as the creature lunged out at him. Anthony grabbed his katana and ripped it out of his sheath, praying for a miracle to happen.

As soon as the tip cleared the sheath, the sword exploded in a flash of green light. Anthony dropped the sword and fell back in surprise as the light filled the entire room. The creature let out a demented gurgle and stumbled backward. Anthony heard the creature hissing in disgust, followed by the sound of something slashing, then sudden silence. When he opened his eyes, the room was dark, except for the faint green light seeping from the sword.

Anthony turned around to see what had happened to his attacker. His eyes widened as he beheld the strangest sight. A tall dragon stood over the shredded corpse of the creature. The dragon was humanoid in body structure, but he had claws coming from his feet and hands. And on his back were a pair of large leathery wings and a thick tail. His scales glittered green and varied in shades, getting lighter around the stomach area and darker on his back. His jaws were long, and ivory teeth shone off the faint green light. Anthony stood up and tried to speak.

"W-w-w-what are you?" stammered Anthony.

The dragon looked at Anthony with piercing eyes that seemed to study his very soul. "The introductions will have to wait," rumbled the dragon in a deep commanding voice.

It reminded him of the voice he had heard his last vision, but the dragon's voice was harsher.

"Right now, we have a serious problem."

The dragon grabbed the corpse of the creature and brought it into the light. Anthony was shocked to see a human in the dragon's clutches.

"This man possessed the dark energy," the dragon confirmed. "That means the day of reckoning is upon us. The Zankrex have taken over Tertalla."

Chapter 4

KEVRAN

*A*nthony stumbled back and landed on his butt. The dragon had just confirmed every one of his worst fears in one sentence. A cold sweat dripped down his face as he tried to gather his thoughts and get his nerves back.

The dragon dropped the corpse and walked over to Anthony.

Kneeling, he put his claw on his shoulder. "I understand that you are terrified, but we have to move. At the very least, get outside. I will take care of everything from there."

Anthony gathered himself together and nodded. He stood up on shaky legs and began to walk toward the door. An image of his mangled brother flashed through his head and brought him back down to his knees.

"I'm sorry," he whimpered. "My brother's on the other side of that door, and there's no way I can walk past his body right now."

The dragon sighed in frustration but nodded in understanding. "Would it help to know that your brother is still alive?"

Anthony shook his head. "If he's alive, and what I've heard is true, then it would only be worse."

The dragon walked up beside Anthony. "Yes, what you are thinking is true. If this Zankrex attacked your brother, then they attacked your parents as well. Zankrex attack for only two reasons: to kill and to contaminate. It is safe to assume they have already been turned."

Anthony buried his head in his hands, but was far too scared to cry. His family had been turned into monsters, and he hadn't even been able to move a muscle to help them. He should have been feeling depression of the highest degree, but all he could feel was rage and anger at himself for being weak. Anger at others for not believing him. Anger at the Zankrex as a whole.

Anthony raised his head and stood back up. "I'm going out there."

"No, you are not."

Anthony turned in anger and faced the dragon. "I have to go out there. My family needed me, and I'm going to go down there and do whatever I have to do to make sure that they are safe."

The dragon let out a short burst of laughter. "What is your course of action then? Are you going to stumble back and hope another dragon arrives to save you? Because I can promise you that will not happen again."

Anthony ground his teeth in rage, tears forming in his eyes. "Well, what am I supposed to do, huh?" he shouted at the dragon. "My whole family has been violated by those demons, and all I did was cower in the corner like a little girl. I couldn't even hold my sword when I watched my own brother get attacked."

Anthony crumpled to the ground and slammed his head into the carpet. "I'm useless as a Divine Blade. I can't even rise up to save those that I love. Why am I so pathetic? Why am I so useless? *Why am I so weak?*"

The dragon walked up to the sniveling Anthony and put a claw on his back. "I understand how you must feel, but nothing will change by you throwing away your life. Come with me, and I will show you the path to strength. Strength to protect the ones you love."

Anthony's sniffing stopped, and he raised his head. "Do you mean that?"

The dragon nodded.

Anthony paused for a moment then nodded his head as well. He sniffed hard and wiped the tears from his eyes as he stood back up. "I can't take the door, but I'll jump out the window. You said I just had to get outside, right?"

The dragon smirked at the change in attitude and nodded.

Anthony stepped toward the window and grabbed his sword. "All right then, I'll trust you. But I'll expect an explanation once we are safe."

The dragon nodded again. "Of course, I will explain everything."

Anthony strapped his sword to his back and opened the window. Not looking back, he put his foot on the sill and leapt into the night air.

It was a cold fall night, and the breeze should have been the only noise, but the Zankrex had other ideas. Sounds of fighting and screams could be heard in the distance as the invasion of Tertalla continued. Dark shapes could be seen patrolling the skies looking for those they had yet to convert.

Anthony hid under a bush as a flying Zankrex passed by. Once it had gone, he turned to the dragon.

"Well? You said that all I had to do was get outside, and you would take care of the rest."

The dragon waved his claws. "First, you must calm yourself. I know what I said, and it may have been inaccurate. I need a wide-open area to accomplish my goal."

Anthony stared in disbelief at the dragon. "Are you kidding me? There's no way I—"

He stopped as a Zankrex flew in low above him.

He peered around to be sure the coast was clear, then turned to the dragon and continued in a hush tone. "I can't get to an open spot when Zankrex fly over every two seconds. You're a freaking dragon. Can't you do something to get us out there?"

He pointed to the spot where they needed to go to. It was his backyard, and it was indeed spacious enough, but the center was too far away for them to get there without being noticed.

The dragon folded his arms and shook his head. "It is regrettable, but I need to save my power to get us to where I need to take you. If I fight Zankrex to open up a path, I will not have the sufficient amount of energy I need to open the portal."

Anthony gave a look of confusion. "Portal? What are you talking about?"

"You will see when you get us out into the center," the dragon responded, not wanting to discuss it here.

Anthony sighed in frustration and prepared himself. "All right, I can use my speed step to get us out into the yard, but there's no way I can get us to the center. And after I use it, the divine energy is sure to attract the Zankrex. I'm going to use it, and then we have to run the rest of the way. That's the only plan I have."

The dragon shook his head. "The plan stinks, but you are right about it being the only option. Fine, just get us halfway. We will pray that it is enough."

Anthony nodded and began to concentrate his power. He grabbed ahold of the dragon and drew out energy for his speed step, but something was different. A torrent of energy flooded his being. He was taken off guard by the wave and activated his speed step. In an instant, they shot forward, and the scenery changed. They stood thirty feet past the center of the yard. Anthony stumbled as he recovered from the burst of power he just used.

"Where the heck did that power just come from?"

"No time for questions," shouted the dragon as he bolted for the center of the yard. "Hurry, there is not much time."

Anthony gathered himself and began to sprint toward the spot. He looked up and saw multiple shapes speeding toward the two of them. The dragon had made it to the center and was opening a portal. Anthony was halfway when the portal was completed.

"Hurry," shouted the dragon as he jumped into the portal.

Anthony gritted his teeth and dove for the portal. He slid in right under the grabbing hands of a Zankrex and fell into the dark hole.

Anthony fell through a dark void, tumbling for what felt like forever. He popped out of the other end of the portal and landed in a heap on the grass. Rubbing his head, he looked up to see the dragon sitting on a chair that looked like a throne. Anthony gazed around the room that he was in. It was dark, but not too dark, thanks to mysterious glowing stones that gave off a faint light. The light itself had a light-green tint to it that made everything around him look green, though the color of the light wasn't a big factor. The whole room was covered in lush thick grass and was close to the size of the gym on campus.

Anthony stood gawking at his surroundings when the dragon cleared his throat. Anthony looked at him. The dragon stared at Anthony as if he was expecting him to come closer first. Anthony steeled himself and approached.

"Who are you? What is this place? Why did you bring me here?" he asked.

The dragon chuckled and held up his claw "Slow down, impatient one. Those are all excellent questions, but before I answer any question, I must first make you understand who you are."

Anthony stared at the dragon in confusion. "What do you mean?"

The dragon stared at Anthony with a piercing gaze. "Anthony, can you tell me what you are?"

Anthony looked at the dragon in confusion. "I don't understand."

The dragon sighed. "What are you, son? Tell me who you are."

Anthony began to think, still not sure what it was that the dragon wanted from him. "Well, I'm an eldest son, a brother. I'm a Divine Blade—"

"*Wrong*," shouted the dragon. "I said tell me what you are."

Anthony looked even more confused now than he ever had before. "I don't understand. I am a Divine Blade."

The dragon shook his head in frustration. "No, you are not. Look deep inside yourself, boy. The answer is there. Everything that has happened: the Zankrex, me, and your sudden explosion of power. It should all tell you the truth. The truth of who you are now."

An idea began to form in Anthony's mind. Then he broke out in a cold sweat. "No, I can't be one. They're cool and strong and always know what to do when the time comes. I'm none of those. I can't even move when my own family is in danger. I can't be one of them."

The dragon continued to pierce Anthony with his gaze. "You are one, but you must say it here and now. You will not be able to grow any further if you refuse to accept who you are. I will ask again: who are you?"

Anthony swallowed his apprehension and fear. He had a feeling from the start of this night what he was, but now it was time to confirm it.

"I'm a God Sword, aren't I?"

The dragon smiled and softened his gaze. "That is correct."

Anthony fell down hard on his butt at the confirmation of this. All the pressure and duty of the God Sword began to weigh down on his shoulders.

The dragon sat back in his chair and sighed. "I understand that this may seem like too much information for you to take in on one setting, but we do not have the luxury of time right now. The Zankrex will not wait for you to take in everything on your own pace. Because of this, I cannot give you the time you need to sort this out. I am going to give you a lot of information in a miniscule amount of time. Are you ready?"

Anthony nodded, having calmed himself down, and waited in silence for the dragon to speak. The dragon rumbled in approval and made himself comfortable.

"Well, I will not bore you with all the details since I know you are aware of the Zankrex history. But I will skim over it. Long ago, when the Creator had first willed Tertalla into existence, there was peace and tranquility. The dark energy had yet to even be created, and life on the planet prospered. Humans lived in perfect harmony with the life and land around them. But an angel in heaven became jealous of the love and care that the Creator gave to the mere mortals that lived on Tertalla. He became angry at Him for seeing the angels, who were far superior in every way, as second best. The anger in the angel grew, and he began to amass followers whom he had seduced with his lies. Soon they revolted against the Creator, and the inevitable happened. He defeated the traitors with a thought and cast them out of the divine paradise. Banished to the pits of the Demonic Lake and stripped of his name, he became known as the Accursed One."

"Deep in the bowels of the lake, he created a dark energy. This energy allowed him to take over the animals that lived on Tertalla. He unleashed his energy on the world, and chaos was sown on the planet. At first, the issue was manageable as the only living things to be taken over by the energy were mere animals. These animals could be killed by mortal ways, and for a while, it seemed that the dark energy would prove no threat to you humans. In fact, for a while, it only served to bring you closer together. But one day, a human by the name of Yadgusril found the source of the dark energy. Instead of running or trying to destroy it, he listened to the whisperings of the Accursed One and became enticed by the power that he promised him. Yadgusril allowed this power to invade him, and the first Zankrex was born. He would forever be known as the Zankrex king. As time passed, he gained more followers who fell for the same delusions of power and grandeur, and soon a whole army of Zankrex was born. This army ripped through the mortals like they were nothing, and the very existence of the human race seemed to be doomed. That is when the Creator intervened. Using his divine power, he forged five blades that you would come to call the God swords. He gave them dominance over one element and imbued in them a massive amount of divine energy. That is also when he created us."

Anthony looked at him in confusion. "Us? Who's us?"

Kevran pointed at himself. "I am referring to myself and the four others like me. Each sword was given a guide to teach the wielder about his or her sword. I was created to guide the wielder of the Earth Katana. My name is Kevran, and from here on, I will be teaching you and guiding you along your way."

Anthony sat in complete and total shock. "Well, it's nice to meet you, Kevran, but what about the rest of the story? What happened with the God Swords?"

Kevran chuckled. "Should that not be obvious? The five wielders mastered their powers and stopped the Zankrex army. There was a standstill at that point. The Zankrex were not powerful enough to defeat the God Swords, and the God Swords could not handle the overwhelming number of Zankrex. That is when the Divine Blades were created. He created a thousand Divine Blades, and the war was soon won by the humans. The only downside of the whole battle was that the Zankrex king could not be killed. He was sealed away in the pits of the Demonic Lake, and as long as he stayed there, Zankrex would never bother the humans again. Or so we thought."

Anthony laughed at that line. "So you thought? Isn't that something you should have been sure about?"

Kevran growled at the attack. "Watch your tongue. We had assumed that the Zankrex were wiped out, but we were wrong. Zankrex can only be bred of other Zankrex. If they had all been wiped out, then there would have been no possible way for the king to return. But some survived. Amassing power and numbers for several centuries, they were able to free their king. Now the invasion of the Zankrex is upon us, and the king sits on the Zankrex throne once again. Only now, he has become stronger."

Anthony gulped. "And I'm supposed to fight him? He's stronger than he was then, and I have to beat him when the five God Swords of old couldn't kill him?"

Kevran chuckled and rose from his chair. Anthony stood up as well.

Kevran walked over and put a reassuring claw on Anthony. "Do not worry. I am here to make sure you are prepared for your battles ahead. From here on out, the history lesson ends and the training begins."

Anthony stood in the middle of the cave with Kevran standing thirty feet in front of him. Kevran nodded, and Anthony unsheathed the sword.

"Now," Kevran started, "tell me the extent of your power."

Anthony looked down in embarrassment. "Well, I can use my speed step twice, but I can't control it very well, and my physical upgrades are lackluster, to say the least."

"*Wrong*," shouted Kevran.

Anthony bobbled his sword from the shock. "Is that the only way you know how to say that word?"

Kevran, ignoring the comment, crossed his arms. "You are a God Sword. You have power that Divine Blades can only dream of. Now, I'll ask you again, what is the extent of your power?"

Anthony began to understand what Kevran was getting at. "My power is greater than even I am aware of?"

Kevran nodded, pleased. "Very good, you catch on quick. I understand that you may not believe that yourself, but as a God Sword, you need to understand that your power far exceeds what even you believe you are capable of. The Creator once told me that a God Sword's power reaches its limit when the wielder's imagination runs dry. Do you understand what I am trying to tell you?"

Anthony sighed. "I kinda do, but you have to understand where I'm coming from. The only time I had any power was when we weren't using our divine power. My sword always had the lowest amount of divine energy. To tell me now that it was a God Sword all along is tough for me to comprehend."

Kevran sighed and unfolded his arms. "I suppose I should explain to you why you had so little power before."

Anthony stared at him, puzzled by what he was saying.

"In school, they taught you that the power you wield is the divine power from the Creator. And for most on that campus, this is true. But, Anthony, you have never wielded the divine power before in your life."

Anthony stared at Kevran in shock, not even being able to form a protest to this ridiculous claim.

Kevran chuckled at Anthony's disbelief. "It is true, the divine energy in this God sword has been locked up for centuries. This night is the first night in centuries that this God sword has been released. Yet it is undeniable that you had some form of power. Do you know why this is possible?"

Anthony shook his head, still stunned to silence.

"It is the same reason why the humans were able to fight off the demon beasts. They used Reichi."

The mention of a new power got Anthony out of his shocked silence. "Reichi? What the heck is that?"

"It is the natural energy inside of every human," answered Kevran. "In the days before the dark energy, humans learned of Reichi through the Creator Himself. They used this power to hunt animals and build mighty structures. But when the Creator brought down the Divine Blades, humans began to rely more on the divine power. Its ability to kill demon beasts with only a scratch was far more efficient than killing them with normal methods. Over time, the use of Reichi became a lost art known only to a select few. Now only Divine Blades of high caliber and God Swords use Reichi."

Anthony nodded. Kevran had just answered a few questions that he didn't even know he had, but he was still confused.

"What does my Reichi have to do with the God Sword? I thought Divine Blades and God Swords could only be used if their divine power was unlocked."

Kevran chuckled. "That is what makes you amazing, Anthony. You used your Reichi to unlock the God sword."

Kevran stared at Anthony, expecting some sort of proud reaction. Instead, Anthony continued to look at Kevran, waiting for him to finish his thought. Kevran seemed upset that Anthony wasn't grasping the ridiculousness of what he had accomplished.

"Do you not understand how incredible that is? To unlock a God sword and still have power left over to fight means that you possess an incredible amount of Reichi. Now, this was only possible because the sword accepted you, but this is why I want you to understand how powerful you are. God Swords fight using both their own Reichi and the divine energy in their sword. Not only are they wielding an abnormal amount of divine energy, but they also utilize their massive reserves or Reichi. This is why no normal Divine Blade can come close to them."

"Wait," Anthony interjected. "What do you mean the sword accepted me? Shouldn't it unlock if it accepts me?"

Kevran shook his head. "For normal blades, that is how it works, but the earth katana is special. Even if it finds its wielder, it will not unlock unless the right time comes. But that is not the point. The point is, Anthony, that you have Reichi."

"Wow," Anthony said. "I'm actually really strong?"

Kevran threw back his head in laughter, surprising Anthony. "Strong? Strong does not even begin to describe you. No one in the history of Tertalla has been able to unlock a divine blade with their own Reichi. Not even the most accomplished God Swords could pull of the feat that you pulled without even knowing it. Are you strong? You are incredible is what you are. Your Reichi dwarfs what even some of the most accomplished God Swords wielded."

Anthony marveled at the news he had just heard. "So, the reason I was having so much trouble with my speed step is because I was straining all my Reichi just to unlock the divine energy for it?"

"Close," said Kevran. "But your speed step is not a God Sword ability. The only ability the God Sword has is the manipulation of the element that it is connected to. Your speed step is a Reichi ability. Because of this, and due to the fact that most of your Reichi was used to unlock the sword, you were unable to use your speed step the way you are now."

Anthony scratched his chin. "Wait, if I had this massive amount of energy deep inside me, then how come I could never use it until this point?"

Kevran almost found the question stupid. "Your body would not be ready for it. The energy raging inside you would have torn you apart. Your body kept it locked away to protect itself. That also explains why you were able to unlock the God Sword without trying. Your body saw an opportunity to release the energy that had been building inside you your entire life."

Anthony was offended at the answer. "I'm not that weak. I'm sure I could have handled the power once I had matured."

Kevran waggled a finger at Anthony. "Overwhelming energy will tear apart even the most trained body if it has no experience holding it. The God Sword gave your body an avenue to get used to having energy flowing through it."

Anthony accepted the explanation and had an epiphany. "Now that the sword is unlocked …"

Kevran nodded. "Your ability training will become much easier."

Anthony began to train his speed step. Kevran said they would get to nature manipulation later, but first he wanted him to get used to pulling and using the massive amount of energy that he now possessed.

Anthony stood thirty feet away from a wooden dummy. The task was similar to his divine-power test. All he had to do was strike it with a killing blow. Kevran had warned him that Zankrex would only die by fatal strikes. Small scratches would do nothing to them as the amount of dark energy that resided in them protected them from the divine energy.

Anthony focused and began to draw out his power. His body began to fill with energy, and he shot off. In the blink of an eye, Anthony's view changed. The dummy was nowhere to be found. He looked around confused and glanced back. There, standing fifty feet behind him, was the dummy. Anthony stood in shock as Kevran flew over to him.

"Astounding, is it not? That you could pull that much power out by accident."

Anthony could only nod his head in awe of what he had just accomplished. He had never used his speed step to cover that much ground before. And if he ever got close to this distance, he would always be too tired to do anything else.

Kevran put his claw on Anthony's shoulder. "May I offer some advice? You are still used to straining to draw energy out. However, that is no longer necessary. Try thinking about it in a different fashion."

Anthony looked at Kevran with a puzzled look on his face. "What do you mean 'think of it' in a different way?"

"Well," said Kevran, "I will try and explain it to you using objects you are familiar with. Up to this point, your energy has been like that last bit of toothpaste that is still stuck in the tube. You have to exert yourself to even get a drop. But your power is not a blob of toothpaste anymore. Think of it as if you are sticking a straw into a lake. There is plenty of water in the lake, so there is no point in sucking up as hard as you can. All this time, you have been pulling, but right now all you need to do is reach and take what you need. Does this make sense to you?"

Anthony squinted. "How do you know about toothpaste?"

Kevran closed his eyes and attempted to keep his cool. "I was not sealed away with the sword. I have been observing the world, albeit in a limited view, but that is neither here nor there. Do you understand now?"

Anthony nodded, choosing not to ask any further about where Kevran was looking. He focused on the dummy and began to draw on his power. He could feel it this time. It was a giant swirling vortex inside of him. The vortex was so vast. It was an ocean compared to the puddle he was used to dealing with.

He dipped into the vortex and took out the energy he needed. Bringing that energy out, he shot forward and slashed. Seconds passed as Anthony observed the dummy in front of him. Time seemed to catch up to the dummy as the top half slid off and landed on the ground. Anthony beamed and jumped for joy.

Kevran flew up to him, clapping as he landed. "Very good, Anthony. It did not take you long to grasp that, though I will take some of the credit for your progress. But do not let this victory get to your head. You still have quite a bit of training to do before you are ready for the outside world."

Anthony continued to train his speed step for two more hours. He tried to get used to the amount of power it would take to go certain distances. By the end of two hours, he had gotten almost perfect with his speed step, only missing the targets when he stretched the distance to the max.

After two hours, Kevran stopped him. "That is enough of the speed step. You have progressed enough with that skill. Right now, it is crucial we get you used to fighting with your upgraded physical boosts."

Anthony nodded and followed Kevran to a makeshift ring he had built.

"Now," said Kevran as they stepped in the ring, "the reason I need to train you with this is because it is a different concept than your speed step. When you use your physical boost, all you need to do is open up your power as if it were a dam. Your body will take what it can handle. The more you practice and train your body, the more energy it can use, and the faster and stronger you become. Do you understand?"

"Yes," said Anthony.

Kevran nodded. "Good. There is also one other thing. From this point forward, you must use your divine energy."

Anthony was taken aback. "What do you mean use my divine energy? Haven't I been doing that this entire time?"

Kevran shook his head. "No, up to this point, the only energy you have been using is your own Reichi. That massive vortex of energy is only your inner strength. You have yet to tap into your divine energy."

Anthony was speechless. To think that he had that much raw energy inside him was mind-boggling.

Kevran chuckled at Anthony's amazement. "It is one thing to think of it, but it is another thing to experience it."

Anthony raised his sword and looked at it. He hadn't noticed it when it first happened, but when Kevran appeared, his sword had changed. He first noticed it when he trained his speed step. When he asked Kevran about it, all he had said was that was the sword's true form. The form he had gotten used to was what it looked like while it was in its locked state. The sword's blade went from a dull metallic color to a bright shining silver color, though not as bright as Hannah's sword. And the guard had gone from a rusty bronze to a brilliant gold, and designs of leaves had been etched in. To tie it all together, the handle had been changed from its nasty leather wrap to a green material woven in intricate patterns. The sword had become a work of pure art and felt perfect in his hands. But he had yet to reach into the sword to see if the power had changed.

He closed his eyes and focused. He reached into the sword and tapped into its energy. Nothing could have prepared him for what he encountered in the sword. The amount of energy in it dwarfed his own Reichi, which, just moments ago, had been the most amount of energy he had ever seen. The energy inside the sword locked with his Reichi and formed a bridge between the two. Anthony allowed them to connect, and the powers combined began to swirl throughout his entire body.

Anthony opened his eyes to see multiple dummies laid out before him. As quick as a flash, he moved and attacked the dummies. His body was a blur as he hacked, slashed, and stabbed the twenty dummies that stood before him. Calm passed over the area, and Anthony stood in the ring with thin slices of wood strewn all about him.

Kevran walked up, laughing and clapping. "That was incredible. It took you all of five seconds to dispatch those twenty dummies. As expected of someone who is a master of their own body. The learning curve was not steep. Are you used to this newfound power?"

Anthony looked at his sword in awe. "This sword, it's almost as if it was forged for me. I've never felt this in sync with a weapon before. And yes, I do believe I have a full grasp over this newfound power of mine."

Kevran chuckled. "Excellent, because now we reach the fun part: nature manipulation."

Anthony stood in the same ring he had just finished slaying dummies in; only this time, instead of dummies, a pile of leaves lay before him.

Kevran finished his preparations and stepped out of the circle. "Now, we are going to begin with a simple exercise. I want you to tell me the exact number of leaves in that pile using only your divine energy."

Anthony was hesitant but decided to play along. He closed his eyes and focused on the pile of leaves. He couldn't feel anything coming from the leaves. The only power he could sense was his own and the faint spark of Kevran's. He strained his mind to try and find anything, but to no avail. He gave up and looked back at Kevran in frustration.

Kevran was holding back a laugh. "Done so soon?" he asked with sarcasm in his voice. "You seemed to be making great progress on your own."

Anthony gritted his teeth and restrained himself from strangling Kevran. "Wasn't it you who told me we were short on time? Or are your jokes part of the training as well?"

Kevran chuckled at his frustration and stepped into the ring. "Nature manipulation is only possible through your God sword. Just then, you were using your Reichi, and your divine power combined to search for it. The connection between you and nature can only be made through your divine energy. Focus your divine energy and examine again."

Anthony calmed himself and closed his eyes once more. He reached deep inside of himself and was greeted with the familiar vortex of energy. Both energies were swirling around together, but Anthony was able to reach back to his sword for pure divine energy. Activating this energy once again, he reached out to the pile. This time, the energy was clear and obvious. Each leaf had its own light and own power source. It took him some time, but he was able to count all of them.

"A hundred and forty-seven," he shouted out, opening his eyes.

Kevran nodded and walked back in the ring. "Good, as usual, you catch on quick. As you may have noticed, when you searched with pure divine power, everything came into focus. This is because your divine power can function as both a power source and a search-light. Your divine power will allow you to scan any sort of natural environment, but it can also be used to detect your enemies. It is important to get used to only using your divine energy at some points in your battle. As you master your techniques, you will be able to use your Reichi with your divine energy and still get the same results, but that takes time and great patience."

Anthony soaked all the information in. It was true that the divine energy made everything clearer, but he didn't feel right using just that power. He decided he would practice this skill with great diligence to quickly master it, so he could use his Reichi with it as well.

"All right," Kevran said, interrupting Anthony's train of thought, "now on to the next part. This part should be easy, though, as you already understand how to use your divine energy. I want you to use your divine energy to raise and manipulate the leaves. Draw out the energy as you did for your speed step, but this time, instead of using the energy, transfer it to the leaves. Once the energy is there, you will be able to manipulate the leaves through the energy. Do you understand?"

Anthony nodded and closed his eyes. Focusing on his divine energy, he took out a large-enough portion and pushed it into a handful of leaves. Once the energy had set, he pulled the leaves upward. They shuttered for a moment and lifted into the air. Anthony opened his eyes and stared in amazement. The leaves were easy to manipulate. It was as if they were a part of his body.

Kevran nodded. "Now that they are in the air, I want you to manipulate them around your body. Think of the leaves as a sword. You must move them with enough speed to kill but without injuring yourself."

Anthony nodded and began to circle them around his body, getting faster the longer he did it.

"Hey, Kevran?" asked Anthony.

"Hm?" replied Kevran.

"You always use the word *Reichi* instead of body energy, but I've never heard you call divine energy by any special name. Do the divine and dark energies have any cool names?"

Kevran rubbed his chin in contemplation. "Well, the divine energy has many names in the angelic tongue, though none of those names will do as mortals cannot understand that language. But there are no angelic terms for the dark energy. Ah yes, there were terms back in the ancient days for the two energies. The ancients called the divine energy Deypia and dark energy was called Onigor."

The word *Onigor* sent shivers down Anthony's spine. "Well, that's a good term for it. Somehow it just sounds evil."

Kevran laughed. "Yes, the ancients had quite the way with words. But enough idle chat. The last phase of your training involves using the leaves as weapons and shields. When the leaves are possessed by your energy, they become indestructible. I want you to use your leaves like a sword to cut through these three dummies."

As he said that, three dummies rose out of the ground and stood before Anthony in the ring. Anthony took a stance and imagined his leaves as a sword that he could use to attack those that were out of reach. Anthony let out a roar and slashed his hand across. The leaves followed the motion and cut the dummies' heads off in one clean swing.

Kevran clapped. "Very good, even if I did expect that outcome. You understand this concept quite well. Now block this."

With that, Kevran charged forward and slashed at Anthony. Anthony's instincts brought his arms up in defense. A thud caused Anthony to peek out. A leaf shield had stopped Kevran cold.

Kevran winced and withdrew his claw. "I never expected your first shield to form on a whim or be that strong. Though I suppose I should have expected that outcome as well."

Anthony let the leaves fall to the floor as Kevran stood up straight and looked Anthony in the eyes.

"Well, that is all that I can teach you right now. The rest will have to wait until another time when you are both stronger and more mature in your power. For now, you should manipulate the leaves a while longer. Then you need to rest up. Once you awake, we are heading back out onto the surface."

Chapter 5

UNDERSTANDING

*A*nthony plopped down on the grass and leaned back against the soft dirt wall. The training had just begun to take its toll. His body ached, and his eyes drooped from lack of sleep since the Zankrex raid had happened at two in the morning. He had no idea how long he had been down in the cave, but it felt like half a day at the very least.

Anthony turned his attention to Kevran, who was lying in the middle of the field. "Hey, Kevran," Anthony shouted out.

Kevran lifted his head. "What?"

"How long have we been in this cave?"

Kevran rested his head back down. "Time in this zone does not pass at the same speed as the time outside. But we have spent a mere six hours inside this cave."

Anthony's eyes widened in surprise. "Only six hours? It seems like I've been training for an eternity in here."

Kevran rumbled in agreement. "Yes, it may seem that way, but that is because you have learned much in such little time. Of course, to you, it would feel as though you have been training for days."

Anthony continued to watch the ceiling as he hummed in response to Kevran. Silence pervaded the room once again. Anthony, still coming down from his workout high, began to inspect the cave. When they had first tumbled in, he had been too preoccupied by the Zankrex event to get a clear view of his surroundings, and the subsequent training he went through kept him from admiring the scenery.

Now that all the hubbub had stopped, he was able to view the cave in its entirety.

The cave was more of a room underground. There were no passages leading to other areas; it was just the single room. The room itself was smaller than the gym on campus, but the ceiling was higher. Though, it wasn't the size that impressed Anthony the most; it was the appearance of the cave. The floor and the ceiling were both covered in lush dark-green grass. The walls were simple dirt walls, but the dirt never fell from its place. He could lean against the dirt, and it felt soft. But when he leaned back up, the dirt wouldn't trickle down or make stains on his shirt. It was almost mystical how everything worked in the cave. The grass was soft and wouldn't prick or cut him in any way. But by far, the most interesting thing in the cave was the ceiling. Scattered about it were stones that shone with a faint green light. A single stone on its own wouldn't be enough to light any space, but all of them together gave off more than enough light for the entire cave. The stones also were absorbing what appeared to be energy floating out of the ground. It was subtle, but when he focused on the air, he could see tiny orbs of light floating up and getting caught in the stones. The grass on the ground varied in length all around the cave. In some areas, it would be up to knee height; but in the areas he had been training, it was trimmed.

The more he looked and observed, the more relaxed and at peace he felt. Then for the first time, he realized how much energy he still had. He leaned back up from the dirt wall.

"Hey, Kevran," he shouted.

Kevran sighed in frustration and leaned his head up. "What is it this time? I am trying to rest."

Anthony smiled at the irritable dragon before continuing to his question. "Why is it that I feel as though I just woke up even though I've been training for six hours?"

Kevran grumbled and laid his head back down. "I am sure you have noticed it by know, but this cave is not a normal cave. This cave was molded by the Creator Himself for me to use as a sanctuary. The tiny orbs of light are the residue of the Deypia that was used to form this cave. It is natural that you would be able to absorb that energy and regain your stamina faster than normal."

Anthony whistled in amazement. There was a pause in the conversation as Anthony's thoughts turned to something he had put off for a while.

In a serious tone, Anthony asked, "Hey, Kevran. Is my family going to be okay?"

Kevran remained silent for a while as Anthony stared at him. He stirred and sat up to face Anthony. The two locked eyes and stared at each other in silence. Anthony fidgeted under Kevran's fierce gaze. After some time, Kevran broke the staring contest and sighed once more.

"I suppose you have a right to know what's going on. I was going to tell you right before we left, but if you refuse to sleep, then I will get all the exposition out of the way now. To answer your question—yes, I believe that your family is alive."

Anthony's face lit up in delight and relief.

Kevran held up a claw. "But they will not be the same if you meet them again."

Anthony's expression turned into a confused one as he walked closer to Kevran. "What do you mean?"

Kevran waited until Anthony sat himself down a few feet away. "Well, as with most things I have told you, I need to explain the past in order for you to understand the present. I told you earlier that the Zankrex attacked at the beginning of human existence. That was just the first attack. Unfortunately, the Zankrex would attack a second time before the Zankrex king could be sealed away. The first war ended with the Battle of a Thousand Swords. This battle took place after the God Swords and Zankrex battled to a stalemate. That was when the Creator sent the Divine Blades for the second battle, and thus the reason for the name. The Battle of a Thousand Swords was the second battle in the first war. The God Swords and Divine Blades earned a total victory."

Anthony looked puzzled, "If the God Swords won the first war, why was there a second war?"

Kevran rolled his eyes. "I am getting to that."

Anthony lowered his head like a child after a scolding, causing Kevran to chuckle. "Anyway, as I was saying, the Zankrex king and a small vanguard of his elite warriors managed to escape from the battlefield and hid themselves away on a far island called Xanto. There they stayed and plotted a way to return their strength to its full potential. Soon the Divine Blades began to rule over the people, and the Zankrex name was made out to be the ultimate evil in the world. After this, the Zankrex king knew that there was no way for him to seduce people to join them, so he began to experiment with ways to inject Onigor without the host giving permission."

Anthony raised his hand at this point. Kevran stopped talking, amused at Anthony, and nodded at him.

"I thought you said that Deypia could be used to detect enemies. Why didn't they use their energy to track the Zankrex down?"

Kevran nodded at the good question. "I suppose that would make sense to you, but you must understand that, at the time, the humans did not understand this new power. Reichi had never been used to track, so they never assumed that technique existed. It was well after the second war when one of the God Swords discovered that use."

Anthony nodded his head in understanding. Kevran waited to see if he had any more questions before continuing his story.

"For fifty years, the Zankrex worked on the island, kidnapping many people to figure out how they could raise their numbers. During this time, they figured out three things: One was that the dark power, or Onigor, could be put into willing victims or orphaned children who were not old enough to understand the world. Second was that forcefully injecting the Onigor into people would only make them subservient toward the Zankrex king. They could not turn them into full-fledge Zankrex through this process. But the third thing they found was the most crucial. The Onigor could not be forced into those that had Reichi within them. At the time, he discovered this 90 percent of the population had some sort of Reichi in them. Knowing this, the Zankrex king attempted to make an army out of orphaned children and wait it out. This is why the second war is not in the analogs of history. Someone spotted a Zankrex kidnapping a child and followed them to Xanto. After discovering the island, they went back and informed the God Swords about it. The second war was not so much a war as it was genocide. The Zankrex were killed without mercy, and the Zankrex king, who was the source of the Onigor, was sealed. The God Swords made those that knew about the island take an oath of secrecy and found a way to seal off the island from human memory. Even to this day, Xanto will show up on no map."

Anthony nodded, taking in the history lesson. "Well, that's all very interesting, but how does that explain the Zankrex plot?"

Kevran looked confused for a little bit; then his eyes lit up in remembrance. "Ah yes, I was explaining the Zankrex plan to you. Sorry I got a bit caught up in the past." He started laughing at his own mistake as Anthony looked on in disbelief.

"Ah, that is funny," Kevran said as he settled back down. "But enough distractions. I need to explain their plan to you."

Even though that whole distraction was because of you, Anthony thought, rolling his eyes.

Kevran cleared his throat. "The Zankrex have been back for quite some time now. The seal was broken almost a hundred years ago. Because the Zankrex king is the vessel for the Onigor, he never ages. He has all the time in the world to prepare these things. He waited for this moment to be unsealed for two reasons: the first being that, this time, a hundred years ago, was about the time that the percent of people with any sort of Reichi in them dropped to below 10 percent. He knew that it was only a matter of time before the greater majority of people would be without Reichi. That is when he wanted to attack. The Zankrex king's goal is to enslave the people of the world."

Anthony stared at Kevran with wide eyes of disbelief. He couldn't even get a word out. The thought of world domination was so large to him that it almost didn't seem real.

"Everyone in the world will be under the Zankrex control?"
Kevran nodded.

Anthony was terrified. "What was the second reason?"

Kevran looked off at one of the walls. "The other reason he chose now is because 90 percent of the Divine Blades are new users, and all the God Swords are still new with their swords as well. This is the first time this has happened in a very long time. The Zankrex king wanted as little opposition as possible and now is as easy as it is going to get for him."

It was all starting to make sense to Anthony. He searched his brain for the words he wanted to use.

"How is that even possible? Why is the Creator allowing this to happen?"

Kevran hit Anthony with an angry glare. "Do not blame the Creator for what you humans have brought upon yourselves."

Anthony shrunk back from the angry dragon. Kevran stared Anthony down for a couple more seconds before exhaling and relaxing. "Of course, the Creator does not want this to happen, but humans have had this coming for a while now. They sin and have become so corrupt I even wonder if there is any good left in them in the first place. Even though the God Swords and the Divine Blades wield the power of the Creator, your scientists would want everyone to believe that it is a reaction to a metal that can only be found in space. They say that demon beasts are just animals with genetic mutations. Humans now have rejected the Creator for explanations that make less sense than anything I have ever heard before. The reason the Onigor was able to gain this much power is because human sin has fed it like a wealthy man would feed his spoiled children. Do not blame the Creator for something that you humans have brought upon yourselves."

Anthony looked down at the ground, chastised at the tongue-lashing that Kevran had given him. His look of shame turned into one of horrible realization. "Those infected by the Onigor will be going to Demonic Lake then?"

Kevran turned his head in confusion. "What do you mean by that?"

Anthony looked away at the wall. "Well, you know that at the beginning of creation, everything was holy. But the introduction of the Onigor caused the downfall of humanity, which I assume is connected to the Zankrex king's birth. After that, the humans were no longer allowed into the Holy Paradise, so the Creator sent down the

Divine Sacrifice to create a way for the humans to get to the Holy Paradise."

Kevran nodded, though he still had a confused look on his face. "I am aware of all that. What are you getting at?"

Anthony looked back at Kevran. "Would those that have been possessed by the Onigor go to the Demonic Lake even if they were covered by the Divine Sacrifice?"

Kevran sat in amazement of Anthony, chuckling at his worry for others. "You worry about others even though you yourself are burdened by so many things. You embody a God Sword in every sense of the word."

Anthony looked up in confusion, and Kevran waved it off. "Do not worry. Anyone who was covered by the Divine Sacrifice before they were infected will still go to the Divine Paradise if they die."

Anthony breathed a huge sigh of relief. He then looked up as he searched his mind for any other questions that he may need to ask before going out. "So those that have been forcefully infected by the Onigor aren't full Zankrex?"

Kevran nodded. "You see, the Onigor still needs the host's full cooperation to be released. Only those that give in to the darkness become full Zankrex. The rest will follow the king's orders but have no special power."

Anthony nodded in understanding, "I won't have to fight my family."

Kevran nodded.

Anthony sat for a little while longer but couldn't think of anything else he might need to ask. It was then that he realized how tired he really was. His vision blurred for a moment as he laid himself down.

Kevran chuckled. "Looks like the exhaustion kicked in. Rest up. I will wake you when it is time to head out."

Anthony mumbled an agreement and fell to sleep.

Anthony's eyes fluttered opened. He stared at the grass ceiling above him for several seconds, trying to figure out where he was.

It didn't take long for the memories of the past day to hit him like a hammer. All the training and the history that he had learned played on fast-forward through his head. He would have laid there for several more minutes, trying to sort things out, but Kevran didn't give him that time. He poked his head over Anthony and stared at him. The sight of a dragon looking over him startled Anthony near to death as he sat straight up.

He breathed a sigh of relief. "Goodness, Kevran, you can't do that to me."

Kevran smiled as he straightened himself out. "I am sorry, but you had this stupid expression on your face, and I did not think that a God Sword should look as confused as you do right now."

Anthony got indignant. "Well, of course, I'm confused. You explained things last night that should have taken a semester to learn. Excuse me for being a little overwhelmed. And I don't think you can play the God Sword card on me just yet. I haven't even tested my abilities out on another living thing. I don't know if I can keep up with the speed that some of those monsters fight at. Right now, I think I am a God Sword in name only."

Kevran stroked his chin. Anthony, now standing, looked a little worried at Kevran. He assumed that Kevran would get upset at him for that outburst, but the look on his face was almost that of agreement.

Kevran nodded his head, as if he came to some conclusion. "You are right," Kevran said to Anthony. "While I have every confidence that you could keep up with the Zankrex out there, your lack of experience at fighting at that level could hurt you. Here is my proposal. I will come at you using my full power with every intention of landing a blow on you. If I do hit you, then not only will we know you are not prepared, but you will be in a lot of pain. But if you can block or dodge the barrage, then you will have the confidence to proceed. What do you say?"

Anthony mulled the offer over. This spar would make a lot of sense, but that part about the intense pain was none too reassuring. *Still*, thought Anthony, *I have to know where I stand, or if I'm even ready to take on the Zankrex.*

"Fine, I'll do it."

Kevran nodded and led him to the center of the cave. Anthony walked out and took a stance. Kevran stopped and turned to face Anthony. He took a stance and began to raise his energy. Anthony could feel the immense power building up in Kevran. But it wasn't suffocating like Clancy's was; it was concentrated.

Anthony calmed himself and accessed his own power. He mixed both his Reichi and his Deypia and prepared to counter Kevran's attacks. In the blink of an eye, Kevran flew forward and struck out at Anthony. Anthony couldn't see the strike and closed his eyes in preparation for the punch, but it never came. When Anthony opened his eyes, he saw that the punch had missed; or rather, he had stepped out of the way. Kevran planted and whirled around for the second strike, and again, Anthony dodged it. He couldn't see either of the attacks, but somehow he had managed to dodge them.

That's when it hit him. *Even though I can't see these attacks, I can still see where they are coming from. I've trained my body for so long to dodge these blows. The speed doesn't matter here. As long as I know how the strike starts, I can dodge it, even if it is just reflex.*

This thought gave Anthony confidence. Instead of looking at the strike itself, he looked at Kevran's posture and stance. Each strike that Kevran threw out, he was able to see where it started from. His body would then move out of habit using the large amount of energy he had inside him.

Anthony was amazed. *This is what it means to be a God Sword—to be able to fight against those who you can't see and who are so much more experienced than I am without even realizing it.*

Anthony continued to dodge and parry Kevran's attacks. He used this fight as a chance to get acclimated with the speed at which he would have to fight from here on out. Fists flew faster than he could have ever imagined possible. Each strike created a small wind that would flutter his clothes. As the battle continued, he began to see Kevran's fists. His eyes began to see more and more of each strike. Before long, he was able to watch each and every strike as it passed by him, and his dodging was deliberate, not instinctive.

Anthony decided it was time to put his strength to the test. He waited and dodged for a few more seconds and then found the strike he was waiting for. Kevran reared back and threw a powerful punch. Antony stood there and waited for it—and caught it in his hand. The thud reverberated across the entire cave and died down after a few moments. Anthony couldn't believe it. By bringing his inner power up to his hand, he was able to stop one of Kevran's strongest punches cold, and there was no pain.

Kevran stood there for a second with labored breath before extracting his fist from Anthony's hand. He shook it a couple of times and began to laugh.

"That was incredible Anthony," he exclaimed. "I thought I would knock you out cold, but you proved me wrong. And not just wrong, I was not even on the same continent as the truth. And the way you caught my punch. I do not think I have ever seen a God Sword acclimate to their powers with the speed that you have."

Anthony smiled at the compliment. He was still in awe of the speeds he had just moved. Kevran moved like a blur at the beginning, but there, at the end, it almost seemed like his was moving in slow motion. *Is this the power of the God Swords? To be able to acclimate to an opponent like that and then outclass him in the same fight is something I never thought would be possible. And yet I just did.*

Anthony continued to marvel at his own strength when Kevran walked up to him.

He inspected Anthony for a moment and then chuckled again out of amusement. "You are not even tired either. That is incredible. You were not using your sword or any of your skills, and yet you were able to fight with that proficiency. I understood your skepticism before, but now there can be no doubt. You are more than ready for the outside world."

Anthony looked at Kevran with a look of determination he hadn't had in a long time. "All right, Kevran, let's go save the world."

Chapter 6

Loss

*T*he portal opened up in the backyard, right where they jumped in the night before. Anthony poked his head out of the hole to examine the area. His sword was drawn, but he had his energy suppressed as low as he could get it. He hoisted himself out of the portal and waited as Kevran flew out and closed it.

Anthony checked his surroundings and was puzzled. It was far too peaceful. When he had jumped in the portal, there were sounds of fighting and explosions. But now he could hear the birds chirping and the morning traffic off in the distance.

They hid themselves in the bushes outside of Anthony's window.

Anthony turned to Kevran. "What's going on here? Shouldn't there be panic in the streets? Why is it so peaceful right now?"

Kevran closed his eyes and stroked his chin. "I told you that the Zankrex king's goal was to enslave humanity. If he has succeeded, then this peace is the obvious outcome. The populace would not realize that the Zankrex were enemies. In fact, they would assume that the Zankrex were their rulers. I told you this, remember?"

Anthony turned and watched his road for any sign of trouble. "I know, but I just didn't think that things would have progressed that far in a single night."

Anthony was interrupted by the sound of his front door opening. He was about to duck out of sight but stopped as he watched his brother trot out to his trito. He walked with no burden at all, and his neck was clear of any marks from the bite he suffered last night.

Anthony almost stepped out of the bushes to go hug him, but Kevran grabbed his shoulder. Anthony looked back in surprise to see Kevran shaking his head and then pointed back to his brother. Anthony turned back around and was shocked at what he saw. Even at that distance, the change was still noticeable.

His brother's eyes were bloodred.

Anthony slinked back into the bushes in total shock as Kevran whispered, "The only way one can tell if a normal mortal is taken over by the Onigor is the color of their eyes. When the dark power has overtaken them, their eyes turn that color. Your brother was still attacked on that night. The Onigor healed him and erased his memories of the attack. Your brother, for all intents and purposes, is now an enemy."

Anthony stayed quite for several seconds before turning back to Kevran with a smile on his face. Kevran leaned back at the sight of this.

Anthony continued to smile. "But my brother is okay. And if he's like this, then he isn't a full-blown Zankrex, is he?"

Kevran nodded, still perplexed about Anthony's reaction. Anthony looked back and watched as his brother drove off to school.

As soon as he left, Anthony stood up and walked out of the bushes. "I guess I should be thankful that the Zankrex have decided to get their revenge this way."

Using a quick burst of Reichi, he leapt up to the windowsill and looked back at Kevran. "I don't know if I could have fought my family. But now I don't have to worry about that. Remind me to thank the king when we see him."

Kevran shook his head and chuckled. "Yes, I imagine that would make him happy."

Anthony stepped down from the window and into his room. To his surprise, the door to his room was brand-new. None of the wood from the previous door was lying around. There was no body or any bloodstains from the fight that Kevran won.

Anthony stood in the middle of his room, amazed. "This is ridiculous. I mean, the memories are one thing, but they even cleaned my carpet. Why would they clean my carpet?"

Kevran shrugged. "Removing physical signs of the takeover eliminate chances of memories resurfacing. The easiest route for them would be to take over everyone in a single night so that they would have less to clean up afterward. The control they have over the mortals is great, but they do not know what would happen if they started to think there was a conspiracy. The human mind is a terrible weapon indeed."

Anthony was amazed. "But to go to such lengths, they must really doubt this power of theirs. Though I wonder what they told my family."

Kevran shook his head. "There is no way to know that. Not without asking your parents or asking a Zankrex. But I would assume they had false memories that you were killed or died long ago. That seems the likeliest option. They would have known that you were a Divine Blade, so they would have already prepared something for the family and friends of all the Divine Blades."

A troubling thought hit Anthony. "Do they know that I am a God Sword?"

Kevran thought about it before shaking his head. "I do not see how they could. They know you are a Divine Blade, but no one could surmise that you became a God Sword overnight. I would imagine that the Zankrex are working under the assumption that the Earth Katana is not around at this point. Why do you ask?"

Anthony still seemed troubled as he paced his floor. "I'm just worried that if they found out that I was a God Sword, they would use my family against me. I doubt they care about sacrificing my family if it meant getting to me."

Kevran nodded. "You are correct in your thinking. I would agree that keeping your identity hidden would be a wise course of action."

The sound of the garage door going up cut the conversation off. The two stayed very still and listened. The garage door clunked as it opened all the way and the sound of a trito starting could be heard. It sat for a while then pulled out and drove off. The sound of the garage door closing was the last thing they heard.

The two stayed still and quiet for several more seconds before Anthony moved. "That was my dad leaving for work. My mother should have already left before my brother, and we saw my brother leaving. That gives us four hours before my father comes back home."

Kevran nodded and moved to the door. "I am going downstairs to see if I can find any evidence the Zankrex might have left behind that can help us. You should get changed into something that you do not mind traveling in for the foreseeable future."

Anthony nodded, and the two broke off.

Kevran stepped back into the room and closed the door. "I could not find anything. The Zankrex were thorough with their cleanup."

He turned and saw Anthony rummaging through his closet, muttering to himself. He was wearing a pair of dark-blue jeans and a skin-tight blue sleeveless undershirt along with blue athletic shoes.

Kevran scanned the outfit. "That is a lot of blue."

Anthony mock-laughed and continued to search through his closet. "Dang it, of all the times for my mother to change up my closet. And it's not like I can call her 'cause—oh, that's right, she's a freaking Zankrex."

He gripped the metal basket and let out a frustrated wheeze.

Kevran looked on, amused by the display. "I feel like you are more upset about the missing clothes than you are about the invasion."

Anthony rolled his eyes and continued to search. Kevran stood in the middle of the room as Anthony muttered curses under his breath and flung clothes out of the closet.

After a while, Kevran spoke up, "What is it you are looking for?"

"A blue pullover," he replied.

"Again with blue," Kevran muttered under his breath and looked at his feet. He stood for a second, staring down at the article of clothing.

"Could this be it?" Anthony stopped and turned around to see Kevran holding up his blue pullover. The two stared at each other for several seconds before Anthony walked over and tried to grab it.

Kevran pulled it out of reach and smiled. "Now, now, what do we say?"

Anthony stared daggers at Kevran and nabbed the pullover.

Kevran chuckled. "I swear if I have to keep up with all of your things this entire adventure, I will kill myself before it is halfway done."

"Ha ha ha, very funny," Anthony said with dry sarcasm. He threw the pullover on and double-checked his shoelaces.

"What is it with you and blue anyway?" Kevran asked.

Anthony stopped and thought about it. "You know, I've never thought about it before. It's always been my favorite color, but I couldn't tell you why."

Kevran shrugged. "It does not matter, I guess. That blue is a good color for hiding in, so I have no qualms."

Anthony continued to get ready, grabbing a pair of fingerless biking gloves and a hat.

"What are those for?" Kevran asked.

Anthony sighed and looked at Kevran. "What are you, my fashion consultant?"

Kevran raised his claws. "I was just curious, not judging you."

Anthony turned back and continued to put the gloves on. "I wear these gloves whenever I am going to be fighting for a long period of time. The gloves have padding on them which keep my hands from getting sore. The material they are made of also helps with my grip, especially in rainy conditions."

Anthony finished putting the gloves on and looked at his hat. It was dark navy blue with *MT* embroidered on the front in silver. He picked it up and put it on backward. "The hat ... doesn't do anything. It's just that it was the hat that my parents got me when I got accepted into Murffana Tech's Divine Blade program. It kind of has some special meaning. Though I guess if I'm going to be adventuring for a long time, my hair might get long and in the way. When that happens, I'll be able to use this hat to keep the hair out of my eyes."

Kevran chuckled and nodded in approval. Anthony picked up his sword and looked at it for a while. After several seconds, he let out a frustrated sigh.

Kevran cocked his head in confusion at Anthony's frustration. "What is it?"

Anthony turned the sword over a couple of times. "I have no idea where I'm going to put this sword. The sheath's going to be in the way no matter how I look at it. Clipping the sheath to my belt would be fine and all, but any movement at high speeds would become impossible. Putting the blade on my back eliminates those problems, but it takes away any tumble options during battle. Also, I doubt I would be able to pull it out from back there. However, none of that matters because there is no strap on the sheath that I can use."

Kevran nodded and walked up to Anthony. "I understand your confusion, but there is a simple solution. The sheath is made from Deypia, so it has certain attributes that make carrying it around much easier. First off, the sheath will stick to its wielder and not move unless the wielder wishes it to."

Anthony was excited about the prospect of not needing any straps. He moved the sword to his back and positioned it where he wanted it. Once the sword felt comfortable, he let it go, halfway expecting the sword to land to the ground and Kevran to laugh. But the sword hung on his back, clinging tight to his clothes.

"Next," continued Kevran, "on the issue of pulling the blade out. The sheath disintegrates into leaves whenever you and only you draw the blade out."

Once again, this prospect excited him. He gripped the handle and began to unsheathe the sword. As he did, leaves fluttered all around him and then disappeared, leaving the sword free from the sheath. Anthony brought the blade all the way around, amazed at the display.

"And," Kevran interjected, "when you want to resheathe your blade, just put it behind your back, and the sheath will form around it."

Anthony did as he was told, and sure enough, the leaves fluttered back around him, and he felt the familiar pressure of the sheath on his back. He pushed the sword all the way into the sheath and nodded in approval.

Kevran nodded as well and turned back to the window. "Well, now is the time to embark, but our destination is a bit of a mystery to me."

Anthony thought for a second, and then his face lit up with an idea. He bounded to his desk and turned his computer on. It took a second to boot up, but soon he was able to access the Internet.

Kevran walked up behind and placed a claw on his shoulder. "I know I said we had no destination, but I do not think that means we get to stay here."

Anthony didn't even look back, and he typed into his computer. "I know that, but there is a site on the Internet that is used only by Divine Blades. It was set up as a message board so that we can stay up to date on demon-beast attacks. If there are any Divine Blade survivors, then they should have posted on this site on where we should meet up."

Kevran seemed skeptical. "I am fuzzy on the workings of this Internet thing, but if that message board is accessible from the Internet, then is it not available to everyone?"

Anthony shook his head. "No, we got special permission from the government to get a site that was disconnected from the rest of the Internet. I don't know all the details, but according to the school, it's impossible for those without a code to get access to it."

Kevran nodded, impressed by the foresight that the Divine Blades had. Anthony typed away at the computer for several minutes before getting to his destination. Kevran leaned in close as Anthony scrolled through to the recent posts. There was a message. The sender was the Head Blade at the academy. Anthony and Kevran leaned in close to the screen and read the message. In it, the Head Blade gave instructions that any surviving Divine Blades should meet up at the gym by sunup. All security systems would be disabled for the day, so they were told to move in the shadows before dawn. There, they would be escorted to a classified location. Anthony's face lit up when the message mentioned that Clancy would be the one to meet with the survivors.

Thank goodness Clancy is still alive. Everyone should be safe as long as he's around. Anthony leaned back in his chair and turned to Kevran. Kevran nodded after rereading the message and stood up straight.

"Well, I suppose we have a plan now," Kevran said and turned toward the window. "Shall we meet up with the group?"

The two leapt down from Anthony's window and landed in the grass. Their detour in the house had cost them precious time. The e-mail indicated that they should gather at sunrise, and the sun had been up in the sky for a while.

Anthony looked up and began to worry. "I hope they wait for a bit. If they don't, then we're all out of luck."

Kevran nodded in agreement. "We need to hurry, but still be careful. Remember, you are the most wanted man on the planet at the moment, even if the enemy does not realize it yet. You need to move without attracting any attention. But to do that, I am going to have to move back to my own space."

Kevran opened up a portal and leapt into it. The portal then closed. Anthony tried not to panic as he realized he was alone, but was comforted by Kevran's voice.

I'll still be able to communicate with you in here, but if it comes to a fight, then you will have to face it on your own. But do not worry, I have not detected any opponent that is powerful enough to challenge you.

Anthony shook his head, still trying to get used to the clarity of the voice in his head and began to move forward. The neighborhood he lived in enjoyed sprinkling bushes everywhere, so his path to campus would be covered. Keeping his power masked, he moved from bush to bush until he made it out of his neighborhood.

Anthony noticed something, and Kevran was quick to take notice as well. *I know what you are thinking, Anthony, and you are right. Even though things have calmed down, there should still be Zankrex patrolling the area.*

Anthony nodded. *That's what has me worried. The only reason the Zankrex wouldn't be patrolling is because they know they got all the Divine Blades. But that's not possible, is it?*

Kevran chastised him. *Stop doubting the power of your friends, Anthony. You know full well that Clancy is capable of handling himself in a fight, and if what you said about that Internet site is correct, then there is no way that the Zankrex could know.*

Anthony tried to reassure himself with Kevran's words, but the doubt never left. Anthony moved on, heading into the small forest that lay within the middle of the town. The forest was used as a training ground for the Divine Blades and connected his neighborhood to the campus. It was a long walk, but it was out of the city, which was all that Anthony cared about at the moment.

With every step he took toward the campus, the feeling of doubt and dread continued to get stronger. He almost wanted a Zankrex to appear just to break the tension that was mounting up inside of him. Kevran attempted to ease his doubt from within, but he could do little to help.

Anthony stepped onto the campus and hid behind a dorm building. He recognized the building and ran over to the building to his left. He continued the path until he came to the familiar square building.

He took the back entrance which led to the locker rooms. Once inside the building, he paused and let his eyes adjust to the darkness. It took longer than Anthony wanted for his eyes to adjust, but the pause allowed him to catch his breath and calm his heart. Once he was ready, he pushed the door open, and the light of the gym came flooding in.

The initial burst of light blinded him for a second, but his vision was quick to return. His spirits rose as he saw the back of Clancy, who was standing still in the middle of the gym.

Anthony breathed a sigh of relief and stepped out of the locker room.

"Clan—"

But the words caught in his throat as he watched Clancy collapse in a pool of his own blood.

And there standing over him with a wicked smile and a bloodied sword was Hannah.

Anthony stood in complete shock as Hannah let out an evil giggle. "Anthony, how good of you to show up here. I see you got the message from the site, after all."

Hannah bent down and used Clancy's shirt to wipe the blood off. She stepped over the body, stepping in the pool of blood, and began to make her way closer to Anthony.

Anthony could only stand in complete shock. "Yo-you cut Clancy? Why would you cut Clancy?"

Hannah stopped and threw back her head in laughter. "Why, you ask? Well, it's quite simple really. I've joined the Zankrex."

Anthony stumbled back but maintained his balance. "You joined them? But you were a Divine Blade. You were chosen by an instrument of the Creator, and you joined them?"

Hannah continued to smirk. "That's right. I gave up my stupid divine power. And in return, the Zankrex have given me a whole lot more of the dark energy to use. Now I'm much stronger than I used to be, though I still had to trick Clancy to cut him. Poor fool was so worried about me he never saw the attack coming."

Anthony's disbelief changed as he stood up straight. He bowed his head and clenched his fists. "You used Clancy's trust to kill him because you knew you couldn't kill him fair and square?"

Hannah scoffed. "Oh please, I still could have beaten him in a fair fight. But that would have taken time and effort, and I didn't want to waste any energy. Besides, I'm going to need it all to torture you. After all, it's my hatred for you that drove me to this point anyway. I guess you could say it's your fault that Clancy is lying half dead in a pool of his own blood."

Anthony's eyes widened, and he stepped forward to say something, but Clancy's coughing cut off what he was about to say. Anthony's shock only doubled at the sign that Clancy was still alive.

Hannah looked back annoyed and sighed. "I guess one cut isn't enough to put down the great Clancy, but you'll bleed out soon enough. Anyway, as I was saying, Antho—"

Hannah stopped talking as she turned back to see Anthony was gone. She stood still for a moment and looked around. She turned back around and saw him at Clancy's side. Anthony kneeled over

Clancy as he tried to continue breathing. Each breath was labored and full of blood. Anthony looked on with tears in his eyes as he tried to think of the words he should use.

Clancy managed to look Anthony in the eye and gasped out. "Run … you need … to run." A fit of blood-filled coughs interrupted the sentence.

Hannah laughed as she began to stroll over. "You wasted one of your two speed steps just to get closer to the dying old fool? Well, if you insist on wasting your abilities, I won't stop you, but don't expect me to hold back."

Hannah took a stance, getting ready for a fight. "Come on, let's duel one more time just for nostalgia's sake."

Anthony didn't even acknowledge her as he continued to look over the wounded Clancy.

Hannah got annoyed at his silence and shouted at him, "*Hey,* I'm giving you one more chance to face me in a duel. If you don't fight me now, I'll just kill you where you stand and be done with it."

Only silence answered her as Anthony continued to ignore her. Hannah slammed her foot down in rage and stomped over to Anthony. She stood over him and prepared her sword. "Even in your dying moments, you manage to piss me off. Well, see if I care. I'll send you to the afterlife first. Be sure to greet Clancy when he comes up behind you!"

With that, she swung her sword down at Anthony's head. The sword halted in midair. Hannah looked at her sword, confused, until she saw it.

Anthony, still bent over Clancy, had caught the blade between his thumb and four fingers.

The blade rattled as Anthony shook with rage. He stood up and looked at Hannah with a murderous gaze. Hannah tugged and pulled but couldn't get her sword out of Anthony's grip. She began to feel fear as Anthony reached for the sword on his back. Leaves danced around, and for a second, all was quiet and still.

Hannah never saw the slash. She could only feel the pain. She looked down and saw a deep gash across her torso. She screamed out in pain and let go of her sword, stumbling to the ground. Anthony tossed the sword to the ground and kicked Hannah flat on her back. He jumped and straddled her, pointing his sword straight at her forehead. But he froze.

For several seconds, the two stared at each other as Anthony struggled inside himself. Hannah's face was full of fear, and tears began to fall down her cheeks. Anthony quivered for a moment longer before screaming out and stabbing down.

The sword went a third of the way down into the wood floor and concrete. And then silence once again fell over the gym.

Hannah turned her head and looked at the blade an inch away from her skull and passed out. Anthony stood up and yanked his sword out of the ground. He looked at Hannah's wounded body before turning back and running to Clancy.

Clancy's breathing was getting worse. Anthony got over the body again and inspected the wound. The sudden realization set on him. *This wound isn't fatal. If we get him out of here now and to a hospital, then he can still make it.*

Kevran was about to interject when Clancy's hand reached up and grabbed Anthony's arm.

Clancy smiled up at Anthony. "I know … that face. You want … to get me out of here … don't you?"

Anthony nodded his head, still unable to talk to Clancy.

Clancy mustered up a rough laugh. "No … you can't take … me with you. I … would only get … in the way."

Anthony shook his head and found his words. "But I can't just leave you here. You could still make it. How am I supposed to live with myself if I let my friend die in front of me?"

Clancy only gripped Anthony's arm harder. "You're a … God Sword … aren't you?"

Anthony was shocked at the change of topic, but he did manage to nod.

Clancy smiled. "I thought so. That power … it wasn't the power … I was used to feeling from you. But … if you're a God Sword … then your safety … is the most important thing. If you take … me with you … you will be caught by the Zankrex."

He is right, Kevran interjected. *You have to leave him here. I know it is tough, and it does not seem right, but you have to think about the future. Do not throw everything away because you were not strong enough to say goodbye.*

Tears began to roll down Anthony's face. "But I don't want to say goodbye. I wanted to fight with Clancy. I wanted to prove to him that I was useful, that I could help, that this boy could save the world. But I can't even save my own friends. How am I going to save the world?"

Clancy continued to squeeze Anthony's arm. "I already know … that you are useful."

Anthony looked at Clancy's eyes; they were full of trust and love. Anthony bowed his head and held in his sobs. "I'm sorry," he whispered.

Clancy shook his head. "No … I should be … thanking you, Anthony. Now that … I know you're the … next God Sword … I can die knowing that … the world is safe."

Anthony kept his head bowed and tried to keep his tears at bay. A commotion could be heard outside the doors.

Kevran cut back in with a worried tone, *I am sorry, Anthony, but we have to leave now.*

Anthony stood and sheathed his sword. He wiped the tears from his eyes and looked down one last time.

Clancy smiled through pain and gave him thumbs-up. "Go … save the world … Anthony."

Anthony nodded as the tears began to reform and sprinted out the back door.

Zankrex were walking all around the gym. Hannah had long since been taken out to a hospital while Clancy's body lay in the center of the floor.

The Zankrex seemed to be lost until the banging open of a door brought them all to attention. A tall imposing figure stood in the doorway and walked in with command. He instantly turned to a Zankrex nearest. "Give me an update on the situation."

The nervous Zankrex saluted. "Y-yes, sir, General. There were two bodies found, one being that of General Hannah, who was taken to the infirmary. The other one is still alive, though he is knocking on death's door."

The general turned toward Clancy and stood in thought for a couple of seconds. "Go ahead and take that body to the infirmary. There's no rush, so if he dies, it's no big deal, but try to get him back to health."

A couple Zankrex began to load Clancy up on a stretcher and walked out of the building.

The Zankrex who had spoken before walked up to the general. "You know that one was a Divine Blade. Not only that, but he's only hanging on by a thread. Why waste time and energy trying to bring him back?"

The general sighed. "There were orders from higher up that said to capture any Divine Blade alive that could be caught. Research and development is looking into things related to the Divine Blades, though I have no idea what they are."

The other Zankrex nodded in understanding, and they all watched as Clancy was carried out of the gym.

The general turned back. "Anything more to report?"

The Zankrex shifted his eyes and cleared his throat. "Well, this next bit is only just speculation, but we have reason to believe that a God Sword was here."

The general grabbed the Zankrex by his collar and hoisted him up in the air. "That's impossible," he growled. "We have intel on all four God Swords, and none of them were even close to this location." Realization spread across the general's face. "You don't mean to tell me that it was the fifth God Sword?"

The Zankrex nodded as he dangled there.

The general let the Zankrex down and stared at him with interest. "What makes you think that it was the Earth Katana?"

The Zankrex twiddled his thumbs. "Well, it's the only thing that makes sense, sir. General Hannah was at the same level as that Divine Blade. But there are no signs of a struggle, which means that General Hannah was taken out in one strike. Only a God Sword has the power to do that. And since we know that the other four are nowhere near here, I have to assume that the fifth one is responsible."

The general stared off into space, a smile spreading across his face. "The fifth God Sword, said to be the most powerful God Sword, has been awakened. And I'm going to be the first to test his legendary skill."

The general turned to the remaining Zankrex. "Begin a search for the God Sword. Keep in constant contact and inform me when you find him."

The Zankrex shouted their understanding and took off into all directions, leaving the gym empty except for the general. He stood in the gym by himself, the smile still spread across his face. "I hope you come out to play, God Sword, because I'm itching to see what you're made of."

Chapter 7

CLASH

*A*nthony ran. He ran faster than he had ever run before.

He ducked through trees and jumped over bushes, never missing a stride. Tears continued to trickle down his cheek and fly off his face. Everything was a blur to him. He wasn't even aware of his surroundings anymore. He just ran.

Kevran stayed quiet but was growing increasingly worried about Anthony. Twenty minutes passed, and nothing had changed. Anthony continued to run through the woods at incredible speeds. Finally, Kevran spoke up.

Anthony.

Anthony gave him no response.

Anthony, he said, louder this time.

Still Anthony didn't reply.

Anthony, stop, he shouted, fed up with being ignored.

Anthony slowed down and came to a stop. He wasn't tired; his massive reserves of energy allowed him to run at that speed for that long without even breaking a sweat.

Anthony stood in a clearing, fists clenched as Kevran came back from his space.

He approached Anthony and tried to put a claw on his shoulder. "Come now, you cannot blame yourself fo—"

Anthony smacked Kevran's claw off his shoulder and stared at him with bloodshot eyes.

"Don't tell me it's not my fault," he growled at Kevran. "I'm the freaking God Sword, yet all I've been able to do at this point is show up too late and cry. I couldn't even save the man that helped me the most in life, and you're going to tell me to calm down?"

Kevran raised his claws in defense. "You could not have shown up any earlier than you did. You did not even know about the meeting place until an hour ago."

Anthony turned away and punched a tree, leaving a sizable dent in the trunk. "None of that matters! A God Sword is supposed to be able to protect all his friends. He has the power to do anything. I couldn't even save a man that was lying right in front of me."

"Enough," Kevran interjected. "There was no way you could have saved him. His wounds were too great for you to heal by yourself, and no hospital would take him in because everyone in the world has been taken over. There was absolutely nothing you could do."

Anthony continued to stare at the tree. "How is any of that an excuse? In the end, I was there, and I still couldn't save him. Heck, I couldn't even kill Hannah. She was pure evil, and I couldn't finish her off. Now she'll be the one to survive while Clancy dies."

Anthony bent down and rested his head on the tree, tears beginning to form in his eyes again. "I go through all that training, and still I couldn't save anyone. And now that Clancy is dead, I don't have anyone to tell me where the other Divine Blades went. For all I know, they could have been killed by Hannah before she killed Clancy."

Kevran watched as his partner broke down against the tree. He fought within himself for a time then made a decision. Kevran took a step forward. "There is a chance that Clancy lives."

Anthony froze; every muscle in his body tensed up.

The tree assisted him as he stood back up and turned toward Kevran. His eyes were filled with confusion and hope. "What do you mean?"

Kevran took a breath and met Anthony's gaze. "Clancy's wound was great indeed, but it would take a while before he bled out. Now this next part is only speculation, but it is speculation that I am confident in."

Kevran looked at Anthony for confirmation to continue. Anthony studied Kevran for a good while before finally nodding for him to continue.

Kevran nodded. "The Zankrex were working on a project before the second war. It was their goal to find out how to implant Onigor into those that had Reichi or Deypia. They fail because they had no test subjects, but now they have control of Tertalla. I am sure that the project will continue, and for it, they will need all the test subjects they can get their hands on. If they have indeed started this project back up, then you can be sure that they will not let Clancy die, though I doubt living would be any better for him at this point."

Finished with his explanation, Kevran studied Anthony. He had no idea how he would take the news. Anthony stared at the ground, his mind racing a mile a minute. He looked up at Kevran. Kevran held his breath and waited for the reaction. Anthony's face turned from confusion to relief, and a smile crossed his lips. Kevran stepped back in shock of the reaction. Anthony continued to smile as he wiped the tears from his face.

He turned to Kevran. "Thank you for telling me that. Even if they torture him, as long as he is alive, I can still save him. And I will save him. Even if I have to scour every prison on Tertalla, I won't let them use him as their lab rat."

Kevran was amazed at the sudden determination that Anthony had. He smiled and shook his head. "Really, you God Swords never cease to amaze me. I have every confidence that you will find him, Anthony, though I feel sorry for the Zankrex that are in that prison when you get there."

Anthony chuckled and nodded in agreement.

Anthony sat at the base of the tree in the small clearing. It had been some time since Kevran had told him about Clancy's probable fate. Despite the fact that he would be tortured and beaten, Anthony was happy with this outcome. Though he knew there was a chance that this wasn't the case, he decided to buy into the scenario that Kevran had played out. It made sense to him that they would want a prisoner of war, and Clancy was by no means dead when he left. He had at least a half hour of life left in him.

Anthony couldn't help but smile. He knew that one day he would find the prison that kept Clancy, and he would bust him out of there. He couldn't save him from Hannah, but he would save him from torture.

Anthony's face lit up in realization. He turned to Kevran, who was also resting against a tree. "Kevran, why in the world did Hannah have Onigor?"

Kevran looked up in the sky and shrugged. "That has been bothering me since we left the gym. Never in the history of this world has a Divine Blade forsaken their power for that of the Onigor."

Kevran's eyes lit up as he leaned off the tree. "Wait, did she not mention you when she talked about the reasons why she turned?"

Anthony sat thinking for a moment, then remembered what she had said. "That's right," he exclaimed in realization. "She said her hatred for me drove her to do what she did."

Kevran looked at Anthony in confusion. "What in the world did you do to that girl that made her join the Zankrex?"

Anthony shrugged in honest cluelessness. "I've been trying to figure out why she hates me for almost a year now. But no matter how I look at it, it doesn't make sense. I only met her in the academy, and even then, I never talked to her unless she started it. She started out hating me. I have literally never had a polite conversation with her."

Kevran shook his head in confusion. "Well, none of that matters anyway. All we need to know is that Divine Blades have the capability to turn to the Zankrex side. We have to hope that there are not more people out there like Hannah. Otherwise, things could become bleak indeed."

Anthony could only nod in agreement.

Anthony sighed, still lying at the base of the tree in the clearing. A substantial amount of time had passed since he had run out of the gym. With no backup plan, they were stuck sitting around until a destination presented itself.

Anthony took his hat off and scratched his head. "Hey, Kevran, what do we do now?"

Kevran kept his eyes shut. "That is an excellent question, Anthony. I wish I had an excellent answer for you, but I am all out of ideas at the moment, which is not good because every second spent here is another second the Zankrex have to catch up. We still have time, though, thanks to your little tearful run."

Anthony rolled his eyes, though he couldn't get mad. He didn't feel bad for the way he reacted. The thought of Clancy dying still dropped a pit in his stomach, but he knew that as a God Sword, he would need to control his emotions a little better in the future. He had a feeling that this wouldn't be the last time a close friend would be lying in a pool of his own blood.

He shook his head to get the morbid thoughts out when something struck him. He turned back to Kevran. "Hey, Kevran, I have a question."

Kevran nodded for him to ask.

"Is there a place that maybe the last Earth Katana would have made to leave some of his knowledge behind for the next generation? You know, since he knew that the Earth Katana would be sealed away, and no one would be there to mentor him. Do you think he left a place that the next Earth Katana could go to find answers?"

Kevran's face lit up like a solar flare. "That is it," he exclaimed. "The sanctuary in Wishitak, Anthony, that is it."

Anthony sat back in surprise of Kevran's sudden outburst. "What's the sanctuary?"

Kevran tried to calm his excitement as he walked over to Anthony. "It is exactly as you said. The last Earth Katana made a hidden area called the sanctuary in Wishitak where he put in a wealth of knowledge for the next Earth Katana. I cannot believe I forgot it—the one thing that Oshuma made me promise to remember. Anthony, I am sorry it took me this long to remember it."

Anthony was too in shock of Kevran's excitement to get angry. "No, it's fine. Besides, if you had remembered, I might not have been in the gym in time to save Clancy."

Kevran smiled and nodded. "I guess it all worked out for the better then."

Anthony laughed. He put his hat back on and turned the bill backward. "We need to go to Wishitak then, right?"

Kevran nodded.

Anthony checked the sun. "We still have enough daylight to start the trip. Wishitak is near the northwestern coast, so it's probably going to take a while to get there."

Kevran thought for a second. "Well, we cannot have you running at full energy the entire time, not unless you want the entire Zankrex army to attack you."

Anthony smiled and shrugged. "It's going to happen soon anyway. Why not get it started now?"

Kevran rolled his eyes and turned west.

Anthony jogged at a brisk pace. He used just enough of his energy to keep himself from sweating, but not enough that would be noticeable to any Zankrex nearby. He ran alone since Kevran had gone back into his space as soon as he started running.

As he ran, he continued to think about all that had transpired. Hannah's betrayal lay at the forefront of his thoughts. *She did say she blamed me for her turn to evil, but what in the world could I have done to make her turn into a Zankrex?*

Anthony pondered that thought for a while until his thoughts were interrupted by a branch smacking him in his face. He regained his composure just to lose it again after tripping over a root. Anthony stopped thinking and focused on dodging the forestry ahead of him.

Angry, he asked Kevran, *Why is it that I can't take two steps without hitting a tree? When I was running away from the gym, I never hit a single plant.*

Kevran chuckled. *I was wondering when you planned on asking that. I assumed your goal was to hit every tree on Tertalla.*

Anthony's face flushed in embarrassment. *Would you just answer my question already!*

Kevran regained his composure before answering, *Well, it only makes sense that you could dodge plants while running. You are the Earth*

Katana. Use your Deypia to feel out the land you are about to traverse. If you run while sensing your surroundings with your Deypia, then you should have no problem knowing where each and every branch is and which path to take.

Anthony realized how obvious that was, shaking his head at his own stupidity. He slowed down and took a moment to access his Deypia. He drew it out and let it flow out in front of him. Just as Kevran said, he noticed where each and every branch was, where every root was positioned, where it came from; and just like that, the forest went from a labyrinth to a wide-open passageway.

He drew out a little more energy to broaden his view of the forest. With this newfound skill, he began to jog again; only this time, it was a little faster and a whole lot more confident. Each step was premeditated, and no branch even came close to hitting him. With a smile on his face, Anthony sped off toward Wishitak.

The sun began to set as Anthony stepped into a small clearing. *Anthony, let us stop here for the night*, advised Kevran.

Anthony stopped, happy to oblige. He had spent the entire day running, and while he wasn't exhausted from the endeavor, he was certainly glad to take a nice break. The only times he had stopped for the past eight hours was to eat lunch and to take a water break. Yet his energy was far from depleted, which astounded him.

He stood in the center of the clearing and looked up. The sky was ablaze with the color of the sunset clashing with the autumn's blue sky. Never had Anthony felt so alive. The world was against him, his family had been turned against him, and all his friends were in the exact same position, but Anthony couldn't help but feel happy—his immense power bringing confidence to match it. He had yet to use this power in any useful way; he had even failed to save his friend. But his mood was still upbeat.

Kevran walked out of a portal and up to Anthony. "You are in good spirits right now."

Anthony chuckled. "I don't know why either. With everything that's happened, I should feel horrible. But I have this feeling that somehow everything is going to be all right."

Kevran smiled. "Well, that only makes sense. A true God Sword would not worry about the troubles in front of him because he knows that he has the strength to overcome them. You seem to be realizing that right now."

Anthony shook his head. "I don't care what it is. All I care is that I feel good. It's nice to know that after everything, I can still feel this way."

Kevran nodded and turned away, walking into the forest. When he came back, he had an assortment of fruits and nuts in his arms. Anthony had managed to find a small outcropping of rock nearby using his God Sword power. The two sat in the clearing and munched away on nuts in total silence.

Kevran sighed as something had been weighing on his mind for a while now. The sigh drew Anthony's attention.

Kevran looked at Anthony. "I'm sorry to bring this up now, but I feel as though it is a topic that we need to discuss."

Anthony folded his arms and nodded his head.

Kevran continued, "I want to ask you why you did not kill Hannah back at the gym."

Anthony sat there in grim silence as he remembered the scene. His rage had made the memories hazy, but he remembered the look on Hannah's face as he pointed the sword at her.

"I couldn't do it because, in my eyes, she was still human. I know it sounds weird, but the fear on her face was all too real to me. Even if all she did was torture me, she was still my classmate. I would have to be rather cold to just be able to kill her off without some sort of hesitation. I mean, I know she's a Zankrex, but she's still a human being."

Kevran stared at Anthony with an intense gaze. "Are you saying that you would not be able to kill any Zankrex regardless of who they were?"

Anthony nodded, understanding where Kevran was going with this.

"Anthony, you cannot win this war if you refuse to kill your enemy. They are not human anymore. They gave that up of their own will. If they turn their blades toward a God Sword, it can only mean that Onigor resides where their soul once did."

"I know," Anthony said strongly. "I understand that, but it still doesn't make it any easier on me. At the end of the day, I would still have to deal with the blood on my hands, regardless of whose it was."

Kevran sighed and became silent for a while. After thinking some, he continued, "I am not going to be able to convince you one way or the other. Just get to the sanctuary in Wishitak. I have a feeling that once we get there, you may change your mind."

Anthony shrugged. "I don't see what the big deal is anyway. Hannah was at a high level for a Zankrex, right?"

Kevran nodded. "The power she had was that of a general. Regular Zankrex will not have even a fourth of that power."

Anthony smiled. "Then there's nothing to worry about. I took care of her with ease, so dispatching of pawn Zankrex without killing them should be a piece of cake. And I'll deal with those so-called generals if that time comes. I'm a God Sword, remember?"

Kevran half-smiled, and the topic was dropped. The two retired to the small outcropping of rocks as the sky turned black. Kevran looked at the sky once more before going in as the unease in his gut intensified.

Anthony's eyes shot open to utter darkness.

The only noise that could be heard was the wind blowing through the trees. He had no idea what time it was, but that wasn't a concern to him.

A horrible feeling of dread covered him and his every sense.

He could feel nothing. No sound was made. There was no scent on the air, and nothing could be seen. But Anthony knew something horrible was about to happen.

He sat in utter silence waiting for his eyes to adjust to the darkness. As his eyesight improved, he reached for his sword, attempting to be as quiet as possible. As he wrapped his hand around the hilt, the sword budged, and the sheath made a small clank against the stone.

In an instant, a blur shot out from the bush close by. Anthony whipped out his sword with all the speed he could and countered the blow. His attacker came into focus as Anthony's worst fears came to light.

The Zankrex grimaced at him, his pointed teeth showing, as he drilled him with his bloodred eyes.

Anthony's mind raced. *I can't let him make a sound. If I do, then I'm sure I'll be swimming in Zankrex before the sun can come up.*

He pushed his sword back with as much power as he could muster and forced the Zankrex to stumble backward. Anthony flipped his blade around and drove the pommel of his sword toward the Zankrex stomach.

As he was about to land the hit, the Zankrex pushed the hilt to the side and slashed back at Anthony with speed he wasn't expecting. Anthony ducked down and let the blade fly over his head. At that moment, the Zankrex began to shout something, getting a word out before Anthony managed to elbow him on the side of the head. The Zankrex was knocked out cold, but the damage was already done.

In the distance, he could hear several footsteps and the sound of those jumping out of the trees. Anthony had no time to debate his next move; he turned and ran as fast as he could into the night.

Anthony sped past trees and bushes. Using his power, he could see a large area of the forest around him, even though his vision was diminished in the darkness. He found that with his power, he could detect anything that touched a plant in his viewing radius. He knew that what seemed like a small army of Zankrex wasn't too far behind him.

Well, this came out of nowhere, Anthony proclaimed to Kevran.

Kevran was very alert at this point. *I cannot help but feel that I could have warned you. I had the worst feeling in my gut last night. I should have said something.*

Anthony struggled to talk and keep his focus on his surroundings. *Don't worry about it. I felt the same thing right before the attack. I felt it last night as well, but I was far too tired to be bothered by it.*

Kevran sighed. *Either way, just hold out for a little while longer. I'll come out to assist you.*

Anthony shook his head. *No, don't. I can handle this on my own. More like I need to handle this on my own. I should start getting some experience on how to handle these situations solo anyway.*

Kevran was hesitant to agree but decided that he could always come out to help if things got out of hand. Anthony focused back on his surroundings, but one thing wouldn't leave his mind.

Kevran, that Zankrex I fought at the campsite had crazy reflexes. He might have even been stronger than Hannah. Is he like a commander or something?

Kevran became troubled at this point. *In the Zankrex army, there are those that wield far more power than the regular Zankrex. They are called the generals. There can be any number of them at one time. The term* general *is used for those in a different power class than the regulars. Hannah was a general, but she would have been considered on the lower level of general.*

Anthony nodded. *So, the Zankrex I fought would have been a general?*

Kevran shook his head. *No, that Zankrex was not a general. The power that a general wields is of a different type than the regular Zankrex. The Zankrex you fought had a normal-type power.*

Anthony became confused at this point. *How could a normal Zankrex be far more powerful than a general?*

Kevran had no answers.

Anthony tried to wrap his head around what was going on, but his thoughts were interrupted by Zankrex. While he had been focused on the conversation, the Zankrex had managed to encircle him and stop him dead in his tracks.

Anthony stood in the middle of a clearing, the dark starry sky illuminating the field. Anthony stood in the center and put his hand on his blade.

We're going to have to continue this conversation later, Kevran. Right now, things are starting to get interesting. He whipped out his sword as the Zankrex charged.

Anthony parried and blocked attack after attack. After his first run-in with the overpowered Zankrex, he decided not to take any risks. He opened up and accessed the full amount of his power. The

Zankrex's movements turned sluggish and anticipating them became all too easy. Once again, he was amazed at the extent of his powers.

It's just like my fight with Kevran. Their movements just don't seem that quick to me anymore.

If there had been a few of them, the fight would have been over in a heartbeat. But the number of Zankrex seemed endless. Anthony spun and slashed with the backside of his sword so as not to kill any of them, but the waves of Zankrex coming from all directions soon proved to be a problem for him. Using his powers, he could tell where the Zankrex were coming from by the plants they touched. But knowing where they were and how to block them all were two different things. Multiple times, he would focus too much on his front and be split second away from getting slashed on the back, or vice versa.

Anthony felt Kevran's mind make contact with his. *Do not forget about your ability to manipulate leaves,* he said right before severing the connection.

Anthony understood what to do. He spun around several times to give him some room and time to concentrate. He focused on all the leaves around him and picked up as many as he could. A mass of leaves flew toward him. Not missing a beat, he maneuvered them behind him and formed a leaf wall on his back. The wall was thin but might as well have been solid steel due to the power in the leaves.

With his back covered, all his focus went to his front. He took full advantage of this and began to take the Zankrex out one by one. He used his fists and the hilt of his sword as much as the actual blade. Behind him, he could hear the Zankrex attempting to break his leaf wall, but he wasn't worried about that.

The battle had turned in Anthony's favor after he erected the wall, and only a handful of Zankrex were left when the fighting died down.

Anthony stood in the clearing taking in labored breaths. The battle hadn't drained him in any major way, but there was a noticeable dent in his power.

The sound of clapping drew his attention.

"Who's there?" Anthony shouted as the power he felt was different than that of a regular Zankrex.

This is what I feared, Kevran said.

A tall man walked out of the shadows. He was different than the rest of the Zankrex. He wore a skin-tight black T-shirt and black pants. His skin was no whiter than the other Zankrex, but his eyes seemed to gleam brighter than the rest. His black hair was long and would flow over his eyes if he hadn't brushed it aside. He was far more muscular than the other Zankrex. He held a hand-and-a-half sword with a long white blade. The hilt held a bloodred stone in the pommel. The Zankrex had a twisted smile on his lips and a crazed look in his eyes. Anthony scowled as realization began to set in.

"Don't tell me, you're a ..."

The Zankrex's smile widened. "My name is Lance, and yes, I am a Zankrex general."

Lance leapt down from his perch in the tree. His hand-and-a-half sword was drawn and gleaming against the starlight. Anthony knew his ability to sense others' powers was not very good, but even he could feel the overwhelming amount of power that Lance was wielding.

Kevran touched Anthony's mind. *You have to be extra careful here, Anthony. You have lost a portion of your energy in the events leading up to now. That should have put you at about even with him, but something very unnatural is going on here.*

Anthony agreed, and Kevran receded back to let him concentrate.

Lance took his time walking a circle around Anthony, smiling all the way around. "I can't believe I finally get to meet a legend such as yourself," he said with honest admiration. "Well, not you the person, but the fact that you are the Earth Katana makes you a legend by default. You have gone this entire night at full power, and even now you can still match me. The legends did not exaggerate when it came to your power."

Anthony held a defensive stance, even though Lance had yet to raise his blade.

"What's even more impressive," Lance continued, "is that you haven't killed a single one of my men. The level that you overpower them is impressive, to say the least. And considering how much more powerful they are right now, thanks to tonight, I could only imagine how this engage would have gone during the day."

Anthony half-smiled. "Oh, do go on. I always love hearing from a fan."

Lance threw his head back in laughter. "Even now, you joke with me, as if you're in an inconvenient position. I throw a small army at you, and you stand here and joke."

Anthony was beginning to get creeped out by this guy. He wasn't used to having an enemy flatter him like this.

"Not that I don't enjoy the lip service, but maybe we can get to the point of you being here?"

Lance stopped moving and turned to face Anthony. "Of course, I can't keep you waiting here forever, now can I? Well, I'll get right to the point then. I want to fight you right here, right now, just you and me."

Anthony continued to keep a defensive stance as he tried to tell if this was a trap or not. "That's quite brazen of you. You of all people must know that even for a Zankrex general, going one-on-one with a God Sword is suicide."

Lance chuckled. "Well, for most generals, that would be the case. But I am a tier above most of the generals. That and this night is a special night."

Anthony started to get annoyed. "That's the second time you've mentioned that. What makes this night so special that all Zankrex become so powerful?"

Lance waggled his finger at Anthony and raised his blade. "Ah-ah, I can't go giving that information away to someone who didn't earn it. If you can defeat me, then I may think about letting you in on our secret."

Anthony sneered at Lance. "Well, if you're going to make it that easy, then you may as well just tell me now."

Lance wore a sinister grin. "Oh, I wouldn't be so sure if I were you. You only defeated Hannah, and compared to her, I may as well be a god. I know you want to get through this whole debacle without shedding blood, but if you come at me without an intent to kill, I promise you, you won't win."

Anthony scowled and switched to an attacking stance. "Enough chatter. I'll let my sword do the talking from here on out."

Lance smiled, the wild look in his eye only intensifying. "You took the words right out of my mouth."

Six Zankrex stood around by the tree line in confusion. Just a moment ago, they were trying to corner the God Sword and failing at it. Then their leader popped up and struck up a conversation with the God Sword. Then before they could even blink, they had begun fighting.

The battle was fierce. Anthony had expected the pace of the fight to be quicker, but he wasn't prepared for how much quicker. Lance had almost sheared off two limbs before Anthony was able to acclimate to the fight. His fight with Kevran was beginning to look like child's play compared to now.

Lance was proving to be more than a match for him. Their swords flew at blinding speeds as they parried and struck at each other. Anthony lost track of time the moment steel touched steel. All that existed in the world for him was this fight. Every inch of the forest was only an object to be used for the fight. Time meant nothing now. Anthony tried to feint and strike at Lance's leg. He had hoped to injure him and get the battle over, but Lance swatted his strike away with ease.

He leapt back and waggled his finger at Anthony. "Didn't I tell you that you would have to fight me with killing intent? There's no way that a strike meant to wound me is going to land. If you want this fight to be over, then you're going to have to kill me."

Lance gave Anthony no time for a rebuttal as he charged right back in. Anthony started to block and counter as he tried to think about what to do. He then remembered his speed step and berated himself for forgetting such a crucial move.

Anthony accessed his power and speed-stepped back. He used it several more times in an attempt to confuse his opponent. Anthony readied his blade as he shot from one corner of the clearing to the next. He saw an opening and charged in, slashing at Lance's back.

Anthony's blade stopped mid-swing.

What should have been flesh and bone under his sword was instead Lance's blade. Anthony stared in disbelief. Lance had put his sword behind him and blocked his attack without even looking.

Lance turned his head and smirked. "You refuse to learn, don't you?"

Lance spun around and pushed Anthony back with force. Anthony grimaced as he was flung back a few feet but regained himself to block the oncoming attack. The two combatants' blades locked.

Lance stared deep into Anthony's eyes with his crazed look. "You disappoint me, God Sword. Even with my current boost, if you had decided to come in with killing intent, then I would have been the one on my toes."

Anthony held his gaze with an intense stare of his own. "I see no reason to bring myself to your level by killing another human being. I don't care how much Onigor is inside them. To me, they are still humans."

Lance let out a curt laugh and jumped back. "You may want to change that mind-set of yours."

Anthony didn't wait around this time. He speed-stepped right in front of Lance and struck out. The two blades clashed in a shower of sparks, and the battle continued. The two leapt from tree to tree, striking at each other in the air.

Anthony distanced himself from Lance and focused. He grabbed as many leaves as he could with his power and created a large swirling mass of green. As soon as they had gathered, Anthony sent them flying toward Lance. Leaves flew like daggers around Lance as he dodged and parried most of them.

Anthony kept some of the leaves and used them like a blade, slashing out at Lance. He parried them twice before ducking under the next swing and darting toward Anthony. Anthony dropped the leaves and focused on his own sword as he blocked Lance's barrage of attacks.

Lance laughed as he slashed. "You can't wield both your sword and the leaves, can you?"

No answer was needed as Anthony continued to block the oncoming attack. He began his counterattack as each strike fell short upon his enemy's sword.

The two opponents stood on the tree limb, neither one moving their feet. The strikes sped up until there was only a blur of motion. Anthony put all of his focus on the moving blades, only taking a moment to notice that Lance too was deep in concentration. The blur of attacks seemed to last for an eternity as neither side wished to be the first to break the attack off. Leaves fell to pieces around them as their blades sheared everything around them except their bodies. Even small cuts were beginning to appear on the branch they stood atop.

Finally, Anthony saw a gap; and in the split-second window, he ducked and slashed at Lance's legs. A normal opponent's legs would have been cut clean off, but Lance leapt up and off the branch and on to one a few feet away. The two stood there staring at each other.

Anthony's chest heaved as he drew in deep breaths. As he tried to catch his breath, he noticed that Lance was still keeping his composure quite well. Lance leapt at Anthony, but Anthony jumped off the branch and landed in the middle of the clearing.

Lance landed and began to laugh. "Looks like someone is running out of gas." Lance stood up, his sword hanging from his side like he had already won. "Well, this has been fun, but I think I'll end it now. The king gave us strict orders to kill any God Sword if we were given the opportunity. So, it's been a blast, but you need to die now."

Lance took an attacking stance and prepared to strike.

Kevran touched Anthony's mind. *You have to get out of there now. I do not know how he is doing it, but he is not losing energy like he is supposed to. If you engage him now, there is no way you can survive.*

Anthony understood, but he had underestimated his fatigue. The lack of sleep and strain he had put on his body had caught up with him at the worst possible moment. He couldn't run now, at least not very far. He took up a defensive position and prayed for a miracle.

Lance landed on the ground and shot at Anthony. Anthony flexed and prepared for the worst as the sun broke over the trees.

Chapter 8

FOCUS

The bright morning sun filtered in through the trees. Anthony could feel the warmth from the sun bathing his back in its light.

But that wasn't what had caught Anthony's attention.

Lance stopped in his tracks and emitted a howl of pain, covering his eyes in anguish. Anthony felt the drop in Lance's power, and it was significant. In an instant, Lance's energy dropped.

Anthony didn't hesitate and made a dash for Lance. He intended to strike a good blow before retreating away. His progress was halted as four Zankrex jumped in his way. Two more appeared behind them and helped Lance up. The four in front seemed hesitant to attack and kept their distance.

Anthony didn't care. He had no intentions of killing any of them, so if they wanted to run, he wouldn't mind. As they began to turn, Anthony remembered something.

"Hey, wait," he yelled out. The Zankrex stopped in their tracks and turned around. Lance could only stare at him in exhaustion. "You said that if I won, you would tell me why you guys got so powerful. I want my explanation now."

Lance let out a tired chuckle. "You only won because of the sun. Don't go getting so cocky."

Anthony smirked. "And I have a feeling you were only winning because of the night."

Lance sighed, understanding that he had pretty much figured it out already. "Fair is fair. I'll honor my promise since I am the one running away, though it seems you may have already figured it out. The night does make us more powerful, but that isn't all there is to it. Not all nights are the same. Some nights are different. We receive better power boosts depending on something specific to the night."

Anthony just stared at Lance. "Are you talking to me in riddles?"

Lance laughed. "Well, it wouldn't be very fun if I told you out-right. Now tell me, God Sword, what do you think gives us our boost?"

Anthony lowered his sword and thought about it. He thought about the night. *What is specific to the night?* he wondered.

It hit him.

"It's the moon," he exclaimed.

Lance nodded. "The moon is what decides how powerful our boost is. I won't say anything more than that, but I'm sure you'll fig-ure out the rest for yourself."

The Zankrex were about to carry him away when Anthony stopped them.

"Wait," he shouted.

The Zankrex stopped, and Lance rolled his eyes. "What? Can't you see I'm exhausted right now?"

Anthony didn't understand one thing. "Why did you tell me that?"

Lance looked at Anthony one more time then looked back toward the forest. "I don't like it when my enemy is defeated because of sneaky means. I'm going to be the one to kill you, God Sword. I couldn't take the chance that one of my comrades would use that information to ambush you and kill you. If telling you the secrets of our power is what it takes to keep you alive until I can kill you, then I'll happily divulge everything."

With that, Lance signaled for the Zankrex to move with a nod of his head. The Zankrex took one weary look at Anthony and then disappeared into the trees.

Anthony stood in the clearing for a few moments, making sure the Zankrex had gone before allowing his legs to buckle. He landed hard on his back, but the relief of resting made the pain seem nonexistent.

He lay there gasping for breath as his aching muscles began to release their tension. He opened his eyes again to see Kevran standing over him.

Kevran bent down and helped Anthony back up. Anthony stood there, leaning on Kevran, trying to gain his balance back. After a couple of breaths, he managed to stand on his own.

To his surprise, the fatigue had already begun to alleviate. Kevran motioned toward the unconscious Zankrex bodies.

"We must talk about a great many things after that fight. But we should leave first before the Zankrex awake and attack you again."

Anthony nodded and followed Kevran away from the clearing.

It took some time for the two to get to a suitable place. An hour after the battle had ended, they made it to the bank of a creek.

Anthony was at his absolute limit. When Kevran motioned for them to stop, he crashed down by the bank and just lay there. Kevran smirked at the display and walked over to a tree. The tree's roots were already poking out of the soil, so it only took a few scoops of Kevran's claws to clear out a small hole under the tree for Anthony to rest.

When Kevran turned back around, Anthony was leaning down the bank and taking great gulps of the clear creek water. After a time, he came up for air and lay back down. His panting had subsided, but the fatigue was obvious.

Kevran sighed and walked over to Anthony. "I suppose our talk is going to have to wait until you rest up. I will bring you over to the tree. You rest there until you feel at least 80 percent. I will go find food while you are sleeping."

Anthony managed a nod as Kevran bent down again to help Anthony over into the tree. As soon as his head hit the soft soil, he passed out into some much-needed sleep.

Anthony awoke to the sound of water splashing about. Birds sang their songs in the canopy above.

Groggy wasn't a strong-enough word to describe Anthony's condition. Soil clung to his face and hair, and his mouth was dry from having it agape the entire nap.

He pushed himself up before hitting his head on the underside of the tree. He cowered down and clutched his head in pain and confusion. It took him a second before the memories of last night came rushing back to him. The battle and the events that transpired afterward all came back to him.

He crawled out from under the tree and stood up. He eased himself into a stretch, expecting some sort of resistance, and found that he wasn't stiff in the slightest. He finished his stretches and tested his range of motion. He found that he was able to move his body just as well as he could have before the battle.

He then took stock of his surroundings. He wasn't in a clearing as trees all around blocked his view of the sky. Even with the trees, he still managed to guess that it was an hour after midday.

He remembered his sword, and his hand flew back to feel for it. Nothing was there. He had a mini-heart attack before turning around to see it leaning up against the tree he had slept under. Relieved, he strode over and grabbed it. With the familiar pressure on his back, he felt a thousand times more confident. He paused and stood there for several seconds, just enjoying the peace and quiet, when an intense hunger and thirst hit him like a ton of bricks.

He knelt down and took several long draughts from the creek. After he had quenched his thirst, he sat back up. His stomach growl echoed through the trees. He clenched his stomach in pain as the hunger doubled. Anthony could only sit as any other movement hurt his core.

A rustle in the nearby bushes caught his attention, and his hand flew to his sword. Before he could pull it out, Kevran walked through the bushes. Anthony breathed a sigh of relief and relaxed his hand.

Kevran chuckled at Anthony's high alert. "Nice to see you so energetic after such a tough fight."

Anthony could only shake his head in amazement. "I figured I would be sore all over after that brawl, but I feel as though I just woke up from a wonderful night's rest. Am I to assume that this is another perk of being a God Sword?"

Kevran nodded his head and set down an arm full of nuts and berries that he had picked from the nearby brush. Anthony didn't hesitate and began to cram his mouth full of the delicious treats.

Kevran continued as Anthony ate, "Being a God Sword will allow you to recover faster than regular Divine Blades. Even then, your recovery would have taken a little longer, but you were resting in a forest."

Anthony said nothing but gave an inquisitive glace up at Kevran before looking back down at his lunch.

Kevran explained, "You know that each God Sword has a certain element attached to the sword. If that God Sword comes in contact with his or her element, they receive certain benefits. One of those benefits happens to be speedy recovery."

Anthony finished off the rest of the nuts and berries and nodded in understanding. "That makes sense, I suppose."

Anthony stood back up, feeling rejuvenated after his meal.

Kevran walked forward and put a claw on Anthony's shoulder. "We have much to discuss about that battle last night, but it would be bad if we made no progress. Let us run until dark, and then we can talk."

Anthony nodded and took one last drink from the creek before tearing off into the forest.

Several hours passed before the sky began to darken. Anthony had been running through the forest alone with his thoughts the entire time. Kevran had decided to go back to his cave to rest up as he had been out watching Anthony while he was resting in the tree.

Anthony had mulled over the fight in his mind hundreds of times while he made his way toward Wishitak. As hard as he tried, he couldn't think of anything that they would need to talk about.

Anthony rolled his eyes. He knew that Kevran was his guide and mentor to the God Sword, which meant that he was going to take every opportunity to teach him something. He just couldn't help but hope that it wouldn't happen after every event.

Anthony came up on a small pond covered by several trees. He had decided early on that a clearing might be a bad spot to rest up, so he chose something with a little more cover.

He found a place to lie down next to a tree and rested for a few minutes before getting back up to drink from the pond. He inspected it first as random ponds in the woods might not be the healthiest thing for him. After determining that it was safe, he took a couple of gulps and went back to his tree.

He still couldn't make contact with Kevran, so he assumed that he was still sleeping in his cave. He wouldn't have cared if it wasn't dinnertime. But it was, and Kevran had been the one to provide food.

Anthony shook his head and stood up. *I always rely on Kevran for this*, he thought to himself. *It's time I start providing for myself.*

He concentrated and used the same technique he was using to dodge trees. Spreading his power out like feelers, he could sense a large portion of the forest, but he couldn't tell what any plant was. He focused harder and really zeroed in on each plant. As he focused, the identity of the plant would reveal itself. Ecstatic at his new discovery, he got to work scanning the forest.

It took a while, but he found a berry plant. With an enormous sense of accomplishment, he trudged off to retrieve his prize.

Anthony strode back into the pond area and was surprised to see Kevran sitting by the same tree cooking a fish.

Anthony could only look on in confusion. "When did you come out of your cave? I never sensed you."

Kevran gave a half smile as he continued to tend to the fish. "I have been out for a while now. I came out when you were searching for berries. I imagine you were so focused on the task at hand that you failed to realize I was there."

Anthony felt embarrassed that he hadn't managed to sense such an obvious thing, but Kevran was quick to wave it off. "You were focusing on one thing at the time. This is a good lesson for you. Focusing too hard on one thing will shut you off from the rest of the world. I am glad you were training your focus, but you need to remember what happens when you do."

Anthony nodded and set the berries down by the fire. He pointed at the fish. "Are you cooking yourself a fish, and you didn't think that I would maybe like one?"

Kevran chuckled and plucked that fish off the fire. He sat it on a stone and slid it toward Anthony. "That is a greedy attitude for a God Sword, don't you think? This fish is not for me as I have no need for physical nutrition. It has been a while since you had a full meal. That fish is for you."

Anthony smiled in thanks as he had been missing not having any meat to eat. The fish was small, but put alongside the berries, it would make an excellent meal. Anthony dug into his small feast as Kevran went about putting out the fire.

By the time the fire was gone, Anthony had finished his meal. After a drink from the pond, Anthony sat back against the tree in contentment.

The sky was a dark shade of blue when Kevran turned to Anthony. "We need to talk about the fight last night."

Anthony groaned. "Do we really need to? I'm sure you have something more to teach me, but I would say everything in that battle was self-explanatory."

Kevran continued to stare at Anthony. "I understand you just want to charge in and do everything on the fly, and that may work for you for a time, but one day you are going to run into something that you know nothing about, and it will kill you. Every battle you survive is a learning experience. If you will not learn from them, then the battle itself was useless."

Anthony sat in silence for a while before turning toward Kevran. He looked annoyed but beckoned him to ask what he wanted to ask.

Kevran smiled. "I only have two things I believe we need to talk about. First would be your stubbornness."

Anthony looked up in surprise then annoyance. "Look, if you want to talk about the battle, then that's fine. But if this is going to turn into a bash fest, then I'm going to sleep."

Kevran raised his claws and motioned for Anthony to stop. "I am not going to bash you. I simply want to know why you never asked for my help when it was obvious there at the end that you were about to lose."

Anthony slumped back against the tree. "I don't know what to tell you. I just had this feeling that Lance wasn't going to kill me. I had it from the very beginning of the fight. It was like his whole intention was to get to know me, to understand me. It was like an introduction, but with a sword fight."

Kevran was stunned. He could only look on in total silence. After a while, he shook his head and continued, "I am failing to think of a good way to follow that up, so I am just going to move on. The last thing I wanted to talk to you about was your focus. In the battle, whenever you used your God Sword powers to move leaves, you always had to stop fighting."

Anthony nodded. "Well, yeah. I have to concentrate on manipulating the leaves. Isn't that what I have to do?"

Kevran shook his head. "The God Swords before you all managed to manipulate leaves without breaking a stride in their sword fighting. You too will need to achieve this if you want to beat the Zankrex king."

Anthony seemed unconvinced. "How is it possible to manipulate leaves and sword-fight at the same time? Wouldn't that take some tremendous focus and discipline?"

Kevran folded his arms. "Not as much discipline as you would think. The hardest part would be mastering it. But becoming proficient at it is the easy part. It is the same principle that allowed you to block me even though you could not see my attacks. We need to get you to where your body is so used to using the power that it can multitask it with sword fighting."

Anthony nodded in slow realization. "If that's the case, then I guess I just need to practice more."

Kevran nodded again. "And I have some great exercises for you too, but those will have to wait till morning. You should get some actual sleep tonight so that your body does not become too reliant on the Deypia to heal it."

Anthony was about to agree when he remembered something. "Wait, Kevran, I have a question."

Kevran seemed surprised but nodded his head.

Anthony motioned back the way they had just came. "I don't understand why I ran out of energy so fast while fighting that little bit but spent so little energy while running all day."

Kevran smiled. "Little bit? You do realize that you were fighting Lance for a whole hour, do you not?"

That was news to Anthony. He took a step back in shock. "A whole hour? There's no way it could have been that long."

Kevran just nodded. "It was that long, if not even longer. You would not have noticed because you were so engrossed in the fight, but it was an hour."

Anthony still couldn't believe it. Kevran couldn't help but laugh at Anthony's dumbfounded look.

He calmed down then looked at Anthony again. "I have no answer for you on why you use so little energy for physical boosts. That has been true for every God Sword before, and no one knows the answer. But when it comes to the next part, I am afraid you are wrong about something. You did not run out of energy."

Anthony couldn't help but feel insulted. "What do you mean I wasn't out of energy? Are you telling me I don't know what I'm feeling? I was unable to draw anything out by the end of that battle. Isn't that running out of energy?"

Kevran remained calm and stoic. "You felt as if you had no energy simply because your body did not allow you take in any more energy."

Now Anthony was confused. "What do you mean?"

Kevran motioned to Anthony. "This is an explanation that I was saving for a later date, and perhaps I will go over it again in the future, but I suppose now is as good a time as any. Deypia and Reichi have a profound effect on the body. I mentioned this on the first night I came to you. A body that is not used to either energy can be torn apart by it. That is why Divine Blades and God Swords must first go through some training before they can wield their power. However, they do not just start off wielding the full extent of their power. Even if a body is used to Deypia, it can still only take so much before the strain begins to affect it. That was what you were experiencing."

Anthony's mind wasn't clicking. "So … wait, I can't use my full power?"

Kevran nodded. "When you access your energy, it does not just all open up and flood your body. That would be inefficient. Your body acts as a filter for this. Think of Deypia as the water, and your body is the dam. The dam will only let in as much water as the container it is protecting will allow."

Anthony nodded his head. "A'right, that makes sense to me now, but how does that answer my question?"

Kevran mimed a dam opening all the way. "What happened to your body is like what would happen to a lake that allowed the dam to open all the way. Water flooded in, but the container was not prepared for it. Your body reacted in the moment of the fight. It brought in the necessary amount of energy to fight Lance. The problem being, of course, that your body is not capable of working with that much energy. It did what it had to, but only for so long. The feeling you had with your 'energy loss' was your body shutting the dam before you hurt yourself."

Anthony let the explanation sink in as he began to realize the gravity of the situation. "Me at my base level was at a complete disadvantage against Lance?"

Kevran nodded his head. "But do not dip too far into depression. Your body is capable of fighting an overpowered general for an hour. That shows your progress is not as far back as you may think. Keep training, and you will find yourself on the winning end of those fights"

Anthony couldn't help but feel uplifted by the thought. "Here's to hoping that next fight waits a little while."

Kevran chuckled. "Yes, indeed. But this night is not waiting any longer. Get some sleep, Anthony. Morning training will come much earlier than you think it will."

Anthony smiled and nodded his head as the exhaustion from the day began to creep back up on him. After some searching, he found a group of bushes clumped next to the pond. He climbed in and fell asleep under their branches.

Anthony's eyes opened to the dawn of the new day. A slight fog had rolled in and brought with it colder temperatures. Anthony curled up tighter, trying to get more warmth out of his body. Soon it became evident that warmth wouldn't find him there, and he crawled out from under the bushes.

Besides his shivering, he felt great. Even though his bed had been the ground and his covers had been the bushes, he had still managed to get a good amount of sleep. He scavenged around and found some breakfast before Kevran showed back up.

"Well, now that you are awake, we can begin the training."

Anthony raised his hand, and Kevran stopped. He rolled his eyes and pointed to Anthony. "A question from the audience?"

Anthony lowered his hand. "I have a concern, actually. If we stay here training, then won't the Zankrex catch up?"

Kevran shook his head and got a devilish glint in his eye. "We will not be staying here and training. That would be too easy. You are going to train and run at the same time."

Anthony groaned as Kevran rubbed his claws together. "No complaining, Anthony. If you want to get stronger, then you are going to have to work for it."

Anthony was still upset, but he shut up.

Kevran nodded his appreciation and continued, "Now, the exercise starts off with you taking three leaves. You are going to use your power to make them fly around in circles by one another in complex shapes. After you get used to maneuvering them, we will add in distractions and other objectives for you to pass."

Anthony nodded and got three leaves. The three leaves floated over Anthony's palm for a minute as he tried to think of a pattern for them. Soon the leaves were flying around in circles, making it look like he had one sphere floating above his palm.

Kevran gave a thumbs-up. "As I figured, the first step is not so difficult. Now you need to maintain that form with your leaves while you walk around this area."

Anthony again nodded in understanding and began to take a few slow steps. The first few steps made his leaves waver a bit off path, but after a few more confident steps, the leaves were once again flying straight.

"Excellent!" Kevran exclaimed as Anthony strode around the area numerous times with ease. "Now it is time to kick it up a notch. You need to run through the forest like normal without letting the leaves deviate from their path."

Anthony looked at Kevran with doubt. "But it's not just as simple as running through the forest. I have to use my power to find the path through the forest."

Kevran nodded. "This is why this step may take a while."

Kevran then grew a smug look on his face. "But I guess if you are not good enough to do it, then we can always take even more baby steps."

Anthony shot Kevran an icy glare and then focused back on the forest. He took a deep breath in then headed off. He only got a couple steps before his leaves crashed into one another and went flying everywhere. He stomped his foot in frustration and picked up three leaves again. After the leaves took their shape, he started to jog again. This time, he got a little farther but rammed right into the middle of a tree. Cursing, he jumped back up and punched the tree in the middle of the trunk, leaving a sizable dent.

He took a few calming breaths before Kevran came back up beside him. Worry covered his face. "Look, if it is too much for you, we can try something el—"

Anthony shot Kevran another icy glare. "I can do this, and I will do this. Don't pamper me anymore."

Kevran raised his claws and backed away. Anthony closed his eyes and took several more deep breaths. After a time, he collected three more leaves and spun them around until the sphere was back. He lowered his hand, and the sphere stayed where it was. With the orb floating in place, he once again began to run. After a few steps, a branch swiped across his face, but he kept going. At times, the leaves would clip one another and threaten to fly apart but never did. In time, Anthony managed to work his way up to a fast-paced run, and the sphere stayed right where it was.

Trees flew past Anthony as he tore through the forest. His breath was heavy, and his pace was faster than he was used to. He wanted to slow down, but the Zankrex on his tail wouldn't let him.

Now would be an excellent time to train your focus, Kevran chimed in.

Anthony elected to ignore him, but he continued, *This opportunity will not present itself again. Why not grab some leaves?*

"Shut up," Anthony said, too focused to speak in his head.

Kevran ignored him. *Holding an orb in these conditions would show considerable progress. An excellent chance to see how you are progressing.*

"Shut. Up," Anthony said with a little more force.

It was once again ignored.

I would be able to tell where you are in your training. It would help me figure out what exercises to do next.

"*SHUT UP!*" Anthony yelled. An unfortunate Zankrex popped out of the bush at that exact moment and was concussed. Anthony didn't wait to see if the Zankrex was out or not; he just kept running.

Kevran seemed miffed. *I am only worried about your training, Anthony. No need to be so hostile.*

Anthony ground his teeth as he found a hole in a tree. He squeezed into it and covered the entrance. Once in, he was able to focus more on the conversation. *Your training is the reason I'm in this mess.*

Kevran took offense to that. *It was not my training that alerted the Zankrex to your presence in the city. That was your inability to contain your own energy.*

Anthony wanted to punch something. *Which is why I wanted to go around the city, but no, that would have been too easy. Heaven forbid, I just want to slink past a large city without risking my life for once.*

Kevran couldn't agree. *You need to learn how to hold in your energy. There will be many times on this journey when stealth will be of the upmost importance. If you do not know how to hide your presence, then we may as well give up now.*

Anthony knew he was right. *I'm aware the skill is important, but there had to be a better way to train it.*

Kevran dismissed the thought. *There may have been other ways to do it, but none as effective as this one. You have learned a valuable lesson, have you not?*

Anthony didn't want to agree, but he knew Kevran was right. Simple distractions and emotions had been his downfall in the town. It was only a small spike, but it was enough to alert the Zankrex in the area. Now he had to wait in the hollow of a tree as the day passed.

Why don't I hide in your space? Anthony realized.

Kevran dismissed the option. *We cannot do that.*

Anthony was annoyed at the response. *And why not?*

Kevran sighed. *My space is not something to hang around in. I allowed you in for training on the first day because of the circumstances. I would never suggest the idea on a normal day.*

Anthony was getting curious. *Why is that?*

Kevran continued, *My space was brought into existence by the Creator Himself. It leaks Deypia just by existing. Humans cannot endure that for prolonged periods. The only reason you were able to train for the night is because you are a God Sword. Any normal human would simply perish from the extreme amount of Deypia around them.*

Anthony couldn't think of any rebuttal to the heavy news. He let the topic alone, and Kevran was happy to leave it.

He sat there for a few hours before daring to exit. He focused on his surroundings. He detected breaks in branches all the way west, letting him know that the Zankrex had long since made their way past.

He reoriented himself toward the north and headed off.

The sun began to set on the seventh day of travel. Anthony reflected on the journey. It had been a quiet trip. Aside from the one city he was chased out of, he had stayed clear of any actual human interaction.

His training had progressed faster than he had hoped it would. It had started off slow. His troubles of keeping the leaves from hitting one another persisted for two days, but on the third day, something clicked. The leaves became easy to move even while running. On that day, he added a second orb of leaves without any trouble. Even Kevran was impressed with the progress.

Now at the end of the journey, he was able to manipulate two orbs of leaves without holding his hands up.

The spinning orbs dissipated as he came to a halt on a small hill. Off in the distance was a quaint little town. It was small, with the whole village being in full view. Anthony smiled with accomplishment as the sun set on his destination. He knew a closer look would be needed, but for now, he was content with knowing the journey was over.

They had made it to Wishitak.

Chapter 9

ASHLEY

$\mathcal{A}$nthony poked his head over the bushes. The village below was small and rustic. There was the center, which seemed to have everything from shops to playgrounds; then there was the outside of the downtown area. Several small neighborhoods sat clustered together, lights emanating from most of the houses.

Anthony was fond of the setup as he had always wanted to live in a small country village.

Twilight was just setting in as stars began to burn in the darkened sky. The air was colder than back in Murffana.

Anthony crouched back down and began to ponder his attack plan. *This is Wishitak, isn't it, Kevran?*

Kevran seemed hesitant. *I believe it is, but things have changed so much since the last time I was awake in this world. If you get me into the village, I will know for sure.*

Anthony didn't quite understand why being in the village was so important. *Why do we need to get into the village? It's not like you can come out and snoop around anyway.*

Anthony could feel Kevran rolling his eyes. *I am well aware of that. But in Wishitak, there is a building that Oshuma created to hide things away for the next Earth Katana. The building will have trace amounts of his energy in it, so if we get close enough, I will be able to sense it. That and the building is a square wooden hut, so it would be impossible to miss.*

Anthony nodded, impressed at the preparedness of the former God Sword. He took one more peak at the village.

It had been a real pain to try and find the village. Since he didn't have a map or any sort of electronics to guide him, he had to rely on his power to sense out villages that were small enough to fit the bill. Kevran had already ruled out two others before telling him to head toward this village.

The village was still far away, so spotting the small cabin they were looking for right now would be impossible.

Anthony started to get up to get closer, but Kevran stopped him. *Let us not get too hasty, Anthony. If we walk into town right now, we may raise some suspicion. That and one look at your eyes, and they will know that you are not one of them. Let us wait for midday where we can walk into town without raising much thought, and when wearing sunglasses is accepted as commonplace.*

Anthony sat back down and sighed. Kevran was right, of course, but Anthony was itching to see what was inside this building. Putting aside his enthusiasm, he turned around and found a place to sleep.

Anthony lay on his back, gazing at the stars. He had already eaten his dinner and was trying to get comfortable. Kevran asked if he wanted to train a little before bed, but Anthony decided to decline. For one, they were too close to the village for him to feel comfortable about training, and he had spent the entire day prior training his focus. He felt pretty trained out for the day.

He was still amazed at the progress he had made. His ability to control leaves while performing other tasks had skyrocketed, which was impressive considering how terrible he was at the start.

Must be the Deypia. There is no way I could have done this all on my own.

Kevran chimed in, *Well, give yourself some credit. You worked hard at mastering that. You are not there yet, but the progress you have made is impressive, to say the least.*

Anthony nodded in self-satisfaction. This past week had been a good week for him. The training had gone well, and there had been only one small Zankrex encounter since his run-in with Lance.

The memory of Lance caused the battle to blur through his mind. He hadn't put much thought into it since Kevran had dissected it in its entirety.

Sudden realization hit Anthony. *Hey, Kevran, how come you didn't talk about the moon after I battled Lance?*

Anthony felt Kevran's confusion.

We never talked about how the moon powered Lance up, Anthony clarified.

Kevran nodded. *I was wondering what you were talking about there for a second. I suppose I never felt the need because I figured it was self-explanatory. We need to make sure to stay away from Zankrex at night. And we still have to be careful until we figure out if it is the full moon or the new moon that gives the better power up. I suspect the best power up is to be had during the new moon since that is when the Zankrex invasion took place.*

Anthony still felt unfulfilled. *But you don't wonder why at all? I always thought that creatures of the night would be at their most powerful when the moon was full.*

Kevran chuckled. *Well, that makes less sense if you think about it. The moon is just a reflection of the sun, so a full moon is the closest that nighttime will ever be to having a sun. Creatures of the night, theoretically, would not like a full moon. They would thrive when there is absolutely no sunlight, reflected or otherwise.*

Anthony felt stupid after the obvious explanation. He decided not to talk anymore as he didn't wish to be shown up. Kevran must have felt his embarrassment because he was sending smug vibes toward Anthony. Anthony chose to ignore it and go to sleep.

The sun rose over the tree line and hit Anthony right in the eyes. He squinted and woke up. Morning had come and with it had brought an even colder day than before. He began to shiver as he wasn't used to the bitter cold this early in the year. *This is why I don't like the north. They seem to forget about fall.*

Kevran chuckled. *Well, in any other situation, I would tell you to raise your power to keep yourself warm, but I do not think that would be a good idea so close to that town. You can feel it, right?*

Anthony nodded. His sensing powers weren't great, but even he had been feeling it for a while now. There were a couple of high powers in the town center, and they were making no effort to hide their strength.

You don't think they could be guarding the building we need to get to, do you?

Kevran could only shake his head. *I have no idea, but I would think that going there first would be a real smart idea.*

Anthony nodded and began to trek down the hill before Kevran stopped him again. *One more thing: you need to put your sword in my room.*

Anthony started to protest but then realized that walking into town with a sword on his back would be one of the most suspicious things he could do. He took the sword off his back as the portal to Kevran's room opened up.

He dipped the sword into the portal and let it drop.

Do not worry about the sword. If you are ever in trouble, the portal will open up beside you. Just reach in and grab it.

Anthony nodded, not excited about going into a Zankrex-infested town weaponless, but he trudged on anyway.

Anthony walked at a casual pace. The sun was high in the sky, and the temperature had risen as a result. There was still a good chill in the air, but with no breezes blowing, the sun was able to keep him warm.

It didn't take him long to make it to one of the outlying neighborhoods. Once he got within distance of people, he decided to keep a low profile. He knew he needed to find sunglasses, but he didn't know how to go about doing it.

At that moment, he watched as a man walked out of his house and tossed a bin of garbage into the larger container outside his home. Anthony watched as useless junk fell into the container, but something familiar glinted off the sunlight. Anthony felt a surge of adrenaline as he realized what they might be. He waited for the man to go back into the house, taking a casual stroll across the road. He didn't have to dig far to find his prize. The man had thrown away what appeared to be a brand-new pair of sunglasses.

Amazed at his ridiculous fortune, Anthony wondered to himself why the man would do that, but decided not to think about it too much.

Even though he was walking through enemy territory, he felt relaxed. He was on the outskirts of town before he ran into his first group of villagers. When they looked over, he smiled and waved but never slowed his pace. Much to his relief, they waved in kind and continued about their day.

He knew the area with the powerful Zankrex was on the opposite side of town, but he decided to take the long way through downtown. He wanted to see if there were any street vendors selling food. He wasn't in any way malnourished, but it had been some time since he had eaten anything cooked or prepared.

He wasn't disappointed.

The streets were teeming with people and outdoor shops. He almost found it weird to see this scene in this day and age. Most shops were indoors, and an outdoor market like this one was rare.

His thoughts were interrupted by the heavenly smell of cooked meats and sweet cakes that were on display. He fished his money out and counted his total before hitting the stores he wanted. By the time he had bought the food he desired, he was out of money.

He sat on the curb munching away at his feast in total bliss. As he ate, he took the time to observe his surroundings. The people went about their lives like nothing had happened. He hadn't expected anything different, but it still bugged him.

But something else popped out to him. No one was wearing any sunglasses. The sun was shining bright in the sky. Even with the sunglasses on, Anthony still felt blinded.

I wonder how all these people are able to walk around without any sunglasses on?

Kevran mulled it over. *It may be a side effect of the Onigor in them. The same energy that turns their eyes red may also grant them better vision. They may see better at night as well. If that is the case, we will not be able to use the sunglasses very long. I am certain word will get out that people with sunglasses on are to be reported.*

Anthony hated that no situation could ever be solved in an easy manner. He decided he wouldn't think about it anymore. All he had to do was get in and out of the shrine.

With those thoughts in his head, he went about eating his food with renewed vigor. When he was done, he stretched out in satisfaction.

Well, he thought to himself, *better head off and figure out if the shrine is indeed here.*

He shot up in excitement but paused as he felt the blood rush from his head. As he stumbled from light-headedness, he knocked over a girl who was passing by. A small squeak escaped her lips as she tumbled to the ground, spilling the armful of supplies she had.

Anthony turned around and began to pick the things up.

"I'm so sorry," he said, embarrassed at the attention he knew would follow.

He looked up. "Let me help yo—"

He stopped midsentence as he looked into the girl's eyes.

They were bright blue.

Anthony couldn't speak for a second as realization hit him. His thoughts didn't get far as the sound of people beginning to turn forced him to act.

In a split second, he noticed a towel lying with the stuff that the girl dropped. He swiped it off the ground and threw it over her head. Just as he did, a man walked over and kneeled down. He looked at the girl for what seemed like an eternity before turning to Anthony.

"Is she all right?" he asked in genuine concern.

Anthony felt relief wash over his body as it seemed no one saw her eyes. He could feel her shaking in fear as his hand was still on her head.

Anthony smiled. "Oh, everything's fine, sir. Thank you for your concern. My sister here just doesn't do well when she's out in the sun for too long. She'll be fine with some rest."

He could feel her start to calm down as she realized she wasn't going to be found out.

He helped her and gave her sunglasses back. She put them on and stood around with the towel still draped over her head as Anthony collected the rest of her goods. After they were all in hand, he put his arm around her and led her off, with everyone walking off none the wiser.

Anthony stood in a dark alley surveying the area. It seemed that everyone was shopping at the bizarre, which left the outlying areas empty. He sighed in relief as it seemed no one had followed them there, and he turned to the mystery girl. She sat with the towel still draped around her head, but her sunglasses were now off. Anthony walked over and kneeled down to her eye level. He took his sunglasses off and showed her his eyes. Her eyes widened in shock as he stood back up.

"You're not one of them?"

Anthony shook his head. "No, I'm not one of them. I'm a God Sword."

Anthony almost laughed at the amount of shock that was on her face. She sat there with her mouth open for a few seconds before realizing what she was doing.

She closed her mouth in embarrassment and stood up. "You say you're a God Sword, but you don't look like Robert or Brandon. Who are you?"

Anthony smiled. "My name is Anthony, and I'm the Earth Katana or the fifth God Sword, if you don't know what that is."

Once again, her mouth flew open in shock; and once again, Anthony almost started laughing, this time being much more obvious about it. The girl's face burned in embarrassment as she closed her mouth again.

She gained her composure and smiled back at Anthony. "I'm Ashley. It's very nice to meet you."

This time, Anthony took a good look at her. She had long blonde hair that reached down past her shoulders. Her face was slim yet slightly rounded. Her bright blue eyes held his gaze, and her smile was vibrant and genuine. Anthony was getting more and more nervous the longer he looked at her. She was skinny, but not athletic skinny. As a whole, she was absolutely stunning.

He quickly shook his head to clear his thoughts and got back to the matter at hand. "I'm glad to see someone managed to make it out without getting turned. Are there any others like you?"

Ashley got solemn as she shook her head. "There aren't any others like me. Not anymore at least. A man that lived on the outskirts of town was still normal like me, but he was found out yesterday."

Anthony smirked at the thought. *That would have been an amazing coincidence if that was the man I saw throwing these sunglasses away.*

Kevran couldn't agree more. *It is tough to be thankful for an event like that, but thanks to them finding him, you had a pair of sunglasses. And that would further cement my theory about the Onigor affecting their eyesight.*

Anthony nodded and continued to pay attention to Ashley's story.

"After the attack, I didn't go outside for a few days, and when I did, everyone just walked around like nothing happened, except their eyes were all bloodred. There, at the market, was the only time I've been out since, and that was just because I was running out of food."

Anthony nodded in understanding. But now he was faced with a dilemma. He couldn't just leave her here as that would be cruel, but taking her along with him would be dangerous, to say the least.

She interrupted his thoughts with a question. "What's happening to everyone?"

Anthony sighed and gave a quick overview of the Zankrex and their world-domination plot.

Ashley's eyes widened in horror as she stepped back and leaned against the wall. "How is this possible? Everyone I know and love is now a Zankrex?"

Anthony nodded. "Some aren't full Zankrex, but everyone is under their power."

Ashley put her head in her hands and began to cry.

Anthony put a supportive hand on her shoulder. "But I'm going to change all that."

She stopped crying and looked up at him, tears still in her eyes.

Anthony nodded. "I'm going to find the Zankrex king, and I'm going to seal him away and the rest of the dark energy with it. When I do that, everyone will return to normal."

Ashley seemed doubtful, but Anthony's confident demeanor reassured her.

She wiped the tears from her eyes and stood up off the wall. "Is there any way I can help you?"

Anthony was about to say no when an idea hit him. He slowly smiled. "Depends. How well do you know this town?"

The two walked down the street, passing vendors and shoppers as they went. Ashley had started out very worried and walked rather stiff, but walking next to Anthony had calmed her down. He walked with such confidence that she couldn't help but feel safer. She knew he had just said he was a God Sword, but even then, she didn't see a sword on him.

As they walked into a clearing, she leaned over to Anthony. "Why are you so confident right now?"

Anthony looked back with a puzzled look on his face. "Why shouldn't I be confident? I am a God Sword, after all."

Ashley was still worried. "But you don't have a sword."

Anthony chuckled and explained the alternate dimension that his sword was stored in and how he could retrieve it at a moment's notice. Ashley was surprised to hear that and wasn't all that convinced it was real.

"Either way," she continued, "you can't have enough power to stand up to an entire village."

"I do."

Ashley just stared at him. His absolute confidence had left her speechless. The two walked in silence again after that as Anthony walked to a secluded corner of the village. After they were safe, he took his sunglasses off and looked across the way. The square wooden shrine stood across from them.

Anthony nodded and turned to Ashley. "All right, we need to figure out a game plan to get those guards to leave their posts. But first, I should introduce you to the other member of our team."

He gestured behind her, and she turned around to see a green humanoid dragon sitting cross-legged on a barrel.

He raised his claw up in greeting. "Yo."

Ashley held in a scream and looked back at Anthony.

He nodded in reassurance, and she turned back around. "N-nice to meet you. I'm Ashley."

Kevran got off the barrel. He gave a small bow. "My name is Kevran. It is nice to meet you."

Ashley couldn't decide if she was terrified or astounded. This dragon looked vicious and mean, but he acted like a gentleman.

Anthony walked in between them and interrupted her train of thought. "I'm glad the greetings are out of the way. Now let's break into that shrine."

Anthony crouched down behind a barrel and observed the two guards in front of the gate and two guards around back. Anthony had counted his lucky stars that word of his existence hadn't reached the village yet. If it had, security might have been ten times more intense around the shrine. But with only four guards to take care of planning, a break-in was easy.

Anthony had outlined the plan. They all knew what they needed to do. Kevran hated it but had decided to let Anthony take the lead. The plan wasn't complicated, but it did rely on Ashley. Anthony could only hope that she wouldn't freeze up.

At that moment, Ashley came running up to the guards. She looked panicked and out of breath, which helped set the scene. The Zankrex tensed up as she came to a halt in front of the stairs.

She looked up at the guards. "There's a Divine Blade in the village!"

The Zankrex looked panicked for a second before calming down and calling the back guards over. The two back guards approached Ashley. "Show us where he is."

Ashley froze for a second.

A spike of panic rose in Anthony as he thought she wouldn't be able to continue with the Zankrex so close to her. He tensed up, ready to charge out and improvise. But before he could, Ashley exhaled and turned around.

"Follow me," she said as she jogged off toward where Kevran was waiting. As Anthony figured, three of them ran off with Ashley while one stayed behind. Anthony got ready for his window of opportunity. He had already retrieved his sword from Kevran's space, which had proved to be a scary venture. It was all Kevran could do to keep his power under wraps yet still activate the portal. He managed it, though, and the Zankrex were none the wiser.

Then he felt it.

Kevran's power spiked for a second as he took out the three guards. Anthony popped out and speed-stepped to the one remaining guard. The guard was powerful, but Anthony was far stronger. Using the element of surprise, he whacked the guard on the back of the head with the back side of his sword. The Zankrex fell to the ground unconscious.

He sheathed his blade and opened the large doors. He turned to see Kevran and Ashley running up the stairs. They had to hurry. If any other Zankrex were in the town, they would have felt his and Kevran's power spike.

Kevran and Ashley ran inside, and Anthony closed the door as he walked in. As the doors closed, he drew out his power, and a swarm of leaves spun around him. He patched the door lining with them and put as much power in each leaf as he could.

With the door reinforced with his leaves, he let out his pent-up breath and turned toward the back of the shrine.

Chapter 10

THE SHRINE

*A*nthony gazed at the interior of the shrine. It was very simple and rustic, yet it was awe-inspiring. Not only was the design epic, but there was an amazing power emanated from deep within the shrine.

Anthony stepped up to Kevran and saw that he held the same expression. Ashley was lost at what the other two were seeing.

She turned to Anthony. "Are you sure this is the right place?"

Anthony could only nod as he approached the single door that would lead him deeper in. As he approached, ancient runes began to glow over the doorframe. Anthony continued to stare on in awe but soon became confused.

Kevran stepped up. "These runes are dead runes from a civilization long ago. Allow me to read them for you. It says, 'Wielder of earth and land, should ye be in need, present your blade, and clarity ye shall receive.'"

A smile spread across Anthony's face. "Man, the ancients sure spoke in a weird way. But that was kind of cool. Either way, I guess I am kind of in need."

Anthony stepped forward and presented his sword. For several seconds, nothing happened.

Ashley looked around in anticipation before becoming annoyed. "Hey, is anything going to happ—"

Kevran stuck his claw out, and Ashley fell silent. As she did, the door began to glow a bright green and creaked open.

Anthony sheathed his blade and started to take a step forward when a loud bang interrupted the moment. A commotion could be heard on the other side of the shrine, but Anthony didn't need to see what was on the other side to know who it was. The power emanating from beyond the door made it quite apparent that some high-level Zankrex were in hiding around the village and had made it to the shrine. Anthony began to turn back around when Kevran stopped him.

"We can manage things here," he said. "Trust the leaves you put in place. They will not give way that easily. And if they do force their way in, I am more than capable of protecting Ashley and defending myself. You go ahead. Whatever awaits inside is going to be vital to our journey."

Anthony seemed hesitant but nodded anyway. He looked over at Ashley.

She forced a smile and nodded as well. "I don't really understand what's going on here, but it seems like whatever is beyond that door is important. I'll trust Mr. Dragon here, so don't worry about me."

Anthony resigned himself to Kevran's plan and sheathed his sword back up.

He turned around and began to walk in, waving as he went. "I'll try not to be too long. Don't die while I'm away." And with that, the door closed behind him.

Anthony stared at the cramped little room. The door had been sealed behind him, and with it, every sound that was outside was also cut off. He could no longer hear the banging of the door or even feel the Zankrex anymore. He was now alone.

He gazed at the inner room. Like the outside, it was very simple and rustic, yet even more awe-inspiring than the outside. He could feel a great power emanating from somewhere inside the room.

He looked at the objects that were strewn about the floor. Most of them looked like ancient training equipment while others looked like trophies of war. He began to rummage through the old swords that were lying in a pile in the corner when a voice surprised him.

"Hey, now, don't touch my memorabilia."

Anthony turned around, startled to see a man standing in the center of the room. He was tall, a good half foot taller than Anthony, and his long black hair was tied off in a ponytail. He was dressed in robes that were from the ancient times, and an empty sheath was strapped to his side. Anthony could feel great power coming off this man, but it wasn't murderous. When he saw the empty sheath, an idea began to turn in his mind. The man smiled, as if he knew what Anthony was beginning to piece together.

He bowed his head. "It is a pleasure to meet you, Anthony."

Anthony was taken aback. "How do you know my name?"

The man laughed and scratched the back of his head in embarrassment. "Ah, I'm sorry. You see, I've known your name ever since the sword was activated. Though I'm pretty sure Kevran told you my name while you guys were on your way here."

Anthony's eyes widened as the realization hit him. "You have to be kidding me. But you can't be him."

The man laughed again and walked over to Anthony with his hand outstretched. "It's nice to meet you. My name is Oshuma, the God Sword before you."

Anthony stood in disbelief. He was trying to think of how to take this whole thing when he realized that Oshuma's hand was still outstretched. Anthony was slow to grab his hand.

Oshuma smiled wide and shook his hand with enthusiasm. "Well, Anthony, it is a real pleasure to meet you. There are so many things I want to talk to you about, but we don't have time for that at all. My time here is limited, of course, so we need to get down to business."

Anthony came to. "What do you mean your time here is limited?"

Oshuma sat cross-legged in the center of the room. "I'll make it brief since we need to get you out soon, so you can protect your friends."

Anthony became panicked. "My friends? What's happening to Kevran and Ashley outside?"

Oshuma waved his hand. "They're fine for now. That leaf seal you put on the door was quite something, considering how long you've been a God Sword and all. The proficiency of your skills is very impressive."

Anthony couldn't help but feel smug as the praise made its way to his head, but he snapped back to reality. "Anyway, you said that time was of the essence?"

Oshuma snapped his fingers. "Ah yes, I did say that. We only have a set amount of time because I died a long time ago."

Anthony was taken aback. "Died a long time ago? But you're right here talking to me."

Oshuma smiled. "Amazing, isn't it? I figured out this technique that allowed me to put a part of my consciousness in a certain area for a long period of time. The catch being that I only have a certain amount of time to do something after I get called out. That and I can't leave this shrine."

Anthony nodded, still a little skeptical about it. But he saw no reason to doubt it, considering he was claiming to be someone who should be dead.

I have to remember that anything is possible with the God Swords.

Oshuma nodded as he was agreeing with Anthony's thoughts. "But let's not dillydally with all these explanations. We need to fix the problem that you came to me for."

Anthony looked at Oshuma in confusion. "But I don't have any problems that need to be fixed."

Oshuma laughed. "Oh, Anthony, everyone has problems. Heck, even I have a lot of problems, a fact that my wife wouldn't let me forget."

Anthony chuckled a little. "I'm not saying I'm perfect, but I don't think I have any problems with the current Zankrex situation."

Oshuma sighed and folded his arms. "I happen to know for a fact that there is a glaring problem you have that is very much related to the Zankrex."

Anthony couldn't help but smile. "Now a dead man is saying he knows more about me than I do?"

Oshuma shook his head. "Ah, I remember when I used to quip like that. It must be a God Sword thing because all the others did it as well."

Anthony sat down and stared at Oshuma. "Now I just have to figure out what I want to ask you."

Oshuma raised a finger and waggled it at Anthony. "No, you need to figure out what's wrong with you first. When you admit your fault, then I will help you. Until then, I'm just going to sit here and stare at you."

Oshuma was true to his word as he proceeded to drill Anthony with a hardcore stare. Anthony squirmed a bit under the harsh gaze. He ignored it by racking his brain about his problems.

He thought about it for a little bit before having an epiphany. "It's my lack of focus, isn't it?"

Oshuma just shook his head and continued to stare. Anthony was upset that, that wasn't it. He was hoping maybe Oshuma would give him a shortcut to better focus.

He began to think again before snapping his fingers with another idea. "Is it the way I don't rely on others?"

Oshuma gave him a what-the-heck face. "That doesn't even apply to you. You haven't had anyone to rely on yet."

Anthony shrugged. "I'm just throwing out ideas. And there was that one time that I told Kevran not to help me."

Oshuma rolled his eyes. "No, you had a good reason as to why you didn't ask for help, and you know it."

Anthony threw his hands up in exasperation. "Well then, I have no idea what my problem is."

Oshuma let out a tired sigh and rubbed his eyes. "Geez, by the time you figure it out, I'll be long gone. All right, since I have limited time here, I'm just going to tell you. Your problem is the fact that you refuse to kill Zankrex."

Anthony was taken aback by this. "How is not wanting to kill someone a problem?" he demanded. "I'm sorry that I have a problem with killing other people, but I don't see that as something that you should waste your time trying to fix."

Oshuma slammed his hand down on the ground, and Anthony became quiet. "I'm not saying that killing people is a good thing to do, but you seem to have some misconceptions about the Zankrex as a whole."

Anthony looked on in confusion. "How am I confused about Zankrex? It's a simple concept, isn't it? They're just humans that are possessed by the Onigor."

Oshuma shook his head. "That description is neither wrong nor right. You keep using the word *human*, but the Zankrex are the furthest thing from that."

Anthony wasn't getting it, and Oshuma could tell. "It's going to be hard to explain what I mean with words. Here, I'm just going to show what I saw all those years ago."

Oshuma leaned forward and touched two fingers to Anthony's forehead. As they touched, Anthony felt himself slip away into darkness.

The scene changed. Anthony found himself in a field. In the distance was the ocean. The crashing of the waves played their soothing melody in the background.

Where am I? Anthony wondered. He couldn't move his body, or whatever body he was in.

Suddenly Oshuma's voice echoed in his head. *You are seeing things from my eyes. This is a memory from long ago. Just watch it all the way through, and it should clear up what I was trying to say earlier.*

Anthony acknowledged Oshuma and watched the scene unfold in front of him. Oshuma was alone in a large field. He was hiding behind a large bush. He suppressed his power as low as it could go as he watched the scene unfold in front of him. A normal man stood a ways off, also alone. Soon a dark-cloaked figure came ashore on a small craft. He lurched toward the man. Oshuma had to strain his ears to make out what it was that they were saying.

"Do you wish to join us?" the creature asked.

The man could only nod. The creature beckoned for the man to follow. The two headed to the small craft the cloaked figure had arrived in. The creature hopped in, and the man hesitated for a bit.

After a second or two, the man also got in the boat, and it pulled off to the open ocean.

Oshuma walked out from behind the bush as the boat became a dot on the horizon. He sat down and started to think things over. Another man ran up beside him. He was dark-skinned and bald, standing a good half foot above Oshuma.

Oshuma smirked. "It's about time you got here, Kintarfus."

Kintarfus stood and caught his breath for a while. "I'm sorry I was late, but I can't navigate fields like you can. Nor can I run as fast as you can."

Oshuma laughed and stood back up. "I know, I know, but I just couldn't help but poke a little fun."

Kintarfus pointed at the dot on the horizon. "Was that the meeting you were talking about?"

Oshuma became serious as he looked back at the boat. "I've never seen one in person, so I can't say for sure. That and master told me that he had annihilated all of them in the purge. But if my memory of the world map is correct, then they are heading straight for it."

Kintarfus looked a little uneasy as he gripped the cutlass at his side. "They are heading straight for Xanto, aren't they?"

Oshuma nodded and folded his arms into his sleeves. "There's no way we can say for sure, but if they are, then we may be looking at the third coming of the Zankrex."

The two men stood staring out at the open ocean. Oshuma admired the vastness for a time. He had always enjoyed staring at the ocean as it always managed to calm him down.

Kintarfus also stood and stared out. He took a few steps and stood ankle deep in the water. He closed his eyes and concentrated. He seemed to be straining, as if something was eluding him before opening his eyes and releasing his pent-up breath.

"The boat's presence is faint, and I can feel even less of the island. It's like someone or something is trying to hide the island from us."

Oshuma stroked his chin. "The generation before did hide the island away from normal people. But we God Swords should still be able to find it."

Kintarfus nodded. "I agree, but the power hiding the island is not the power that the God Swords use. No, the power concealing the island now is a far darker power."

He shuddered as he remembered the feel of it. Oshuma remained stoic as he thought things through. He turned to one side and saw a large dead tree that had washed ashore long ago. An idea began to form in his mind as he moved to the log. He placed his hands on it and began to strain his power. The tree remained still for a while but soon shuddered and began to morph. The tree took the shape of a medium-size canoe.

After it had stopped changing, Oshuma took his hands off the tree and let out labored breaths, as if he had just done some heavy lifting.

Kintarfus went up and patted him on the back. "I see you have yet to master the wood-shaping art."

Oshuma chuckled between gasps of air. "It would have been a piece of cake if the tree had still been alive. Dead wood is so much harder to shape than living wood."

Kintarfus nodded and looked at the boat. "What do you expect to do with that then? Are you planning on paddling to Xanto all by yourself and solving this problem now?"

Oshuma lowered his head and chuckled with a somewhat evil tint to it. Kintarfus took a half step back as worry spread across his face. Oshuma looked up at Kintarfus with a smile and an odd twinkle in his eye.

Sudden realization hit Kintarfus. "Oh no, I'm not going to join on this stupid venture. You can forget it."

Oshuma said nothing and continued to stare at Kintarfus.

He began to grow uneasy as the stare just kept boring into him. "It doesn't matter how long you stare at me. I'm not going to charge headlong into enemy territory without the others."

The smile continued.

"Stop looking at me! I'm not going, and that's final!"

The ocean was calm, with small swells coming every once in a while. Oshuma sat cross-legged on the prow of the boat as it shot off toward the mystery island Xanto.

"I must say this is going so much faster than rowing the boat." He turned back. "Am I right?"

Kintarfus was sitting in the back of the boat with his face in his hands in exasperation. "I despise you, you know that, right?"

Oshuma turned back and laughed. "Oh, come on, how often do you get a chance to fight Zankrex? I just couldn't wait for the others to get there."

Kintarfus took his head out of his hands and sighed. He was using his power over water to push the boat along. He could also tell that they were heading in the right direction as the God Sword of water gave him perfect directional abilities on the open ocean.

"You do remember how the masters would always tell us not to rush headlong into any battle, and they always warned us to be extra cautious around anything that might be Zankrex?"

Oshuma brushed the worry aside. "They only meant that if it had anything to do with the Zankrex king, and they sealed him away for good anyway. These are probably just some regular old Zankrex, and if we can't take those out, then we aren't worthy of being God Swords."

Kintarfus sighed again, realizing that arguing with him now would be pointless. The two sat in silence as the boat sped along the water.

After a while, Kintarfus perked up. "The boat ahead of us just left the water. That means that we will be hitting land soon."

Oshuma just nodded as the two prepared for whatever would be on the island.

The two God Swords snuck up on the island. Xanto was everything that they thought it would be. A constant swirl of clouds was over the island, giving it a bleak and dark atmosphere.

The two had suppressed their power to get by unnoticed. It took them a while, but soon they found the creature and the man on a stone dais farther in the island. The two hid and listened in on the conversation.

"Are you ready to give yourself to the darkness?" the creature hissed.

The man seemed a tad panicked, but there was an evil gleam in his eye. He was excited to do this. The man nodded. The creature cackled and summoned a dark ball of energy.

Oshuma shuddered, as the energy in the creature's hand was vile and horrible. Kintarfus looked over and nodded in understanding. It was the same power he had felt when he tried to find the island.

The creature held the ball and then pushed it into the man. There was a pause before an energy explosion occurred around the man. He doubled over and cried out in pain as the power in him began to take over. The ground began to shake as the dark aura around the man only got bigger. That's when Oshuma felt it. He could feel the man's humanity, his very soul, leave his body and was replaced by the dark energy. After a while, the rumbling and scream-ing stopped, and the man stood up straight. His eyes were bloodred, and the evil power was seeping out of his body.

The man began to laugh, and he flexed his muscles and threw punches into the air. "This power is amazing. I feel like I could destroy the entire world with this power."

The creature threw off his cloak. Under was another normal man, except for the red eyes and the evil power that was emanating from him.

The original Zankrex laughed. "And it only gets better. Right now, it's just you and me, but soon we will grow stronger and seduce others to join us. After we get more converts, we can resurrect our king."

The new Zankrex didn't seem to understand, but he nodded anyway. The two started to walk off. Kintarfus grabbed his weapon and started to get up.

Oshuma stopped him and looked at his sword. "What are you planning to do?"

Kintarfus stared at him. "I'm going to kill those two before they can get any more followers."

Oshuma shook his head. "We can't kill them! That man was a human just a second ago."

Kintarfus smacked Oshuma across the face. Oshuma froze. He wasn't expecting that, and he looked at Kintarfus in confusion.

Kintarfus grabbed Oshuma's shirt and brought him up close. "Those two aren't human anymore. You felt it too, didn't you? When that man accepted the dark power, he lost his very soul. That man was willing to give his humanity to become one of those monstrosities."

Oshuma's head had been cleared by the slap he had just received. He knew what Kintarfus was saying was correct. He sighed as Kintarfus let him back down.

Oshuma looked at Kintarfus and unsheathed his sword. "You're right. Thanks for the wake-up slap."

Kintarfus smirked. "The slap was for everything up to this point, but I'm glad it cleared your head."

Oshuma couldn't help but smile. "With friends like these."

With that, the two God Swords charged out from their hiding place.

The battle had lasted all of five seconds. Neither of the Zankrex had a weapon, and the two God Swords were far more powerful than they were.

Oshuma stood over the original Zankrex and pointed his sword at him. The Zankrex was bleeding out and could barely breathe.

"Tell me now, are there more of your kind? Why are you doing this when my master had already sealed away your king?"

The Zankrex let a weak chuckle out as he stared Oshuma straight in the eyes. "You can't stop us." He wheezed. "We will come back no matter how many times you kill us. As long as there is evil in the hearts of humans, we will always be able to rise up. One day we will have enough strength to free our king and take our revenge on you stupid humans."

The Zankrex coughed up a whole lot of blood and then stopped breathing. Oshuma was haunted by the Zankrex's words as he looked to Kintarfus.

He could only shrug. "Do not concern yourself with his riddles. We've done all we can do at the moment. Let's inform the others of what happened and then go from there."

Oshuma nodded and looked at the two corpses before heading back off to the boat.

The scene changed as Anthony was now staring at Oshuma in the shrine. He let out a heavy breath and slumped back. Oshuma gave a sympathetic half smile as he watched Anthony try to process what he had just seen.

"You understand now why you calling them human is wrong."

Anthony nodded as he regained his composure. "That was something else. I didn't realize that you could lose your soul before you died."

Oshuma nodded. "It was a sobering experience, to say the least. But that's not the point. Have you taken away what you needed from that?"

Anthony nodded, not happy about it, though. "I can't say it sits right with me, but I understand that they aren't humans anymore."

Oshuma nodded. "And I won't say that this knowledge will make killing them any easier. The first few times won't feel right at all. But you don't have a choice. They won't hold back against you, and if you keep holding back against them, they will take advantage of that and use it to kill you."

Anthony continued to sit and stare at the ground.

A silence pervaded the two for a bit before Oshuma broke it. "My time is getting short, and your friends are about to be in need of your help. Is there anything else you wanted to ask me?"

Anthony thought about it for a while before thinking of something. "Yeah. Why did the Earth Katana become hidden?"

Oshuma smiled. "That's a good question. I was the one that sealed it away. As you grow with the Earth Katana, you will come to the same understanding I did, but I'll go ahead and tell you the whole story now. As I grew with the sword, I found that the power it contained was far above that of any other God Sword. At first, I thought that this would be a great thing to pass down to the younger generations. But the Creator opened my eyes to the reality of it. He made me realize that the awesome power that it contained would be abused if it was passed down from generation to generation. The Creator explained to me that the Earth Katana was different from the other God Swords. He told me that the Earth Katana would pick its own wielder depending on the state of affairs between the other God

Swords and the power of the Onigor. As I was at the final days of my life, I sealed the sword away with a promise that it would be found by the proper wielder in times of need. I also took a piece of my power and conscience and sealed it in this shrine. Does that answer your question?"

Anthony nodded and couldn't help but smile.

Oshuma looked at him in confusion. "What are you so happy about?"

Anthony shrugged. "Well, the sword chose me out of all of the people in the world. I know that's an incredible responsibility, but it's also the greatest compliment."

Oshuma smiled. "It is. I have the utmost confidence in you. I have only known you for a short while, but I can tell that you have a good soul. You will save the world. Of that, I'm sure."

Anthony nodded in appreciation.

Oshuma's figure began to disappear. "It looks like my time here is up. And it's a good thing too. Your friends are in a bit of a bind right now."

Anthony shot up and drew his sword. "Thank you for everything, Oshuma. I'll be going now."

He spun around and shot out the door. Oshuma smiled as he faded away.

He looked up to the heavens. "You know how to choose them, don't you?"

Ashley and Kevran watched as the door closed behind Anthony. Silence followed, breaking only for the Zankrex outside still trying to find a way inside.

Ashley leaned up against a wall and slid down it. She brought her knees up to her face and wrapped her arms around them. This was the first time since the market that she had any time to rest and think about everything that had happened today. She was still trying to digest the story that Anthony had told her. She had no reason to not believe it, but that didn't make it any easier to accept. Kevran stood in the center of the room, arms crossed, looking off in space.

He looked over at Ashley. "Are you going to be okay?"

Ashley looked up, startled, as she had gotten used to the quiet.

She lowered her head back into her knees. "Yeah, I'll be okay, I guess. I'm just having a little trouble believing everything that's been happening."

Kevran nodded in sympathy. "Anthony had a similar reaction. Even though he knew exactly what was going on, he still did not want to believe it. Though the Zankrex outside do not care if you believe in them or not, they are still going to come in here and try to kill us."

Ashley sighed as she knew that Kevran was right. Then the quiet came back to the room. Kevran shuffled in discomfort. Ashley looked up at him in confusion when he turned back to her. "Please do not ever call me Mr. Dragon again."

The request came out of nowhere. Ashley had to take a minute to be sure she had heard it right. She pointed at him. "Is that what you were acting all uncomfortable about?"

Kevran nodded. Ashley froze for a little bit, trying to figure out how to react. She smiled and then started to laugh. She tried to hide it at first but failed.

Kevran could only look away. "It is not that funny, you know."

Ashley waved her hand. "I know, I know, but I just loved how much it bothered you."

Kevran tried to hide his scowl. "Of course, it bothered me. My name was given to me by the Creator. I appreciate when people use it."

Ashley stopped laughing and took a deep breath. She unfolded her legs and laid them out in front of her. She bowed her head. "My apologies, Kevran. I will be sure to call you that from now on."

Kevran nodded in appreciation. The room got quiet again, but the mood had changed.

Ashley leaned back. "I guess I knew that this Zankrex invasion was coming."

Kevran looked over in confusion, in part at the statement but more so at the random change in topic. "How could you know? Not even the God Swords knew that this was going to happen."

Ashley waved her hands in defense. "No, I didn't know for sure that it was going to happen. It's just looking back on it now, it makes sense. The woman that guards this shrine was always so in tune with the dark energy. She had been acting very strange for the last few days. I can only hope she escaped the city before they attacked."

Kevran remained stoic. "Well, with only that, no one would say you should have known this would happen. I hope you are not beating yourself up about it."

Ashley shook her head. "I know there was nothing I could do, even if I knew for sure it was going to happen. But there was another thing that, looking back on it now, should have kind of tipped me off."

Kevran looked on. "What was that?"

Ashley scratched at the floor. "My boyfriend had always liked things that were related to the source of the God Swords' power. He also liked to look into the dark energy that the Divine Blades would fight. A couple of weeks ago, he started to act strange. He started poring over videos and records of fights between the Divine Blades and demon beasts. Our relationship was always a little rocky, but after that, we were always fighting. One day, I told him that he had changed. He started to laugh in this creepy way and then looked me straight in the eyes. He told me that this whole world was going to change very soon, and then he left. I haven't seen him since."

Kevran scratched his chin as he took in Ashley's story. "Yes, I suppose in hindsight that would be a huge tip-off. But even still, I would have been amazed if you could have taken those things and come to the conclusion that the Zankrex were going to invade."

Ashley smiled at Kevran. She was about to say something when a large boom shook the entire building. Ashley looked at the door in panic. Kevran walked over and put a comforting claw on her shoulder as the ramming continued.

He looked over at the door that Anthony had walked into. "That door has shut Anthony off from the outside world. I cannot feel anything coming from that room."

Ashley looked up in fear. "He may not come out in time?"

Kevran sighed and looked at Ashley. He couldn't help but feel sorry for her as he tried to comfort her.

"It is going to be okay. I am stronger than most Zankrex. I can hold them off and protect you until Anthony comes out."

Ashley gave a half smile, but she couldn't help but feel that even Kevran was having trouble believing that. She could only sit there and pray that Anthony got out soon. The pounding continued for some time, but the leaves that Anthony had put up were holding very well.

The pounding stopped. Kevran and Ashley held their breath for a while before Kevran started to walk over to the door. As he reached it, he tried to listen to see if he could hear any activity outside.

The door exploded in splinters of wood, sending Kevran flying back. Ashley screamed as she was showered in debris. Four Zankrex sprinted in and surrounded Kevran. He stood up and took a fighting stance. His anger turned into fearful confusion as he felt the enormous power emanating from the four of them.

"How are you that strong? You should not have been able to hide that kind of power from me."

A fifth Zankrex walked in, laughing. "Tell me, dragon, do you believe you are the only one that is capable of suppressing his power?"

Kevran's face contorted in a scowl. The fifth Zankrex was a little stronger than the other four Zankrex that were surrounding him. If it was just him in the room, he wouldn't be worried. But he knew there was no way he could protect Ashley and fight the five of them at the same time.

Please hurry, Anthony.

The fifth Zankrex walked up to Ashley and smiled wide at her. Ashley's face was full of emotions, everything from fear to joy.

Kevran looked at her then at the Zankrex. "Do you know that Zankrex, Ashley?"

She could only nod as the Zankrex laughed. "I would hope she would know me. After all, I am Devon, her boyfriend."

Ashley couldn't move. It had been so long since she had seen Devon that she had thought she would never see him again. She wanted to run into his arms and hug him, but his red eyes confirmed her darkest suspicions.

"Do not go to him," Kevran yelled out, as if he knew what she was thinking. "He is a Zankrex."

Ashley wanted him to be wrong. She wished she could just close her eyes and open them up to see him with normal eyes, but she knew nothing would change.

Devon seemed to enjoy the turmoil that Ashley was going through as his smile got wider. "Nice to see nothing has changed, Ashley. You still can't function without me."

Ashley's eyes got wide as he struck home.

He laughed and stepped closer to her. "You could never do anything without me. Even now, you know that without me, you are just lost and alone."

Kevran was frantic as he realized what Devon was trying to do. "That is not true, Ashley. You cannot listen to him."

Devon laughed as he turned to Kevran. "Oh, and she's supposed to believe a dragon? Stay out of this. You don't know her at all." He turned back to Ashley with his evil grin. "Isn't that right, Ashley? If you really wanted to leave me, you would have left the town when the attack happened. But you stayed because you knew that, without me, you are nothing. Even your very survival is connected to me. You stayed hidden because you had to wait for me. You were incapable of making any decision on your own."

Ashley bowed her head as he laughed even more. "Let's change that now. Come with me, Ashley. If you come on your own now, then I will convince the higher-ups not to kill you for this little act of insubordination. Of course, you will have to work under me for the rest of your life, but that's nothing new."

He raised his hand. "Now come with me before you make another mistake on your own."

Ashley started to grab his hand.

"Wow."

The word destroyed the tension in the room.

"That's a whole lot of crap you've been talking there."

Ashley looked up startled as Devon got a scowl on his face. She turned her head to see Anthony standing in front of the door.

The door behind Anthony began to close. He stood there staring Devon down. He hadn't been out long, but it had been long enough for him to hear most of what Devon had been saying to Ashley.

The door closed all the way, and Anthony took a few steps forward. "Ashley survived by herself in a town full of Zankrex without getting caught for a week. The only reason she would have been discovered was because I bumped into her at the market. She was doing absolutely fine by herself."

Devon laughed, trying to play it off, but his worry was showing. "You only say that to try and comfort her. I know who she really is, and that's someone who needs me there to function."

Anthony drew his sword and pointed it at Devon. "I don't have time to prove you wrong. Step away from her and leave."

Devon laughed, shaking off his worry. "Or you'll do what? I've heard from the platoon at Murffana. You won't kill any of us. We've already figured out how to fight you."

Anthony continued to stare at Devon showing no emotion at all. "I'll give you one more chance. I don't want to kill you in front of Ashley."

Ashley looked at Anthony in surprise. She knew he had just said horrible things to her, but she couldn't stand him being killed. She stood up and blocked off Anthony's path to Devon.

Anthony scowled, and Devon laughed. "You see, God Sword? I already have her wrapped around my finger. I can do whatever I want, and she will continue to come back to me."

Ashley's face was full of pain, but there was also determination. Anthony saw it in her eyes. She was dependent on him.

Anthony's face grew dark. He continued to point his sword. "Will you leave?"

Devon laughed even harder. "Leave? Why should I leave when I have the upper hand here? I'll use her to kill you, then I'll take her away and make her part of the king's army. Though I doubt there will be much need for a useless girl like he—"

Devon never got to finish the sentence. In the blink of an eye, Anthony disappeared from in front of Ashley. She looked around in confusion before turning around. Her eyes widened in horror as she looked at the scene in front of her. Anthony stood in front of Devon with his sword clean through his chest. Devon's face was contorted in pain, and life drained from his face. Blood splattered to the ground as Devon tried to croak out a word, but it caught in his throat. A final breath escaped his lips as he hunched over and fell to the ground. Ashley began to tear up and fell to her knees and screamed.

Anthony quickly turned. "Kevran, get her out of here!"

Kevran was standing in total disbelief with the other four Zankrex when he snapped back. He shot past the Zankrex and grabbed Ashley. "Meet me outside town. I will let you know where when we get there."

Anthony nodded as Kevran flew off with Ashley.

Chapter 11

ESCAPE

*A*nthony watched the two fly out the door and out of sight. With them gone, he knew he wouldn't have to hold back.

He looked at the four Zankrex with the same dark glare he had given Devon. "Will you run away?"

The Zankrex were shaking in fear but still charged at him.

He sighed. "Wrong answer."

The first Zankrex had no time to react before Anthony cleaved him in two. That slowed the other three down for just a moment, but it was all the time Anthony needed. He took a step forward and stabbed the second through the chest. The third slashed down at Anthony while his sword was still in the second one. The sword made it close, but there was never a chance of it making its target. A single leaf stopped the blade's progress inches away from Anthony's head. He whipped his sword out of the second Zankrex and cut the third one across the chest. The second and third Zankrex both fell to the ground.

The fourth one had stopped. He was frozen in his steps. Anthony turned to him, blood still dripping from his sword.

"Will you leave?" he asked one final time.

That snapped the fourth Zankrex out of his fear. He charged with his sword overhead. Anthony didn't wait for him to even get close. A leaf shot through the air and straight through his head. The Zankrex fell as the momentum carried his body to a sliding halt.

Then there was quiet.

Anthony let out a weary breath and looked down in disgust at the blood on his sword. He stooped over and wiped it off on the shirts of his enemies. He ran outside to see if there were any more.

The short answer was yes.

The courtyard was filled with Zankrex, all of them taking battle stances. He took up his sword and charged the crowd. He was outnumbered thirty to one, but it made little difference. Anthony was a whirlwind of death. He moved through the mosh pit ducking and parrying every blow that came close to him. After every block came a counterattack, and each strike found its mark. No one in the crowd was fast enough to block any of his attacks. One by one, the Zankrex fell until there were none left standing.

Anthony stood in the center of a massacre. Bodies lay strewn about the courtyard, and the blood was beginning to get deep.

He couldn't look down at the bodies. With the knowledge he had on the Zankrex, he was able to kill them, but that didn't make the act any easier. He knew he had to do it, but he still wasn't used to the feeling of taking a life. He wasn't used to the scene of carnage. The blood. The fear in his opponents' eyes the moment before his sword ended their existence. He ran off, knowing that if he stayed, he would vomit. He could feel Onigor coming toward him from the east. Kevran had flown off west, so Anthony was spared another battle. He wiped his sword off then sheathed it and ran.

Kevran flew over the town, going as fast as he could without dropping Ashley. She continued to cry, her sobs having been reduced to sniveling. He dared not say anything for fear of how she would handle it.

I am no good with humans and their emotions, he admitted to himself.

He continued to fly, ignoring the frantic screams of the denizens below. He knew that the Zankrex would be far more interested in Anthony than they would be in him. It only took him a couple of seconds to get out of town, but finding a suitable place to land and hide was another matter.

After some searching, he found a dense group of bushes under a large tree. He flew straight down and landed by the bushes. He put the teary-eyed Ashley down next to the tree and then went about clearing out the center of the bushes. As he went about his task, he, every once in a while, would look over at Ashley to see if she was doing any better. But every time he looked over, she was still in the same position. He began to worry.

What if she believed everything that Devon had said to her? What if she blames Anthony and runs off to betray us? Either way, if she does not get over this soon, it could be very detrimental to our trip. Of course, the trip stands at a halt without a destination.

Kevran thought about their next destination for a while before he finished his task. The bushes were a lot larger and denser than they had seemed. But that made for a perfect hiding spot now that the center was clear. He shuffled out and walked over to where Ashley was. She was at least sitting up on her own now, though tears still filled her eyes.

"Are you going to be okay?"

She shook her head no and continued to stare at the ground.

Kevran sighed. "Can you at least get up and get to the center of the bushes over there?"

She sniffed and wiped her nose and nodded. She struggled a bit but was able to get up. Kevran put a supportive claw on her shoulder and started to lead her toward the bushes. At that moment, Anthony came jogging through the trees.

Anthony stopped in his tracks as he saw Ashley for the first time since the shrine. An awkward silence hung over the forest as he waited to see what would happen.

Ashley stood there staring at Anthony. After a pause, she walked over and stood right in front of him. She slapped him as hard as she could. Anthony saw it coming but stood there and took it. When he turned his head back, he was greeted by a tearful and angry face. Ashley was distraught as her whole body shook with rage and despair. She gritted her teeth and slapped him again. Anthony stood there and took it with a solemn look on his face.

"Why did you kill him?" she yelled at him. "You were always telling me how strong you were. How nothing in the town could stand up to you. Yet still you killed him. You could have just knocked them out, and we could have escaped without anyone following us. But you killed him. Why?"

Anthony wanted to answer her. He wanted to explain everything to her. To try his hardest to dispel her anger. But he was wracked with his own personal guilt and couldn't bring himself to defend his actions.

He bowed his head, and Ashley stormed off. "I'm sleeping here, but in the morning, I'm leaving. I don't want to be with a murderer like you."

She slipped into the bushes. Anthony could hear her sobbing even from deep within the cluster of bushes. He plopped on his rear and buried his face in his hands. Kevran watched Anthony for a second, trying to figure out what to say. After consideration, he walked up and lowered himself down next to him.

The two sat in silence for a while before Kevran broke it. "Were you followed here?"

Anthony shook his head. "I sprinted off to the south and then cut my power and ran here. The Zankrex will be scouring that area for a while before they think about coming over here."

Kevran nodded and smiled. "That was an intelligent move."

Anthony looked up from his hands with a small half smile. "Yeah, I can do those things every once in a while."

Silence pervaded the two once again.

Kevran got serious again and turned to Anthony. "If you are willing to talk about it, I do desire to know what happened in that inner room."

Anthony nodded and recounted the experience he had. He told Kevran everything from Oshuma's apparition to the vision that he was given. After he wrapped it up, Kevran sat in silence and soaked it all in.

He turned it over in his mind for a bit before continuing, "I remember that day. Oshuma told me to rally the other God Swords for fear of a Zankrex. By the time I came back with the other three, he had already returned from the island. He never told me exactly what happened. All he told me was that there were Zankrex and that he and Kintarfus had already taken care of it. But it was obvious that something more had happened to him. To hear the full story is news to me. Though it makes perfect sense."

Anthony nodded and continued to look at the ground.

Kevran sighed. "That also explains why you killed all those Zankrex. I must say it took me by surprise. Why would you change that ideology of yours in such an aggressive manner?"

Anthony sighed and looked up at the sky. It was still bright out, though the sun was fading fast. "When I saw that man give his very soul up just to get power, it made my blood boil. I don't let much get under my skin, but people who take shortcuts in life to gain something have always ticked me off. Someone willing to take a shortcut using the dark power and giving up their very being is something that I just can't tolerate. I was riding that anger high when I walked out of the inner room. When I saw all the Zankrex, all I could think about was how, at some point in time, all of them gave up their very being just to receive power they hadn't earned. Then couple that with the horrible things that one Zankrex was saying to Ashley. At that point, I was far past my limit. I ignored Ashley's pleas, and I killed that Zankrex. Now I'm starting to wonder if it was the right thing to do."

Kevran put a reassuring claw on Anthony's shoulder. "You did what you needed to do. You cannot let your personal feelings get in the way when it comes to Zankrex as they will exploit them and kill you using them. I know this may sound tough and heartless, but the sooner you get used to killing the Zankrex that have personal meaning, the better off you are going to be."

Anthony cringed at the thought of that, but deep down, he knew that Kevran was right. Silence fell over the camp once again. Ashley's sobbing had died down, the quiet indicating that she was asleep. Kevran went about other tasks while Anthony sat and turned everything over in his mind.

Soon the sun began to sink over the horizon, casting the world into twilight. Kevran looked over at the still somber Anthony. He hesitated for a moment before addressing him. "Sleep would serve you well. Ponder those things in the morning."

Anthony nodded and got up, still weighing the deaths of the Zankrex on his mind.

Ashley tossed and turned in the dirt. Her dreams were filled with visions of Devon. In every one of them she kept hearing the words that he was saying to her back in the shrine. She kept hearing the words useless and pointless. Then visions of his death would flash over and over. She was forced to watch it time and time again without being able to do anything about it, all while his voice echoed the words 'useless' in her mind.

Ashley's eyes bolted awake as she felt something covering her mouth. She tried to let out a scream, but it was far too muffled to even make it out of the bushes. She thought she would die then and there when Kevran's familiar face appeared in front of her. She calmed down, surprised at herself for not freaking out at seeing a dragon, and Kevran released his claw.

"Sorry about waking you like this, but you were tossing and mumbling to yourself. It looked like you were having a nightmare, so I decided to wake you up."

Ashley smiled in appreciation as she rubbed her eyes. She didn't feel rested at all. The nightmares had kept her from getting any meaningful rest, and the hard ground had helped nothing.

Kevran studied her for a second. "You were dreaming about Devon, were you not?"

Ashley nodded her head, tears beginning to form in her eyes again.

"Do you blame Anthony?"

The question took Ashley off guard. She knew that she had said some horrible things to Anthony, and she knew that killing Zankrex was his job; but no matter how much she tried to think about those things, she still couldn't find a way to justify him killing Devon. She nodded, a tad embarrassed by it.

Kevran sighed and scratched his chin. He seemed to come to a conclusion and motioned for her to follow him. Ashley looked at him in confusion, but he didn't give her any time to question it. He turned around and slipped through the bushes. Ashley scrambled to keep up with him, and soon they were out in the open air.

The night air was several degrees cooler than the day, and it had been a cold day. She was used to colder air since she had lived there her entire life, but that didn't stop her from shivering. She hadn't had any time to bring an extra layer for the night, so she wrapped her arms around herself and jogged up to Kevran.

Kevran continued to walk through the forest, unfazed by the cold. They walked for almost a minute before he stopped and motioned for Ashley to come see. She walked up and looked out at the clearing. Her eyes widened in shock. There in the clearing was Anthony, but surrounding him were broken branches and dented logs. He was bent over on his hands and knees, clenching the ground. It took her a while to see what it was that he was doing, but soon she made it out.

He was crying, even sobbing at times. She was so confused that she had to look up at Kevran to be sure that she was seeing the same thing. Kevran looked on with pain and compassion in his eyes. It was obvious that seeing Anthony like that was hurting him as well. He pulled her back and walked her to camp. There they walked back in the bushes. She looked at Kevran with concern and question.

Kevran sat down and stared at Ashley. "There is something you should know about Anthony. When this all began and the Zankrex attacked, he was just as scared as you were. But he pushed his fears aside because he knew that he was needed by his fellow man to save the world. He met up with a former classmate that had turned to the Zankrex for power. That classmate had injured one of his close friends. Anthony was filled with rage and hate, but even with all that, he still could not kill her. He also battled a small legion of Zankrex and their powerful leader. He was at a major disadvantage, yet he still did not kill a single one."

Ashley was still confused. "Why would you tell me all these things?"

Kevran pounded his fist on the ground and stared her straight in the eyes. "Because you need to know that Anthony had not killed a single person up to that fight in the shrine. He had never even harmed another being. Before you blame him and hate him for killing someone, even if that was the man that you loved, think about how it is affecting him. He could not sleep at all because the faces of those he killed were haunting him. I told him to go find a clearing and just let his emotions flow out. He was trying to bottle them up because he did not feel right mourning over Devon when you were far more upset about it."

Ashley looked away from Kevran's piercing gaze. She began to feel guilty about how she had treated him, though she still couldn't erase all her hate.

Kevran seemed to understand that and settled back. "I am not going to ask you to forgive him. But please hear him out. He has far too much to deal with, and the knowledge that you hate him is a rather big burden for him."

Ashley nodded and looked back up at Kevran. "I'll let him talk before I judge him."

Kevran half-smiled and bowed his head. "That is all I ask."

The two got silent as neither knew what to say. After a while, Kevran exited the bushes. Ashley let him go as she had some things to ponder.

Anthony sat outside the bushes as the first rays of sunlight shone through the treetops. The night had been the coldest of the season. It was made even worse by his inability to use his energy to keep himself warm. The Zankrex were no doubt searching, and he wasn't going chance anything.

He rubbed his eyes and cringed as his knuckles pulsed with pain. He had done what Kevran advised him to do and went to a clearing to let his emotions out. He hadn't been able to sleep at all as the scenes of every kill replayed in his mind over and over again, and the voice of a pained Ashley kept blaming him. It had been the worst night of his life by far. He had punched as many things as he could but without any of his Reichi. He was thankful he hadn't broken any knuckles, but at the same time, the constant pain reminded him that without Deypia or Reichi, he was just a normal human being.

He rubbed his eyes again, trying to clear away the drowsiness. He continued to sit until a rustling from the bushes snapped him back to reality. Ashley climbed out of the brush and walked over to where Anthony was sitting. An awkward silence ensued as neither of them knew what to say.

Anthony noticed her shivering and leapt up. "I'll get a fire started."

Ashley nodded in appreciation as Anthony jogged off. He soon returned with an armful of logs. He arranged them on a dirt patch and then shuffled inside the bushes. He managed to find some leaves that weren't soaked by the morning dew and put them at the bottom of the pit. He then pulled out two stones that he had found on his way to Wishitak. It took several strokes of the stones to create the right amount of sparks. After some care, he got a small flame going. He nursed it up into a nice-sized fire and then sat back. Ashley bent over closer to the fire and absorbed as much warmth as she possibly could.

The two sat in an awkward silence once again with the crackling of the fire being the only noise to keep the perfect quiet away. Kevran had long since returned to his room, and Anthony had a feeling he wasn't going to return until he and Ashley found some closure. Anthony sat and thought about what he could possibly say to her now.

Before he got anything out, Ashley broke the silence. "Kevran told me you didn't want to kill anything when you first started this journey."

Anthony looked up, startled, but nodded his head.

"Why did you kill yesterday—and not just Devon but all the others as well?"

Anthony sighed and recounted the tale of what he encountered in the inner room. When he got to the part about the man giving his soul to obtain the dark power, Ashley's eyes widened.

"That means …"

Anthony nodded. "It means that each and every one of those Zankrex, Devon included, had given up their souls to be who they were. They may have talked and acted like normal, but they were no longer themselves."

Ashley didn't cry, but she bowed her head at the realization.

Anthony continued, "I don't know if you will ever forgive me, and I understand that, but please see it from my perspective. All the Zankrex in that room were nothing but monsters to me. Then there was that one in the center—Devon, I guess, is who that was—who kept belittling you and using you. I saw how much pain that was putting you in. I just lost myself in the collected anger that was building up. You were right about me being able to defeat them without killing them, but if I hadn't killed them, then they would only come at us again and again."

Ashley remained silent. Anthony also got quiet as he waited to hear what she had to say. Several moments passed as they sat there and stared at the fire. The sun was making its way up the sky. Off in the distance, the chirping of birds could be heard as they flew about, getting ready for winter.

This would be a wonderful morning if it wasn't for the current circumstances, he thought to himself.

Ashley stirred and stretched out. She brought her arms back down and looked at Anthony. "I'm not mad at you anymore."

Anthony felt relief and surprise flow through him but was interrupted.

"But I can't say that I've forgiven you. I can't explain it to you, but all I do know is I'm not angry at you anymore."

Anthony half-smiled. "Well, I don't know if I've forgiven myself, so I guess that's all I can ask of you."

The two smiled at each other as the awkward air that was hanging around them began to lift.

"What a nice moment you two are having right now."

The two leapt up in surprise. They turned to see Kevran sitting cross-legged by the fire.

"When did you get here?" Anthony asked.

Kevran waved his claw. "I just got here, but that is not important. What is important is how we plan on getting out of here now that we have Ashley to tow around with us."

Anthony crossed his arms and stared deep into the fire. Kevran had indeed posed a serious question.

Ashley looked at the two in confusion. "Why do you need an escape plan? Why don't we just leave in the vehicle he came in?"

Anthony twiddled his thumbs. "We didn't drive here. I ran the whole way."

Ashley looked at the two in total disbelief. He just said he ran across almost half the continent by himself, and in a week no less.

Anthony noticed her looks of indignation and dismissed her surprise. "I'm a God Sword, remember? I have an immense amount of power at my disposal. That power can be used to give me amazing physical boosts and awesome endurance."

Ashley just nodded as the two continued to think. She wasn't so much amazed at the feat as she was at the way that Anthony treated it like no big deal. She shook her head and brought her thoughts back to escaping. *If they want to escape with me, then they will need a vehicle. It will have to be incredibly fast as well.* A thought popped into her mind. She turned it around and debated it for a while, but she liked it. She raised her hand and got the two's attention. "I think I have an idea. How fond are you of grand theft?"

Anthony sat in the space between two houses with Ashley. He tapped his foot and looked around. Soon the trito that they were focused on pulled into the house next to them. They ducked behind a trash can and waited for the man to step out of his car, lock the door, and go inside. They waited a minute before relaxing again.

"I don't like this plan," Anthony bemoaned. "Theft just doesn't sit well with me."

Ashley half-smiled. "And you think it sits well with me?"

Anthony looked at her. "You were the one that suggested it. It was also the first thing you suggested, which leads me to think that you've had this on your mind for a while now."

Ashley looked at the ground. Anthony rolled his eyes and took another look at the trito. It was the new Snaudi 243Z. He had seen commercials for it all over the place. It was supposed to be one of the faster tritos out on the market right now. It also cost a fortune, but the size of the man's house told him that money was no object.

"How rich is this guy?" Anthony asked.

Ashley looked at the house with a twinge of envy. "He's the owner of the cheese factory up here. The famous Wishitak cheese that everyone loves was created by his family. He's the richest and most influential person in the area. My family moved to this neighborhood because of him. They wanted me to get with his son, but I found Devon instead."

She stopped at the mention of his name and tried to hold back tears.

Anthony changed the subject. "I don't understand why he would buy a trito when the newer quadtos are so much nicer."

The original vehicle that was first invented was three wheels, thus the name *trito*. But in recent years, someone added a fourth wheel, saying that it gave more traction and more control, thus the name *quadto*. Anthony wasn't interested in vehicles, but a few of his friends were, so he picked up a few things.

Anthony looked over to Ashley to see if she was still sad but was surprised to see a gleam in her eye. "The quadtos are nice, but when it comes to speed and general attractiveness, the tritos are where it's at."

She proceeded to talk about the engine and all the inner workings of the car with such passion that Anthony couldn't help but get sucked in. He must have worn a shocked face because when she did look over at Anthony, she seemed to realize how much she had gone off.

Her face turned bright red, and she turned away and looked at the ground. "Sorry, I was rambling, wasn't I?"

Anthony shook his head and smiled. "That was amazing. You know more about tritos than most of my friends."

Ashley seemed a bit surprised but managed a half smile at the praise. "Well, my dad did work at a garage for a while, so I kind of picked up on a few things. But I've always been obsessed by tritos. I just love them so much."

Anthony gave her a thumbs-up. "You certainly know your stuff, or at least you make it seem like you know your stuff. I wouldn't be able to tell if you were lying or not."

Ashley laughed as Anthony rubbed his head. He was happy. He and Ashley had yet to share a nice moment. He knew that she had good reason to hate him, but he still wanted to get along with her. There was also the fact that they would probably be traveling together for a while before he could find a safe place for her. The thought of traveling with someone that he couldn't have good conversation with sounded horrible to him.

He was brought out of his daydream by the sound of the lawn mower starting up in the man's backyard. The two got serious as Ashley nodded to Anthony. Anthony nodded back and sent the mental signal to Kevran.

Kevran lay flat on his stomach on the roof of a random house. It had been a long and laborious process of getting to that spot without being detected. He was still in shock of the whole process that had led to this idea.

"We can steal a trito."

Anthony and Kevran just sat there looking at Ashley like they were waiting for her to finish some joke. After they realized that she was serious, they had tried to blow it off; but try as they might, they couldn't think of another good alternative. They needed a vehicle. The Zankrex were on edge and would be all over them if Anthony tried to carry her out of the town's vicinity. The logical choice would be to take a trito out of town so that Anthony could keep his energy hidden, but buying one was out of the question. Ashley had stated that she didn't own one. The only other options were to steal one or to hope to find an abandoned one.

"Fine," Anthony conceded. "We can steal a trito, but I have no idea how to do that, and I doubt Kevran does either."

Kevran shook his head in confirmation.

"Unless you know how to, then we—"

"Yeah, I know how to steal a trito."

Anthony and Kevran just stared at her, mouths agape in complete disbelief.

"I also know the perfect one to steal. All I would need is a distraction and a little of Anthony's power."

Kevran sighed as he waited for the signal. He was happy that Ashley was contributing to the group, but ever since she had shown up, it had been nothing but trouble.

No point in bemoaning her presence. I know Anthony will never force her to leave. As long as she is not too much of a burden, then I suppose it is fine for now.

He received the mental cue from Anthony. He sighed and rolled over into a crouching position. *Well, if I am going to be the distraction, then I may as well go all out.*

An explosion rumbled the ground where Anthony and Ashley were.

He smiled and turned to Ashley. "The distraction has started."

Ashley recomposed herself after being caught off guard by the explosion. "No kidding, but don't you think that may be a bit much?"

Anthony shrugged. "We can talk about that later, but for now, let's get this trito before Mr. Rich decides to come check things out."

The two ran out front and got up to the trito. They had gone over the plan several times before now. He was to use his God Sword powers to mold a leaf to open the door, but the trito didn't have a key slot to start it. The newer tritos were all push starters. That meant that the key had to be inside the trito in order for the button to actually start the car. That was where Ashley would take over and hot-wire it.

Anthony molded a leaf and unlocked the door. As soon as the door opened, Ashley went to work. Anthony stood outside and looked around for people who would notice. Just as Ashley said, most everyone was away at work, so there wouldn't be any witnesses. Anthony wasn't worried about that so much as he was about a stray Zankrex noticing the little bit of power he had to use to open the door. That's why Kevran had to make such a spectacle. He needed to drown the town in his power so that no one would notice the little bit of Anthony's power.

The seconds ticked by. Soon they turned to minutes. Anthony began to grow more and more anxious. He began to tap his foot and looked back. "What's taking so long?"

Ashley cursed as she messed with the wires. "If this thing was easy to steal, then every lowlife with a pair of wire cutters would be driving one."

Anthony watched her work for a little bit. The hair on the back of his neck rose up. He turned around just in time to see a sword flying toward his face. He accessed his power and ducked under the swing and slashed the opposing Zankrex. The Zankrex fell dead, but Anthony knew better than to relax. That short outburst of power would be enough to let other Zankrex know he was there. Sure enough, he felt dark power closing in fast.

Anthony kept his sword out and turned to Ashley. "We need to leave here now."

As if on cue, the car started up. Ashley hopped in the driver's side. "Get in," she yelled at him.

She closed the door before Anthony could argue about who should drive. He darted around the car and got into the passenger's side. Ashley backed out of the driveway and shot off down the street.

Kevran clawed, ducked, and punched through what seemed to be an endless horde of Zankrex. None of them were as powerful as the ones he met in the shrine, though their numbers were going to be a problem. Even though he was trying to focus to feel it, he couldn't sense Anthony's power. He wondered if he had missed it already. If he missed it, then the Zankrex did as well because none of them turned around. They continued to fly at Kevran in waves, which wasn't a problem since his space was only a short portal ride away.

In a moment, the waves of Zankrex stopped as a much more powerful foe stepped forward.

"Where is your master, dragon?"

Kevran gritted his teeth. "He is not my master, and even if I did know, I would never tell demons such as yourselves. He left long ago. I just stayed behind to sharpen my claws on fresh meat."

The head Zankrex curled his lip in disgust. "You think I'll believe that lie? If you don't tell me now, then I will be forced to beat it out of you."

This is bad, thought Kevran. *If I don't continue to fight, then they aren't focused on me. If something goes wrong and Anthony needs to use his power, then they will detect it for sure.*

"You can try, but incompetents like yourselves could never beat me."

The Zankrex crowd began to stir. They were seconds away from flying at him.

The lead Zankrex held out his hand. "Fine then. Just remember that you were the one that asked for this."

He motioned forward with his hand, and the Zankrex flew at him. Kevran prepared to fight when a power spike caught everyone's attention. Kevran's eyes widened in fear as he realized that it was Anthony's power. Anthony's foe was defeated, but his power was already noticed.

"The God Sword is in the city. You know where he is now, so go get him."

Kevran tried to fight a few Zankrex, but they shot off in Anthony's direction. Kevran realized that he could no longer do any good here and teleported back to his dimension.

The trito flew through the suburban area at amazing speeds. Ashley had changed the second she had stepped on the gas pedal. She turned from normal girl to a speed demon. She had a crazy look in her eye as she drifted around turns and flew through stoplights and intersections.

Anthony's knuckles were white from gripping the door handle. "Do you think maybe you should slow do—"

"Shut up, I'm driving," she snapped back.

Anthony receded. "Yes, ma'am."

It was then that Anthony noticed that Kevran had returned to his dimension. Anthony had hoped that they would have a little more distance between them and their pursuers. The wave of Zankrex behind them dashed those hopes. He wasn't worried about getting caught, though, as the trito was hitting speeds that no one could keep up with. The Snaudi brand was living up to its name.

After several twists and turns through town and some residential areas, they hit the highway. The large road provided the perfect place for Ashley to punch it. She shifted into the highest gear, and the trito propelled itself forward.

Anthony wiped his forehead and relaxed in his seat. "It's nice to know that we are out of that town now."

Ashley wasn't as relaxed. "But it seems that they aren't going to let us go without a fight."

Anthony looked back to see four police tritos behind them. He scowled as he could feel the Zankrex that were in them. He thought for a moment before an idea came to him. He sighed as he didn't like it, but he knew that it was the only thing to do. He rolled the window down.

Ashley looked over at him in disbelief. "What do you think you're doing?"

Anthony looked back. "I'm going to stop the police."

Anthony stuck his head and torso out of the car. Whatever protests that Ashley was giving were drowned out by the wind.

He hadn't thought this through at all. All he knew was that if he could get on the roof of the trito, then he could finish the job. He didn't like the idea of hurting police officers who were being controlled by the Zankrex; but he knew that right now, if he didn't do this, then they wouldn't have any peace for a good while, though his plans would be pointless if he couldn't get on the roof.

He thought about it for a couple of seconds before Kevran interjected, *Put leaves on the bottoms of your feet and use your power to make them sticky. It is a natural process for the leaves, so it should not take much to force them to do that.*

Anthony nodded and acquired some leaves. He focused on them for a little bit and found that what Kevran had told him was indeed true. It wasn't natural for the leaves to secrete sap, but he found that all the components for making sap were in the leaves. He stuck the leaves to his feet and, in a single motion, leapt on the roof. The wind threatened to blow him off, but his feet stayed stuck to the roof.

Good idea, Kevran, though I have no idea how I'm supposed to move now.

Kevran acknowledged the problem but didn't seem worried. *It was a simple matter to get them to be sticky. I am almost positive that there is a way to make them unstick.*

Anthony tried out Kevran's suggestion. As he worked to make them unstick, he began to slide off the roof. He panicked for a second before sticking back to the roof.

Kevran chuckled. *Graceful as always. I've connected you and Ashley telepathically for the time being. We all should be in contact right now, so we can escape.*

Ashley seemed unnerved by having people in her head but was pushing through it. *Does anyone have a plan?*

Anthony nodded. *I have a plan. I'm going to speed-step over to the police tritos and take them out. That's as far as I've gotten, though.*

Ashley rolled her eyes. *That won't do us much good. The cops will just radio in to the next junction, and a new group will be waiting for us at the next town. We have to find a way to leave the highway without them knowing which way we went.*

Anthony couldn't think with the wind whipping in his ear. He had already pulled his sword out and was staring the Zankrex down. They had also managed to make it to the top of their cars, but they used their claws to hold on to the roof.

Ashley spoke up, *I have an idea. Up ahead there is a fork in the road, but in the middle of the fork is a hidden path that leads to another road. If we can take that dirt path without them knowing we went that way, then we should be clear. It will be up to you to give us that cover, though.*

Anthony was impressed, and Ashley must have felt it through the mental link because she couldn't help but feel a tad prideful.

Anthony smiled at her response and prepared to move. *Give me the word on when to move.*

Ashley came back to. *All right, it's coming up here real fast. When I say go, you should have about ten seconds to pull this off in order for this to work. Can you handle it?*

Anthony smiled as he took a stance. *We're about to find out, aren't we?*

The atmosphere got intense as everyone waited for the signal. Finally, the tension broke as Ashley shouted, *Go!*

Anthony shot off the car. He found that softening the amount of stick to the smallest amount needed would allow him to speed-step to and from each trito. He landed on the trito farthest away. He knew he had no time to waste, so he ducked under a Zankrex slash and slashed the hood on the vehicle, killing the engine. He managed this routine with the next two tritos before making it to the last one. Two Zankrex waited for him on the roof of this one. He ducked under the first slash but was forced to block the second one with his sword. He tried to step, but he couldn't move his feet because of the leaves. If he was going to take out the Zankrex, then he would have to do it from that spot. He ducked under the first Zankrex's second slash and slashed back, killing him. As he flew off the roof, he deflected the next strike from the second Zankrex and stabbed him through the heart. The second one flew off the roof. Anthony killed the last engine and speed-stepped to the Snaudi. He stood there and began to gather leaves. He was going to give them cover in the only way he knew how.

If I cloud the vehicles with a bunch of leaves, then they won't be able to focus on my power source. I'll cut it off, and the trito will go out of sight.

A storm of leaves began to form around him as Ashley shouted, *Here comes the fork. It's about to get bumpy, so hold on. Hitting it in three, two, one—now!*

As they approached the fork, Anthony let loose his storm of leaves. A few straggling Zankrex were attempting to fly after them.

The leaves ripped through them and cut the visibility down to zero. The police's line of sight was completely cut off. Anthony was admiring his work when Ashley drove off the road. He nearly fell off the trito before he could properly stick himself back to the roof. He suppressed his power and held still. As they flew down the dark wooden trail, Anthony held his breath. He couldn't sense their powers chasing after them, and after a couple of long painful seconds, he let out his pent-up breath.

They had escaped from Wishitak.

Chapter 12

WARNING

*A*nthony slipped back into the trito and rolled the window up. Silence pervaded the cabin as Ashley tore down the dirt road.

"I didn't even see this road. I'm surprised you found it on your own," Anthony said, trying to get a conversation going.

Ashley's face was expressionless.

She continued to stare straight ahead. "I wish I had found this on my own. My ex-boyfriend showed me this when we were dating."

She never said another word after that, though Anthony never tried to talk to her again.

I don't understand this. She's acting like a completely different person.

Kevran chimed in, *Some people become something different when they are doing certain activities. My guess is that driving does that for her. I would just let her be until we have to stop.*

Anthony agreed and turned to look out of the window. The trees were zipping by as they shot down the road. Soon the dirt path met with an intersection to a real road. It was almost as big as the highway they had just gotten off. Ashley turned on to it and continued at her normal breakneck speed. As they went, the awkward air dissipated. Ashley's demeanor relaxed just a little bit, and she reached over and turned on the radio. Anthony had always enjoyed long rides in his trito, both driving and riding along. The songs played on as the scenery buzzed by. The forests would turn to fields, and the fields would turn back to forests. They were able to drive by unnoticed for the most part. In only two instances did Ashley slow down as they passed by towns.

It was about midday when they ran out of gas. Anthony had been keeping track of their progress with his God Sword ability. They had made far more progress in little less than three hours than he had been able to make in a single day. The trito was amazing. He was sad to see it go, but at the same time, he was happy about getting old Ashley back. Trito Ashley was cold and boring.

They parked the trito in some bushes in an attempt to hide it before trekking off. They had been heading back east, so Anthony decided it would be best to continue that route. They walked for about an hour before Ashley stopped. It was obvious that the journey was wearing on her, yet she didn't complain.

Anthony smiled at her determination and walked over to her. "There's no need to push yourself. If you're tired, then just say so."

Ashley shook her head in between breaths. "No, I'm good. I can keep going."

Anthony chuckled. "Of course, you can, but I'm getting hungry. So, let's take a lunch break, as long as that's okay with you?"

Ashley looked at him with thanks and pushed herself back up. They found a clearing, and Ashley dropped down and leaned up against the nearest tree. She breathed a sigh of relief as she caught her breath. Anthony looked around the clearing. It was a tad larger than he would like as he preferred to be in tight hidden spaces, but it would do for a short break. Anthony closed his eyes and reached out into the forest. The nearest berry bush was still a ways off.

He opened his eyes and turned to Ashley. "I'm going to go get us some food. I'll only be a bit, but Kevran will be here in case anything happens."

Ashley nodded as she made herself comfortable against the tree.

Anthony tripped over a bush as he stumbled back into the clearing. He looked up to see if Ashley had seen his ungraceful moment. He was relieved to see she was sound asleep against the tree, but not so thrilled to see Kevran trying not to laugh. Anthony shook his head and brought the berries he had collected over.

He put them down on a patch of grass and went over to Kevran. "How long has she been asleep?"

Kevran looked over. "For as long as I have been out here. She was asleep by the time I emerged."

Anthony smiled as he looked at her. She seemed so calm and peaceful when she was asleep.

Kevran nudged him with his elbow. "Be sure to keep impure thoughts away."

Anthony flushed red. "I don't know what you're talking about."

Kevran laughed at the reaction. "Of course not."

Anthony sighed and looked back at Ashley. "What are we supposed to do with her?"

Kevran became serious again. "I have been trying to figure that out for a while now. It is not like she is a burden, but it would be safer for her if we could find a place of refuge against the Zankrex."

Anthony nodded in agreement. "If I could figure out where the others from school went, then I could take her there. But I have no idea where they would have run off to."

Kevran nodded as he crossed his arms to think. "I have been out of it for far too long to have any idea about a safe house. I am afraid I will not be of any use to you right now."

Anthony smiled. "That's fine. I told you, didn't I? It wouldn't be right of a God Sword to keep relying on others."

Kevran half-smiled and nodded at Anthony. The two sat thinking in silence for a while. They were still deep in thought when Ashley stirred and woke up.

Anthony gazed up at her and smiled. "Good morning, or I guess it would be good afternoon now."

Ashley wiped the sleep from her eyes and looked around the clearing in a daze. Anthony remembered that look from the time he wore it after he woke up in Kevran's cave.

"We escaped Wishitak, remember? Now we are in the forest."

Realization struck her, and she nodded her head. "Sorry about that. I just couldn't, for the life of me, figure out how I got here."

Anthony brushed it off. "Don't even worry about it. I did the same thing the morning after the Zankrex attacked."

She smiled at him and stretched her body out.

She looked down and noticed the pile of berries. "Is that our lunch?"

Anthony nodded. "Sorry it's so meager, but that's all I could find for the time being. I'll find something more substantial come dinnertime, but for now, we are going to have to make do with this."

Ashley accepted this fact and dug into the berries. She was hungrier than she thought she would be, and by the time she had finished, only a couple handfuls remained. When she noticed how much she had eaten, she panicked and looked up at Anthony.

They made eye contact as he looked on in amazement. "I've never seen a girl eat like that before. I turned my head away for one second, and most of the food is gone."

Ashley blushed and turned her head away. "Well, I was super hungry. Sorry, I'm not a normal eater."

She looked back to see Anthony trying hard not to laugh. She became indignant. "Stop laughing. Is it really that funny that I eat like that?"

Anthony raised his hand as he continued to try not to laugh. "I'm sorry, it just struck me as funny. I didn't see you as the hurried eater."

Ashley turned away, her face still beet red. "Well, I'm sorry, but that's who I am."

Anthony managed to get his laughing under control. "No, I think that's wonderful. It always bugged me how daintily some girls would eat even when they said they were super hungry. It's nice to know that some girls don't mess around when it comes to food."

Ashley turned back around to see Anthony finish off the rest of the berries. "I'm sorry I ate most of them. You are the one who needs to keep his strength up the most."

Anthony waved it off. "I ate a few berries at the bush, so I didn't need a whole lot to begin with. That and I am not a heavy eater, so don't worry about me."

Ashley looked at him in confusion. "Really? I thought men always ate a whole lot of food."

Anthony laughed. "Yeah, that's what everyone says, but I've never been a heavy eater. Don't know why either, but my friend would always make fun of me for how little I would eat in the cafeteria at school."

Ashley smiled. "That doesn't seem very nice to do."

Anthony chuckled. "Maybe not, but what are friends for if not to make fun of you?"

They both laughed. Anthony was enjoying talking to Ashley like this. Not about the Zankrex or about anything serious, just talking. He hadn't had a normal conversation like this since he talked to Christian at school the day before the attack. He knew that Christian would have made it to the gym in time to leave with the group. He lived on campus, so he would have been one of the first ones there.

Suddenly an idea hit Anthony. It must have showed on his face because Ashley was looking at him in confusion.

He stood up in excitement. "I know where we can go."

Kevran looked over in anticipation. "You thought of something?"

Anthony nodded. "We need to go back to Murffana."

Ashley continued to be confused, but Kevran looked shocked. "Go back to Murffana? Why in the world would you go back there? You have the greatest chance of having your family used against you there, and since that is where the Divine Blade academy is, I am almost positive that it will be crawling with powerful Zankrex like Lance."

Anthony did lose some of his enthusiasm after thinking about fighting multiple Zankrex like Lance, but he still remained determined. "I understand it's the most dangerous place for us. But if they are guarding it so well, then they won't be expecting us to go there."

Kevran just shook his head. "You are trying far too hard to out-think them. If they have that many soldiers there, then it means that they are prepared for you."

Anthony shook his head. "We can argue that later. The main reason I think we should go there is because the Divine Blade academy is there. We know that a group of survivors was supposed to meet in the gym. It's safe to assume we missed them since the only other option is that no one survived."

Kevran was getting impatient. "Where are you going with this?"

Anthony pointed to the east. "They left Clancy behind to have someone to lead the stragglers away, which is a smart thing to do. But they might have left a clue somewhere on campus for anyone else who didn't make it in time. I think our best chance right now is to hope that a clue like that does exist in the academy."

Kevran didn't look sold on the idea, but he had no rebuttal for it either.

Anthony could tell he was getting to him. "Right now, we are traveling blind. If it was just you and me, then I would be fine with just roaming around till we found somewhere to go. Heck, if it was just me and you, then I would be far more confident in this plan. No offense, Ashley."

She raised her hands. "None taken. But I don't understand what's so significant about Murffana."

Anthony sat back down. "Murffana is where the academy for Divine Blades is. It's the school where we Divine Blades receive our training and our schooling. When the attack happened, all the Divine Blades met in the gym on campus before relocating some-where. Kevran and I were too late, and we didn't get to see where they went off to. I think that if we go back, then we could find a clue as to where they would have relocated to."

Ashley nodded. "That makes a whole lot of sense. Though I could understand why Kevran would be hesitant to go there."

Kevran chuckled. "Hesitant is a nice way of putting it. As Anthony said, it would be one thing if it were just him and me. But we have to protect you as well. Either way, I would not want to go there. However, Anthony is right. We have no idea where to go, and time is of the essence here. We cannot afford to be wandering around the world hoping to stumble across something."

Anthony stared Kevran down. "Does that mean you're okay with this plan?"

Kevran sighed. "I am far from okay with it. But it is our only option."

Anthony smiled as he was happy that he was the one to come up with the plan. He looked up at the sky and squinted at the sun. Based on its position he assumed that it was around midday.

He stood up and stretched out. "Let's get started then. Thanks to Ashley's driving, we have made far more progress than I thought would be possible in such a short time. If we keep moving now, then we can get to Murffana long before I would have thought possible."

Kevran nodded and also stood up, but Ashley wasn't as sure. "How could we get there in better time? In case you've forgotten, I'm not a God Sword like you are. I won't be able to run with you."

Anthony smiled. "That won't be a problem at all. I can carry you and still run fast at the same time. And don't worry, I won't let any branches scrape against you."

Ashley looked uneasy. She made a face like she was going to protest, but the words never came out. She didn't like the plan, but try as she might, she couldn't think of a better option considering the circumstances.

"Fine, I guess I have no choice anyway."

Anthony nodded and helped her stand. He scooped her up, holding her back in his right arm and her legs in his left arm.

He adjusted her to be sure she would be fine. "Are you comfortable?"

Ashley nodded, and she folded her arms up against her chest. Kevran couldn't help but chuckle.

The two looked over at him in confusion as he raised his claws. "I am sorry. It is just that you two look so cute like that. It is like a prince holding his princess."

Both of them looked at each other but turned away as soon as their eyes met, their faces as red as they could get.

Anthony was quick to change the subject. "We better get started. We have a long way to go, after all."

Ashley was quick to agree with him. "You're right. No reason to hang around here any longer."

Anthony shot off into the forest and headed toward Murffana.

Kevran chuckled. "Oh, this is going to be a lot of fun for me."

Anthony ran through the woods as fast as he felt comfortable running. He knew he could run faster, but with Ashley in his arms, he didn't feel confident in his ability to keep her safe from branches at his top speed. It was obvious that Ashley was having a hard time getting used to going this fast and not being in a trito. She was tensed up and wasn't looking. She had long since buried her face in his chest. Anthony had tried not to let that get to him as he knew that he needed to focus on where he was going. But he found himself looking back down at her. The feeling of a girl cuddling up to him for support was a new feeling for him. He almost let a branch smack him in the face as he brought his attention back to the forest.

I can't be thinking about these things now. Besides, she's probably still in high school. It would be weird for me to go after her since I am in college, after all.

Kevran quickly butted in, *That is not entirely true. Even if she was in high school, that would only put her two to three years below you. That is not that big of a gap.*

Anthony found himself agreeing with Kevran before shaking his head. *It's a moot point anyway. I need to focus on this Zankrex thing. I don't have any time to deal with relationships.*

Kevran couldn't help but chuckle. *Sounds to me like you are trying to convince yourself there.*

Anthony didn't respond, choosing instead to focus on running faster. He knew that time was of the essence. The chance that a Zankrex would find the clue he was looking for raised with every passing hour.

With this thought on the forefront of his mind, he ran on until sundown.

Anthony slowed down and stopped by a creek next to a small clearing. Ashley had long since fallen asleep in his arms, so he was careful to lay her down without waking her.

He turned back toward the creek as Kevran popped out of his portal next to him. "You ever notice how many clearings there are with creeks next to them? It seems like these things are everywhere."

Anthony shrugged his shoulders. "I'm sure they're not that common. I can just detect when we pass one. My forest-feeling ability has gotten a lot better since we started this trip."

Kevran held in a laugh. "Forest feeling? How long did it take you to think of that name?"

Anthony ignored his jabs. "You never gave me a name for it, and it's more convenient to have names for my abilities so I don't have trouble telling you about it. If I didn't have a name for it, then I would have to describe my ability every time we talked about it."

Kevran lifted his claws in defense. "All right, all right, you do have a point. It just seems like there could be a better name for it than *forest feeling*."

Kevran suppressed another laugh as Anthony looked away in annoyance. "Well, if you think of a better name, then please let me know."

"A better name for what?"

Kevran and Anthony turned to see that Ashley had woken up. She was rubbing the sleep from her eyes as she stood up.

Anthony sighed. "I have an ability that allows me to use my God Sword power to map out the layout of the forest so that I can take the safest route and find food. I was just telling Kevran how that skill had gotten better since we had left, and I called it forest feeling so he would know what I was talking about."

Ashley snorted as she tried to hold in her laughter.

Anthony looked at her in exasperation. "Not you too."

Ashley struggled to keep from laughing and got it under control. She took a calming breath and looked at Anthony. "I'm sorry, but *forest feeling* doesn't seem like a name I would give to a God Sword ability."

Anthony threw his hands up. "Well, great, glad I know that now. If you come up with something better, please be sure to let me know."

He stormed off into the forest as Ashley and Kevran began to laugh.

Anthony walked back into the clearing with an armful of berries.

Ashley looked over at him, impressed. "Ridiculous name or not, your ability to find berries every night is amazing. I didn't even realize there were that many berries in the wild anymore."

Anthony chuckled. "That's where you'd be wrong. It's amazing how many bushes full of berries we pass every day."

Anthony sat down next to Ashley and placed the berries in between them. He had noticed that two small fish were cooking on the fire they had started.

"Did you catch those?" Anthony asked, pointing to the fish.

Ashley shook her head. "Kevran caught those. He said that you would need more than just berries if you were going to keep your strength up."

Anthony nodded. He didn't want to be the one to complain, but his diet of berries had been tough on him. He had never been a big eater, but even he needed meat and variety in his meals.

"I'm glad he caught them. I've never been good at catching fish."

Ashley looked at him weird. "But with your enhanced speed, shouldn't you be able to catch fish no problem?"

Anthony smiled. "Yeah, it should be easy to catch them now, shouldn't it? I didn't really think of that."

Ashley could only just sigh as Anthony rubbed the back of his head and laughed. He brought his attention back to the fish. Two fish meant that he could split it perfectly with Ashley.

"We can split the fish and berries fifty-fifty then?"

Ashley shook her head. "Thanks, but I'm going to have to pass. I don't like fish at all. I'll just eat the berries, and you can have the fish."

Anthony shrugged. "That works for me."

They spent the next minute or so in silence as they ate their dinner. Anthony had just finished his last fish and was turning to Ashley to say something when a piece of wood hit him on the back of the head. He cringed for a second and turned around. Kevran stood there smiling as he tossed another wood piece up and down.

"You ready to continue your focus training?"

Anthony grimaced as he stood. He knew Kevran would start his training again. He had hoped to avoid it with Ashley there, but he knew that Kevran wouldn't listen to any protests. Ashley didn't understand what was going on, but she knew enough to slide out of the way and watch from the sidelines.

Anthony sighed and prepared himself. "What kind of training am I doing this time?"

Kevran smiled an unnerving smile as he tossed the wood piece over to him. Anthony caught it and looked at it. It was just a normal piece of wood, with nothing special about it. Anthony was about to ask him what it was about, but Kevran was already holding a claw up to silence him.

"I shall now explain the training. You are going to close your eyes and sense where I am using the forest. I will drop my energy level so you will not be able to detect me. You will have to detect me using the forest to detect my movements."

Anthony sighed in relief. "Okay, that doesn't sound too bad."

Kevran's smile only widened. "However, you will also be spinning two leaf orbs with ten leaves each. You must maintain their shape and hit me with that wood piece before I hit you with mine. If you can do this multiple times in a row, then I will consider your focus training complete."

Anthony became deflated. Spinning one leaf orb had been tough enough for him. The jump to two orbs had been a huge step in his training. And even those orbs held half the amount of leaves that Kevran was now asking for. But that wasn't the part he was worried about. Just running and maintaining the leaves had proven to be a tough task to master. But now he had to detect the slightest disturbances in the forest to find Kevran.

He closed his eyes and gathered the leaves. He took his time getting the orbs spinning. Making sure that each one was spinning the way he wanted it to. After a time, he dropped his hands and prepared himself. Seconds passed as he felt around to the best of his abilities. A sharp whack on the back of the head signaled the failure of his first attempt. The orbs spun out of control as his focus was shot. He snarled and got the leaves spinning again. This time, he put a little more focus on his surroundings; and this time, the leaf orbs spun out of control. He clenched his teeth in frustration. He had always hated practicing things that he wasn't good at. It was the same feeling he had training his speed step before the invasion. He wasn't all that good at it, so he hated to practice it.

Kevran's voice brought him back to reality. "Hey, we are not done until I say we are done. Now let us do it again."

They practiced for the better part of the hour. Anthony never once hit Kevran. He had gotten close once or twice, but he would always regress afterward. His frustration was keeping him from making any real progress.

Kevran called it off, sensing that Anthony wasn't going to make any progress at this point. "I am upset with you, Anthony."

Anthony was already in a foul mood. He ignored Kevran because he didn't feel like having a shouting match in front of Ashley. She had sat there and had never once laughed, or at least not where Anthony could hear it.

Kevran shook his head. "There is a reason why you continue to fail, but I want you to figure it out on your own. Think about it tonight and see if you can have an answer by tomorrow night."

With that, he stepped through his portal and disappeared. Anthony sat down on the opposite side of the fire from Ashley. She kept quiet for a time, letting Anthony cool down a bit.

After a minute, she got up and sat a little closer to him. "I'm not going to pretend to know you guys after just meeting you. But it does look like Kevran is trying to help."

Anthony sighed. "Yeah, I know. I'm not mad at him. I'm not even mad at all. I'm just frustrated."

Ashley gave a half smile as well and stared into the fire. The two of them just sat there like that for several minutes.

Anthony turned to Ashley. "Why were you dating him?"

Ashley looked up, stunned. "What?"

Anthony continued to stare her down. "Why were you dating that guy that was bad-mouthing you in the shrine? And why did you continue to stay by his side?"

Ashley didn't know how to react. "Where did this come from?"

Anthony sighed. "It's been bothering me ever since we left the shrine. I tried to get it out of my mind, but no matter how hard I tried, I couldn't. I can't think straight anymore because of it."

Ashley almost wanted to laugh. "Why does it bother you that much? It's not like it matters anyway."

"I know," Anthony answered. "I know it's none of my business. But at this point, I don't care anymore. Please just tell me why."

Ashley looked down at the dirt and hugged her legs. "You might think he's the worst man on the face of the earth, but for a while, he was my hero. I was in a bad relationship before that one. The guy was about as abusive as Devon was at the shrine. It was a part of who I was. My father wasn't around growing up, so I never knew how a male should treat me. I also developed real early on. It made me the envy of every girl and the aspiration of every boy. I found the attention of males to be wonderful as I had never known it before. But that must sound super clichéd. Another girl with daddy issues. It must sound like a lazily written backstory in some cheap soap opera, huh?"

Anthony shook his head. "I don't think so. And I also don't think that was the only reason why you let him use you like that."

Ashley nodded her head. "You're right. Growing up in middle school as a girl is the hardest thing. I was the most attractive girl, so I became the target of every rumor. No girl wanted to associate with me because they were either jealous or too scared that they would be shunned if they talked to me. Of course, they would act nice in front of the boys, but when it was only us, they wouldn't have anything to do with me. I became desperate for friends. That's when he showed up. My first boyfriend, the one before Devon, befriended me and took me in. It only made sense that a guy would befriend me. The girls' rumors never reached over to the guys, and even if it did, the other guys didn't pay any attention to them. I thought that if I made guy friends, I would be safe from the girls. I became far too dependent on his company. He used it to keep me tied to him. He would verbally abuse me all the time but would always finish by saying that he was all I had. At some point, I believed him and accepted my fate. That lasted through middle school and well into high school before

Devon came along. He told the guy off and convinced me to break up with him. It wasn't long before I was going out with him. For a time, everything was fine. I fit in perfectly with his group of friends, but because of that, I didn't branch out to find other friends. It was around senior year that he began to change. He started acting like my first boyfriend did. Even his friends started to question his actions. They tried to convince me to leave him several times, but I was too blind to see what he had become. Devon's friends left him, and then high school was over. I had no plans for college, so I went to the same one as Devon. At college, things got worse. It was like I was dating my first boyfriend on steroids. Then of course, the Zankrex takeover happened, and the rest is history."

Anthony stayed quiet for a while as he tried to soak it all in. "Wait, if you had just started college when the Zankrex incident happened, then that means that you're around eighteen years old?"

Ashley looked at him in confusion. "Odd that that's the first thing you say after that story, but yes, I am eighteen. Why is that an interesting thing to you?"

Anthony looked at the dirt in embarrassment. "'Cause I figured you couldn't be out of high school yet. I thought you were still sixteen."

Ashley sighed, not surprised. "Yeah, I get that a lot. I guess I look like I'm still in the middle of high school."

Anthony nodded and became serious again. "But thank you for opening up to me. I know it must have been tough to say all that to someone you only just met."

Ashley shrugged. She didn't feel great about the topic, but somehow it was carrying less weight than it used to. "It's no big deal. It's in the past in any case. But why did you want to know?"

Anthony stared into the fire. "I just wanted to confirm that I made the right choice."

Ashley looked at him in confusion. "When Devon said all those bad things in the shrine, I got so mad. But when I got to thinking about it, I started to doubt my choice. 'What if that was just the Onigor talking?' was my biggest doubt. But after hearing your story, I'm 100 percent sure that I made the right choice in killing him."

Ashley's eyes widened in shock as Anthony raised his hands up so he could finish. "Everything that I've learned about you during our short time together had been positive. You are a wonderful woman who's been nothing but helpful. You're attractive, and you know how to think and act for yourself. You've gotten us out of two jams already, and you don't even have any powers. This is the fastest I've ever befriended someone. To see that man not only agree to let the dark power take over his life but also trying to abuse you into joining their side was more than I could take. I know you loved him, even if it was misplaced love. But I have no remorse for my actions."

Ashley had no idea what to say. He had said things that, under normal circumstances, would have been considered a confession. But at the same time, he had also said that he felt no remorse for killing her ex-boyfriend. This didn't faze her like it should have.

Maybe I'm realizing that that was the right decision to make.

She let a small smile grace her lips as she turned away. "I'm glad we could have this talk. Let me sleep on it before I answer you back." She walked away and curled up on the edge of the clearing.

Anthony couldn't help but smile. *Heaven forbid, I just have a normal conversation with a girl.*

Kevran chimed in, *Well, that would require you to be a normal person, and we both know that is not the case.*

Anthony smiled. *Yeah, I suppose it is silly of me to think that anything normal will happen around me.*

The two laughed as Anthony sat down in front of the fire. Kevran seemed to be pleased with something, and Anthony didn't know why.

What's got you in a good mood?

Kevran took a second. *I am happy because I did not have to explain something to you.*

Anthony was confused, but Kevran continued, *I told you, did I not? There was a reason you were having trouble with training today. It was because you had Devon on the brain. I was worried that I was going to have to force you to talk that out with Ashley, but you did it on your own. I guess I am just pleased that you managed to figure your own thoughts out.*

Anthony understood what Kevran was saying. He wasn't the best at understanding his own feelings. He was just proud of himself for even having the conversation.

It wasn't easy, but you're right. I needed to talk to her about that. Now that I have, I feel a thousand times better.

Kevran smiled. *Then I will look forward to you doing a little better during training tomorrow.*

Anthony smiled as well. *I'll look forward to it as well.*

With that, he doused the fire and found his own corner to sleep at.

Ashley didn't get much sleep that night. She couldn't stop thinking about the conversation she had just had with Anthony. Every word bounced around in her head. Her feelings ranged from flattered to outrage all at the same time. But the one thing that stuck out to her the most was his conviction. There was no lie in his eyes. He was being 100 percent honest with her. She couldn't help but admire that.

He told me everything he was thinking even though it was tough to say. That is impressive.

But no matter how impressed she was with it, she couldn't feel great about him. She wanted to feel great about him. It was obvious that he was a great guy and a wonderful person to be around. She agreed that this was the fastest she had befriended someone in a very long time, but even then, she still had reservations. She just couldn't get something out of her mind. She just couldn't understand why he had to kill. She knew the Zankrex were evil, and it wasn't like she didn't believe the story about them giving up their humanity, but she just couldn't accept that killing was the best way to go about it. But even then, she couldn't hate him because of it. She gripped her head in frustration. She sat like that for a few minutes and just cleared her mind. After calming down for a moment, she relaxed her body and stretched out.

I'll stay quiet then, she concluded. *I don't know if I can forgive him yet, but I won't bring it up again. I'll stay with him and try not to think about it until I can get a clear answer.*

It, by no means, solved her problems, but it pushed them aside for the time being. The weight was off, if even for a moment, and that gave her the mental peace she was looking for.

The journey continued on without a hitch. Even though Anthony continued to carry Ashley, they were making the same progress that Anthony made on his own toward Wishitak.

Ashley was still afraid of the speed of travel, and she never got used to it. She got to the point where she wouldn't cower in fear as soon as they started, but she could never watch the forest for more than thirty seconds. Anthony didn't mind. He didn't need someone to talk to while he ran. Kevran made him maintain two leaf orbs anyway, so the less talking that happened was best for him.

Every night, Kevran would continue his training with Anthony. After the first night, and after Anthony got to talk with Ashley, he had been doing much better. He still couldn't quite get consecutive hits, but his focus with the leaf orbs was top tier. He got hit often as well, but he was always the one to throw his piece of wood first. Afterward, he would stay up and talk with Ashley for as long as they both could stay awake. They had yet to address the conversation they had the night after their escape, but Anthony didn't care. He could sense that there was a greater understanding from Ashley. Either way, he had said what he wanted to say, so he didn't care how long it took for her to respond.

Their conversations were always so therapeutic for him. They never talked about heavy things. They would just talk, letting the conversation go where it wanted to go. He never felt any pressure to continue to talk to her. They always knew when to stop anyway. For once in his life, he looked forward to conversations. Even when he talked to Christian, there was always a little pressure to say some-thing funny. With Ashley, he never worried about that. He also got to know her better as a result. No matter how bad the training before had been, the conversation would always get his mind off the stress and allowed him to relax.

Anthony also tried to be sure to keep his sword skills up. Every night, he would go off by himself and defeat imaginary enemies. He looked ridiculous swinging his sword around in the forest with no one around, but for him, it was a great way to practice his moves. It wasn't much, but it made sure that he never forgot, even a little bit, what the sword felt like in his hands.

The trip was also less stressful as they managed to avoid every town along the way. This was thanks to their journey out. He had remembered significant landmarks and where they were in relation to towns. The detours would take just a little longer, but the peace of mind was always worth it. Roads were a different matter, though. It seemed like they couldn't go two hours without running across some busy road. It never proved to be that big of a deal, but it forced them to stop and proceed with caution. No matter how busy the road was, they would always get across without a problem. The whole trip was very quiet.

Anthony relaxed next to a tree. Ashley and Kevran were talking about something, but Anthony was zoning out. He was in a very good mood that night. The training had gone his way. He had managed to hit Kevran almost every try. He couldn't help but think back to the first night of training.

It took a little longer than I wanted it to, but all that matters is that I made the progress. If I do what I did tonight again the next night, then Kevran will have no choice but to graduate me. Though I only have Ashley to thank for that. If she hadn't opened up to me, then I would have never made this much progress. I guess I underestimated just how much that whole Devon thing bugged me.

Anthony couldn't help but chuckle. It was all in the past now. The group dynamic they had was great. Kevran had bonded with Ashley, which had surprised Anthony. When all three of them talked, it was never anything special; but when those two talked alone, it was like they had been best friends forever. He had heard them talking about people in general and how rude they could be. He also overheard a conversation about tritos. Kevran had taken an extreme liking to tritos after they had escaped Wishitak. Anthony smiled. He was glad to see that Kevran was getting along with her.

Maybe now he won't be so eager to get rid of her. It would be nice if she could stick around. He realized what he was thinking. *That's ridic-*

ulous to think about. Of course, she has to leave. No matter how fun she is to have around, I have to find someplace safe for her to stay. It would be far too dangerous for her to stay with us anyway, and I would be selfish to want her to stay around.

He knew that answer was obvious and the safest, but a part of him couldn't help but feel sad at the thought of having to say goodbye.

An energy level approaching fast scattered the thought from his mind. He sprung up and looked at Kevran. He must have felt it too because the worry was written all over his face. Ashley looked at the two in confusion, but before she could ask anything, another voice broke the silence.

"Hey there, God Sword. Didn't think I would see you here again."

Anthony knew who it was the moment he spoke. The figure walking into the light only confirmed his fears.

Anthony managed a half smile as he pulled out his sword. "It's a pleasure to see you too, Lance."

Lance grinned wide as he walked forward. His sword was drawn and gleamed in the firelight.

He looked over at Ashley and bowed. "And who might this stunning beauty be?"

Anthony scowled. "Kevran, get her away from here!"

Lance laughed a genuine laugh at Anthony. Both he and Kevran stopped and looked at him in confusion.

Lance caught his breath and wiped a tear from his eye. "Sorry, I keep forgetting that you two don't know anything about me. The thought of me using a hostage is laughable. I don't need to use such tricks to take you down."

Anthony chuckled at him. "Oh? What do you call attacking me in the middle of night while you're at your strongest?"

Lance shrugged. "It's a natural phenomenon. I don't see how that's cheating. And I wasn't the one who attacked you first, now was I?"

Anthony shook his head. "No, you just stood back and watched, waiting for your chance to strike at me once I got weak."

Lance wagged his finger at him. "Now, now, don't say that. You make me sound like a coward. I was observing you to see what your true strength was. If you couldn't even handle my minions, then I wasn't going to waste my time on you."

Anthony smiled. "You should have fought with them. Then maybe you might have had a chance to win."

They tensed in their battle positions. "That's some big talk coming from someone who couldn't even stand after the fight. But enough chatter. I didn't come here to talk. I came here to fight."

Anthony became serious and shot forward. Lance's eyes widened at the quickness of his attack but refocused. Anthony slashed and stabbed at Lance, chaining his moves together and trying to keep on the offensive. Lance played the defensive game while he waited for his opening. His eyes lit up as Anthony came slashing in from the high left. He ducked under it and struck out. The blade came inches away from Anthony's ribs before his sword was stopped. The tide turned as Anthony was forced back. He blocked and parried each of Lance's strikes as the two circled around each other looking for an opening. Their swords moved like blurs as they struck and counter-struck. Neither side was making any progress in normal battle.

Anthony changed up tactics and used his speed step. He darted around the forest, disappearing and reappearing behind every tree. Lance looked frantic for a moment, but then he seemed to dial in. Anthony went in for a strike but was blocked. It was as if Lance knew where he was going to be and, at the last second, managed to get his sword around to block it. Anthony tried this technique several more times, with each one ending up the same as the last one.

If he knows where I'm going to strike with the speed step, then I should reserve it for escape use only.

He changed tactics again and speed-stepped to a tree branch. He gathered as many leaves as he could and shot them at Lance. Lance sprinted through the forest and dodged the leaves at every turn. Using the trees around him, he managed to dodge them for a time. After a while of the chase, Anthony managed to shoot his leaves where Lance was going and not where he was. Lance managed to fend off the surprise attack. From that point, he started to block the leaves with his sword as much as he dodged them altogether. But Anthony wasn't paying attention to where he was on the battlefield. He had let him get far too close to him. Lance had noticed this and charged forward at blinding speeds. Anthony was able to block the attack and went on the defensive. Lance landed several blows on Anthony's sword before he felt something. The leaves that were chasing him were flying straight at his back. Lance had just enough time to leap up and out before the leaves tore the space he had just occupied.

Then a silence filled the battlefield.

Both Anthony and Lance were breathing heavy. The battle hadn't lasted all that long, but the intensity had been full bore from the very beginning.

Anthony chuckled. "You aren't quite as strong as you were that one night."

Lance managed a half smile. "The night isn't as kind to me this time around. But enough about me, you seem to have gotten better at controlling your leaves."

Anthony smiled. "I wouldn't be much of a God Sword if I didn't work on my abilities, now would I?"

Lance laughed. "No, I don't suppose you would be."

He stood up straight and sheathed his sword. Anthony looked at him, confused by his apparent surrender.

"What are you doing?"

Lance shrugged. "I don't feel like deciding our match tonight. No matter how it ends, I won't get to see what kind of interesting things you will do. I'm still going to kill you. But I want to have a little fun before that happens."

Anthony couldn't believe what he was hearing. He couldn't help but shake his head and laugh. He sheathed his sword and stood up straight. "I won't argue with you then. I have no love for bloodshed anyway."

Lance laughed. "Oh? But I heard about what you did at Wishitak. There were quite a few casualties there, according to the report."

Anthony shrugged. "A lot changed in Wishitak. I don't want to kill, but I will if you force me."

Lance nodded. "It's just more fun that way. It would be real boring if you refused to kill anyone."

Anthony was quick to move on. "Why did you come here if you weren't planning on finishing our little match?"

Lance's face lit up as he remembered something. "That's right. I came here to tell you something. Sorry about that. But whenever I see that ugly mug of yours, I just can't help but want to fight you."

Anthony sighed. "It's not like you're a sight for sore eyes either."

Lance laughed. "Sticks and stones, God Sword. But I actually came here to warn you."

Anthony furrowed his brow. "Warn me? Warn me about what?"

Lance became far more serious than he had ever been. "To warn you about where you are going. Don't go back to Murffana."

Anthony could only look at Lance in confusion. "What?"

Lance continued to stare on. "Don't go back to Murffana. Nothing good can come of you returning there."

Anthony tried to process what was happening. "Why shouldn't I go back to Murffana?"

Lance turned around and crossed his arms. "I don't have any reason to tell you that." He looked back with a sly grin on his face. "Though, if the young lady over there would introduce, herself then I may consider telling you."

Anthony rolled his eyes and looked back at Ashley. She seemed hesitant, looking to Anthony. Anthony gave a reassuring smile and nodded.

She smiled back and took a step forward. "My name is Ashley Flowdrid."

Lance turned around and bowed to her. "It is a pleasure to meet you, Ms. Flowdrid. My name is Lance Zater. I trust the God Sword here has kept you protected?"

She could only nod as talking to a Zankrex that had just gone blow for blow with Anthony was kind of stressful to her.

Lance couldn't help but laugh at her hesitation. "Don't worry, miss. I don't kidnap or harm people that can't protect themselves.

Though, if you go back to Murffana, there is someone there who doesn't think the way I do."

Anthony became interested. "What do you mean?"

Lance folded his arms. "There is another Zankrex general there by the name of Shane. He hates Divine Blades and God Swords just as much as the next Zankrex, but he is a genius tactician. He can find anyone's weak point and exploit it for all it's worth. He will kill you using your own family. Unlike me, he doesn't care how you are killed, just so long as the job is done."

Anthony nodded. "That would be a tough opponent to face back in Murffana. Thank you for the information."

Lance shook his head. "You can thank me by not letting that pipsqueak kill you."

Anthony couldn't help but smile. "That's why you're helping me?"

Lance looked indignant. "I'm not going to help you out of the kindness of my heart, now am I? I will be the one to kill you, God Sword, and I'm going to do it without using any stupid tricks. Don't you ever forget that."

Anthony nodded. "I won't."

Lance nodded and ran off back into the night.

Ashley fell to her knees and exhaled. Anthony looked over worried, but she raised her hand in reassurance.

"I'm fine. It's just that I wasn't ready for that. Your battle with him was incredible. I couldn't even see you guys moving half the time. And yet you both acted like it wasn't a big deal."

Anthony couldn't help but smile as he sheathed his sword. "That Lance is an interesting character. I know I shouldn't trust a word he says, but for some reason, I never get worried around him. It's a shame. If he wasn't a Zankrex, I think we could have been friends."

Kevran shook his head. "Getting too familiar with your enemies can be a bad thing, you know—though, I have this weird feeling that you are right about him."

Anthony smiled in agreement. "Well, enough about that. We need to get some sleep for the big day tomorrow."

Ashley looked up, confused. "What's happening tomorrow?"

Anthony looked up with a determined gleam in his eye. "Tomorrow we make it to Murffana."

Ashley was taken aback. "Wait, tomorrow we get back? But didn't we just start our journey?"

Anthony looked at her funny. "No, we've been on the march for five days now."

That blew Ashley away. "Five days? It can't be five days. There's no way it's been five days."

Kevran laughed. "I can understand how the days would blend together for you, but it has indeed been five days. It took us around a week to get from Murffana to Wishitak, and we are a day's journey away from Murffana, so it makes sense that we've been on the road for at least that long."

Ashley shook her head and ignored the fact that time seemed to be zipping by and addressed the main concern. "But didn't that guy just tell us that it was super dangerous to go back? And didn't you just say that you trusted him? Why would you ignore his advice then?"

Anthony sighed and sat back down. "I know what he and I said, but that doesn't change that fact that Murffana holds our only real chance at finding where the others went. I can't let some Zankrex get in my way of that. If worst comes to worst, then I have to fight. Even then, I'm not worried. My leaf skills work a lot better in a crowd."

Ashley tried to think of something to say to talk him out of it but couldn't. She looked over at Kevran for some help, but he too couldn't think of anything.

"I do not like heading into a situation where we have to face a tactician since none of us are good at making plans. It is one thing to be stronger, but sometimes brains can more than make up for your lack of fighting power. But even with that said, Anthony is right. Murffana is our only hope right now for finding the others. Lance delivered his ultimatum. If he hates this other Zankrex as much as he made us believe he did, then we do not have to worry about him leaking any details. No matter how you look at it, we still have the element of surprise."

Anthony nodded, and Ashley just resigned herself to the stupid plan. "Do you even have a plan when you get there?"

Anthony shook his head. "No plan now. Just keep low and find a way into the gym. Using distractions in Murffana would be tough since it's such a big city, and drawing attention to ourselves would be a bad idea. I know this town like the back of my hand, so a covert operation is our best bet."

The other two nodded in agreement. Anthony stood back up and put the fire out. Kevran went through his portal, and Ashley curled up in a soft patch of grass. She fell asleep as Anthony stared up at the stars.

Tomorrow, he thought, *tomorrow is going to be interesting.*

Chapter 13

RETURN

*A*nthony's eyes opened. The sun was shining bright, and birds were singing in the trees. Anthony got up and stretched out. The weather was immaculate. Fall time in Murffana was one of the most sporadic times. The weather could go from cold and miserable to warm and wonderful in the blink of an eye.

Anthony made his way to the stream and leaned over it. He cupped his hands together and took several drinks. After he quenched his thirst, he splashed the ice-cold water on his face. As the water dried, he scanned the clearing and enjoyed the view. Soon his eyes landed on Ashley lying under the tree. She was still fast asleep.

Anthony couldn't help but smile.

I'll let her sleep for a while longer, he thought to himself. *We still have a little bit of time before I want to go.* He didn't have a real specific plan to get into the town, though he didn't need a plan. *I don't want to start looking today. I just want to get into town.*

Anthony nodded at his own thoughts and trudged off to get some berries.

When he came back into the clearing, Ashley was awake. She must have just woken up because she looked dazed and confused.

Anthony smiled and walked over. He sat down next to her and poured the berries on the ground. "Good morning, sunshine."

Ashley grunted at him and crammed as many berries into her mouth as she could.

Anthony couldn't help but chuckle. "You've been like this every morning since we left, and it's funny every morning."

Ashley mock-laughed. "I'm so glad you get enjoyment out of my misery."

Anthony could only laugh. Knowing how Ashley was in the mornings, if he said anything else, he would be in danger of getting hit. He shook his head and leaned back and looked up at the sky. There was a slight breeze rustling the area. The leaves on the top of the trees swayed, and the clouds floated by.

Anthony let out a content sigh. "This day is so peaceful. I almost just want to stay here."

Ashley smiled and nodded. "We've been traveling for so long I've almost forgotten how to relax."

They both just sat there enjoying the weather for several more minutes. Neither of them wanted to move. Soon the sound of a portal opening up brought them back.

Kevran stepped through, and the portal closed. "It is nice to see that you are enjoying nature. It is a wonderful day, after all. But if we do not leave soon, then we are going to miss our window of opportunity."

Ashley looked back at Kevran. "Window of opportunity?"

Kevran nodded as Anthony stood up. "I want to get back to my house to set up a base of operations. If we get into town before midday, then everyone will either be at work or in school, so my neighborhood will be pretty much empty."

Ashley nodded. "I see. It's like my neighborhood. Well then, I guess we should be leaving, right?"

Anthony nodded and helped her up. "Indeed, we should. Let's head over to my house."

Anthony lifted up a branch and allowed Ashley to pass under it. After the warning from Lance, Kevran advised Anthony against running with his energy boost. He had made the argument that if Shane was as crafty as Lance said, then the odds were pretty good that he would also be good at sensing energy. Anthony agreed with Kevran's hypothesis, so they decided to walk.

They were close to the outskirts of town, but walking at the pace they were going increased the time it took to get there. It was prolonged even further by Ashley's constant need to rest. Anthony was reminded about ten minutes in that Ashley wasn't in the best of shape. The landscape did nothing to help her along as every step was over a root or up a hill. They had to take frequent breaks in order for her to catch her breath. Anthony tried to help her along by keeping a conversation going. For the most part, it helped her keep her mind off the travel; but in the end, it only delayed the next break by a couple of minutes. But no matter how many breaks she needed to take, Anthony never got upset.

It only makes sense, I guess, he thought to himself. *She's been carried around for the past few days, and she was already weak to begin with. I suppose I would have been more surprised if she managed to go the entire time without stopping.*

With all the breaks, the journey took about two hours. After the second hour, the first houses came into view. Anthony and Ashley stopped on a small hill that overlooked the suburb.

Anthony smiled as he looked upon the familiar landscape and turned to Ashley. "Welcome to Murffana."

Anthony and Ashley crouched behind a bush as a trito passed by. They waited for several seconds afterward before they made their move. They were far from any busy part of town, but they stayed cautious.

Anthony had been right about the state of the town. It was deserted, even around houses. Every once in a while, there would be one house that had some activity, but it was simple to sneak by. Anthony had long since put his sword in Kevran's realm, so when they put on sunglasses, they blended in well. Anthony still took no chances. If they saw someone, they would hide out until they found a clear avenue for escape.

They didn't have to keep it up long, though. It only took a few minutes for them to reach Anthony's neighborhood, and once they got there, Anthony and Ashley moved down the lifeless streets. They stayed cautious as Anthony's house lay deeper in the suburb.

As they went, Anthony could only feel unease. All the silence and peace was making him more than nervous. It must have shown because Ashley was looking at him with some concern. Anthony shook his head and gave her a reassuring smile.

"I'm fine," he said, not believing it himself.

Ashley could tell he lacked conviction as her concerned look continued. "The silence and peace is what's bothering you, isn't it?"

Anthony sighed and let an uneasy smile cross his lips.

She gave a half smile as she realized she was right. "I know because it's bothering me too. All these people living like nothing's wrong. Did you hear the children laughing at that one house we passed a while ago? They laughed like nothing was wrong. Even their parents looked content. I know I'm supposed to hate this enemy, but it's tough to hate them when they treat their victims like this."

Anthony could only look forward. He knew exactly what she was talking about. It had gone through his head when they were walking around in Wishitak.

I know they are the enemy. Nothing they do will change the way I look at them. But even so, I have no rebuttal to what Ashley is saying. Anthony hated himself for not being able to argue with her. He wanted to give her some reason to hate them. *But she didn't see the vision that Oshuma showed me. Of course, she would have no reason to hate them. Even though they tried to take her, they still didn't do it by force. Her boyfriend said horrible things to her, but he still tried to make her do it on her own accord. They could have just barged in there and infused her on the spot, but they tried to recruit instead. If anything, she should hate me. I killed them all and with no warning. Sure, I knew what I had to do, but she still has no idea why we have to kill them.*

Kevran was quick to interject. *Anthony, you know full well that this peace is not a good peace. People are being forced to live their lives under the Zankrex king. They have to obey his orders and his laws now, and none of them have a say in anything that goes on. You can convince Ashley of their true evil, but it will have to wait until we are safer.*

Anthony nodded, grateful that Kevran had interjected. Ashley seemed to notice the peace that washed over Anthony because she didn't bring it up any further. It didn't matter anyway as they were out of time to talk. They slowed to a stopped as Anthony's house stood before them.

Anthony speed stepped up to the window that led to his room. *You idiot*, Kevran shouted.

Anthony cowered at the sudden rebuke.

Kevran continued, *Speed stepping like that in enemy territory is asking for trouble. What happens if the enemy senses your energy?*

Anthony realized Kevran was right and bowed his head in anger.

Ashley could only look on in confusion. "What's wrong?" she whispered.

Anthony explained the situation to her. Ashley got scared at the news. "Does that mean they're on their way now?"

Anthony paused for several seconds before shaking his head in relief. "Kevran just confirmed that we made it out safe this time."

Ashley let out a sigh of relief. "Thank goodness."

Anthony and Ashley continued to crouch outside the window to Anthony's room. Due to the shape of the house being a dome, there was an area right outside his window that allowed for people to sit. Anthony sat there and stared at his window. It had been locked tight since he had last left. He had left it unlocked when they left, but it made sense that his parents would have locked it since then.

Anthony couldn't help but shake his head. *My dad did always have an eye for things being unlocked. I shouldn't be surprised that he noticed it.*

He racked his brain trying to think of a way to get in when Kevran offered his help. *I think you could slip a leaf in through the cracks. It would shave the leaf down, but all you need is a little bit, and you can unlock the window with it from the inside.*

Anthony agreed as that was their only option at the moment. He got a leaf from the bush nearby and went to work. Ashley kept watch, but the area they were in kept them pretty much covered from the outside world. Anthony took his time finding the largest crack in the side of the window that he could. The window was well sealed, but the area where it rolled up offered the best option.

Anthony took a deep breath in and focused his energy. He had been suppressing it as much as he could since he got into town, and he wanted to keep it that way. He broke off just the smallest piece of energy that he could. A single leaf only needed a small amount of energy to begin with. The amount of energy he put in allowed him to move the leaf, but that was it. Anthony positioned the leaf by the crack. He began to move it in with extreme care. The first little bit got in, much to Anthony's pleasure. He began to work it in more, keeping the pace he had set for himself. He was halfway done when Ashley sucked in a sharp breath. The sudden sound caused Anthony to lose focus for just a second, and the leaf broke in two. He cursed himself for being too careless and turned to Ashley. She had her mouth covered as a trito drove away.

She looked embarrassed as she uncovered her mouth. "I'm so sorry, but I wasn't paying attention to the road, and when I looked over, I saw that trito. It startled me so much I forgot to stay quiet."

Anthony sighed and gave a half smile. "It's fine. I've got enough of the leaf in there, so I can still manage."

He turned his focus back to the half leaf sitting on the floor. He reached out with his energy and brought it up to the locks. They were simple flick locks and in no time at all he had managed to unlock the window. He dropped the leaf and hid his power. He had used it for too long as it was. With how many Zankrex were in this town he didn't want to use any more power than was necessary.

He opened the window and stepped in. He helped Ashley in as well and then shut the window. They stayed quiet for several seconds. Anthony had figured that everyone would be away, but with the garage door down, he had no way of knowing if someone was home or not.

After several heart-pounding seconds, he let out a sigh. "I don't think anyone is home. And at the very least, no one has noticed my power. Or if they have, they aren't acting right now. Either way, we need to move fast. I came here to set up a base of operations, but making it here in the house would be far too dangerous."

Ashley nodded. "I thought so. It seemed weird to me that we would be trying to stay in the same house as your family that had been turned."

Anthony nodded. "And I would like to not get them involved if possible. If Lance was correct about Shane, then the last thing we need is for him to know about my family. As of now, I don't think there is anyone who knows who I am besides Hannah. If she's still here, then we may have a problem. But even then, as long as they don't know I'm in the city, then we should be fine."

Ashley nodded in understanding. "What do we need to grab?"

Anthony thought it over. "Food would be nice, of course, but it would have to be small things that wouldn't be missed. Also, we should grab some clothes from my room, so we have some things to keep warm when we make camp outside."

Ashley nodded in confirmation and began to scrounge around the room. She grabbed a sweater and something else before she looked up to see Anthony standing frozen.

Ashley looked at him in confusion. "What's the deal, Anthony?"

She turned to see what he was looking at and froze as well.

There, standing in the doorway, was Anthony's mother.

Anthony couldn't move. Too many emotions were flowing through him for him to make a decision. Of course, he was happy and relieved that his mother was alive. But on the other hand, he was alert and distraught because the bright-red eyes made it obvious that she had already been taken over. He had no idea how to handle this situation. She wasn't making any moves toward him, which only made him more confused.

I know she isn't a full-fledge Zankrex. If she was, there would be far more energy emanating from her. But even then, she should have some sort of orders to turn in any Divine Blades that they run into. What is she going to do?

Kevran was just as lost as Anthony was. He could only hold his breath and hope that everything would work out well.

Anthony's mom continued to smile. "Is there anything I can help you with, dear? And who is this girl you brought home?" She took a step forward, and Anthony took a quick step back. Anthony's mother looked at him strange.

Anthony decided to not dodge around the subject. "Mom, you know I'm different from you, right?"

Anthony's mother stood there in thought for a while before nodding her head. "Yes, I knew it when I walked in, though I already knew that you were a Divine Blade. We were told to turn you or any like you in as soon as we saw you."

Anthony got real tense. "And did you?"

Anthony's mother's face contorted in confusion, almost as if she were battling within herself for something. "No, I haven't yet. Though I have this amazing urge to do so right now."

Anthony nodded as he motioned for Ashley to move behind him. As she moved, Anthony questioned further. "You said yet? Does that mean you still will?"

Anthony's mother looked at him with worry in her eyes. "I may. The higher-ups said that the Divine Blades and the rebels were dangerous and out of control. They said that they've killed many soldiers that are trying to keep the peace and even more innocent civilians. Anthony, you aren't a part of that, are you?"

Anthony couldn't answer right away. *Darn them for spinning it like that. Now, if I tell her that I am, she'll feel there's no other option than to call the Zankrex.*

Kevran agreed. *I do not like lying, but it may be necessary here, though I did not expect this to happen.*

Anthony could only question what he meant, and Kevran was quick to explain, *The Zankrex hold over regular humans is supposed to be complete, so much so that even parents will obey an order to kill their children. But here, your mother stands disobeying what she has been told to do. I have no idea how you should handle this.*

Anthony mulled it over as his mother waited for a response. It wasn't an easy conclusion to come to, but he knew what he had to do.

Kevran seemed less than optimistic about the idea. *It is your call, but be ready to face the consequences if it does not go like you planned it.*

Anthony nodded and looked straight at his mother. "Mom, I am part of the Divine Blades, and I have killed those soldiers."

The room was filled with silence for a second as Anthony took a pause.

He was quick to continue, not wanting his mother to say anything until he had said everything that he wanted to say. "I have killed those men, but not without reason. I never sought out any conflict. They would always attack me first with no intentions of taking me prisoner."

Anthony's mother remained calm, the words of her son bouncing around in her head. She stared him down with discerning eyes as she asked him one question. "Why are you being attacked all the time?"

Anthony let out his breath as he thought about how to answer her.

Kevran was quick to step aside. *I am going to leave this up to you. I do not know your mother well enough to help you. Only you can say the right thing here.*

Anthony was grateful for the confidence and began to piece together his answer. "I don't want to get you into any trouble, so I can't tell you why."

Anthony's mom nodded her head as if she had expected him to say that. "You're saying I should go against the officials who tell me everything and trust you who won't tell me anything?"

Anthony couldn't help but chuckle. "When you put it that way, it sounds a lot worse. I understand that this seems sketchy and weird, but you have to trust me on this. Something isn't right with the way things are now, and I'm fighting to fix that and make it better. Please, Mom, you have to believe me."

Anthony could only look at his mother with pleading eyes as he waited for her response. She continued to ponder the situation. Seconds ticked by as everyone in the room waited for the outcome.

In a moment, Anthony's mother looked up and smiled. "How could I not trust my eldest son? Fine, I won't tell the authorities about this."

Anthony released all of his pent-up breath and smiled wide. He walked over and hugged her. "Thank you, Mom. I promise you won't regret this."

Anthony's mom hugged him back and then focused on Ashley. "Now, who is this cute girl that was alone with my son in his room?"

Anthony ignored the remark and motioned for Ashley to come over. "This is Ashley. She helped me escape from the … authorities, and so now they want her too. She's traveling with me until we can find a safe place for her to stay."

Ashley smiled and shook Anthony's mother's hand. "It's a pleasure to meet you, Mrs. Multan."

Anthony's mother shook her hand back and smiled. "Oh please, call me Judy. And it is a pleasure to meet you too. I guess I should thank you for saving my son."

Ashley lowered her head. "Oh no, it was nothing, at least not compared to how he helped me."

Anthony couldn't help but feel awkward as he knew that she was referring to the shrine. And it was obvious that Ashley also felt a tad awkward as she wondered if she should have even brought it up. But Judy seemed to sense that it was a sore topic and looked past it.

"Now, I know that I have welcomed you in with open arms, but I'm not real sure about your father. A week or two ago, we had officials come to our house asking about you. They said you were a wanted fugitive and an enemy of the state. We had no idea where you were at the time, so we were of no help to them. After they left, we had a hard time figuring out how to take that news. I have decided to look past it and trust you. I had decided that a while ago, but your father is still thinking about it. Or if he came to a conclusion, then I have no idea what it is."

Anthony nodded. Dad had always been a little more straitlaced than his mother had been. If anyone was going to rat him out just based on principle, then it would be his dad.

We should prepare to leave now so that if the worst happens with him, then we can jet.

Kevran agreed.

Anthony turned to his mother. "When is Dad going to be home?"

She thought about it for a second. "I believe that he will be back in around five hours. But I can't be sure of that."

215

Anthony nodded and turned to Ashley. "Let's prepare like we are going to leave. That way, if things go south with my dad, then we can jet real quick without having to get our stuff together."

Ashley nodded. "That seems like a sound plan, but can that include a shower? I think we both need it right now."

Anthony looked at his clothes hard for the first time in a while. His pants had dirt and mud all over them, and his blue pullover was in no better shape. His gloves were fine except for sweat, as was his hat.

Anthony conceded. "All right, I guess we can do that."

Judy chimed in as well, "I can also clean your clothes if you want me to."

Anthony was going to think about it, but Ashley gave him no time. "Yes, please, that would be wonderful."

Judy smiled and headed downstairs.

Anthony sighed and looked around his room. "Let's get a backpack and fill it with hoodies and water containers, maybe some food items, but food has never been a real problem. If we head any farther north, then the hoodies will be a welcome item."

Ashley nodded. "That sounds like a good plan, but you can go ahead and get all that put together. I'm going to take a nice, long shower."

She turned around and headed off before Anthony could even argue. He sighed and began to rummage around his room.

Anthony had never waited on a girl to get out of a shower before, much less one who hadn't showered in a while. He learned real quick that time had little meaning for Ashley while she was in the shower.

It took Anthony all of ten minutes to pack a backpack filled with hoodies and various other cold-weather gear for him and Ashley. He also packed canteens and a knife. He didn't figure on needing the knife, but if Ashley was alone, he wanted her to have protection of some sort. In the ten minutes, he also changed into some sweatpants so his mother could wash his clothes. She had said that she would call him down when they were done, so Anthony spent the next thirty or so minutes walking around his room and rummaging through various things.

He found his way to the wooden sword that he had used to spar before he won the nice one that was still in his locker at school. He stared at the wooden sword in fondness. Many training sessions and severe beatdowns were attached to that sword. Clancy had given it to him at a young age when he first talked about wanting to learn how to sword fight.

Remembering Clancy brought him close to tears. It had been a while since he had thought about him. He couldn't help but bring up the image of Clancy the way he had seen him last: bloodied and dying on the gym floor.

Anthony shook his head and sent the image scattering. *I can't think about that. Clancy is fine. He's imprisoned, but he's alive. I have to believe that.*

Anthony could feel Kevran sending him comforting vibes. He was thankful for that much. Words weren't necessary about that subject. They had already said everything that needed to be said.

It doesn't matter how long it takes, Anthony thought. *I'll find him, and then I'll rescue him. It's as simple as that. Then we will go and fight with the others from the academy.*

Anthony nodded, feeling more self-assured, when a knock at his door snapped him back to reality. He spun around to find Ashley poking her head around the doorframe.

"What's up?" Anthony asked.

Ashley looked around the room then back up to Anthony. "Do you have anything to wear?"

Anthony furrowed his brow. "What happened to your clothes?" he asked while walking over to her.

She shrunk back. "Don't come over here," she shouted.

Anthony stopped, still confused.

Ashley's breathed a sigh and then shot him a stern look. "Of course, I don't have any clothes. Your mom took them to wash them. All I have is this towel on. I would appreciate it if you would throw me some clothes."

Anthony blushed at the realization of what he almost saw. He stood around with a stupid look on his face before snapping out of it and throwing her a pair of athletic shorts and a hoodie.

She took them and stared daggers at Anthony. "Don't you dare try and peek."

Anthony's face turned an even brighter shade of red as he shook his head and turned around. "I would never dream of such a thing." His thoughts betrayed him, but he stayed put until she walked back in.

"I'm decent," she declared.

Anthony turned around.

Ashley looked down out of embarrassment. "Thanks for the clothes."

Anthony mumbled something of an acknowledgement, but he was far too enthralled by Ashley. He had spent almost a week with her, and she had always worn the same thing. But seeing her in his clothing was almost more than he could handle.

This is why my friends always had their girlfriends wear their hoodies. It makes perfect sense now.

Ashley noticed that Anthony was staring. Her face burned red as she threw the towel she had in her hand in Anthony's face. "A-anyway, you should take a shower. You really stink."

"O-okay," Anthony stuttered. He walked out of his room and into the shower.

The warm water cascaded down Anthony's back as he stared at the ceiling. He hadn't wanted to take a long shower as he knew that time was of the essence, but the warmth of the water made him change his mind. He hadn't felt this warm since he left Kevran's cavern. His whole body let go of the tension that it had been carrying for almost two weeks.

It hit Anthony just how long it had been since he had started this journey. *It doesn't seem but two days ago that the Zankrex were first attacking, but two weeks have passed. I've really come a long way since that point.*

Kevran agreed. *The amount of progress you have made in such a short amount of time has been unbelievable. When we started, you could not even hold a leaf up while you ran. Now you can manipulate a tree full of leaves while fighting against Zankrex generals. At this rate, Tertalla will be saved in no time.*

Anthony smiled at Kevran's praise. He was right, of course. He wasn't pathetic, but his ability to use his power in battle was lackluster, to say the least. But thanks to Kevran, his progress had been exceptional.

I can't take all the credit. Your teaching technique is amazing. All the trials and exercises you made me do honed my skills in a way I could have never achieved on my own. Thank you so much for that.

Kevran conveyed his thanks while trying to hold back his pride. Anthony could feel it, though, and smiled at his feeble attempt to be humble. But Anthony became solemn again as his thoughts turned to Ashley. He tried to shake her out, but he found that she just wouldn't leave. *I don't understand it, Kevran. Before now, I had no trouble keeping focused on the goal. But now my mind keeps slipping to … other things.*

Kevran smirked. *You mean Ashley?*

Anthony blushed and looked down. Even though Kevran wasn't there, he felt like he still had to avoid his gaze.

She's a wonderful girl who's smart and handy. In normal circumstances, she would be the girl that I wouldn't be brave enough to say anything to. This journey has put us alone for pretty much the entire trip, yet I never felt self-conscious or nervous. Why is it now that my mind is wandering toward her?

Kevran chuckled, amused by Anthony's struggle. *I would say it is obvious. Now that we are out of danger, you feel like you have a chance to make something romantic happen. Of course, you are attracted to her. She is beautiful and has proven to be very capable on her own. If you want to get her out of your head, then you need to start focusing on the mission at hand and the greater goal. Start thinking now on how you plan to get to and investigate the school while it is under Zankrex hold. And if that is not enough, then think about this: you are not strong enough yet to take on the Zankrex king.*

That caught Anthony's attention. *What do you mean I'm not strong enough? I thought you said that I was the greatest power on Tertalla?*

Kevran was quick to say otherwise. *I did not mean that you are currently the strongest. I meant that you are capable of becoming the strongest. The Zankrex king holds the source of all Onigor. He has been alive for several millennia now and has had far longer to hone his skills. You have only had your power for two weeks now. You could never hope to beat him at this point. That is why I have been a proponent of you finding the other Divine Blades. The quest to find them gives me more time to train you and will put you in situations where you can grow. Not to mention that unifying the remaining Divine Blades would be a good idea regardless. An army behind you will only help in beating the king.*

Anthony nodded. His paradigm of the world had been shifted. The task ahead had just become more daunting. He would have to train a lot more if he wanted to save everyone. Yet the knowledge of a powerful foe did nothing to curb his determination. Thinking of an all-powerful evil being sitting on the throne made his blood boil.

He couldn't help but smile at his newfound determination. *Thanks, Kevran. I'll focus on making it a peaceful world that I can sit around being awkward with Ashley in. But until that point, I don't have the luxury of thinking about it too hard.*

Kevran chuckled. *Though, I do not think you should give up on it, not that I think you will anyway. Having a girl to fight for will only make you stronger. And if you do not think about how to interact with her, you will do it just fine on your own. Focus on your goal and enjoy her company. You can balance both.*

Anthony was about to retort when a sharp knock at the door brought him out of the conversation.

"Anthony, don't take forever in there, okay? I would like some hot water to myself when I shower later tonight. Also, your clothes are out of the dryer."

Anthony reached for the soap and got on with his shower. "Thanks, Mom, I'll be out soon."

Anthony walked out of the bathroom clad in a towel. Ashley was sitting on the couch in the room outside Anthony's room. She had already gotten dressed and was flicking through channels on the TV. Anthony snuck behind her and slipped into his room, closing the door behind him. His clothes were folded on his bed in a neat pile. Anthony changed into his now clean clothes and walked back out of his room. He sat on the other side of the large couch and watched what Ashley had on at the moment. It was a news program. They were on the tail end of a discussion about some sports team when the story switched over.

The head anchor looked at his papers before looking back up at the camera. "We now switch over to a story that had been developing for the last two weeks. For those of you that don't know, there have been a string of attacks on our peaceful land by radical revolutionists that appear to oppose the current world government. Nothing of any serious nature has occurred, but minor skirmishes have led to multiple deaths on both sides. We now go to our correspondent in the field."

The screen cut away to a man standing in front of the shrine at Wishitak. Ashley and Anthony perked up and leaned in.

"Thank you, Dave. I am standing in front of an ancient shrine here in the town of Wishitak. This shrine was the scene of a massacre a little less than a week ago. This story is just now being released as officials have kept it hidden to get everything under control. According to sources, two revolutionists stormed the shrine and locked themselves in for a time. They emerged some time later, killing several officers before making their escape in a Snaudi trito. The trito was found days later abandoned. The police have no leads as to where they could be but urge citizens to report anything unusual as soon as possible to the local authorities. It is also unknown why the revolutionists broke into the shrine in the first place. Back to you, Dave."

The screen cut back to the anchor who was wearing a very serious face. "It is tragic to think about the lost lives of those brave officers. We keep their families in our thoughts and also pray for the quick capture of these horrible people who only seem to want to destroy our peaceful lives."

Anthony switched the TV off and lay back on the couch. Ashley looked over at him in concern.

Anthony sighed and rubbed his eyes. "The Zankrex have taken on the mantel as the police, huh? I guess that makes sense, but it doesn't make things any easier."

Ashley stood up and stretched out. "Yeah, kinda makes you wonder if we are doing the right thing."

Anthony remained silent, allowing Ashley to look at him and smile.

"I don't mean it like that, of course. I trust you, and I also believe that you are doing the right thing. You have seen a side of them that I have never seen. But it's just tough for me to hate them after seeing them mourn their dead like that. It also doesn't help that everyone looks so peaceful."

Anthony looked up and smiled. "I really hope that you keep that outlook, Ashley." Ashley looked at him in confusion as he continued, "'Cause to change your mind would require you to see their evil side. And that's not an experience that I want you to have. For your sake, I hope you never find a reason to hate them."

An odd silence filled the room. Neither one knew how to follow that up. The silence was shattered by Judy running up the stairs. By the time she made it to the room, Anthony was already up on his feet.

"We have a problem," Judy said. "Officers are coming door to door and searching houses. And we're the next house."

Anthony didn't panic. His mind raced with possible options on how to avoid this when his mother continued, "This is a lot worse than you think. They will probably search the house, and I have to tell them everything I know. I'm not sure how you plan to get out of this one."

Ashley looked up at Anthony. She didn't panic or look overly concerned. In her eyes, Anthony could tell she trusted him. She was waiting for him to think of something.

Anthony scratched his chin and thought, *The Onigor in mother will make her tell the Zankrex where we are. Trying to leave the house would just result in us getting caught. It would be nice to hide here in the house and hope they don't do a rigorous search.*

Anthony's face lit up. Ashley breathed a sigh of relief. "You thought of something?" she asked.

Anthony nodded and turned to his mother. "If you know where we are and they ask you, then you will have to answer them, won't you?"

Judy nodded her head.

Anthony smiled. "In that case, Mother, I'm going to go hide somewhere in this world."

Both the women looked at him like he was an idiot.

"I don't get it," Ashley said.

Anthony waggled his finger at the both of them. "Mother, you are going to go downstairs and wait for the officers to show up. By that time, I will have found a place to hide somewhere on this planet. I may hide in this town. I may hide in the next town. I may hide here. I don't know yet. And since I don't know where I'm going to be in two minutes, then I know for sure that you won't know where I am in two minutes."

Ashley didn't seem to follow along, but Judy's face had already lit up in understanding.

"I still don't understand," Ashley said, scratching her head.

Judy smiled. "It's a stupid plan, I'll give you that. But it just might work. If all they ask me is if I know where you are, then I'll be able to say no. But that's hoping for an awful lot. If they start asking more serious questions, then I may not be able to dodge around them."

Anthony nodded. "I understand. I'll think of a backup plan before then. For now, just go downstairs and wait."

Judy nodded and headed downstairs.

Ashley looked over at Anthony. "It seems weird that that would be a loophole. But if both of you are confident in it, then I guess I'll have to go along with it. Where are we hiding?"

Anthony waited for a moment to be sure his mother was well out of earshot before motioning for her to come over to a cubbyhole. He got down on his knees and opened the small door and crawled in. When Ashley had crawled in, he muffled the door closing so that his mother would be as ignorant as possible. He stood up and rummaged around in the dark.

"Where are you taking us?" Ashley whispered.

"Just wait." Anthony grunted as he stretched out and moved a board in the wall. "There is a little passage way here that only I and my brother know about. It leads to a crawl space in the ceiling. I doubt we will be found here. Now let me boost you up. When you get up there, you will be able to crawl in a ways before it stops."

"Okay," Ashley said.

She stood up and stepped on Anthony's hands. He boosted her up far enough for her to slither her way into the crawl space. The space wasn't much more than two feet high. She could only belly-crawl, and the dust made that a bit tough. She held in a sneeze and crawled forward until she couldn't anymore. The area was pitch-black and quite unnerving for her. She wasn't claustrophobic by any means, but it was still tough for her. She heard the sounds of what she could only guess were Anthony sliding into the crawl space. The sound of a board being put into place let her know that they were entirely closed in. She tried not to freak out, but their current predicament was making it difficult. The situation as a whole was rather intense, and the close quarters weren't making it any easier.

She was close to hyperventilating when she felt a hand grasp her own.

Anthony sidled up close and whispered in her ear, "Don't worry, we are going to be just fine."

A wave of calm washed over her. She was glad for the dark in that instance as she knew she was blushing hard. Thoughts started to fill her head about Anthony as she could only focus on his hand and his presence so close to her.

She realized what she was thinking and dashed the thoughts. *I can't be thinking like that now*, she thought to herself.

Then they waited for what seemed like an eternity. No sound could be heard. She hadn't noticed it when she had crawled in, but there was a pinprick of light shining in. It appeared to be a spot where the ceiling fan had been installed. Anthony had positioned himself over it to see out in the room.

The silence was broken by a knock at the door.

The silence that followed the knock at the door was maddening. It seemed to take his mother forever to get there. After what seemed like ages, they heard Judy's footsteps walking toward the door. She reached the door and unlocked the dead bolt and opened the door. Three men stood on the porch.

The first tipped his hat to her. "Good evening, ma'am. We are with the police, and we would like to ask you about something."

Judy nodded her head, and the officers continued, "Have you heard about the rumors that a member of the radicals that have been terrorizing the world has come here?"

Judy shook her head. "No, I haven't heard those rumors."

The police officer smiled. "Understandable, ma'am, as they are new rumors. But in any case, we believe there may be a shred of truth in them, so we are going around seeing if anyone is holding the members in their house. Are you hiding any members or suspicious people in your house?"

Judy shook her head.

The officer continued, "Do you know where members would be hiding if they were here in Murffana?"

Judy once again shook her head. The officer nodded and jotted down something on his notepad.

He looked up at her once again. "Now, ma'am, if you would be so kind, we would like to search your house."

Judy looked at them in confusion. "Well, of course you can, but do you not believe me?"

The officer walked into the house and waved his hand dismissively. "Of course, we believe you are telling the truth. But there have been reports that the members have snuck into houses without the owners knowing about it. And seeing as you are alone right now, your house would be the perfect one to sneak into."

Judy nodded, starting to feel a little worried.

The officer seemed to take notice of this and turned toward her. "You don't look so good, ma'am. Is it possible you were lying to us, after all?"

Judy hid her shock and looked up. "No, no, that's not it at all. It's just the thought of one of those evil people having snuck into my house right under my nose makes me sick."

The officer stared at her for several seconds while the other two officers began to rummage around the house. He smiled at her and put a comforting hand on her shoulder. "Don't worry, ma'am, we won't let anything bad happen to you."

She smiled at him as he turned back to help the other two officers look around the house. They were thorough in their search of the house. They swept every nook and cranny of the downstairs in record time. After they finished, they began to walk upstairs. Anthony and Ashley heard them coming up and almost forgot to breathe as they came into the main room. There, Anthony got his first look at the Zankrex. The two in the back were huge. They were muscular and easily six foot ten. But it was the guy in the front that really caught his attention. He was almost two inches smaller than Anthony was, but that wasn't the shocking thing. He was paler than the other two, as if he were suffering from an illness. His thin black hair hung over his eyes. His body was tiny, and his large coat and uniform made it tough to see any muscle. His face was the only contradiction on him.

His eyes were bright with life.

They were the eyes of a man who was powerful and knew what he was doing. And his smile was confident and smug. It was the face of a man who was tested and proven. The two behind him were his underlings. They saw him as the alpha and were quick to stop behind him and waited for him to make moves. He pointed in different directions, and the two got to work. They examined every place they could. At one point, one of them crawled into the cubbyhole. After he lost sight of him, all he could do was wait and hope that he didn't check the board. A tense few seconds passed before the guy crawled back out of the cubbyhole and gave the all-clear sign. They rummaged around the upstairs a bit longer before reconvening.

"Well, ma'am, it seems that this home is free of unwanted guests."

Judy breathed a sigh of relief. "That's good to hear. I was worried that one of those evil men were in my house while I was alone."

The leader smiled and shook her hand. "Well, that does it here. We will be leaving now. And if you see anything suspicious or see anyone out of the ordinary, then please be sure to contact me."

Judy nodded. "May I please get the name of the brave man who is protecting us?"

The leader smiled and did a half bow. "But, of course, madam. My name is General Shane."

Chapter 14

EMOTIONS

*A*nthony's eyes widened at the revelation of the man's name. *That's Shane? Kevran, isn't that the guy that Lance warned us about?*

Kevran nodded his head. *Yes, that is the name. Though it is tough to believe that man is him. Lance seemed to be worried about his capabilities. There is more there than meets the eye.*

Anthony agreed. He continued to wait as Shane and his goons walked out of the house, bidding one final goodbye to Judy. He waited several seconds after the door closed before he made any move.

Ashley looked over at him. "Can we get out of here now? This place sucks."

Anthony cracked a smile and nodded. "Yeah, this place isn't the best. But it was the greatest hiding spot I ever found."

He slid his way over to the exit and moved the board. He turned himself around and slid out feet first. After he was out, he helped Ashley down and put the board back in place. They exited the cubbyhole and flopped on the couch.

Ashley gave out a satisfying sigh. "I hope that's the last time I have to be in a cramped space like that. I think that gave me claustrophobia."

Anthony chuckled. "Yeah, I haven't been up there since I was a kid. I have fonder memories of it back then than I do now."

Ashley smiled. "That makes sense, I guess, considering that you were smaller back then."

228

Anthony shrugged his shoulders. "Well, either way, I agree with you. I don't think I'll be going back up there anytime soon."

They sat in silence for a little while, letting the sun and open space act as therapy against the tight space they were just in.

Anthony's mind continued to stay on Shane. *Kevran, I couldn't feel any energy from him like I could from the other two.*

Kevran thought it over. *Neither could I, but that makes sense. If Shane is on the same level as Lance, then it makes sense that he could hide his energy as well. The other two did not have that skill.*

Anthony understood, though it still didn't ease his worry. *An enemy that you know nothing about is a terrifying enemy indeed.*

Kevran chuckled in agreement.

Ashley looked over at Anthony. "Hey, that guy said he was Shane. Do you think that it was the same Shane that Lance was telling us about?"

Anthony shrugged his shoulders. "There's no way to be sure, but I would be willing to bet that that was him."

"Are you guys talking about Shane?"

Anthony and Ashley turned around to see Judy standing in the doorway.

"This was the first time I've seen him, but they say he is the head of police here in Murffana. He has brought many of the revolutionaries to justice and is seen as one of the strongest men in this area."

Anthony nodded. "Then that's the Shane that we've been hearing about also."

A weird silence enveloped the room. Anthony could tell that his mother was still having a hard time understanding why her son was a part of this so-called revolutionist movement.

Anthony smiled at his mother. "Don't worry, I'm not here to disturb the peace or hurt anyone. I'm just here to get information and then be on my way. I won't cause a ruckus."

Judy smiled, still not feeling at ease. But she appreciated her son's efforts to calm her down.

Anthony looked out the window and sighed. "Now all that's left is to wait for Dad and James to get back home."

Anthony and Ashley waited patiently in the upstairs room. They didn't want to venture downstairs as there were more windows there. That, and if someone knocked on the door, they would have less time to hide, so they stayed upstairs. They would shift every now and again from the family room to Anthony's room. They also managed to keep themselves occupied by talking about various things. Anthony's mom came up at one point with a family album and proceeded to embarrass Anthony. Ashley began to feel more at ease as well. She was hesitant at first at the thought of meeting Anthony's family, but she got over it as Anthony's mother made her feel right at home.

The three of them were laughing at a funny picture of James when the sound of a trito pulling into the garage cut them off. Anthony took a deep breath and stood up.

Judy was quick to stand up as well and turned to Anthony. "I'll bring him upstairs, but you're going to have to do the convincing."

Anthony nodded, and Judy walked downstairs.

Anthony's dad was hanging up his coat when Judy greeted him. "Hello, dear, how was work?"

Anthony's dad rolled his eyes. Classes were in full swing at the university, and so were his problems. "Things could always get better, but I don't have a good feeling about my class this time around."

Judy nodded. "That's always how it is with you."

An awkward silence followed as she didn't know how to segue into getting him upstairs. Her hesitance must have been obvious as Anthony's dad gave her questioning look. "Is something the matter?"

Judy sighed and nodded. "There's something upstairs that you have to see."

Anthony's dad gave her a concerned look but followed her up the steps. As he turned the corner, his eyes widened in surprise.

Anthony stood in the doorway. "Hey, Dad," he said with a half-smile.

Anthony's dad just stood there, trying to process what was standing before him.

Anthony didn't give him a chance to saying anything yet as he quickly started talking. "Dad, I know that you know that I'm a part of this revolution, and I know that you were told to turn us in. But please don't. I can't go into all the details, but I'm not an evil person. There's something going on in this world that I have to fix. I don't want to hurt anybody, but it's necessary to right the wrongs that are happening. Please just believe me and don't say anything."

Anthony had said all of that almost as fast as he could. He was far too nervous about what his father would say and had spoken a lot faster than he had intended. His father had always been a big rules person. If there was anyone in this world that would go to the police about him, he was almost sure it would be his dad.

"Okay," his dad said.

Anthony's mind stopped racing as he looked up at his father. He was smiling at him. Anthony shook his head, trying to clear it. "What?" he asked.

"I said okay. I won't tell the police about you."

Anthony could hardly believe it. "Just like that? I don't have to explain anymore? But haven't you heard all these horrible things about me?"

Anthony's dad laughed. "Well, gosh, it sounds to me like you almost want me to turn you in. I said okay because you are my son. You say that there is something that needs to be fixed, then I'll believe you. Of course, I can't support you in your endeavors, but I can keep quiet about this."

Anthony paused for a bit, almost as if he was waiting for his dad to say "gotcha!" and call the police. But as he waited, his father's smile never changed.

Anthony breathed a sigh of relief and ran up and hugged him. "Thank you, Dad. I promise I won't cause you any trouble. I just need to look into something, and then I'll be gone."

Anthony's dad chuckled and hugged him back. After a time, they disengaged. Anthony's dad looked past and saw Ashley. He gave Anthony a knowing look and gave him a soft punch on the arm. "Well, well, I see that running from the police hasn't stopped you from finding a pretty lady."

Ashley and Anthony both blushed. "It's not like that, Dad. Ashley was just someone that got caught up with me, and now the police think she is part of our group. Though she did help me escape from somewhere, so I guess she is part of things now."

Anthony's dad walked over and shook Ashley's hand. "If you helped save my son, then I guess you and I can be friends."

Ashley smiled. "It wasn't that big of a deal, Mr. Multan."

Anthony's dad raised his hand and stopped Ashley. "Please, call me Vincent."

Ashley seemed hesitant but nodded all the same. The room was filled with a nice atmosphere as everyone was getting along.

But before they could change the topic, a voice broke the silence. "What's going on here?"

Everyone turned around to see James standing in the hall.

James was confused. He had heard it from the officer himself that Anthony was part of a revolutionist group that was harming people and bringing chaos. He didn't want to believe it, of course, but the evidence was overwhelming. Now his brother stood with his mother and his father, and they all looked like they were having a great time. He just couldn't understand it. Anthony could tell that James was struggling with himself.

He walked up. "James, I understand what you have heard about me. And I'm not going to say that it didn't happen. The stories of my actions are true, but please understand that the motive behind them was different. There is something very wrong going on, and I'm fighting to fix it. I can't tell you what it is because you would be drawn into this mess with me. All I can ask of you is to trust me."

James didn't know what to think. His mind was swimming with all sorts of emotions. He wanted to believe his brother, but all logic was telling him not to. The struggle was giving him a headache. He turned and walked into his room. Anthony wanted to go after him, but his father stopped him.

Anthony turned back to see his dad shaking his head. "Give him time. He was the one that took the news about you the hardest. I think he will come around, but you will need to give him time."

Anthony looked back at his brother's room. The light was off, and no sound came from within.

Anthony sighed and nodded his head. "All right, I'll give him time."

Vincent gave a half smile and patted his son on the back.

The rest of the time spent before dinner was awkward. Anthony didn't know what to do after the incident with James. He elected to sit in his room and talk with Ashley. They talked about nothing important, but Ashley was determined to keep Anthony's mind off James. She was concerned about him. She had spent almost a week with Anthony, and in that time, she felt that she had gotten to know him. With all they had been through, he had always managed to stay upbeat. She could only remember two incidents where she saw him downcast: the night after the shrine and after failing his training session. During those times, Anthony's face was always full of grief or anger. This was the first time that Ashley had seen this face of Anthony's.

It was that of rejection.

He must love his brother if he's that depressed about being rejected by him.

She did everything she could to distract him. They talked about the town and Anthony's schools before starting in the Divine Blade program. Sometimes they would go out to the family room and watch some more television. Nothing was ever on, and every news program only brought more depressing things about how everyone hated him. Soon Ashley had run out of conversation topics, and a heavy silence fell on the room. It was obvious that Anthony's mind was still concentrating on James.

Ashley let out a sigh and decided to stop avoiding it. "Tell me about James."

Anthony looked up in surprise, having been brought out of his deep thought. "What?" he asked.

She smiled and rolled closer. She was sitting on his computer chair at his desk while Anthony himself had been lying on his bed.

"Tell me about James. You never talked about him on our way here, or any of your family for that matter. Tell me about them."

Anthony sighed and lay back down. "What's the point of talking? You're going to figure out about them one way or the other while we are here."

Ashley continued to stare at Anthony. "And I'm sure I'll come to my own conclusions about them. But for now, I want to hear what you think of them."

Anthony continued to lay there, and Ashley continued to stare. Anthony soon relented and sat up. He crossed his legs and looked up at the ceiling as he thought about it. "Well, you've already been around my mother enough to understand what she is like. She's always been so kind over the years. She was the one that would always spoil my brother and me. If there was something that we wanted, we would talk to Mom about it. But she was the one that got onto me about practicing my swordplay. Even though she never coached it herself, she always took an interest in my competitions. My dad was into it as well, but my mom was the more aggressive one when it came to the actual tournaments. But I love her a lot. She's always worried about me no matter where I go. If there's an accident around where she thinks I am, then I'll get a call asking if I'm okay."

Ashley laughed. "She sounds like a wonderful mother."

Anthony smiled. "Yeah, she is."

"What about your dad?" Ashley asked.

Anthony continued to smile. "My dad was the one that guided me the most. I think I am the way I am because of him. He was always there for me and always understanding when I messed up. He was the one that punished me, but he was also the one to come in after and talk to me about it. He always seemed to know what to say when I was having problems. That's not to say everything he said was perfect, but he always gave it a shot. He was also into my swordplay competitions. Even when I would screw up and lose, he would always say he was proud of me. My mother would be the one to get on to me the most about it, so I think he forced himself to be the one who said he was proud. Of course, he meant it, and I was always thankful."

Ashley chuckled. "It's funny to hear that your mother was that into your sword competitions."

Anthony also chuckled. "*Into them* isn't the right word. Either way, she was very vocal. Early on, when I would lose a lot, she would berate me in the car ride home to the point that I would start crying."

Ashley's eyes widened in shock as she tried to keep herself from laughing. "Your mother would make you cry after you lost a match?"

Anthony nodded. "She was rather scary back in the day. She says it was because she was frustrated by the fact that I wasn't fighting to the full extent that she thought I could. She was right, of course, as I was one of the best in the sport during high school, but it's still something that the family likes to joke about every now and again."

Ashley shook her head in amazement. "That's too funny."

Anthony nodded. The room got quiet again.

Ashley hesitated before asking, "And what about James?"

Anthony's smile faded.

He looked out the window and let out a long breath. "James is one of the people I am closest to. Being my younger brother, of course, means that we grew up together, but it goes beyond that. We've always gotten along so well. Our personalities couldn't be more different, and yet we always seem to find a way to get along. Of course, we fought over the years, and we still do. But we always get past it. We grew up liking the same things, so I feel like that helped. But even without those things, I would still be close to him. He's my brother, for goodness' sake."

Ashley half-smiled. "That's why this thing is bugging you so much with James."

Anthony nodded. "I'm terrified that we won't be able to go back to the way things were. That somehow I'm going to lose them."

Anthony began to tear up and was quick to wipe them away. Ashley was surprised to see tears in his eyes. She put a comforting hand on his arm. "It's okay. We are going to figure this out. I'm sure that soon your brother will come out of there and accept you again. And you will fix this. You will stop the Zankrex king and bring everything back to normal. And when that day comes, I look forward to meeting your normal parents."

Anthony smiled and put his hand on her hand. "Thank you, Ashley."

They stayed like that for a while, just sharing in the reassurance that Ashley had brought out. A sudden knock at the door tore them out of the moment.

Anthony's mother poked her head out and gave a knowing smile. "My, my, look at you two. Sorry to interrupt your little moment, but dinner is ready."

Their faces became beet read as they yanked their hands back. Anthony jumped up and walked out of the door, feeling just a little bit better.

Dinner was silent. They ate downstairs, which had been a concern for Anthony. All the windows were blocked off by the blinds, so he felt a tad safer, but he stayed on his toes in case something happened. His mother and father sat opposite of him and Ashley. His parents tried to get conversation going, asking Ashley about herself. She told them, trying hard to avoid any details connected to Zankrex. Anthony couldn't get into the conversation. The food was good, as they were having hamburgers, but he just didn't feel like eating. He nibbled on a few things, but for the most part, he just stayed in his own thoughts. His parents and Ashley were concerned about this, but none of them knew what to say. Ashley knew that this went beyond just his brother, but even knowing that, she couldn't figure out what to say. James hadn't come down for dinner. His dad had called him down, but he never responded.

After some more silence, Anthony's father let out a sigh. "Look, Anthony, I know you're upset about James and all, but you need to get past this."

Anthony gave a halfhearted smile. "I'm not really upset about that. I'm just lost in thought right now."

Anthony's mother continued to eat, seeming content to let her son figure his own problems out. Anthony's dad wanted to do more but decided against it.

James appeared in the room. Anthony looked up in surprise and caught his eyes. James looked at him long and hard before making a move. He walked over to his spot and picked up the hamburger. He began to walk back to his room but stopped short of the exit.

He paused and then looked back. "Anthony, I don't think I'll be able to talk to you or be around you during this time."

He paused there as Anthony began to deflate more. "But," he continued, "I won't tell anyone that you are here."

With that, he took a bite of his burger and walked back up to his room. Anthony processed what James had just told him and began to brighten up. Soon he looked content, like whatever it was that he was thinking about had vanished. The rest noticed this change and smiled. Peace had been restored in the house.

After dinner was over, they broke off into two groups. Anthony's parents remained downstairs as both of them had work to do for their jobs. Anthony and Ashley went back upstairs to Anthony's room. When they got there, Anthony closed the door and let out a relieved sigh.

Ashley smiled. "Well, it's not full acceptance, but I guess that's all you can ask from James, huh?"

Anthony nodded. "I was just so worried that we were going to have to leave town tonight. I was planning on it at dinner. That's why I was so solemn. I couldn't wait all night for James to make a decision, not when he could have decided the other way and told on us. But now that he said that, I can rest easy tonight."

Ashley nodded and looked around. "Where am I going to sleep?"

Anthony thought about it for a bit. "I guess you'll sleep in my bed tonight."

Ashley's eyes widened, and her face turned red. Anthony noticed her reaction and realized what that sounded like.

He shook his head. "No, no, no, that's not what I meant," he said. "I mean, I'll sleep on the couch in the other room, and you can sleep in my bed."

Ashley realized that, that was obvious and looked down in embarrassment. "Oh, I guess that was obvious."

The two sat there for a while, not knowing how to proceed.

Anthony spoke, "I have some athletic shorts in my closet if you want to sleep in something other than your regular clothes tonight. I also have plenty of shirts in there that you can wear."

Ashley nodded. "I'll do that, thank you."

Anthony nodded and grabbed his own pajamas. He exited the room.

"Good night," he said before closing the door.

Ashley smiled. "Good night."

Anthony stared into the darkness of the family room. He was regretting not taking the bed as it was a thousand times more comfortable than the couch, but he knew that he couldn't do that to a lady. And his bed wasn't big enough for the two of them to sleep separate. An image of them cuddled up on the small bed flashed through his mind before he scattered it.

Wow, this is starting to get annoying.

Kevran chuckled. *What is? The constant thinking that you have been doing about Ashley?*

Anthony nodded. *I know we already talked about this, but I still can't help it. I almost want to leave now so that we won't have any more of these awkward moments.*

Kevran agreed. *Yes, you two almost never had any of those types of moments on the trip here. It must be the house atmosphere. Everything here just seems so normal. It is tough not to get sucked in.*

Anthony nodded. *I noticed that. With all the talk about police as opposed to saying Zankrex and hanging out with my family in my own house. It's not normal, but it feels so far away from troubles we just encountered. I almost need to fight a Zankrex to remind myself what's happening here.*

Kevran half-smiled. *I know how you feel. We should finish everything that we need to do here as soon as possible. The last thing we need is to get dulled by this kind of life. That and the longer we stay, the better the chance is that we get found. And if we get found, then there is no way your family gets off easy.*

Anthony got solemn. *I won't cause them trouble. I've already caused them enough trouble by being a God Sword during this invasion. And yet they fought the power and accepted me.*

Kevran nodded. *I am still amazed by that. I always thought that the hold on the humans would be complete. But I guess it's not strong enough yet. They can still fight it if the right emotions are there.*

Anthony smiled. *I am glad that is the case.*

Kevran changed topics. *I forgot to talk to you about your fight with Lance.*

Anthony wasn't sure why they needed to talk in the first place. *What about it?*

Kevran seemed excited. *You may not have noticed it while so focused on battle, but it did not escape my notice. Lance's energy was lower than the first time you fought him.*

Anthony remembered everything about the first fight. *That means we were right about the moon?*

Kevran confirmed it. *With a larger moon in the sky, Lance had less energy to work with. The moon does indeed affect how much energy a Zankrex possesses, and the larger the moon, the less Onigor they acquire.*

Anthony felt closure on the topic. *Well, that's good to know. Each fight at night is going to get a little easier then.*

Kevran was careful not to get so relaxed. *At least until the next new moon. But for a little while, we should be okay.*

Anthony allowed the new realization to relax him a bit. Tomorrow would bring its own challenges, and he needed to focus on them. *I can't keep my family in danger. I need to get in and out of campus quick tomorrow and then leave as soon as I can.*

Kevran agreed. *That is the best course of action, but you will not be able to function at peak efficiency if you do not get some sleep. Rest now, worry later.*

Anthony didn't need to be told twice. He rolled over and pulled the cover closer. Images of campus raced through his mind until he fell asleep.

Chapter 15

EMPTY

*A*shley's eyes fluttered open. As she rose, she looked around the room. After processing it for a few minutes, she remembered that she had fallen asleep in Anthony's room. She got out from under the covers and stretched out. The sun shone through the cracks in the blinds on the window, illuminating the dust that was floating about the room. The beams somehow made things far more peaceful for her. She let out a content sigh. It had been a while since she had felt this rested. The bed that Anthony had was amazing. She had fallen asleep the moment her head hit the pillow.

Looking at the time, she saw that it was nine o'clock. *I think Anthony's parents said they would be gone by this point. I wonder if Anthony is up yet.*

She walked to the door and cracked it open. She was greeted by Anthony's sleeping face on the couch. She chuckled to herself and was about to walk out to wake him when she saw movement in the other doorway.

She looked over to see James.

He was just standing there looking at his brother. He had a pained look on his face, as if he wanted to say something but just couldn't bring himself to do so. Ashley stood there behind the door wondering what to do. She really wanted to talk to him, but at the same time, she didn't know how he would respond. She shook her head and decided to go for it.

She pulled the door open and whispered, "You care for your brother, don't you?"

James looked up, startled, and then breathed a sigh of relief when he realized who it was. He went back to looking at his brother, taking a while to reply back. "Of course, I care about my brother. What kind of brother would I be if I didn't?"

Ashley walked out in the room. "Why won't you talk to him? You do know that it's hurting him for you to act like this."

James laughed. "Oh, it's hurting him? Try feeling the way that we did when they told us that he had joined the resistance and was killing officers. Don't you think that we felt pretty crummy when the officials came and told us that? And yet he comes back and just expects us to keep quiet about him being here."

Ashley understood where James was coming from. She was on Anthony's side, and even she was questioning why he had to do what he was doing. But she kept her convictions. "You heard what your brother said, didn't you? He has a reason for doing what he is doing. I know that they have told you a different story, but why can't you just consider that maybe he's right?"

James sighed and looked out the window. "Of course, I've considered it. But what reason could there be for killing officers?"

Ashley thought hard. *I can't tell him anything about Zankrex. Anthony wouldn't want me to anyway. And if I do, then they might get dragged into all of this as well. But I have to say something.*

She chose her words with care. "When Anthony found me, I was being chased down by the officials. They were trying to kill me, and I didn't even know why. But Anthony risked his own safety because I said that I was innocent. He trusted me, a complete stranger, so maybe we can trust him. Even if it's just for a little bit."

James looked over at her in confusion. "You're saying that you don't know why you're following him?"

Ashley let out an awkward laugh. "No, I don't know why I'm following him. I just know that he is a good guy. And you should know that too, even more than I do."

James looked pained now. "But they said he killed people. Didn't he kill people?"

Ashley got solemn. "Yes, he did."

James raised his hands in indignation. "Then how am I supposed to trust someone who kills people that are protectors of the people?"

"I don't know either," Ashley said with force.

James was taken aback.

Ashley stared a hole into James. "I don't know how either. But what I do know is that Anthony isn't just a cold, heartless killer. He only killed the officers that where trying to kill us. And after he did it, he stayed up all night regretting and hating himself for doing it. If someone does that after they kill, then they aren't a murderer. Anthony believes in something. He kills because his goal is forcing those people to come for his life. No matter how bad it seems to me, I'm still going to follow him because I trust him."

James was at a loss for words. It was clear that she had managed to throw doubt into his mind. He turned and paused before looking back.

"I have to get back to school," he whispered and walked down the stairs.

Ashley heard the door close, and she didn't relax until she heard his trito drive off down the road.

Ashley sighed and rubbed her eyes. She wasn't used to this much activity right after waking up.

"Thanks for that," Anthony cut in.

Ashley almost hit the ceiling out of surprise. She turned to see Anthony looking at her.

He chuckled and sat up. "Sorry, I didn't mean to scare you."

Ashley clutched her chest as she waited for her heartbeat to return to normal. "No, it's okay. I just thought you were still asleep. How long have you been up?"

Anthony thought about it. "Right around where James asked if I had killed people."

Ashley thought about the conversation and looked down in embarrassment. "You heard all of what I had to say, didn't you?"

Anthony smiled and nodded. "That's why I was thanking you. You had every right to agree with my brother and doubt me, but you said you would trust me. I can't think of a nicer thing for you to say at this point."

Ashley found that humorous. "If that's the nicest thing that I can say about you, then you should start reevaluating your life."

Anthony laughed, which in turn caused Ashley to laugh as well. Anthony quieted down and looked out the window. It was a gorgeous day. Anthony stood up and stretched out.

Ashley looked out the window and decided to change the topic. "What are we going to do today?"

Anthony looked back at her. "Well, *we* aren't going to do anything."

Ashley looked at him in confusion. "What do you mean?"

"We won't be together today," Anthony clarified. "I'm going to the school alone to look for clues as to where the other Divine Blades went off to."

"What about me then?" Ashley asked.

Anthony shrugged his shoulders. "You will have to stay here. I can't bring you there because the both of us will draw more attention than just me. I'm sorry, but you will have to stay here and wait. My mother should be home in an hour or so. I asked her if she would take half a day off to keep you company."

Ashley wasn't too sure how to feel about that. "It's going to be just me and your mother while you're away?"

Anthony nodded. "I understand it isn't the best situation, but she will be able to help cover for you if anybody sees movement in the house. Or if Zankrex decide to search houses again."

Ashley sighed. "I'm not worried about that. It just seems that being alone with your mother will be awkward."

Anthony paused and then chuckled.

Ashley looked at him weird. "What?"

Anthony waved his hand. "No, it's nothing. Just that the mention of Zankrex doesn't freak you out as much as being alone with my mother does. It was just funny to me."

Ashley rolled her eyes. "Well, I'm sorry. I guess they don't intimidate me as much since you're around."

Anthony paused then smiled. "Well, thank you."

Ashley realized what she had said and tried to cover it. "I mean you're supposed to be the strongest being, aren't you? Of course, I would feel safe around you."

Anthony laughed and nodded. "I understand. And I will do my best to not disappoint you."

Ashley smiled. "I'm glad to hear it."

Anthony spent little time dawdling. After he got up, he ate breakfast and got dressed. He threw on some cargo shorts and a shirt with a zip-up track jacket. Kevran seemed a tad confused. *Why the change in wardrobe?* he questioned.

Anthony finished getting dressed before answering, *Well, I figured that the Zankrex we lost on the road at Wishitak only got a good look at my clothes. If that's the case, then they would've reported it. And after my little leaf display and Lance's report, I imagine they know that I am a God Sword, which means that any details related to me would be important. So, I changed clothes.*

Kevran chuckled at the complexity of it all. *It seems that you put a lot of thought into this.*

Anthony nodded. *Of course, I did. The last thing I want to do is cause an uproar because I wasn't paying attention to detail.*

Kevran was impressed. *Well, I am proud of you. You are thinking things through, which is important. Speaking of which, what is the plan when we get to campus?*

Anthony chuckled with a smug grin. *We're going to wing it.*

Kevran was stunned silent. He shook his head in disbelief and sighed. *I take back what I said.*

Anthony laughed and walked out of his room. He made his way downstairs where Ashley was waiting.

She wrung her hands as she peered out the window. "I haven't seen anyone going up or down the street yet."

Anthony peeked out and looked around. The coast was clear on the road at the very least. Anthony nodded, confirming what Ashley had said, and got up from the window. "The coast is clear. I'm heading out."

"Be careful," Ashley blurted out.

Anthony paused to give Ashley a reassuring smile and a thumbs-up. "I'll be back safe and sound before you know it."

With that, he opened the door and shot out.

The streets were devoid of any activity. He had expected it, but it didn't make it any less unnerving. Kevran was there for moral support, but he knew that he was on his own if anything were to happen. Once he was off his street, his apprehension diminished. He was only worried about being caught on his street. There was no one whom he knew in the rest of his neighborhood, so if they saw him walking, they wouldn't think anything of it. He also had sunglasses on, which helped ease him. He had always felt just a tad safer when he was wearing his sunglasses. But the weirdest part was that he had no hat. He had fixed his hair in a different way in an attempt to further hide his true identity, though he wasn't all that worried about it. All of the people that he knew were in the Divine Blade program. He didn't know anyone in the normal university. That would make walking through campus easier, but the real test would be trying to get into the Divine Blade buildings.

Kevran seemed to echo his concerns. *There is no way the Zankrex will leave those buildings alone. There has to be some type of security surrounding it.*

Anthony agreed. There were two buildings designated for the Divine Blade program: the lecture hall, where lectures happened and where all the teachers' offices were. Then there was the gym, the large two floor building where they were supposed to meet to flee the Zankrex invasion.

We should go to the gym first since that was where we were supposed to meet the others. It's possible that they left a clue behind.

Kevran couldn't argue with his logic, but he was still feeling uneasy. *That makes sense, of course, but we cannot hope to just walk right in there without a game plan.*

Anthony nodded. *I'm aware of that. I have a plan, but it's going to have to count on a number of things for it to work.*

That threw up a red flag.

A number of things? Kevran asked in confusion. *What does it count on?*

Anthony scratched the back of his head. *Well, it only counts on one thing. If the Zankrex are guarding the building, then it's a no-go.*

Kevran was indignant. *Well, of course, that is the case. If they are not guarding the building, then can we not just walk right in?*

Anthony shook his head. *There is a camera surveillance system watching the outside of the building at all times.*

Kevran perked up at the mention of this. *We have to get through Zankrex guards and cameras?*

Anthony shrugged his shoulders. *Maybe. Though that's why I hope they won't be guarding the building. If they think that the camera system is enough, then maybe they won't post guards. 'Cause if they post guards, then the people might begin to get worried, and it appears that they want to avoid that. That and from all the experiences we've had with Zankrex, it seems to me that they don't like the sun too much.*

Kevran nodded. *I see, so if all those factors do come into play, then there is a good chance that there will not be any guards.*

Anthony nodded.

Kevran was impressed. *You cannot call it a plan, but it was still impressive how you came to that conclusion.*

Anthony smiled. *Well, I couldn't fall asleep, so I ended up thinking about this all night.*

Kevran chuckled. *Whatever works. I am guessing that you know a way past the cameras?*

Anthony nodded. *I'll explain it when we get there, but for now, we should focus on getting there.*

Kevran agreed, and the two remained silent for the rest of the trip.

The university was bustling like usual. Thousands of students were either walking away from or walking to classes. Anthony couldn't help but feel that he was standing out. He was one of few people who were wearing sunglasses. The sunglasses never attracted attention, however, as the students walked past without even a second glance.

Anthony couldn't help but feel relieved. *Thank goodness college kids don't care about anyone other than themselves. Otherwise, I could have been in some trouble.*

Kevran found it amusing. *I am just surprised by how little they pay attention to their surroundings. I feel like I could walk across the campus, and they wouldn't bat an eye at it.*

Anthony couldn't help but smile as he knew that Kevran was right. The trip to campus had taken far longer than he had hoped. He walked the entire way on purpose so that he could pay attention to his surroundings. The last thing he wanted to do was tip anyone off about his presence. Tritos had driven past, but there would be no way for them to find him suspicious just passing by. Now that he was on campus, he felt even more vulnerable. It was in times like this that he missed his sword. He felt a thousand times more comfortable in any situation with its familiar weight on his back.

He shook his head and focused again on the task at hand. The gym was approaching. As he had suspected, there were signs out front that prohibited anyone from entering. Anthony scanned the premises as he walked by. He followed a crowd of people as they detoured around the building. Anthony scanned long and hard until they were out of range. He walked to a shady spot in the courtyard he had just entered. His heart was racing a mile a minute in excitement.

I didn't miss anything, did I? he asked Kevran.

Kevran was just as relieved as Anthony. *I felt no Zankrex presence on that building. There would have to be a high-level Zankrex in there in order for me not to be able to sense him.*

Anthony nodded in excitement. *I didn't feel anything either, and I also didn't see anyone in the building.*

Kevran got to the point. *How about the cameras?*

Anthony brought himself back. *There is a small corridor of privacy, a narrow strip of land behind the building that the cameras can't see. My friend Christian showed it to me my first year here. I used it to come in after hours and train, but now we can use it to get in and out undetected.*

Kevran was a tad leery but didn't see any reason to bash the idea. *It seems a bit too easy to me. Are there cameras in the building?*

Anthony nodded. *Yeah, but they're only in the equipment shed. There are no cameras in the locker rooms and none in the gyms either.*

Kevran felt a bit more secure now. *That's fine, I suppose. Or at least it will have to be as it is our only option.*

Anthony nodded. *We'll make it work. The hardest part will be walking up to the building without being caught.* Anthony stood up and turned back toward the gym. *Let's do this.*

Despite his strong words, Anthony still had to wait awhile before he made his move. The gym was located on the outskirts of campus, but the back of the building was facing a more crowded walkway, so charging straight in would be difficult. He waited and waited for the traffic to die down before trying anything.

Soon the walkway was empty, and Anthony was quick to make his move. He strode around the border of the cameras' viewing field, making his way to the corridor. It was a straight path to the door. The only thing in the grassy area was a tree that was standing tall right next to the path he would have to take. He remembered walking this path several times when he would sneak into the gym for some after-hours training. He walked with confidence straight toward the building. He could see both cameras from here, and anyone who didn't know any better would believe that they were within viewing range. He remembered Christian telling him that it was that way because of a mistake by the team in charge of setting it up. The blueprints they sent to the installation company were wrong. The costs to fix it would have been too great, so they ended up leaving it like that. The argument they used was that the corridor was small, and there would be no way for anyone to find out about it due to the fact that it looks like the cameras can still see you.

Anthony recalled all of this as he marched toward the gym. He still had no idea how Christian had found out about this as he had refused to tell him. But at this point, all he was happy about was that he had told him in the first place.

If not for Christian, we would be up a creek without a paddle right now.

Kevran agreed as Anthony continued his approach. Anthony's speed walking had brought him to the tree that marked the halfway point when something caught his attention. It was a faint sound, but in the current silence, even the slightest noise would be audible. There was no mistaking the sound. Someone was walking up the path. They were close, far too close. Anthony had seconds to decide as time seemed to slow down.

Thoughts raced through his head as he analyzed his options. *I can't make it to the building now even if I run, and even if I could, I wouldn't be able to open the door, get in, and then close the door again before he noticed me. And I can't play dumb. Or maybe I could?*

But that thought was dispelled by another haunting feeling. The man walking up was a Zankrex. Not a high-powered one but a Zankrex all the same. If he saw him, there would be no way to explain his way out without giving something away. He could incapacitate him before he did anything, but the small burst of energy would be his downfall. Dread began to creep up on Anthony as he realized a confrontation was imminent.

Until, an obvious answer arose. Without even thinking, he made a mad dash for the tree. He had never climbed it before in his life, but he shot up the branches like he had climbed it a thousand times. He settled in midway up the tree when the man came walking around the corner. He was whistling to himself as he read some sort of book. Anthony held his breath and waited for the man to walk by. A slight wind blew, and the man stopped. He looked up from his book and stared straight at the tree.

Anthony's heart stopped as the wind also died down. The man continued to stare at the tree. Seconds ticked by, and Anthony began to panic more and more. He was determined not to move until the bitter end. The man squinted and almost seemed to lean toward the tree. Everything stood still after that.

Then, as if someone pressed Play on a remote, the man shrugged and looked back down at his book as he walked away. Anthony waited until he rounded the other corner before letting out all of his pent-up breath. His heart was racing, and he had broken out in a cold sweat. He climbed back down from the tree, being sure to stay in the corridor. When his feet hit the ground, he found that his hands were shaking with the adrenaline rush he had just received.

He stood there in a daze for several seconds before Kevran snapped him out of it. *Hey now, this is no time to be standing around. Get inside before that happens again and we get caught.*

Anthony came to and sprinted toward the door. He jiggled the knob a certain way, and the door opened like it always did. He stepped into the room and let the darkness close in around him as he shut the door.

Anthony slid down the door to the ground. His heart was still racing as he stared into the darkness. He tried to remember the layout of the locker room but found his mind was far too jumbled to think. He took several deep breaths and began to calm himself down.

Kevran waited for Anthony to get his bearings back before interjecting. *Are you all right?*

Anthony cracked a half smile and nodded. *Yeah, I'm fine. I just needed a minute to calm down. I thought we were done for.*

Kevran agreed. *I cannot believe I let him get that close to us without sensing him. I am sorry about that.*

Anthony waved it off as he rose to his feet. *No reason to worry about it now. Let's focus on finding any clues that we can about where the others might have gone.*

Kevran was thankful for Anthony's understanding and dropped the subject. The locker room wasn't pitch-black. It had just seemed that way at first due to how bright it was outside. Anthony stumbled on the wall as he made his way deeper, all the while waiting for his eyes to adjust. In time, his vision improved to where he could navigate the room without tripping over things. His next goal was to find any sort of light. He thought he had remembered hearing about an emergency locker that had a flashlight in it, but he couldn't remember which one they said it was.

He spent the next few minutes stumbling around lockers until he hit a bit of luck. He opened up a locker and saw a lump. He reached in and fumbled around. It felt like a first aid kit and some other random tools that they never used. He was about to give up when his fingers brushed against a plastic object. He pulled it out. His spirits rose when his fingers hit the switch, and the light illuminated the room. His happiness was short-lived as he soon realized the task in front of him. The locker room was two-storied, along with the gym. There were several hundred lockers in total, which meant that Anthony was going to have to check them one by one to see if anything was left behind.

He sighed in dismay and began to search. The minutes ticked by as he checked each of the lockers, to no avail. He trudged up the stairs to the second floor and continued his search. It didn't take him long to make his rounds, and he soon found himself in front of the last two lockers: his and Christian's. He gulped and opened Christian's locker. He shone the light in and checked every corner, but it was as empty as his hopes were. He almost didn't want to check his locker anymore, but decided to check it all the same. He opened it up and shone the light inside. He was greeted by his wooden sword. After inspecting the locker further, he found that the sword was the only thing in there.

He sighed and laid the light down. It shone off the wall and created a weird sort of ambient light. Anthony reached into his locker and pulled out his wooden sword. The grip and the weight brought back fond memories. He had had so many different fights with this sword. All the spars he had with Clancy and Christian. The one time he beat Hannah in training drill. Anthony couldn't help but smile at the blade. He took a stance. It had been too long since he had swung a sword, so he decided to not let this trip be a total waste. He bent his knees and stared forward hard. He then launched himself into a series of attacks and parries, fighting off invisible monsters like he used to do in his backyard.

But those monsters morphed into Zankrex. Anthony's face of joy turned into a face of hate and anger. His moves became more powerful, and he found himself "slaying" Zankrex after Zankrex. There was no end to them, but Anthony didn't care. He killed each and every one of those evil creatures that had turned his family against him.

That thought brought Anthony to a standstill. He paused and found that he was quite a ways away from his locker. His breathing had also become labored.

How long was I doing that? he asked Kevran.

Almost five minutes, he answered. *I did not butt in because it seemed like you were battling something.*

Anthony looked down at the ground. He hadn't realized how much the situation with his family bugging him. *I don't understand. It's not like they hate me.*

Kevran sighed. *It is only natural. They do not hate you, but they do not trust you either. Not having your own family trust you is a hard thing to accept. And when it is caused by someone else, then it is only natural that you would hate them.*

Anthony understood what Kevran was trying to say. But it didn't make it any easier on him.

He shook his head and cleared his thoughts. *I don't have time to be sitting here thinking about it. Let's check the main gym real quick, and then we can leave.*

Kevran wanted to talk to Anthony a little more about the subject but decided against it as they walked back down to the first floor.

Anthony cracked the locker-room door open. The sound of creaking hinges echoed throughout the empty gym. He pushed it open after he realized that he was indeed all alone. Closing the door behind him, he walked to the center of the gym. He tried to remember fun memories here, but the only thing that he could think of was the encounter he had with Hannah here.

Worry began to bubble up as he thought about Clancy, but Kevran was quick to pull him out of it. *Let us keep a sharp eye out here. This area is big, and there is a good chance that they could have hidden something small here.*

Anthony nodded his head as he focused on the huge room. Kevran was indeed right. The room was large enough to hide a great number of secrets. Anthony went about the task of searching every nook and cranny. He sifted through mounds of pads and baskets full of various workout equipment. The work was long and tedious as he was extra careful to not miss anything. At the end of it, the fruits of his labor were exhaustion and frustration. He let out a heavy sigh as he walked toward the center of the gym. He was soon greeted by a familiar landmark. A small hole in the floor still existed from where he had jammed his sword into the ground beside Hannah's head. The blood had been cleaned away as there wasn't even a drop left.

Anthony bent down and slid his fingers over the small hole. That hole represented his weakness and his hesitance back then.

If that were to happen now, I wonder if it would be different.

Kevran seemed perplexed by the question. *Why would it not be different? You know things now that you did not know before. Of course, things would be different.*

Anthony half-smiled at Kevran's confidence. *I'm glad one person thinks so, though it's pointless to think about now. I'm just not so sure I'll be able to kill her when the time comes.*

Kevran had no response for him, instead allowing him to think it out on his own.

Bells snapped Anthony back to reality as looked up, panicked. *Oh crap, that's the eleven-o'clock bell. Classes will be getting out soon.*

Kevran shared in Anthony's panic. *If we do not leave now, then we won't be able to get out of this building for a while, and who knows who might come in during that time.*

Anthony agreed and bolted for the locker-room door. He made it inside the dark room and felt his way to the back. Once he reached the door, he put his ear to it and strained to listen. After a second or two of listening, he consulted Kevran. *Do you feel anything?*

Kevran confirmed the vacancy outside, and Anthony opened the door. Blinding light filtered through, and Anthony was forced to squint as he waited for his eyes to adjust. He peeked outside and found that no one was there. He then opened the door all the way and stepped out. He wasted no time shutting it behind him and dashed back through the corridor. He had just made it out of the camera range and had settled into a nonchalant walk when the first wave of students walked out of the building nearby. Anthony tried to remain calm as he walked by the first group, almost expecting someone to call him out. But they just passed him by. Anthony was halfway around the gym by the time he started to relax.

That was far too close, Anthony thought to himself.

Kevran agreed. *Next time, maybe you should not take so many trips down memory lane.*

Anthony looked down, chastised, as he continued to walk away. *In any case, the gym didn't have any clues, which is upsetting.*

Kevran concurred. *There was a whole lot of risk and zero reward there. What is your next course of action?*

Anthony thought it over for a second before deciding. *Let's go home for now. I'll want to check the lecture hall next time. If there isn't anything there, then we will go ahead and leave.*

Kevran had no complaints with that as the drama of today had left him drained. Anthony could relate. The sudden adrenaline highs he had experienced had left him tired.

As he walked back toward home, his thoughts drifted toward Ashley. *I hope she managed to stay out of trouble*, he thought to himself. He sped up his pace, leaving the gym behind, but failed to notice the dark figure watching him from its rooftop.

Ashley turned her head and sneezed. She rubbed her nose in surprise at the sudden sneeze and turned her head back to the window. She had been sitting there for most of the time since Anthony had left. He had only been gone for about twenty minutes, but she still couldn't help but feel anxious about this whole endeavor. She let out a loud sigh as she pulled herself away from the window. *No reason to sit here and stare out the window*, she thought. *Let's see if I can do something helpful around here.*

She knew that she technically had free range around the house since the windows were closed, but she still felt nervous about walking around downstairs. But there was nothing to do upstairs besides clean Anthony's room, and she wasn't about to try. His room was a typical boy's room, and she knew that even touching some of it would only make Anthony mad. She decided to swallow her fears and make the journey downstairs.

She tiptoed down the steps, as if there were someone asleep downstairs that she shouldn't wake up. She then made her way toward the kitchen. She knew that there were dishes in the dishwasher that hadn't been taken out yet. She decided she could at least do that while she waited. She got to work. There were more dishes in there than she thought there would be, which didn't upset her. It just meant that she would be putting away dishes longer. She went about getting them all put away in their rightful place. After she finished that, she looked around downstairs for other things that she could do. To her surprise, there wasn't anything left.

This house is clean for a family with two boys in it, she mused to herself.

She then realized that Anthony hadn't been home in around two weeks. *That would explain it then. Mrs. Multan would have one less person to clean up after.*

In that moment, something struck her. It was something that she hadn't felt in a long time. It was the feeling of normalcy. She was at a house, cleaning and thinking about normal things. No Zankrex or cross-country journeys were being discussed.

Ashley couldn't help but smile to herself. *I'd almost forgot what normal felt like. It's kind of nice to have this.*

But even in that moment, it still didn't feel right for her. She realized that she had gotten caught up in all the fuss and excitement. She enjoyed the treks across the forest and running from the enemy. There were some things that she wasn't too fond of, like all the killing and the uncomfortable sleeping situations; but all in all, she was missing it.

She continued to stew in these thoughts as she made her way back upstairs. She didn't get to think about it for too long as Anthony's mother's return brought her out of her deep thought. Judy closed the garage door behind her and made her way inside. She put all her stuff away and looked in the dishwasher. She had intended to clean it out when she got home but found it empty. It perplexed her to see it empty until she remembered that Ashley was home. She then made her way upstairs. Ashley was sitting on the couch looking off into space when Anthony's mother walked in the room.

"You didn't have to do that," she said.

Ashley looked at her in confusion. "Didn't have to do what?"

Judy motioned downstairs. "You didn't have to clean out the dishwasher. I was going to take care of it when I got home anyway."

"Oh, that," Ashley said in realization. She shrugged it off. "It was no big deal. I was bored and needed something to do anyway. Plus, I am freeloading in your home right now, so it was the least I could do."

Judy almost seemed offended at that statement. "You most certainly are not a freeloader, Ashley. You helped my son stay alive. That alone is enough for me to feed you for the rest of your life."

Ashley smiled in appreciation, but before she could say anything else, the doorbell rang.

Both the ladies froze at the sound of the bell. Ashley felt the panic begin to creep up on her and was about to freak out. Judy was quick to calm her down. She grabbed Ashley's shoulders and looked her in the eyes.

"It's going to be okay," she said in a calm voice. "Just hide somewhere and wait for me to come and get you."

Ashley was still on edge, but Judy's calm voice helped her keep her composure. She waited until Judy had exited the room before going straight for the cubbyhole that she and Anthony had hid in last time.

I won't go all the way in like last time, she thought to herself. *I'll do that if things get too intense.*

Judy walked down the steps and prepared herself. She opened the door and was shocked to see General Shane standing outside.

He smiled and bowed his head.

"General Shane, what a surprise to see you here," Judy said.

Shane laughed. "A pleasant one, I would hope."

Judy nodded. "Oh, of course. It's always a pleasure to have someone as important as you visit. Would you like to come in?"

Shane raised his hand to pass. "No, thank you. I just came by to follow up on my investigation yesterday. I remember that you had said how nervous the thought of having a criminal break into your house would be. I decided to come by again and check on you."

Judy smiled while cursing herself on the inside for saying such a thing. "Well, thank you so much, General. It's nice to know that the authorities have such a concern for the well-being of the citizens."

Shane laughed again. "I would hope we would. It's our job to protect you, after all. I wouldn't be much of an officer if I didn't have concern for the people I'm supposed to protect, now would I?"

Judy laughed. "No, I suppose you wouldn't be."

Shane waved his hand around. "Ah, but I didn't come here to make small talk. I came by to ask if there was anything out of the ordinary that you would like to report."

Judy thought about for a bit. "No," she said after a while. "There's nothing out of the ordinary that I've seen."

Shane's face changed for a fraction of a second, as if there was something that seemed off to him. But it was soon gone, and the regular pleasant face he had been carrying was back. He gave a slight bow and turned around. "I am glad to hear that. Now, if you will excuse me, I am off to continue my rounds."

Judy waved to him. "Thank you for all your work." She said, just before turning and closing the door behind her.

Ashley waited in the dark room. She couldn't hear anything that was going on downstairs, so she had no idea if something bad was happening. The sound of the door closing grabbed her attention, and footsteps coming upstairs only raised her apprehension. She began to panic. She had never faced this kind of situation alone before. If Anthony was around, he would have reassured her, but now she had to make a decision herself. She didn't know if she should jump up into the ceiling or not. Before she had any time to decide, a knock on the cubby door brought her out of her thoughts.

"The coast is clear," Judy's familiar voice said.

Ashley breathed a sigh of relief before opening the door and crawling out. Judy smiled at her as she closed the cubby door behind her.

"How did you know I was in there?" Ashley asked.

Judy shrugged. "I didn't know for sure. It was just an educated guess."

Ashley walked over to the couch and plopped down. "Who was at the door?" she asked.

Judy sighed and sat on the couch with her. "It was General Shane."

Ashley's eyes widened at the mention of his name. "Him again? What did he want this time?"

"He just wanted to check up on me is what he said," Judy said.

Ashley scratched her head. "Well, I guess that's okay. But how did you manage to lie to him this time? I doubt he asked such a simple question this time."

Judy laughed. "It wasn't easy. He asked if I had seen anything out of the ordinary. I had to reason with myself that you had become ordinary in my household. I battled with it in my head for a tad too long, I think."

Ashley cocked her head in confusion. "What do you mean you thought about it too long?"

Judy looked down in worry. "I don't know. It's just that when I gave my answer, Shane had this look on his face like he didn't believe what I said. He ended up accepting it, or at least he pretended to."

Ashley didn't know how to react. "You're saying there is a chance that he might be on to us?"

Judy nodded.

Ashley didn't have a comment after that. She had a horrible feeling about the whole situation, but decided to wait to talk about it until Anthony got back. After that, a long pause filled the room. Ashley had underestimated how hard it would be to keep up a conversation with Anthony's mother by herself. No matter what she thought about, it just didn't seem appropriate. Her mind kept coming back to one certain topic. She wanted to ask Judy about it, but she just didn't feel right asking it.

Her struggle must have been obvious as Judy soon caught on. "What's bothering you, dear?"

Ashley almost jumped up in surprise. She looked down at the floor in embarrassment. "Well … there's something that I want to ask you, but I don't know if I should."

Judy laughed. "Oh, please don't worry about it. Ask me what you want to ask me."

Ashley felt a little relieved to hear that but was still nervous.

She took a deep breath and let it out again before asking, "Why are you helping us?"

Judy was shocked to hear that question but was also confused. "I'm not quite sure what you mean."

Ashley thought about it a bit before asking again, "I mean, you know that we are lawbreakers. We've done horrible things. Anthony even admitted that. Why are you helping us if you know we are the horrible people that you've been hearing about?"

Judy's face saddened a bit at the question. Ashley felt immediate guilt. "I'm sorry," she said. "You don't have to answer."

Judy smiled and waved her hand. "No, no, it's fine. I'll answer. It's just that it's something that I haven't thought about myself." Judy thought about it for a little bit before answering, "I guess I don't know why I'm helping you. At first, I thought it was because he was my son, but I've always told myself that if my children became convicted criminals, I would turn them in. I had to battle with it for a little bit. When I first saw him, I got angry. It was like every angry memory I had of him came bubbling up at once."

Ashley looked perplexed. "Why did you agree to it if you were so angry?"

Judy smiled. "Because for every bad memory I have of Anthony, I have ten good ones to block it out. It didn't take me long to remember that Anthony was a good boy. Though, even still, those memories try to creep up and get me angry at him."

Ashley was still confused. "It just seems weird to me that only those memories would be the ones to rise up on their own."

Judy nodded. "I thought it was odd too. I talked to Vince about it, and he said that the same thing happened to him."

A sudden moment of clarity hit Judy. "If that is true, then it would make sense that James has such a hard time accepting Anthony. James would have a lot more bad memories of Anthony than we would since they are brothers and would always get in fights with each other."

Ashley nodded. "You're right. That would make a lot of sense. But how do bad memories play into this?"

Judy's face was vacant for a bit then snapped back as she remembered where she was going with that story. "That's right. I was saying that to say this. When all I remembered was the bad memories, I really wanted to turn Anthony in. But after I listened to him speak and after I remembered all the good things about him, the urge to turn him in was all but gone. It was like my anger was connected to my desire to turn him in. I still don't agree with him or what he's doing, but I don't think he's the demon that the news says he is."

Ashley's head was swimming in the new information that she had just gained. She smiled. "Thank you for telling me that. And I'm sorry I brought up that topic."

Judy waved her hands. "Don't worry about it at all. It was nice for me to talk about that as well."

The two smiled at each other, and Ashley began to feel a lot more at home.

Ashley and Judy went about their day talking and working for a while. Ashley was still deep in thought about the conversation she had with Judy when a knock at the window in Anthony's room brought her out of her daydream. She turned to see Anthony sitting outside the window. He pointed at the locks. Ashley ran over and opened the window for him.

"Thank you," he said as he jumped into the room.

"How did you manage to jump all the way up here?" she asked as she closed the window.

Anthony sighed. "I had to use my speed step."

Ashley looked at him in alarm. "Did you alert anyone?" she asked panicked.

Anthony shook his head. "I only used enough power to get me from the ground to the window. And there was no one in the immediate area. Kevran told me that as long as I kept it suppressed, no one outside of a certain range would be able to feel it."

Ashley seemed unconvinced. "How does that work?"

Anthony sat on his bed and took his shoes off. "I asked the same question. Kevran explained it to me like this: no matter how good someone's hearing is, they won't be able to hear someone whisper from a mile away."

Ashley nodded at the example. "That makes sense, I suppose. And if Kevran says it's okay, then it's going to be okay."

Anthony smiled. "I agree." He lay on his bed and let out a sigh.

Ashley remembered his whole reason for leaving. "Did you find anything?"

Anthony shook his head. "I found nothing. Not even a footprint of someone I knew. I'll have to check the lecture hall tomorrow."

Ashley was uneasy with that. "I don't know if staying here is the best idea."

Anthony sat up and looked at her in confusion. She explained what had transpired after he left.

After she finished the story, she followed up with her feelings. "After Shane left and your mother told me what he said, I got this terrible feeling. Like something bad was going to happen if we stayed here."

She waited for Anthony to answer. He was sitting on his bed, thinking hard about it.

He soon snapped out of it and looked at Ashley. "I'll trust your bad feelings. But I have to check inside that lecture hall. Let's do this. I'll go to the lecture hall early tomorrow morning. It's the university's day off tomorrow, so there won't be anybody on campus in the morning. I'll sneak in, do a quick check, and get out of there. Then when I get back, we will leave. How does that sound?"

Ashley still didn't feel comfortable with it, but she knew that checking the lecture hall was important. She really wanted to leave, but she knew Anthony would never agree to that. She smiled and nodded, thinking that this plan was better than waiting till the day after tomorrow like he had wanted to do. She also wanted to tell Anthony about the memories that Judy had talked about, but Judy walking up with lunch ended their conversation before she could bring it up.

Anthony and Ashley spent the rest of the day relaxing. Anthony was exhausted after his adventure, more so from stress than actual effort. Ashley too was a little tired. She had to worry about so many things in a short amount of time. The two spent most of the time sitting around upstairs doing nothing in particular.

Anthony's mother brought up board games for them to play. They spent a good portion of time playing those. Before they knew it, Anthony's father had come back home as well. He came up and decided to join in the fun. Time seemed to fly by for Anthony. He remembered playing board games with his family a lot when he was a kid. Ashley could tell that Anthony was enjoying himself. She understood why, though. Even though this wasn't her family, she still felt at home here. Anthony's parents were quick to welcome her even though she should be their enemy.

I guess since they love Anthony so much, that love just kind of runs over onto me, she thought to herself.

She hated the thought of having to take Anthony away from all this, but she knew it was for the best. The last thing they needed was for something to happen to his family. When James came home, he went straight to his room. No one tried to get him to come out, instead leaving him to his space. As it got late, Vincent went downstairs and got dinner ready. They ate and continued to have a good time, but soon Anthony's parents got tired and decided to turn in. They left the two upstairs for the night and went downstairs.

Anthony sighed as he lay on his bed. Ashley couldn't help but smile at his contentment. But that smile faded at the thought of having to leave tomorrow.

"Cheer up," Anthony said, smiling at Ashley. "I know we have to leave tomorrow, but that doesn't mean we won't ever see them again. I'm going to be sure to free them from the Zankrex hold so that I can enjoy myself like that again in the future. I won't be sad tomorrow, and neither should you."

Ashley smiled at his reassuring words and nodded. "You're right. It won't be a goodbye, just a 'see you later.'"

Anthony nodded and yawned. He started to get up from his bed. "Well, I have an early day tomorrow, so I think I'll be heading to bed now."

"Ah, then you sleep here tonight," Ashley interjected.

Anthony paused. "Are you sure? You can have the bed. I have no trouble sleeping on the couch."

Ashley nodded. "Of course, I'm sure. I can sleep on a couch tonight. And you need a comfortable bed more than me anyway since tomorrow is going to be tougher on you."

Anthony smiled. "Well, thank you. I'll be sure to sleep it up real good then."

Ashley laughed as she walked out of the room. "You do that. Good night."

"Good night," Anthony said as Ashley closed the door.

Ashley got all ready for bed and got herself comfortable on the couch. As she got comfortable, she remembered that she needed to tell him about the anger thing that Judy had told her about. She got up and opened the door, peeked her head in. She was about to ask if he was still awake when his rhythmic breathing answered the question.

She sighed. *Oh well, I'll tell him about it tomorrow.*

She took one last look at his sleeping face. It was so tranquil and content. She couldn't help but smile as she closed the door behind her.

I hope that contentment doesn't leave you, she thought as she drifted off to sleep.

Chapter 16

TROUBLE

*A*nthony's alarm clock rang out, drawing him out of his deep sleep. He squinted at the clock. It was only six in the morning, but Anthony had planned it that way. He got out of bed and quieted the insistent clock. He stretched himself out and got dressed. He put on the ensemble that he had worn to Wishitak. He knew that he would be leaving as soon as he got, home and he didn't want to use getting dressed as an excuse for staying longer than he had to. After he got done putting on his fingerless gloves, he grabbed his hat and tiptoed out the door. Ashley was still sound asleep in the other room. It was a Saturday, so everyone in the house was still asleep. His parents would be getting up soon, but he knew they weren't up yet. He had chosen to get up at this time for that very reason. No one in any of the neighboring houses would be up yet, so he could leave his house without people noticing. He remained silent going down the stairs and scribbled a note to Ashley, telling her to be ready to leave when he got back.

Are you positive it is safe to leave right now? asked Kevran.

Anthony was more or less confident about it. *I've never seen people up and about in this neighborhood at this time of the day for as long as I've lived here. And I used to be outside this early on Saturdays all the time due to my training for the sword fighters' club that I was in for high school. I'm hoping that hasn't changed, but if it has, then we will just have to leave earlier than expected.*

Kevran, not at all convinced, dropped the topic and just moved on. *What is the plan this time?*

Anthony shrugged. *Since we are leaving today, we won't have to worry about the security cameras as they only check those after the fact. We should be long gone by the time they check them, and since my parents don't know that I'm going there today, they won't be punished for it.*

Kevran felt better knowing that things wouldn't be as complicated as the last time.

It is simple, but I like it, he replied.

Anthony smiled as he walked out the door. *It will be a little easier than yesterday, to be sure.*

Anthony waited for a trito to pass before darting across the road into the forest that connected his neighborhood and the campus. When he was deep enough in, he stopped running and settled into a nice walk. The silence of the forest was deafening. Neither he nor Kevran knew what to talk about. Something was holding the conversation back.

Anthony was the first to realize why. *Something doesn't feel right, does it?* he asked Kevran.

Kevran sighed and agreed. *I was just thinking the same thing. I cannot put my finger on it, but something feels off.*

Anthony looked up at the sky. It was gray and dark, even for how early it was. It was obvious that it was going to rain at some point today.

Maybe it's just the bad weather that's getting us in this funk.

Kevran didn't seem convinced. *It could be. I do not think it is, but I hope that is the reason. Either way, we should be careful on campus. Feelings like this can be accurate sometimes.*

Anthony agreed as he trudged through the woods. The weather was still just as warm as it was yesterday, maybe even warmer, but that's how the weather worked in Murffana. It would get warm, and then a rainstorm would bring in the cold. As it closed in on winter, that warm weather would be replaced with cold weather, and the rain would turn into snowstorms, or it would rain and bring even colder weather. Anthony didn't want to get caught up in the rain if he could help it, but he hadn't looked at a weather report, so he had no idea when it would start.

I guess all we can do is pray and hope that the rain holds off until we get home. I would like it to wait until we leave, but that may be too much to ask for.

Kevran remained silent as they closed in on the campus.

Anthony poked his head out from behind a building. He scanned his immediate surroundings. There was no one on campus. No one was walking about. Anthony breathed a sigh of relief and walked out into the open. With the uneasy feelings both he and Kevran had, Anthony was certain that there would be people walking about on campus. That thought proved to be untrue as he made his way to the lecture hall.

The silence was a blend of peaceful and maddening for Anthony. On one side, he enjoyed the peace and relished in the tranquility that it brought. But on the other hand, he knew from experience that silence could sometimes lead to a battle. Anthony wanted to avoid a battle in town if he could because he knew that the city was most likely crawling with Zankrex and a general. A battle against them here would be a bad idea, to say the least. He kept his head down as he walked up the steps to the lecture hall. He walked up to the main doors and tried them. Much to his dismay, they were all locked tight. Anthony hadn't considered this an option and berated himself for not thinking about this sooner.

Kevran was quick to intercede, *Beat yourself up about it later. Right now, we need to find another way in. You said that they do not check the cameras until after the fact, but that means that there is a chance that someone is watching the cameras right now. We may not have all that much time to spare.*

Anthony agreed and thought of a different path. He was reminded of the faulty window on the side of the building and sprinted off. He approached the window and looked around one final time to be sure that no one was watching. The coast was still clear, so he proceeded. He jiggled the window back and forth for a second or two until he heard that familiar click. He smiled as the window slid up.

Kevran was baffled. *How did you know to do that?*

Anthony shrugged. *I was part of the reason that the window broke. And in an attempt to show that it was still good, I moved it like that to show that it was still set in. It stayed on, but it would unlock if you shook it too hard.*

Kevran could only shake his head in amazement. *There sure are a lot of convenient ways to get into the buildings that are supposed to house the future of the world.*

Anthony brushed off the remark and climbed into the room, closing the window behind him. He looked around, trying to remember where he was in the building. After noticing the plants everywhere, he remembered which office he had landed in.

This must be Professor Troh's office. He was a botanist before he became a Divine Blade. He was one of our real-world professors.

Kevran didn't follow. *Real world?* he asked.

Anthony thought for a bit on how to word it better before answering. *He was a normal professor. He would teach us the things that we would learn in a normal university. You understand now?*

Kevran was catching on at that point. *I see what you mean. But does he have any connections to your group?*

Anthony thought about it as he searched the room. *Doubtful,* he answered after a while.

Then we should probably head to someone's office that would be part of the group, Kevran said.

Anthony nodded as he did one last check around the room before heading out. As he sprinted down the hall, his thoughts turned toward Ashley. *I hope she's doing okay*, he thought to himself.

Ashley waited until she heard the door close before she got up. She had had a horrible time trying to fall asleep on the couch, which was odd to her. She had fallen asleep on the ground for almost a week before they got here, and the couch was far more comfortable than the cold, hard ground. But for whatever reason, she just couldn't sleep. She picked herself up and trudged off to Anthony's room. She locked the door and fell asleep on his bed. The next thing she heard was activity outside the room. The television was on, and the volume was far too loud for whatever it was that was being watched. She tried to sleep through it but found that she just couldn't. She got fed up with it and walked out. James and his father were just sitting there when she poked her head out.

"Could you turn it down, please?"

The request seemed to shock them as they turned it down without saying much. She then receded back into the room and fell asleep for another hour. After an hour, she woke back up feeling refreshed. She got up and stretched herself out. She then got dressed as her clothes were sitting in a neat folded pile. After that, she ventured out into the family room again. The two were still sitting there when she walked out. Anthony's dad couldn't help but smile as he saw her again.

Ashley looked at him weird. "What?" she asked.

Anthony's dad shook his head. "Oh, nothing. It just surprised us when you poked your head out like that. It almost felt like you lived here with us. I just found it funny."

James was smirking as well, trying not to laugh.

Ashley sighed as she took a seat at the far end of the couch. "I suppose you're right. I didn't mean to come off that way. I was just tired and wanted to sleep."

Anthony's dad shook his head. "Don't worry about it. No one was offended."

Ashley smiled. "Well, that's good."

Silence followed for a while as they sat and watched television.

The day hadn't gone very far for Ashley. She was still sitting on the couch watching television even though the others had wandered off to do other things. She found it was hard to get up. It was then that she realized how much of a rut she was in. All she seemed to do was sit around upstairs and wait for something to happen. She hated doing that. All she wanted to do was get underway and leave this town. She was getting antsy staying in the same spot for too long. Her discomfort was apparent as James walked back into the room.

"What's wrong with you?" he asked.

Ashley sighed. "I just hate all this sitting around I've been doing. I would like to move about and do something."

James remained stoic as he stood in the doorway. After a brief silence, he nodded his head. "I guess I could understand that."

With that, he turned back around and walked into his room. Ashley couldn't help but smile at James's awkwardness. It was clear that he was still trying to keep his distance around her since she was a "bad person," but every now and again, he would struggle with it.

Ashley shrugged it off as she focused back on the television. She watched the news in an attempt to learn anything about the whereabouts of the Divine Blades. So far, she had come up empty, but she had learned a little bit about where the other four God Swords were. Robert and Brandon were pretty much staying on their own continents: Robert on Austaria and Brandon on Eufrin. Neither of them seemed to be creating that much of a stir, but they were seen as leaders of the rebellion. The other two were a little more unpredictable. Hizaki was mainly staying in Shinjiko but would bounce around Amaraitia and Rugashin. She would start squabbles here and there, but nothing major. It was Vanessa that the Zankrex seemed to be most worried about. She had been spotted at least once on every continent on Tertalla. She would also cause a great deal of disturbance wherever she turned up. There was a huge search for her and a large reward for any information on where she might be. That would always be the report if anyone talked about the leaders of the rebellion. But it would always end with a quick bit on the fifth and unknown leader. Ashley knew they were talking about Anthony since the God Swords were considered the leaders, and he was the fifth God Sword. But whenever they brought up the fifth leader, they could never attach a name to him. Ashley breathed a sigh of relief.

If that ignorance will hold out until we leave, Ashley thought to herself, *then everything will be just fine.*

She continued to watch as the news transitioned into the weather. It appeared that it would start raining soon. Ashley hoped that Anthony would get back sooner than later as traveling in the cold rain wasn't the most pleasant thing for her to think about.

A sudden knock on the door grabbed her attention. Almost on instinct, she rushed for the cubbyhole.

Please don't let this be anything big, she prayed, but a horrible feeling in her stomach kept her from getting to hopeful.

Ashley had secured herself when she heard the door open. Vince had taken his time so Ashley could hide. He got to the door and turned the locks. As he opened it, he was greeted by an unfamiliar sight. It was only when Judy walked up that he realized who it was.

"General Shane, what a surprise," Judy said, trying her best not to sound nervous.

Shane smiled. He extended his hand to Vince. "Very nice to meet you, Mr. Multan. I've already had the pleasure of meeting your wife. I'm General Shane."

Vice shook his hand, taking note of the five burley officers standing behind him. "It's always a pleasure to have such a high-ranking official come to my home, but what, may I ask, is the occasion?"

Shane's face took something of an almost sinister look. He cleared his throat before continuing, "We have reason to believe that your son has infiltrated this town."

Vince and Judy were shocked, but not for the reason that Shane thought.

"Yes, I know it is a tad shocking to hear about your son after so long, but you are aware that he is a part of the rebellion, are you not?"

The parents nodded, afraid of where this was going.

Shane nodded, pleased. "Well, we were afraid that Anthony may somehow come here and try to use you to his advantage. We are here to make sure that doesn't happen."

Vince was worried now. "What are you going to do?"

Shane's sinister look took a more evil form. "For now, I'm going to have to ask you and your other son"—he pointed at James, who was sticking his head around the corner—"to come with me."

Ashley couldn't hear any of the conversation going on at the door. All she knew was that it was taking longer than it should.

It couldn't be a friend. The conversation would be louder than that. And it can't be a random passerby. They would have sent them off by now. Who is it?

Ashley was afraid that she already knew the answer to the question she was asking. She waited and waited until movement made her catch her breath. She heard someone walking down the stairs.

James is the only other one upstairs, she thought. *Why is he going back down?*

She listened as he walked all the way down, and then she heard the door close. She waited for what seemed like hours until she realized that no one was still in the home. She cracked open the cubby door and peeked outside it. No one was in the room, so she got out and closed the door behind her. She crawled to the window and took a peek outside. Her eyes widened, and she dropped to the floor. She was afraid now. Trembling, she crawled into Anthony's room and shut the door. She leaned back on the door and slid down it until she was sitting. She had no idea what to do, and she could only think one thing.

Anthony, please hurry back.

Anthony walked down the hallway. Unlike the gym, there were cameras on the inside of the lecture hall. He didn't pay them much mind as he knew that he had already been seen by the outside ones. But not paying attention to them was a tough task. He tried to put them out of his mind as he walked into the large lecture room. The room was two-storied and full of seats. There was a large presenting area in front of a huge chalkboard. Anthony never understood why the board was as big as it was. He had only seen Hazblazen write up top once or twice, and even then, he could only do it because of his Divine Blade power. Anthony then turned his attention to the seats. A flood of memories came back to him as he gazed at them—some good and some bad, but all of them nostalgic.

He shook his head to avoid getting lost in the memories like he did in the gym. He walked up the steps to get to the second floor. As he passed by the last few rows, he stopped and looked at his seat. It wasn't his assigned seat as university didn't do that, but it was the seat that he would sit in most often. He hesitated, almost wanting to go and sit down on it.

Kevran jumped in, *Time is of the essence here, Anthony.*

Anthony nodded and turned back toward the door. He jogged up the last few steps and opened it. He turned back and took one last look at the room before closing the door.

Anthony walked down the familiar hallway. He knew this walk like the back of his hand as he had made it several times before. Hazblazen's office was a place that he had found himself in multiple times. He wasn't a bad student, but he did have a bad tendency to daydream during lecture. And since Hazblazen knew Anthony from before university, he would often call him out. Anthony had been grateful for this, of course. If he hadn't done it, then Anthony would have done a lot worse in lecture the first semester.

By the time he had finished his mental recap, he was standing in front of the room. He tested the doorknob and breathed a sigh of relief when it opened without any resistance. He stepped in and looked around. The room was dark, which was to be expected, and empty. He flicked the light switch on and glanced around the room again. Nothing popped out at him. He checked the desk for anything that would tell him the whereabouts of the others. Nothing jumped out at him, so he intensified his search. He looked for anything that would even look like a connection to a note or a communication. Nothing came up. Anthony sat down hard in Hazblazen's seat and breathed out a sigh of frustration.

Soon memories began to surface in his mind. The many number of one-on-ones that he had with Hazblazen. Every berating talk and every disappointed lecture flew by in his mind, but one thing burned through it all. He could feel it on his chest. He couldn't help but reach up and rub his sternum. The point that Hazblazen would always thump when Anthony was feeling down. Every uplifting conversation always ended with Hazblazen's fingers to Anthony's chest. He never knew why he did it nor why he started it, but all he knew was that it worked. Even now, he felt a small peace just remembering it, but soon reality came crashing back in.

He pounded his fist on the desk as he stood back up. *This is ridiculous. There should be some sort of message left behind for anybody that missed the group. That's just common knowledge. I find it hard to believe that nobody would have thought of it.*

Kevran calmed Anthony down before agreeing with him. *Let us not get too worked up, okay? I agree that they should have done that, but let us take into consideration that they may not have had enough time to put a message out. The attack was abrupt, to say the least.*

Anthony looked at the floor. He knew that Kevran was right, but that didn't make it any less frustrating. He got up and made his way out of the room, turned the light off, and closed the door behind him. He looked down the hall and walked past two doors.

Kevran was confused. *Where are you going? Is the exit not the other way?*

Anthony nodded as he stopped in front of a new office. *I know, but this is Clancy's office. It's small, but there is a chance that he was the one that left a note behind.*

Kevran understood as Anthony opened the door and turned on the lights. Clancy's office was much cleaner than Hazblazen's was. This made the search much shorter, though Anthony did give it the same vigorous once-over that he had given Hazblazen's office. But the only thing he found was the same dejection he had found before.

He sighed again and was walking out when a voice over the loud speaker stopped him in his tracks.

"Anthony Multan," the voice said.

Anthony nearly jumped into the ceiling out of surprise. He stopped and looked around for the source of the voice before realizing it was the loudspeaker. A sense of dread began to fall over him as he guessed the identity of the voice. He looked for a camera, finding one at the end of the hall. He walked to it and looked at it, waiting for the voice again.

"Good, I see I have your attention."

Anthony wanted to shout back at the voice, but the loudspeaker was only one way. Shouting now would only be a waste of energy.

The voice continued, "That was a very brave move, Anthony, coming into this building in broad daylight. We don't monitor the cameras on campus during the days off, but you slipped up yesterday. One of my subordinates saw you leaving the gym, so I put someone on guard duty today."

Anthony cursed himself inside for being so careless. He should have figured that someone saw him and left that very day. Now he could only begin to imagine the amount of trouble they were in.

Kevran calmed him down. *Keep a cool head, Anthony. No one ever got out of a sticky situation while panicking.*

Anthony agreed and did his best to calm his nerves.

The voice chuckled. "But forgive me, I've been talking all this time and haven't introduced myself yet. My name is General Shane."

The pit in Anthony's stomach grew larger. He knew he had recognized that voice from somewhere but hadn't been able to remember. Now the situation was at its most dire.

Anthony began to look to the exits, but the voice cut him off. "Before you go, I feel as though I should tell you something: I'm not in the security booth."

Anthony looked back at the camera in confusion.

"No, I'm at your house."

Anthony's eyes widened as fear began to wash over him.

"And I have your family with me. And unless you turn yourself in to me here in one hour, I will kill them all one by one. So be a dear and hurry over. It would be a shame if they died because you were too slow."

Chapter 17

RAIN

*T*he loudspeaker clicked, signaling that the conversation was over. Anthony trembled in a mix of fear and rage.

Kevran stopped him before he could take off. *Do not be rash, Anthony.*

Anthony became incredulous. *Rash? You don't want me to be rash? My family is about to be killed, and it's all my fault. I'm sorry, but I'm going to be a bit rash.*

Kevran sighed. *That is not what I meant. Of course, you have to go, but do not just fly in without a plan. Think this through, even just a little bit.*

Anthony tried his best to calm down and think. *Of course, I'll need my sword out. And sneaking up would be a good idea instead of just running in. But I have no idea what the layout is, so I can't make any plans right now.*

Kevran agreed. *You are right. And the journey there is not short either. I believe you can use your energies in the forest, but as soon as we get to the edge, you will have to go it on your own if you want to sneak in. Otherwise, they will sense you and use your family to stop you.*

Kevran opened the portal to his dimension. *Take your sword. It is smarter to get it out here instead of closer in.*

Anthony agreed and reached in. He grabbed his sword and pulled it out, feeling ten times more confident in himself as he put it on his back. The familiar pressure was a welcome sensation as he looked out the window. It had taken him about an hour to get to campus on his own power. He knew he could half that time if he used his Reichi to run faster, and that would give him more time to scout out the situation before having to act.

He nodded his head and sprinted down the hall.

No time for stairs, he thought as he opened the window and leapt out. *This is my mess, and I'm going to clean it up.*

Trees blurred past as Anthony sprinted his way through the forest. He knew he could go faster, but if he used his full strength to sprint there, the enemy would be alerted to his presence long before he could get there and assess the situation. Stealth would be necessary here. That was why he waited until he was five minutes away to hide his power and go on.

I need to see what the entrance to my neighborhood looks like before I can make any sort of move, Anthony thought to himself.

As he neared the road, he walked slower and slower. He was worried by the silence. *The road separating my neighborhood and the forest is a busy road. I should be hearing some sort of activity or at least a trito or two passing by.*

As Anthony neared the edge of the forest, he found the reason for the silence. There were several Zankrex standing around by the entrance to his neighborhood. A quick glance down the street confirmed that there were other Zankrex down there cutting off the flow of traffic from entering the road.

They don't want me using the traffic to get in, Anthony realized.

He cursed them for being so smart and drew back into the woods to think up a strategy.

You have thirty minutes to think this through, Anthony, Kevran reminded him. *There is no need to form a brash and stupid plan. Think this through.*

Anthony got annoyed. *None of my plans are ever stupid. They just aren't your plans, so you never like them.*

Kevran sighed. *Yes, yes, either way, my statement still stands. This is a tough situation, but I am certain there is a way for us to get in there unnoticed.*

Anthony agreed, but he just couldn't see it at the moment. As soon as he walked out of the forest, he would be in the open. With how many Zankrex there were, it would be impossible for him to hope to run in while they weren't looking. He also couldn't use his speed step. He had noticed the Zankrex in front of him were hiding their energy.

If they're good enough to hide energy like that, then they are plenty good enough to sense it, especially if it's right in front of them.

Kevran concurred.

Anthony sat down and crossed his arms. He thought long and hard about it, using the silence to concentrate. An idea began to form. He decided to take Kevran through his thought process.

Kevran, I'm having a thought right now.

Kevran chuckled. *Oh dear.*

Anthony shot a glare at a tree as if it were Kevran. *Enough of your sarcasm. This is going to be awesome, so just listen.*

Kevran shut up and listened.

There isn't any rational way for us to get in there since they aren't letting anyone in at all. I thought about going around, but I have to assume that it's going to be the same around the entire neighborhood. The more I thought about it, the more I realized that a good distraction is the only way to get in.

Kevran interjected, *I am not going to rampage alone while you sneak in if that is what you are thinking.*

Anthony shook his head. *No, no, that wouldn't work anyway. We should assume that Shane is smarter than that. What I thought I should do is give them what they are looking for.*

Kevran didn't follow, but he was already not liking the sound of it. *I am afraid to ask, but what do you mean?*

Anthony smiled. *These Zankrex are posted here to look for me. If I use my power through the leaves, they will think it's me and run in after me. I then make the leaves fly into the woods and dissipate them so that they lose sight of where the power was. While all this is happening, I've already used my speed step to fly in past them and hide among some bushes until I can move farther in.*

Kevran pondered the plan. He didn't want to agree, but he knew that, for Anthony, this was the best plan he was going to think of. That and he himself was unable to think up a plan better than that.

It might work, but that does not mean that I like it. It is risky.

Anthony agreed. *I know it's risky, but at this point, I can't see a better option, and the more time we waste here, the less time I have to make another plan when we get in there.*

Kevran sighed one final time before consenting. *All right, we will do it, but please be careful.*

Anthony nodded and got up to start putting his plan into motion.

It had taken Anthony longer than he had wanted to get everything ready. The stretch of road was long, and he wanted to use it all to make them more confused. The more road he had to work with, the more leaves he could use, and that meant that there were more targets for his enemies to mistake as him. Each leaf had to be injected with his Deypia. This process proved to be the most difficult as he had to do it without raising his energy up too high; otherwise, the Zankrex on the other side of the road would sense him. Every leaf he set was another tense episode. Then keeping his energy attached to the leaves was even tougher for him. The string that connected the leaves had to be thin and untraceable. Several times, Anthony would drop a leaf on accident because he lost his concentration.

Twenty minutes later, Anthony was back at the spot he first showed up to. He did one last check to be sure that he was still connected to all the leaves that he had put down. He was straining at this point to keep the thin connection between all of them.

Keep focusing, Anthony, but let me give you a piece of advice, Kevran said.

Anthony almost lost his focus but managed to hold on.

Kevran continued, *Raising the power of the leaves will not be that difficult, but the moment that you use your speed step is the most important moment. When you use your speed step, you will be using all Reichi. This will make it that much more difficult to keep all the leaves connected and powered up. I know you can do it, but keep that in mind. Keep your focus, and all should be well.*

Anthony nodded as he knew that was going to be a problem. He had thought it through as such: if the Zankrex are focused on the Deypia, then they shouldn't notice a tiny burst of Reichi. But to do this, he would have to keep his Reichi and his Deypia separate. All his practice up to this point had been trying to get him to combine the two.

Anthony took a deep breath in and focused. A second passed, and then another as Anthony waited for the moment. His eyes flashed as the moment he was waiting for appeared. The two guards closest to him turned around to where their backs were facing each other. Anthony triggered his leaves. Twenty leaves flared up with Anthony's Deypia energy. The Zankrex perked up as they sensed his energy across the way. That's when Anthony made his move. Drawing out just enough Reichi, he shot forward into the bushes across the street. He tensed and gritted his teeth as he felt his hold on the leaves start to slip, and for an agonizing second, he thought he had lost it.

The thought of this going wrong shot through his head. It passed in a microsecond, but to him, it felt like an eternity. He watched as the Zankrex would turn around after the leaves disappeared and spot him. He saw his parents getting murdered on the spot as he tried to fight his way there. The thought of his family dying triggered something in Anthony. He gritted his teeth with a newfound determination and held fast to the leaves. The connection grew stronger, and the amount of energy they began to put out increased. The Zankrex began to panic but still held their ground. They started to head toward the forest, which was what Anthony was waiting for. He forced the leaves to shoot deep into the forest before taking away their power. The Zankrex all shot off toward the power sources. Soon the leaves were cleared of Anthony's power, and the Zankrex were looking around the perimeter of the forest in utter confusion. Anthony breathed a sigh of relief and crawled deeper into the bushes. He waited until it was clear and began his trek to his house.

Anthony had never realized how large his neighborhood was until now. It seemed like it would take him forever to get to his house. It was probably just a combination of the time limit he had and the sneaking he had to do to get to his house, but right now all he could think about was how far it was.

It was never this big when I was walking away this morning. Did the neighborhood grow while I was away? Did Shane use some sort of magic I'm not aware of?

Anthony's thoughts continued down that path until Kevran had had enough.

Oh, be quiet already. The neighborhood is the same size it always was. Just now you are under the stress of a time limit, so you think it is larger than it is.

Anthony's mind stopped racing. He knew that was true; he just couldn't help but worry that he wasn't going to make it. His progress through the neighborhood had been slow. Zankrex were patrolling the streets inside the neighborhood as well, so Anthony wasn't able to walk in the open like he thought he would be able to. But that wasn't what he was worrying about.

There are so many Zankrex here right now.

Kevran agreed. *Yes, I do not like how many are here. It is going to make escaping a lot more difficult than it already was going to be.*

Anthony nodded as he ducked back under a bush. He waited until a Zankrex had sprinted by and then got back out and crept closer to his house. Anthony raked his brain for an idea of how to escape without going into an all-out war with the small battalion that appeared to have taken up residence in his neighborhood. But no matter how he thought it through, casualties seemed inevitable.

Kevran was quick to console him, *I know you are still hesitant to kill, but look at it this way: it is daytime right now. If the Zankrex do decide to fight you, then you will have the upper hand. That means that you could end it all without having to kill as much.*

Anthony chuckled. *That's comforting, but knowing Shane, I doubt it will be that easy.*

It was Kevran's turn to chuckle. *I like how you said "knowing Shane" like we have confronted him several times already.*

Anthony gave a weary half smile. *I know, but even so, I feel like I understand what kind of enemy he is without even having to fight him.*

Kevran agreed.

An uneasy silence fell over the two as Anthony continued his slow trek toward his home. The two kept silent for the rest of the trip. Anthony was grateful for this as trying to sneak about in enemy territory wasn't the easiest thing in the world. He was starting to wish that he could just pop out and start rampaging. He knew that wasn't his style, but it would make him feel better than sneaking around like he was.

Anthony was sure he was running out of time and was starting to think he would never make it when his street came into view. He got excited and nervous all at the same time. The moment of truth was fast approaching, and Anthony still hadn't made a plan. His mind began to race for a strategy as he also turned to Kevran. Kevran was also stuck on a plan. Neither of them seemed to be able to think of a way to get out with everyone. Anthony made it to his street and took a peek down it. What he saw was the worst possible scenario. A multitude of Zankrex stood around in a circle protecting his family from any outside force. On the inside were five more Zankrex. He assumed those to be an elite guard. Then standing in front of his family was Shane. His hands were behind his back as he paced back and forth. Anthony was too far away to discern anything else, but he had seen enough. He backed off and took a long sweeping path around the road's entrance. He headed to the road behind his road and made his way up. The street was empty, which made it easier for Anthony to get to his destination.

Where are you going? Kevran finally asked.

I'm going to get into my backyard through the backyard of the house behind us, Anthony answered.

Kevran understood and remained silent as Anthony made his way to the house. When he got there, he spent a second observing the home. The blinds were closed, and there didn't appear to be anyone inside, or at least anyone who was looking outside. Anthony nodded and made a break for their backyard. He ran straight up to their fence and vaulted it without missing a beat. Once over, he checked his surroundings one more time before vaulting over the fence and into his own backyard. He did a quick tuck roll before making a break underneath his deck. The underside of his deck was wet and muddy, even though it hadn't rained in a while. He could hear various animals scurrying away from him. He didn't have any time to be grossed out.

He went to Kevran. *Kevran, can you connect my and Ashley's thoughts again?*

Kevran was hesitant. *Maybe, but do not go expecting too much. I was only able to do that last time because you two were so close together. I am going to be honest when I say that I do not understand this power.*

Anthony shrugged it off. *Please just do what you can.*

Kevran sighed. *All right, I will do my best.*

A long pause followed that. Seconds ticked by in silence as Anthony became more and more apprehensive. He was on the verge of giving up when Kevran broke the silence.

It is done, he said out of breath.

Anthony tried to contain his shock and thought out to Ashley. *Ashley, can you hear me?*

He could feel Ashley's obvious confusion.

Yes, I can, but why can I hear you? When did you get back? Do you know what's going on? Ashley thought in a hurried and scared tone.

Anthony was quick to try and calm her down. *Yes, I know what's going on, and I don't have time to explain everything. I'm going to make a move to save my family. When I do that, I need you to be ready to move.*

Ashley was still in a panic, but she managed to stay calm enough to nod.

Good. Then, Kevran, I need you to be ready to come out and take Ashley away when things start to get bad.

Kevran was hesitant to agree to leave his partner behind on such a whim, but he also knew Anthony well enough to know that arguing here would be pointless. *I will keep her safe, but first you need to tell me the plan.*

Anthony nodded and was about to explain when Shane's voice interrupted, "God Sword, I grow tired of waiting. Now, would you please come out so we can talk?"

Anthony froze. All he could do was stare at the ground in horror. He tried to tell himself that it wasn't real, that it was just a voice in his head. But that hope was shattered by a second callout.

"God Sword," Shane yelled, annoyed at this point. "I hate to treat you like an infant, but if I reach the number three and you're not out yet, then I'm going to have to kill a member of your family."

Anthony's eyes widened in shock as his body began to react on his own.

"One," Shane started.

Anthony got out from under the deck when Kevran stopped him.

What now?

He knew that this was the only thing that Anthony could, or would, do. But even now it was hard for Kevran to see a good ending to all of this. Anthony stared at the fence on the other side of the yard. He didn't move or even shake. He just stood there.

"Two," Shane shouted out.

Anthony turned and looked at his house. He smiled. *I don't know, Kevran.*

"Thre—"

Anthony shot into the circle of Zankrex before Shane could finish his countdown. The Zankrex all jumped in surprise but regained themselves. The lowered their weapons and encircled him. Some had spears while others had axes and swords. The group was no doubt strong, but Anthony knew he could take them all if push came to shove. He wasn't even worried about fighting Shane as he seemed to be one of those smart-but-can't-fight types. But there was no way he could even start fighting at this point. Five elite-looking Zankrex stood around his family. No matter how Anthony played it out in his mind, he just couldn't see any way for him to defeat all five of the guards before one of them would be able to kill at least one of his family members.

I'll have to wait until an opening shows up before I can do anything, he realized.

Shane walked up to Anthony with a smirk on his face. Anthony scowled at the scrawny Zankrex. He was starting to hate this guy.

Shane seemed to get even more amusement out of Anthony's hate as his smirk grew into a full out grin.

"Well, God Sword, or should I say Anthony, it is nice to meet you in person. Tales of your resistance in Wishitak have reached my ears. I thought you would be harder to catch than this. I guess you just got lucky there."

Anthony gritted his teeth at the jabs and tried to keep his cool. "I'm here now. What do you want?"

Shane waggled his finger. "Tsk, tsk, Anthony. I'm ashamed of you. I also heard that you had quite the sharp tongue on you. But here you are demanding things like a barbarian."

Anthony's eyes flashed in rage as he reached for his sword and started to take a step forward, but swords pressed against his family's throats made him stop.

Shane chuckled. "Yes, I don't think it would be wise for you to make any moves right now. My men have orders to kill your family if you should start to act up. And don't even bother trying to use your Deypia to control leaves like you did at the entrance. I can detect energy better than any living being on this planet. If I even sense you trying to pull a stunt like that, I'll have them executed one by one."

Anthony clenched his jaw even harder as he took his hand off his sword. "That's how you knew I was in my backyard."

Shane nodded. "My ability to detect energy is so good that even the king says that it is better than his. I knew where you were the moment you stepped in the neighborhood."

Anthony thought of something. "Why didn't you know that I was here in the city from day one?"

Shane's face changed. He scowled at Anthony. "I can't detect what isn't there, you know. I'll concede that you are good at keeping your energy levels hidden, but I figured that you wouldn't be able to keep it under wraps with the kind of pressure that I was putting on you."

Anthony kept facing Shane. "How did you know that I was here? How did you know to look at the cameras today?"

Shane regained his smile as he turned to look off in the distance. "I told you, didn't I? It's because you messed up."

Shane continued to stare Anthony down as he let the gravity of his words sink in. Anthony ground his teeth as he remembered what Shane had said over the intercom.

"Someone noticed me coming out of the gym yesterday."

Shane laughed. "Yes, they did. You almost had us too. If you had left even a minute earlier, you might have been fine, and this whole situation wouldn't be happening. But one of my scouts said he thought he saw a strange figure hovering around the gym area and went back to investigate. Once on the roof, he saw you walking away from the back of the building. After giving me your description, I figured out who it was from the other descriptions we have received."

Anthony cursed himself. *I knew I should have left last night. I should have listened to Ashley after she confirmed my own fears. But now isn't the time to beat myself up about it.*

Anthony had another question. "How did you manage to speak to me through the intercom if you were here?"

Shane chuckled. "What a stupid question. My minion in the security room connected this receiver here to the intercom system." Shane held up a small black receiver. "I told him to tell me when you had gone through all the rooms you were planning on going through, and when it looked like you were about to leave, then he would patch me through. I figured it would add to the effect after you went through all that trouble to find nothing."

Anthony furrowed his brow as he processed what Shane had just said. "How did you know it would be pointless?"

Shane dismissed the question with a wave of his hand. "That's rather obvious, don't you think? I was surprised you would come back to this town after knowing about her."

Anthony wasn't following, and Shane saw it on his face.

At first, he was in disbelief, but then he started laughing. "Oh man, you don't understand, do you?"

Anthony began to get annoyed again. "Are you just going to sit there and laugh, or do you plan on actually telling me?"

Shane wiped a mock tear from his eye as he settled down. "We have Hannah, you buffoon. She searched all the rooms and looked for any clues."

Anthony's eyes widened in surprise at the mention of her. "Hannah's alive?"

Shane nodded as he began to recall. "Yes, but not by much. She was in a very bad way after you got done with her, or at least I assume that was you. The immense Deypia from your blade caused a horrible reaction to the Onigor in her body. She wasn't healing the way she was supposed to be healing. It took three days of constant surgery to save her. And even then, it took her a week to get back to full strength, even with the advanced healing that the Onigor should have given her. It was an amazing wound, I must say."

Anthony felt a little relieved.

Shane looked over and chuckled. "You shouldn't feel relieved at all, God Sword. She now has more Onigor in her than Lance has right now. That wound caused her Onigor to grow at a tremendous rate, not to mention all the energy we had to transfuse into her just to keep her alive. She will not be a pleasant foe to fight the next time you meet her."

Anthony was about to say something back when Shane held up his hand. "Enough talk, God Sword. I've already gone on far longer than I wanted to. Now we come to the part where you surrender."

Anthony tensed back up as he stared Shane down. "You would have to be nuts to think that I would surrender myself to you."

Shane laughed. "Yes, I suppose I am a little nuts, but it's the crazy ones that always play unfair." Shane pointed back to Anthony's family. They had no blindfolds on, but they were gagged and bound at the ankles and the wrists. James was avoiding eye contact, but his father and mother were staring at him. Their eyes were filled with worry.

Anthony's heart sank as he realized the gravity of the situation. "You would sacrifice your own people to catch me? That's low even for a demon."

Shane threw back his head and laughed. "Oh, God Sword, it's cute how you try to hold me to some sort of standard. You know full well that we care not for these people. Even then, this family is under arrest for a different reason."

Anthony looked at him in confusion as Shane continued, "This family is under arrest for harboring a fugitive from the law and lying to officials. The penalty for these crimes is very steep indeed. I'm not even sure that turning yourself in now will pardon them. But if you allow yourself to be captured, then I'll do my best to see that they are not harmed."

Anthony's mind began to race. *Of course, he would have seen through their lies. He must have known about it the first time he ever came in but didn't say anything, so he could somehow get this situation. I have to think up of some way for all the blame to be put on me. But how? He won't just accept that I made them. I have to think of some plausible way for me to have made them lie for me.*

An idea popped into Anthony's head. It was a long shot, but he didn't have any choice.

"You're wrong, Shane."

Shane looked at Anthony in confusion. "What am I wrong about, God Sword?"

Anthony pointed at his family. "They didn't lie to you on their own free will. I made them lie to you."

Anthony's family's eyes widened as they all looked at him in surprise. James was the most confused in the group, but his mother and father weren't far behind.

Shane squinted his eyes, but he didn't dismiss the statement. "And how did you manage that, God Sword? Did you just walk up and say to do it or you would kill them?"

Anthony shook his head. "I used my Deypia."

Anthony now had Shane's full attention. "A technique that allows you to take back control of the already infected? There is no technique like that."

Anthony began to sweat as he put his thoughts in order. "It's a secret technique that the previous owner of this sword taught me."

Kevran chimed in for the first time at this point, *Anthony, it would be unwise to tell them about the shrine.*

Anthony shrugged him off. *It's too late to go back at this point. I'll deal with the consequences if they arise. For now, let me concentrate.*

Shane looked like he wanted to laugh, but it was obvious he knew something.

Anthony realized what he was thinking about and decided to take a leap of faith. "Yes, Shane, it is what you are thinking about."

For the first time, Shane looked up in shock. "You mean that old shrine in Wishitak actually held something?"

Anthony smiled on the inside but remained stoic on the outside. "Yes, I was able to get in touch with the spirit of the owner of the God Sword before me."

Shane seemed baffled yet excited. "I thought the king was just a stubborn old fool when he said to be sure that the shrine was sealed off. We didn't believe him when he said it could aid the enemy. I mean, I went in there myself and checked it for energy, and I couldn't find any." He turned and look at Anthony. "It must have reacted with your Deypia then. That would explain it all."

Shane cracked a huge grin. "Well, this is a game changer. A technique that even I can't detect. It would be a good thing to research that."

Anthony held up his hand. "Don't get ahead of yourself. I have some demands."

Shane stared Anthony down. Anthony stared back, unnerved by the Zankrex's stare. Shane sighed and closed his eyes. "What are your demands?"

Anthony pointed at his family. "They go free. You know now that they aren't guilty of anything. They go free, and I'll give myself up."

Shane thought it over for a couple of seconds. "Fine. I will agree to your demands."

Shane signaled for Zankrex to approach Anthony. They were holding handcuffs.

"Put these on, and I will free your family."

Anthony shook his head as the Zankrex stopped. "No, you free them of their bonds first and lower the weapons. Then I'll give myself up."

Shane smiled. "Very well, but you put your sword down first."

Anthony hesitated for a second before reaching back slowly and taking his sword off his back. He was reluctant to part with his sword, even for a little bit, but he knew he had to do it.

I'll break out of those handcuffs after my family is safe. Then I can go wild on the Zankrex and leave with Ashley.

Anthony set his sword down and kicked it a couple feet away from himself. "There, I did it. Now you do as you promised, and I'll allow the handcuffs."

Shane nodded and turned to the guards. He flicked his hand, and the guards broke the ropes and ungagged his family. As soon as his father was free, he tried to say something, but Anthony shot him a glance that deterred him. Anthony tried to get his dad to understand with a look. His dad hesitated but then stayed silent. Anthony breathed a sigh of relief and looked back at Shane. Shane gestured toward the other Zankrex, and they moved in. Anthony put his hands behind his back and allowed them to cuff him. He fell to his knees. His head started to swim as he felt like he was about to pass out. After a few painful seconds, he gained his vision back, but he felt weak. He tried to reach out to Kevran, but nothing happened. He reached for his energy but found that he couldn't. Something was stopping him from accessing it. He looked around in a panic, but Shane's laughter got his attention.

Shane strolled over and squatted down to Anthony's level. "Confused? I would think so. Those handcuffs are not normal, though you know that by now. Those handcuffs were forged using Onigor. Onigor in that density has the ability to block out other energies. It won't last forever, but those should last long enough to get you to a secured location."

Shane chuckled as he started to stand up.

"Wait," Anthony managed to say. He was struggling with the sudden loss of energy. His body wasn't used to being cut off from it completely. He looked up at Shane. "My family goes free."

Shane smiled. "Well, I admire your persistence on the matter. But yes, they do go free. Guards, set the prisoners free."

The family looked relieved as they began to turn around—when blades shot through their chests.

Anthony stared on, mouth agape and eyes wide in horror, as he watched blood pour out of the wounds in his family's chests. Time seemed to move in slow motion as he watched every detail of the scene unfold. The swords were soon retracted out of their bodies. Even more blood began to pour out as all three crumpled to the ground. He watched as his mother took her last breath, followed by his brother. He turned and looked at his dad. He was barely breathing, but in the agony, he looked up straight at Anthony. He expected to see eyes filled with hate and accusation, but what he saw was the exact opposite. Eyes filled with love stared at his very soul. His father smiled at him before going limp. Anthony couldn't think. He couldn't breathe. He couldn't say anything, nor could he move. He simply sat there, allowing tears to well up in his eyes. A cackling laughter snapped Anthony from his dream world. He didn't look as he already knew who it was. All he did was bow his head to the ground.

Shane cackled to sky. He walked over to the dead bodies, kicking them to be sure that they were dead. He turned to see Anthony crumpled up on the ground. "Well, I set them free, God Sword. I set them free from this miserable existence that you humans have."

He continued to laugh as Anthony struggled to find words.

"They were your subordinates," he managed to squeak out. "They would have followed you anywhere. They were innocent, and you just killed them."

Shane started laughing even harder after hearing this. "You think I care about them? I couldn't care less about them. I couldn't care less about anyone on this forsaken planet. Everyone here is just an object that I can use to get what I want. I would kill everyone here with my bare hands if I thought it would help me get closer to killing all the Divine Blades. Humans are weak and worthless. Though I have to say that your family was the worst of the bunch. They whined and sniveled when we bound and gagged them. They were so afraid and useless. They didn't even last after getting stabbed. All they did was die. I don't think I've ever met any family that was more useless. It brought me great joy to see them get killed."

Shane waited in silence, waiting to see what kind of reaction Anthony would have. Anthony sat there, his head still bowed to the ground. He gritted his teeth and began to shake. No power was coming out; the handcuffs had seen to that. Shane's words about his family echoed in his head. They kept getting stronger, mocking him. The only image he had in his head was his father smiling at him.

Shane, annoyed at the lack of a reaction, signaled to the guards. "Get him on his feet. We need to get him to the lab before the cuffs give out. Not that, that will happen any time soon. The handcuffs have made him useless."

The word rung out in Anthony's mind.

Useless.

It echoed louder and louder in his head.

Useless.

Images of Clancy lying in puddle of blood.

Useless.

His brother being dropped by a Zankrex.

Useless.

His family lying dead in a pool of their own blood in front of him.

Useless.

Then Anthony's mind went blank in rage.

The guards turned around to pick up Anthony but found that he was already standing.

Shane turned in honest surprise. "Oh, you can stand now? Well, I am impressed. I thought all you were good for was lying there and crying."

But then he stopped and looked at Anthony's face. It was still bowed, but there was no indication of sadness.

"Don't tell me you're mad—"

He was cut off by an intense rumbling. At first, he looked around as he thought it was an earthquake, but then he felt it. An immense power that he hadn't felt since leaving the king's castle. He turned and looked at Anthony. His head was now raised. His face was contorted in rage. And his eyes were solid green.

Shane stumbled back as he tried to process what was happening. *That's impossible. The only way that his power could get through those cuffs is if his power was as strong as the king's.*

Then his eyes flashed in realization.

"Everyone, get bac—"

Before he could finish, the sound of metal snapping brought everyone's attention to Anthony. His hands were free. He then grabbed the cuffs and ripped them off his wrists, the metal breaking like it was wet paper. The three guards behind him hesitated for a second but then charged at Anthony. They hadn't even taken their first step when the leaves cut them down. Anthony never looked back. His concentration was on Shane. He walked forward for his sword.

Shane realized what was going to happen.

"He's gone mad with rage. Protect me," he squealed.

The Zankrex all rushed him. There were over fifty Zankrex that rushed him. Only twenty made it to Anthony as a flurry of leaves cut every which way, leaving a pile of mangled Zankrex bodies. The twenty that survived were the elite. They were able to detect and block the leaves before they were killed. They rushed Anthony as quick as they could, but he had already picked up his sword. He continued to stare Shane down as he tried to rush him but was interrupted by a Zankrex slashing out at his side. Anthony swung his sword and destroyed the Zankrex blade in a single shot before cutting him in half. He tried to refocus on Shane, but the rest of the Zankrex were upon him. He cut the next one down and then a third before his rage shifted. He was now focused on the Zankrex in front of him.

Anthony snarled at the remaining Zankrex and went to work. He speed-stepped to the back of the group and cut the straggler in half. He took another step forward and stabbed another and pulled his sword out and beheaded the next before the group was able to turn around. Two Zankrex attacked him at the same time. One slashed at his head while the other slashed at his legs. Anthony blocked the leg shot with his sword, but the other blade continued its path. It came inches away when Anthony caught it with his bare hand. The two Zankrex had only enough time to widen their eyes before Anthony picked the one Zankrex up by his sword and crashed him on top of the other Zankrex. The sound of skulls cracking signaled their deaths. The other twelve hesitated at the brutal display before charging once again. Anthony wasn't going to wait. He shot into the middle of the crowd and went about slashing and hacking.

His mind was blank.

All that fueled him was rage. His face was contorted in pain and fury. His blade held no physical form. It was only a blur. No Zankrex could see, much less react to it. Any sword that made it close was destroyed by the overwhelming force that Anthony wielded. The only thing that made it to him was the blood of his hewn enemies. Zankrex flew in from the outskirts of the neighborhood. They paused at the sight of the massacre. Suddenly, the commotion died down. The flying Zankrex were confused by the sudden scene change, but the immense energy behind them turned their confusion to fear. Anthony grabbed the one in the back by the head and shot down. The Zankrex skull was crushed on the road. A crater formed as Anthony forced the limp body further and further down. The rest flew in to strike, but Anthony disappeared once again. His speed step put him above the group. He sliced the wings off the highest one. The Zankrex plummeted into his comrade, and Anthony's blade skewered both bodies. Only three remained. They tried to flee but were caught in the midst of their allies' corpses. Anthony decapitated the three airborne Zankrex with one swing. Their bodies tumbled and slid to a halt.

After the tornado of blood and steel settled, only one Zankrex remained. He was terrified. He looked down at his clothes to find them soaked in the blood of his comrades. He looked back up to a terrifying sight. Anthony stood in the middle of the Zankrex corpses. His breath was calm, as if he had just done a mild workout. His face was looking more and more like a wild beast. The Zankrex couldn't move. All he could do was stand there as Anthony appeared in front of him.

"He's a monster," the Zankrex managed to whisper before Anthony's blade ended his life.

Anthony stood in the center of the street. His eyes still glowed green as he scanned the surrounding area. All he could think about was finding Shane—and killing Shane. He scanned the mass of corpses that was left behind in his wake. Yet the only bodies that he saw was those of his families. He looked at their bodies as they lay side by side with the other Zankrex that he had just slain. He watched as their blood mixed in with others. He couldn't see Shane. He couldn't sense Shane. Shane had long since left when Anthony had turned his attention to the other Zankrex. He had failed at killing the one man that he had wanted to kill.

Useless.

The word continued to echo in his mind. He clenched his fist. He gritted his teeth. Power began to radiate from him even more than before. Leaves began to rise up and encircle him. Then they began to spin around him. Slow at first, but as his rage grew, so did their speed. Soon Anthony let out a feral scream of frustration and agony, which prompted a typhoon to start around him. The leaves whipped around him at amazing speeds. The winds got caught up in it and began to drag loose items into the vortex. But in the center was Anthony, and all he could hear was *useless.*

Ashley didn't know how to react. Tears were streaming down her face, yet she wasn't crying. She had watched it all take place from the second-floor window. She watched as Anthony talked with Shane. She watched as the cuffs were placed on Anthony.

And she watched as Anthony's family was killed.

She had only known them for a little while, but even still, she felt a strong connection to them. Her emotions were in limbo as she watched Anthony suffer. She watched as the leaves began to swirl around him. She watched the vortex form, cutting off her view of the scene. That's when she heard something. She whirled around to see Kevran standing behind her. His face was grim, or at least what she assumed a dragon's face looked like when it was grim.

She tried to swallow her sadness as turned back toward Anthony. "What's going on with him?"

Kevran walked up and shook his head. "I do not know. I cannot get into his head to talk to him. His emotions are making it impossible to contact him."

Ashley continued to watch. "Will he ever calm down?"

Kevran's face remained grim. "I have never witnessed something like this in a God Sword before, but I would think he will calm down when he runs out of energy."

Ashley gritted her teeth. "But if he does that, then we will be sitting ducks for the other Zankrex."

Kevran nodded. "This is a dire situation. We need to calm him down as soon as we can. Otherwise, escaping from here will be impossible."

Ashley stared out the window at the vortex. Anything that got close to it appeared to get caught up in it and thrown about. Ashley saw no way around it.

She turned to Kevran. "Is there any way for you to protect me from the vortex?"

Kevran had an uneasy look on his face. "I could, but I do not know for how long. Why do you ask?"

Ashley pointed out the window. "We need to calm him down now, and at this point, I think the best way to do that is to interact with him face-to-face. If you can't reach him through his mind, then I'll just have to go over there and use my voice."

Kevran hated the idea, but there was no way he could argue against her. He thought that he should go, but as much as he hated to admit it, her voice would work better than his.

He sighed. "I will do my best to protect you, but if you hear me telling you to get back, then get back."

Ashley nodded and shot straight for the door. She tried to open it, but the vortex was keeping it shut tight. She struggled with it for a few seconds before Kevran came down and punched the door off its hinges. It flew into the vortex. Ashley felt the pull as soon as the door left, and she looked back at Kevran. He was struggling but nodded to her. She nodded and turned back to face the outside. She took a few cautious steps to test the waters. She could feel the pull of the vortex, but at the same time, she felt the protection of some unforeseen force. Feeling confident in Kevran's power, she started to walk down the porch steps.

Be careful, Kevran said. *I can block most of the smaller things, but if you see a larger object coming, it will be up to you to dodge it.*

Ashley acknowledged him and began to walk. In any other conditions, the walk from the house to the road would take two seconds, but the wind made it seem like walking ten miles. She took step after cautious step being sure to keep an eye on her surroundings. Out of the corner of her eye, she saw something coming in hot. She dropped to the ground as the screen door flew inches over her head. She struggled to get back up and continued to trudge on. The wind was deafening, and her visibility was low. After what felt like a lifetime, she saw him.

Anthony was only a dim outline at first, but he came into focus as she approached. His head was thrown back as he continued to roar to the heavens. She pushed past into the center of the vortex and ran up to embrace him. She hugged him tight, but there was no response.

"Anthony," she yelled in his ear.

Nothing.

"Anthony, please snap out of it."

Still nothing.

"Anthony, we have to go," she screamed even louder at him, but still nothing.

She began to cry; it wasn't loud. She just started to cry.

"I'm so sorry, Anthony. Please, come back," she whispered.

The vortex stopped, causing all the debris and leaves to drop.

Then there was nothing. No sound was made, and nothing stirred.

They stood like this for several seconds. As they stood, water droplets began to fall. Small smacks could be heard against the leaves as a gentle rain fell, but it didn't take long for it to pour down hard. The constant beat of the rain brought Ashley back to her senses. She lifted her head out of Anthony's chest and looked around. She gazed at the ground to see that all the bodies had been pushed to the curb along with every drop of blood. They stood on an island among a sea. The rain began to clear away the blood as a stream formed on the side of the road. But even through all that, three bodies still remained undisturbed. His family lay just as they had been.

Ashley looked back up at Anthony through tears. Her eyes widened in surprise to see Anthony's eyes back to normal. His rage was now gone, replaced with despair and sorrow. He looked down at Ashley, searching her for anything that he could grab on to, but her face offered no reprieve. Anthony began to whimper as he dropped to his knees. Tears welled up in his eyes as he looked at Ashley. She had no words; all she could do was try not to cry. Anthony bowed his head and began to weep. Quiet at first, but then he let out cries of deep agony as Ashley hugged his head into her chest.

A Zankrex fell across the dead body of one of his comrades. The large gash in his chest made doing anything painful. He tried to make a move toward his weapon, but water wrapped its way up and pinned his hand to the ground. He couldn't move through the liquid.

"Why can't you just die?"

The Zankrex only had a moment to look at his attacker before a cutlass ended his life.

The woman sighed. She looked up at the sky. The dark clouds seemed to indicate that rain would be coming in soon. She could sense the moisture in the air, but she still wasn't good enough to sense exactly when it would fall. She made an annoyed face.

Dear, if you keep your face scrunched like that, you'll get wrinkles. That would be a travesty on you.

The woman rolled her eyes. *I'm already going to have gray hairs dealing with you every day. Why not add some wrinkles to it and look like a grandma when I'm thirty?*

She could feel the pained feelings. *You say I give you gray hairs? Oh, well then, I suppose I'll just keep to myself then. I'll remain locked away here to stay out of your way.*

The woman rolled her eyes once again, an act she found herself doing often, and sighed. *I'm sorry, Strisis. I'm just fed up with Zankrex grunts, not knowing anything about anything. I don't mind killing them by the dozens, but I would love to get something useful out of them, you know?*

Strisis was quick to recover. *Oh, sweetie, I know. That reminds me of the time I started training the twentieth Water Cutlass. A nasty sort at first, but wouldn't you know it, he loved bear cubs. Well, needless to say, this got him in all sorts of trouble.*

The woman could only look on in pain as the story continued. She wanted to bash her head against the nearest tree trunk. She stepped over Zankrex bodies as Strisis continued on about the man who apparently made it his goal to hug every bear cub on the planet. All she had wanted was to find the Earth Katana. She knew he was awakened. She had heard whisperings of him from Zankrex she faced. Rumblings of a powerful man roaming the northwest area of Amaraitia. She had heard he was heading toward the middle of the continent, but she had no idea where.

And that's when I told him tickle fingers are the best, but tickle claws make a mess. Strisis laughed at the end of her story.

The woman could only thank the Creator that it was done and over with.

Oh dear, but if you want to hear about a real character, then you must listen to this one about a shoemaker named Trill. He had the weirdest love for porridge.

The woman held back a scream and was about to tell Strisis off when it happened. The earth almost shook beneath the weight. The trees rustled in the wind it created. The power was overwhelming. It washed over her like a tidal wave. The force caused the grass at her feet to wave like a gale-force wind had just hit. The wave passed, but the energy could still be felt.

The woman began to sweat under the pressure.

Is that him? Strisis inquired.

The woman could only nod. A smile began to form on her face. "Looks like I underestimated how powerful he was. I think he might just be able to help, after all."

Strisis chuckled. *Well then, what are you waiting for? Shall we go introduce ourselves, Vanessa?*

Vanessa smiled and put her cutlass away. "I think we shall."

With that, she took off toward the source as the rain began to fall around her.

Glossary

Tertalla (Tare-tall-ah). The planet where the events of God Sword take place

Deypia (Day-pee-ah). The holy energy of the Creator

Onigor (Oh-knee-gore). The dark energy that the Zankrex wield

Reichi (Ray-chi). The energy that humans wield

Zankrex (Zan-krek-s). Humans who have allowed Onigor inside of them

Kevran (Kev-ran). The dragon guide for the Earth Katana

Strisis (Stir-eye-sis). The unicorn guide for the Water Cutlass

Oshuma (Oh-shoe-ma). The second wielder of the earth katana

Kintarfus (Kin-tar-fuss). The second wielder of the water cutlass

Yadgusril (Yea-jew-sir-ill). The man who became the Zankrex king

Amaraitia (Am-ah-ray-she-ah). The largest continent on Tertalla

Shinjiko (Shin-gee-koh). Long, slender continent directly east of Amaraitia

Eufrin (You-fur-in). Continent northwest from Amaraitia

Austeria (Aw-stare-ee-ah). Continent southwest from Amaraitia

Rugashin (Rue-gah-shin). Southernmost continent on Tertalla

Xanto (Zan-toe). Hidden island northeast of Amaraitia, where the Zankrex are

About the Author

A. A. Mullane was born in Phoenix, Arizona, but grew up in Tennessee. He is the middle of three siblings. He followed traditional schooling all the way through university where he received a bachelor's in science, but all the while growing his writing and storytelling abilities. Mullane grew up feeding his imagination with such video games as *Pokémon* and *Mega Man* and enjoying the works and adaptations of many action/adventure series such as *Lord of the Rings* and the *Inheritance Cycle*. Eventually, he was shown the world of anime where he drew some of his heavier inspirations. Christianity has also brought an inspiration and has influenced his whole life. He currently lives in Tennessee.

CPSIA information can be obtained
at www.ICGtesting.com
Printed in the USA
LVHW03s0420180818
587009LV00001B/15/P

9 781643 001982